Autograph Page

To Ma Petite

_____

_____

_____
Date

BAYOU BISHOPS
Book One

By: Lucian Bane

© 2021 by Lucian Bane

All rights reserved. No part of this document may be reproduced or transmitted in any form or by any means, electronic, mechanical, photocopying, recording, or otherwise, without prior written permission of Lucian Bane or his legal representative.

To all the readers, fans, and/or reader's clubs, thank you for supporting my work. I'd also like to ask nicely that you please not pirate my work. That basically means don't give it away just because you bought it.

If you need a different format, please contact me, the author.

Dedicated to all my romantic fans. Thank you for helping me build this story. You'll find a list of all the games we played and the winners in the back-matter of this book!

CHAPTER 1

"I don't like the smell of what's cooking," Sahvrin said from the round table in the Roulette Club.

His father Lazure leaned back in his chair with those pissed grooved lines on his forehead. "I knew this would come when Romero passed. No disrespect to the dead, but this brother is as bright as a bayou on a cloudy night." He slid methodical fingers over his mustache while eying Sahvrin then his four brothers. "Our agreement is with Romero, and that's what we're here to honor. Nothing else."

"Don't want to say it too loud in case Murphy's law is eavesdropping," Sahvrin said, "but if the new Roulette prez reneges on our contract, we have the option to fold." He eyed his four brothers, who nodded, glad to see he wasn't the only one wanting to cancel the useless pact they'd made with a now dead man. Only reason they agreed to it was out of mutual respect for Romero, not out of necessity. The Roulettes needed the Bishop's protection in the swamps, but the Bishops sure as fuck didn't need the protection of the Roulettes on land. Never did.

"That pissed pot's been dumped," August said, sliding a finger inside the collar of his white dress shirt. None of them liked wearing official Bayou Bishop attire, but it was that time of year which meant few chances to change out of the vintage black suits and wide-brimmed hats. Official club land meetings and annual festivals, that's what they were for. September was a busy month with the Crawfish Festival, the annual Bayou Bishops air boat races, and Alligator Wrangling Competitions they did for charity. And of course Mah-Mah wouldn't dare let Sahvrin miss his birthday with all that going on. The woman was ruthless when it came to all things celebratory. You participated or became gator bait.

Sahvrin didn't mind the clothing since it called for wearing their Judges loaded with bone shattering .45 hollow-point bullets. Just what you wanted when dealing with unscrupulous thugs like Thadious Landry.

"Well," Bart said, peeking from under the brim of his hat. "I've heard nothing but great things about Thaddy The Meat-patty, and all of it points to him giving us a reason."

"He's an asshole," Zep agreed. "Pretty sure your prayers 'll be answered in a timely manner."

Jek clasped his hands behind his head. "Wish he'd hurry the fuck up so I can get back to actual work." He looked at Lazure. "Did I tell you your son here has us booked till mid-summer next year?"

Lazure swerved a signature chilly gaze to Sahvrin. "Good to see you sinking your teeth in. But don't think you'll be too busy to make it to Mah-Mah's parties."

Zep gave a low chuckle. "Cuz you'll be too dead if you don't." He looked at Sahvrin then, chucking his chin at him. "You ever find that part I wanted for my mod? Bros before doughs, don't forget."

Sahvrin gave a single head shake. "Went ahead and made it myself."

"Damn," Zep said, grinning at him. "Soon this whole town 'll be outfitted by the infamous Swamp Rats Mods -n- Rods."

"All I wanna know is will my Swamp Dragon be converted before the boat races," August said, his sky-blue gaze fired up. "You're going down this year, big bro."

Sahvrin chuckled, angling a look at him. "Mon *Dieu*," he said with a headshake. "Like I'd ever modify your boat to beat mine. Lil T-*Aug*."

August snapped a pissed look at Lazure, pointing at Sahvrin. "Tole you he cheats."

They all laughed, except for August who shook his head at Sahvrin.

"You can always modify it yourself," Lazure said, getting more laughter.

"Maybe while our sister wrangles the gators, you can collect their piss and use it in your fuel injectors," Jek suggested, guffawing now.

"Jack off one of them males," Zep assured with a wide-eyed nod. "That'll fly your dragon straight up ur-anus."

When the laughter settled, Sahvrin looked around at the empty bar, pulling the edge of his sleeve over his watch. "If he's not here in five, I'm leaving. I have things to do in town before the festival traffic gets fucking ludicrous."

"Speaking of..." Bart said lowly, "...we find any more unusual traffic in the swamp?"

"I haven't," Sahvrin said. "Thinking it was dropped by one of the tourists."

"Yeah, cuz they're always dropping used condoms, baggies of coke, and ripped to fuck panties," Jek said, suddenly banging the table with his fist. "Dammit! I still need to make a run to the Sale Barn to stock our surplus before one of these hurricanes visits our front porch."

Like a well-timed curse, the door opened at the rear of the room and a Mr. T looking dude called, "Boss is ready."

They waited for The First Bishop to move but he only sat and stared at the man for several seconds. He finally rose slowly, and they all followed.

****

"Well if it isn't The Bayou Bishops!"

The overly dramatic welcome came from a bull-built man with a densely inked bald head.

The unnamed hostility in his blaring welcome put Sahvrin in mind of the three men on the left and the one behind them at the door of the small office.

"Names Thadious. Have a seat. You must be the father, Lazure."

"I am," his father said, taking the seat across from the desk while he and his brothers moved in to stand directly behind him. "These are my sons with me. Jekon, August, Zephrin, Bartholome, and my oldest Sahvrin."

"Well, it's good to meet the infamous Bayou Bishops in the flesh." He took a seat with the air of a king, his throne's hardware squawking under the weight of his royalty. "My bro Romero said good things about you and your family." He eyed his brothers and Sahvrin recognized the kind of tight smile he wore. Those nearly black eyes gleamed with everything Sahvrin committed to killing. He never mentioned it to Lazure or his brothers, but Sahvrin had a thick hunch that whatever they were finding in the swamp came directly from the pig-head he stared at. Who else would be trespassing their laws except those already approved to pass?

"Your brother was a fine man," his father said, only half meaning it since they didn't really know any of them, nor they them. "You said you wanted to talk. What about?"

"Well, I'm gonna come right out with it." He leaned back in his chair wearing the look of a man who always got his way. "We've picked up some new contracts with our brothers down in New Mexico. The usual arms trade." He gave a weird nonchalant twitch before jutting his chin. "Wanted to offer you a deal. You let us set up shop in the swamps, and you get ten percent of sales."

His father sat speechless and still long enough for Sahvrin to move his hand in reach of his Judge. "Last I checked, the contract said no arms business in the swamp. It also says you have safe passage as long as you follow the laws of our land. If you have a problem with that, we no longer have a contract."

Sahvrin became keenly aware they were now a roadblock to a whole lot of dirty money.

"Maybe you need time to think it over," the man said, his threat loud and clear. He sat back and added, "Your boy Old man Francois and his crew said he had no problem with it."

Sahvrin felt the air around his father thicken. "You should talk to him about setting up shop, then?"

The man narrowed his brows at the obstacle across from him. "You and I have a contract."

"Not anymore. But I'm sure Old Man Francois will be happy to work out a deal with you." His father's tone had gone lethal and daring.

The man's chair screeched loudly as he leaned forward, locking his hands together. "Mr. Lazure... I should remind you that our contract is a two-way street. You give us protection and we give you protection."

His father also leaned forward. "We don't *need* your *fucking* protection. But... you *do* need ours."

The dead calm in his father's tone had Sahvrin tense as their stare-off stretched in the silence. Thadious suddenly angled his head with a weird smile. "Lazure..." he began, like he wanted to redirect the conversation to a less fucked end. "These are legal arms trade. But the gun laws aren't the same in every state, you know that, I know that. We're both in agreement that the laws of the land aren't always just. That's why you have your own set of laws, right?"

"It is."

The man smiled with wicked glee like that solved everything. "Same for me and my brothers," he said, spreading meaty arms.

"My answer stays. We want no part in it."

Lazure rose, and the man shot up from his chair, bringing five Judges aimed at his head.

"That was a big mistake, Bishop," the man warned with his hands up, glancing nervously.

"Wach his boys," Sahvrin said, not taking his eyes from the prez. "Take your fucking seat and tell your men to do the same or my brothers 'll blow their knees out."

The men sat quickly on the floor not needing to be told and Sahvrin backed out of the room, keeping the barrel aimed at the face of human filth.

"You leave, Lazure, and our contract is broken," he bellowed behind them.

"Au revoir, you gras son of a putahn," his father called, not looking back.

"Francois will take the contract, you dumb sonofabitch!" he yelled as they exited the front door.

"Bart!" Sahvrin called when his brother spun and headed back for the entrance.

"Get in the truck," their father ordered.

Sahvrin hopped in the driver's seat and his brothers jumped in the back like watchdogs. "Those sonofabitches are already running in our swamp, this I'm sure," Sahvrin muttered, revving the engine. "We need to talk to Francois."

"That cocksucker was bluffing," Lazure assured, propping an arm on the back seat. "And Francois knows better."

"It's not Francois I'm worried about, it's his crew which can only mean his two sons."

"Then you'll pay them a visit. Make sure they understand that if they cross The Bayou Bishop codes, they pay the price."

****

By the time Sahvrin got back to their Dry Dock, he was racing the clock. Climbing on his bike, he headed back into town, meeting traffic as foul as his mood. It was another fifteen minutes to find a place to park then a race-walk through roads and sidewalks crowded with early tourists. All for a fucking tube of JB Weld. Thanks to the new postal worker who delivered his shipment five doors down to his one and only thieven neighbor.

D batteries, don't forget that. He didn't like running swamp traps at night without his high beam light, especially with the Roulettes up to no good. He might have to let Lucas take it over with how busy things were getting at the shop.

"Ahhh, fuck! No!" he muttered, yanking on the locked door of the hardware store. He searched for a familiar face inside that he could bribe. He couldn't wait till Monday for this, he was already fucking behind.

"Excuse me."

Sahvrin turned to find a woman smiling at him. "What?" he demanded, not in the mood to be hit on by empty headed tourists.

"I was here for the festival and was wondering if there was maybe a map of the streets so that I don't get lost." She smiled more somehow and did a strange eye flutter. "I'm staying at the Breaux Bridge Inn and wanted to make sure I could find my way back."

Anger gnawed on his last nerve at what she'd just said. "Where you from?" Definitely not there.

"Oh, up north!"

The vague yet obvious answer annoyed him more. "You tell me the exact hotel you're staying at and only the geographical location of where you're from."

"Sorry! North Dakota!" she gushed, mistaking his sarcasm for him actually wanting to know that.

If he'd been one of his fornicating brothers, he'd seize the opportunity this woman was likely offering. But as the leader of The Twelve, code dictated he have no dealings with women unless absolutely necessary, and this definitely didn't feel necessary other than to point out her reckless stupidity. "You're here from North Dakota, a woman travelling alone obviously, and the first stranger you talk to, you give them the name of your hotel and ask for a map so you don't get lost. Ma Petite, if all you get is lost, you can thank whatever God you serve. And if you're wanting more than a map, try giving your room and phone number to make it simpler."

The look of shock on her pretty face reminded him how little practice he had with the opposite sex. "The gas stations have maps of local attractions," he said, attempting to clean his social mess. He moved to leave, but her oddly modest black dress stopped him in his tracks. "Are you going to a costume party?"

Her attempts at composing herself were painful to watch. He recognized anger in her bright gray eyes now as she presented a huge smile. "To think I was told everybody in the south was soooo hospitable. What are the odds I'd run into the town prick on my first try at socializing. And no, I'm not going to a costume party, Mister…" she looked him over, "whatever you're supposed to be."

The insult humored him. "Bishop," he said, deciding to introduce himself.

She shot out a laugh with wide eyes. "A bishop!" Her disgust added to the comedy, and by now he was kicking himself for being so far out of line with a woman who was obviously the opposite of what he'd assumed.

"My name is Sahvrin Bishop, I was introducing myself. I dress this way during festivals, it's a tradition."

And just as suddenly, other odd emotions chased off her anger, leaving her wordless and somehow more socially awkward than he was. "Where is your chaperone, Miss…"

Like a match on gasoline, those gray eyes flashed with fire again, right on him. "I am not a child."

He was sure she'd had this argument with somebody else many times judging by the amount of pissed she was. Brother? Father? Boyfriend? Surely not boyfriend or he'd be with her. "I wasn't saying you were, I was wondering why you're out here alone in a city you know nothing about."

She shot a finger at him, like they were having a fight. "I know plenty about this town, I've studied it and have planned to come here my entire life. I probably know more than you do!"

He glanced around. Mon Dieu, her dramatics were a calling card for trouble. "I don't know what chaperone means where you come from," he said, angling his look at her, "but here it's another adult individual, preferably male, that makes sure you're not mugged or worse."

"I know what chaperone means--"

Sahvrin pulled his chirping phone from his pocket and looked at the screen. "Excuse me," he said, answering his sister's call.

"Mah-Mah is wondering if you have her grocery list still."

Sahvrin turned a little with closed eyes. Fffffuck, why did he have to agree to everything she asked of him? "I do."

"Ooookay, so you do but you don't," she interpreted, knowing him too well.

"Tell her she'll have her list before the night is up."

"Sahvrin will have your list before the stroke of midnight," she called out on the phone. "Where are you? Sounds loud."

He turned, remembering the girl. Shit, where'd she go? He looked around the crowd. "I was in town, trying to pick up something from the hardware store." He finally spotted her, engaged in conversation with a group of girls. She had that same bubbly joy, confirming her genuine naiveite.

"Hellooooo, earth to Sahvrin, come in Sahvrin."

"Sorry, it's hectic here." He glanced at her once more, debating on what to do. There wasn't much he could do, and he damn well wasn't volunteering to chaperone anybody.

He headed in the opposite direction, ready to get the hell out of there. "Tell Mah-Mah I'm getting it now. See you tonight."

CHAPTER 2

Sahvrin quickly strode across the pier, angling his head to get a read on the night sky through the dense canopy of trees. It was nice to finally be back at his tiny, isolated swamp home. He reminded himself this was why he didn't give the night run job to anybody else. He wanted it. Needed it. This was where he unwound from the constant needs and demands of his land business.

Shit, the storm was close.

He tossed his bait sack and supply bag into the pirogue and climbed in. Being the week of the crawfish festival meant drunks would hopefully put off sabotaging livelihoods till next week. Maybe. But that didn't account for the other shit brewing in the swamp.

The second he cleared his hidden cove, lightening greeted him with a spidery handwave across the dark sky. Thunder followed ten miles behind like a prelude to the sinister things on the horizon. It had only been two days since they broke off with the Roulette Gang, but it was a fucking glorious two days to be rid of that filthy tie.

His mind returned to the girl in town, followed by anger. Mon Dieu, she was like a mental plague, nagging at his conscience. He couldn't take back how he'd acted, it was done, over with. He'd had a bad day and a bad week before that, and now he was arguing with himself again about it. All his years of avoiding women had turned into him being married to himself. And his other half-- apparently Saint fucking Sahvrin--cut him no slack.

The sky lit up again with another light show but this time the thunder dragged its feet, putting the storm twenty miles away. He could make it. Old man Pierre and Leblanc paid him plenty to babysit their traps even in the rain.

Come Monday, he'd have his drone shipment unless the new postal worker delivered it to Canada by accident. The replacement would let him patrol traps from the convenience of his front porch. This time he wouldn't let his alligator buddy Gras Jean mistake it for a snack. And if he did, he'd make a fat wallet with his hide.

Sahvrin finally made it to Pierre's fish traps. He shut off the small engine, ready to enjoy some night tunes from the bayou. Only ten minutes in, he picked up a trap, along with an odd sound. Carefully baiting it, he lowered it back in the water, straining to hear around a deep roll of thunder.

The noise came again, and he grabbed his shotgun. Definitely human. He listened harder, his mind going through any animals that might make this sound while fighting to pinpoint the location it'd come from.

A distressed cry rode the air, and he yanked the cord on the motor, turning the boat around. Pulling out his flood light, he stood and scanned the trees slowly around him. "Help! Please!"

He jerked the beam left and it landed on a small head in the water near a cluster of trees. "Mon Dieu," he swore, hurrying the boat in their direction as fast as the motor could manage.

He set the light down and stopped next to a woman, stretching his hand out to her. Reaching her arm, he latched on and pulled her up a little and froze. "Mon fucking Dieu!" he whispered at the blood and gashes all over her face. Her left eye was nearly shut, and her lower lip split and swollen. He carefully pulled her into the boat. "I got you, I got you, ma-petite. I'm not going to hurt you."

His rage burned at seeing she only had underclothes on, her whole body black and blue. The noises she made said she'd been badly hurt. He looked around for the evil he felt crawling along his skin while getting the motor going. Clicking the light off, he sped as fast as he could toward his home with one hand on his shotgun.

"Please don't hurt me, please, please," she begged between sobs.

The terror in her voice made his blood boil but something else sickened his stomach. Fuck, please, no, no, no, don't let it be her. "Ma-ch`ere, I'm not going to hurt you," he said, fighting to keep his voice soft. "Can you tell me what happened to you? I'm taking you someplace safe."

She only answered with sobbing mixed with painful groans that threatened to undo him.

"Shhh, shhh, it's okay, Ma Petite, don't talk. On-est proche-la, it won't be long, I promise you. Save your strength. We'll get you help, just hold on for me."

Sahvrin hated to but he took the long way back. He couldn't risk being followed. The woman from town's naïve, happy face kept cycling in his head until he craved to kill.

If it was her, she'd obviously escaped being trafficked. And being as beautiful as she was, whoever was responsible would definitely be down a lot of money. They'd come looking. God, he prayed they fucking did. Even as his guilt ate at him, he had to acknowledge the miracle of finding her. And he did, with a soul burning gratitude.

Back in his cove, he shut off the motor and tied the boat secure before climbing out. He glanced at the girl and panic hit him at how quiet and still she was. He found his small flashlight and knelt next to the boat, shining it on her. Please don't be fucking dead, please. He laid the light on the pier and reached out to touch her neck for a pulse.

She bolted up, screaming, arms flying. "Shhhhh, shhh, ma-ch`ere, you're okay," he called, holding his hands up to show he wasn't a threat. "I'm not going to hurt you," he added, watching her slowly realize her surroundings. "I found you in the water? You're safe, I promise." He drew a quick cross over his heart, the shadows hiding her face from him.

She let out a sob and he aimed the light beam just to her left, not wanting to blind her. But he needed to see. His stomach knotted with sickness at finally getting a good look. Fucking Dieu, it was her.

She didn't seem to recognize him and now he wasn't sure giving his name was the best idea. But her knowing he wasn't a threat was more important. "You know me, Ma Petite," he said gently, lowering the flashlight to the pier. "We met a couple of days ago? I was the town prick, Sahvrin Bishop?"

She suddenly gave a loud sob and reached for him, the act cutting him to pieces as he hurried and took hold of her upper arms. "Can you stand for me Ma Petite? You're safe here, I promise you."

Her body shook as she fought to get to her feet. "Yes, that's it, come to me." He managed to get her on the pier, fighting the need to scoop her up in his arms. "Can you walk?"

Her jaw shook and she crossed her arms over her chest, reminding him she was in only undergarments.

"I will go get a blanket to cover you, Ma Petite. Can I do that?"

His eyes adjusted in the darkness, making out that she looked at him for many seconds then nodded.

"Don't try to move, I don't want you to hurt yourself. You'll wait?"

She nodded more and he went quickly, not wanting to leave her alone. There was no logical reason to fear anybody finding his place, not unless they knew him and even then, he'd likely have to lead the way.

Returning with his heirloom patch quilt, he held it out toward her as he came. "My mother made this quilt when I was a young boy," he said, hoping to put her at ease as he carefully wrapped it around her shoulders.

She held it closed tightly, staring up at him. Shock and trauma had her eyes wide and wild, her trembling lips shut. "Can you walk, Ma Petite?" he asked very gently. "Please, let me help you." He put his arms around her, relieved that she didn't fight.

Her jaw rattled loudly as she took a step then choked out a sob.

He scooped her up in his arms. "I got you, I got you, shhhh. No walking for you."

He hurried down the pier, needing to get her in the light to see how bad she was hurt. He may end up having to put her right back in his air boat and get her to a hospital.

****

Beth fought to stop her jaw from clattering as he carried her. She clung to his neck and hid her face in his shoulder. How was it possible, how did he find her? Why was he out there? Was he looking for her? Did he know she was missing? He'd all but predicted what happened to her and that caused her to feel so *stupid* and dirty down to her soul.

She tried to see where they were but hurt too much to move. Every time he spoke, his kind voice and words pushed back her fears while making her wonder if he was really the same person. But unless he had a twin, she'd never forget his hauntingly handsome face.

But no sleeping, she had to stay awake, she had to keep her eyes open and remain alert. There were too many crazy questions for her to blindly trust and she swore never to do that again. She needed to be ready and able to fight if she had to.

"Welcome to my humble abode, Ma Petite," he said softly as he walked with her.

His humble abode. *Ma Petite.* He'd called her that before when they'd first met. It was sandwiched between an insult and the meaning of it was lost in what she'd construed as mockery. But she'd spent every terrifying second during that nightmare knowing just how stupid she'd been, down to the depths of her hurting bones.

Things filled her vision as he walked with her and a row of family pictures on a mantle gave her a shot of hope.

"I'm going to lay you down," he said softly, lowering her to what felt like a bed.

Try as she might, she couldn't unlatch her arms from around his neck or stop the sudden sobs.

"Okay, okay," he whispered, lowering so she could hold on to him. "You don't have to let go." He cooed soft shhhhh's, over and over until her sobs finally subsided.

Nightmare fragments flashed in her mind, bringing a wave of panic. "I need to call my dad," she mumbled, shakily, holding tighter to his neck. "H-he'll worry."

"Okay, okay, please," he said. "Let me make sure I don't need to take you to the hospital."

She wondered how he'd figure that out, finally letting go of him. She watched him turn and pull a chair over, placing it next to the bed. He sat, seeming to study her face with an angry look. "Mon Dieu, Ma Petite," he said, looking into her eyes now. "Who did this to you? Do you know?"

Tears flooded her vision, and she shook her head.

"Okay, okay," he cooed, making the tears come faster. "You don't need to talk. Just nod your head while I ask you questions, can you do that for me?"

She nodded, her jaw back to banging together again.

"Please forgive me for having to ask these questions," he said softly. "But...were you sexually assaulted?"

She closed her eyes at the regret in his gaze, pain shooting through the left, swollen one. They'd hurt her in every way but that one. She shook her head, not wanting him to take her anywhere, especially a public place. He sighed out a long string of words in French and for some reason it helped him seem safer to her. The relief that gave her brought on a wave of tears.

"Shhhh, okay, ma-petite catin." He stroked her forehead, and the sudden boom of thunder made her jump and latch onto his arm. "It's just the rain," he soothed, letting her hold on to him. "Nothing will hurt you here, I promise you this. What is your name Ma Petite? I never did get it."

She swallowed, wondering over the regret in his voice. "B-beth. Elizabeth Sweetling."

"I should call you Beth?"

She nodded, her whole body shaking now.

"Are you cold?"

She nodded again and held his arm tighter when he stood.

"I'm just getting you another blanket, I won't leave you."

He waited as she fought with herself to release him.

"That's a brave girl," he said when she managed it, stroking her forehead again. He turned and she watched him disappear around the wall. She listened to him in another part of the room, talking about the rain and his fishing traps and how he'd found her, the miracle of it.

So, he lived out there and fished? He returned with a blanket and shook it out before laying it carefully on her then pressing it down around her shaking body.

"I'm going to make you some tea that will help with the pain, would you like that?"

"Yes," she croaked when the pain of nodding became too much.

"Does it hurt a lot, Ma Petite?"

He wiped the tears that ran again, shhhhing her as she mumbled another *yes*.

"Do you think anything is broken? I need to know some of these things," he said, full of tender regret.

"I don't…I don't know," she said. "Maybe yes," she strained, fighting back a sob and losing the battle.

"Ma Petite," he cooed more tenderly than ever, stroking her forehead. "Let me fix you the tea, it will help you."

She managed a nod. "Then I can call my dad?"

"I'm sorry to say that my phone reception here is no good. I can take the boat not far from here if you insist, and call him for you?"

She shook her head, not wanting him to leave. "Tomorrow I can go with you?"

"We can do this if you are able?"

She nodded and he went back to she guessed the kitchen area on the other side of the half wall. Another crack of thunder shook the little room, making her tremble more. She didn't want to close her eyes and see the nightmare. She couldn't take it.

The smell of food soon filled the air and her stomach said she hadn't eaten in days. She needed to use whatever she had to keep her out of the nightmare flashbacks. The only life preserver was him. Sahvrin Bishop. What a unique name and man he was turning out to be. Nothing like the horribly mannered *prick* she'd first met.

He appeared with a cup and sat on the chair with it. "I'm going to help you sit up just a little so you can drink this, can you do that for me?" he asked.

She nodded and Sahvahrin worked his arm under her shoulders and lifted her just enough to get the cup to her mouth. The smell of mint reached her nose. And lemon.

"Drink as much as you can for me, Ma Petite. The more, the better, it will help you. Forgive the taste."

The first careful swallow brought the memory of being strangled. Whimpers fought to overtake her, and she focused on getting the liquid down before they could.

"So good, Ma Petite," he praised when she drank it all. He carefully lay her back down and set the cup on the floor. "This will help the pain and help you sleep." He was back to stroking her forehead and the feeling was suddenly the best thing in all the world.

"Sah…varin?"

"Yes?"

The words got trapped in her throat and she forced them out. "Thank you."

He spoke another soft string of French and she fought to open her eyes, managing slits.

"What did that mean?"

"I said no need to thank me, but it was a miracle that I found you."

She nodded as he pressed the covers gently around her. "Don't…leave."

He took her hand in his and she held it as tight as she could. "I won't leave. I'll be right here."

This time when she closed her eyes, she couldn't open them. Wow…whatever he'd given her was amazing. So amazing. "Don't leave me," she managed, then remembered she'd already said that.

His warm fingers moved across her forehead. "I will not leave you, Ma Petite."

There was regret in his deep voice and she wondered over it. Did he blame himself? She hoped not.

Ma Petite. She repeated it in her head. "What does that mean?"

"What does what mean?"

"Ma Petite."

"Means my little one."

Little. And naïve. And stupid. They all felt synonymous now. She'd proven him right on every turn. "I'm…not that little," was the only truth remaining and not worth mentioning, but she did.

"To me you are just a little thing," he said, still stroking her forehead.

"I like your tea," she murmured. "And…your mom's quilt is warm. And pretty."

"How old are you, Ma Petite?"

She wondered why there would be pain in his soft voice with that question.

"I'm…I'm twenty-four."

"No no noooo, surely you cannot be, Ma Petite," he said, sounding doubtful.

She fought to open her eyes, failing. "I know…I look way older."

His low chuckle helped lift her heavy eyelids but the smile on his lips and light in his dark brown eyes made her forget what he'd said. Gosh, he was…"so handsome."

She tried to be embarrassed at hearing the slurred thought out loud, but then his smile had grown and told her it was okay. She was so high, she realized. What was in that tea?

"Try to sleep, Ma Petite. I will stay awake while you do."

She couldn't even nod as a warm darkness wrapped her mind.

****

Sahvrin needed to get his head together. Twenty-four. The same age as his baby sister. He'd thought she couldn't be more than seventeen, not a day over eighteen. How exactly did she end up in that situation? How did she escape? He couldn't ask why they hadn't raped her, but it was surely something he wondered. There was nothing he could do but wait for her to wake up and answer those questions and now that he knew she was more than of age, it would make that part easier.

When she was sound asleep, he got in his boat and rode to the reception spot about a mile out, the clean night air doing not a damn thing for his blood lust. Twenty-*fucking* four. Was she alone? Were there more girls with her?

At location, he opened the group chat with his brothers and Pah-Pah and typed. *Tonight, I found traffic in the swamp. They dropped something, or something escaped. Keep your ears pricked and send out feelers for anybody looking for missing persons with the name Elizabeth Sweetling. They'll come looking for this one. Lazure, this could have been our baby sister. I'll call you and set up a meeting at The Weigh Station. She will stay with me until we figure out what we're doing.*

He hit send and checked for any messages. He spotted one from Juliette and opened it. *Hey lil-bro, you coming to the party, right? I have a friend I want you to meet.*

"Mon Dieu," he muttered as he typed. *Not if you're setting me up, no. Did Mah-Mah and Pah-Pah turn this job over to you, petite soeur?* Ever since his twelve-year celibacy code had lifted, they'd been busy trying to find him love. But unless love hunted him down and fell right into his lap, he wouldn't be looking.

He started a new paragraph on his phone, glancing briefly around. *Listen. I found bad traffic in the swamp not far from here. Don't go anywhere alone until we find out who it is. This pit is deadly, do you understand me, petite soeur?*

He hit send and waited for a bit for any replies. He recalled the bruises all over her body, remembering she needed clothes. He then remembered the modest black dress he'd first seen her in and her bright smile, followed by her hurt and anger when he'd been a dick.

He opened Lazure's box this time. *She needs clothes. Bring whatever you can from Juliette, they are about the same size. Bring Mah-Mah to check her injuries too.* He needed to inspect her closer and needed a woman to do that.

The storm picked up steam and he pocketed his phone, then started the boat. She needed ointments for her wounds. More pain medicine. Food. She needed to eat and rest and that was it.

Several hours later, a fresh fish coubion simmered with every medicinal herb he could find on hand thrown in it. He made another concoction of his tea and set it to steeping. She could use a hot soak but all he had was a shower.

Another round of whimpers reached him, telling she needed more medicine. He went to her side, shhhhing away the demons with a stroke of his finger across her forehead. Merci Dieu it seemed to work every time. In sleep, she was more petite seeming than ever. But definitely not a child and he needed to be careful. The look in her eyes when she'd called him handsome wasn't the same look women normally had, but one a lovestruck teenager might have with their savior. Only, she wasn't a teenager, but a traumatized woman prone to vulnerabilities.

He needed to wake her for more tea and see how she was feeling. At some point, she'd need to relieve herself, and Mon Dieu, he was not looking forward to that.

****

The first light of dawn came, and he fixed a cup of his special tea with a bowl of hot food then pulled a small end table next to the bed and sat. He carefully touched her shoulder and called softly, "Ma Petite." He did that several times, not wanting to startle her. She finally woke with a sharp gasp, and he stroked her forehead, shhhhing her. "It's Sahvrin, Ma Petite. Are you hungry?"

She whimpered and tried to get up, gasping on pain.

"No, no, no, don't try to move," he chided softly.

"I...I need to pee," she squeaked around trembling breaths. Even in her broken condition, she had enough self-esteem to be embarrassed. That was a good sign, he thought.

"I will help you to the bathroom."

She shook her head even as she reached for his hand.

"I will get you to the job and you will finish, yes?"

"My clothes," she said, worried.

"I'm not looking. I have a sister your age, this is how I see you, okay? And I have clothes I will give you to wear after you take care of your emergency."

She nodded, seeming desperate, so he eased the blanket off and lifted her, forcing himself not to think about the black and blue all over her body. Mon Dieu, what had they fucking done to her? And why had they, if they had intended on selling her?

"I will set you down in the bathroom and you will fight the rest of the way, yes? You are a fighter, right ma-petite?"

He caught her nod as he stood her carefully in the small bathroom. "The towel bar is sturdy, you can hold on to it."

"Yes, hurry."

He exited the bathroom and shut the door releasing a breath.

"Go," she pled to him in distress.

"I'll go out of the house," he called back, hurrying out. "Call me if you need."

He pulled his phone out and checked for messages again. Sometimes when the weather was clear, he got a signal. But likely they'd not see messages for another few hours. All drunk no doubt. Sahvahrin remembered the clothes and hurried back inside, going through his drawers. Flannel pants and a t-shirt would have to do for her.

"Ma Petite, I have some clothes here for you," he called loudly. "I will put them on the floor by the bathroom, yes?"

"Thank you," she answered after a few seconds, her words frail sounding. "I want…to take…Please."

He went closer to the door. "Say it again?"

"A shower, please."

Mon Dieu, already? "Can you manage?"

"I think so," he barely heard her say.

"I will put the clothes on the floor here."

"Thank you."

He stood, tense with the idea of her attempting such a thing so early. "I have food and medicine for you when you're done. Please take your time and don't hurt yourself. Call me if you are in trouble?"

He caught her "Yes," and he nodded, setting the clothes down. "Everything is there that you need. The towels, if you can't reach, call me."

He hurried to the boat and made his way out of the cove, speeding to his reception spot. 15 new messages.

He opened the main screen. Two from his sister, one from the group and several from each brother and his Pah-Pah.

He started with his sisters, worried about her. *What kind of "foreign" snake pit are we talking about? I won't bring my friend if you promise to come in person and tell me everything. I miss your hairy face.*

Sahvahrin absently stroked his short beard, opening the group message next.

Lazure: *We'll talk when you come today. Keep details sparse.*

He went to each brother's box, finding much of the same. Questions about specifics and warnings to be careful, each ending with them seeing him later that day. And how was he supposed to leave her? Should he bring her?

No. He couldn't. They'd have to just meet near his place.

He decided to give the message to his father. *I can't make it. Babysitting petite snake bait and can't leave it alone. Let's meet at the Bayou Boudin dock by my lil shack. Tell my brothers, I need to get back. I'm at reception point. Set the time and I will be there.*

His phone rang shortly after he sent the message.

He answered it. "Lazure."

"Sahvrin, what's happened?"

"I was checking traps when I found her."

"Is this a child?"

"A girl. A young woman," he corrected. "Twenty-four. They hurt her bad. But no sexual assault for some reason. "And…" He held his jaw shut for a few seconds, his rage burning.

"What?"

"I met her a couple of days ago, the same day we left the meeting at the Roulettes. She asked for help, and I was a fucking prick, that's what she called me, and she was right. I didn't…" He realized he was about to make the same stupid excuses he'd been making on repeat. "I let this happen. She was naïve, I saw this, and I let her go into the devil's lair."

"What could you have done?"

"Chaperone her, I don't know, something besides be a cocksucker. I'm responsible for my actions and they were *not* honorable, Lazure."

He was silent for a few seconds before sighing. "You are responsible for your words and actions but beyond that we don't know, we just don't know. We *will* find who did this. This can't happen again in our land."

"Agreed."

"Are we sure it's what we think?"

He shook his head, looking around. "I need to ask more questions. She's taking a shower and I don't know how with how beat up she is. This says something about her, yes?"

"Qui," he said quietly before sighing a "Mon Dieu, Sahvrin. When will you know how this happened and what exactly happened?"

A familiar rage tightened Sahvrin's gut at hearing the cold hardness in his Pah-pah's voice. Life had settled down a lot since the war against the swamp demons fifteen years before. A lifetime ago and yet like yesterday. "I will find out in the next hour."

"Call me when you know, and we will meet after at The Weigh Station. I think we need to gather The Horde."

CHAPTER 3

Beth stood still in agony under the hot water. She felt like if she could bathe and wash herself, it would remove some of the nightmare staining her pores. The pain would be worth enduring for that.

It took her thirty minutes just to wash her hair with breaks every few minutes, The citrus, minty smell of the soap seemed to clean her from the inside, and she couldn't stop from washing her hair with it a second time. She borrowed the suds from the second wash to take care of the rest of her body. Feeling the lumps and bumps all over brought a sudden avalanche of sobs up her chest.

No more, no more, no more, please. She needed to move forward. Get well. She allowed her thoughts to latch on to Sahvrin. Sahvrin her strange savior. Where was he? God, he was right, it was a miracle that he found her. She considered the tender sounds in his voice, the endearing words he used with her. How handsome he was. Very. Very, very handsome.

It wasn't good to fixate on him, but he was the only distraction she had. As long as she remembered that, then she could protect her emotions. It was the one thing her college professor had drilled into her head—don't lose track of your emotions. Use them, but always return them where they belong. Psych 101.

She got back to Sahvrin. How old was he, anyway? Maybe his thirties. He had a sister her age. That's how he saw her he'd said.

By the time she'd managed to wash every inch of her aching body, she'd ended up in some odd corners with him. She might have thought he was religious if it wasn't for her first meeting with The Mean Bishop man. Then again, his anger had been almost a righteous one if not common sense. Could be a kind of…swamp priest. Was that even a thing?

He'd ask more questions soon and she was ready to tell him all the answers she knew.

"Ma-Petite?"

Her stomach jolted at the sound of his deep yet soft voice. "Yes?"

"Are you okay?"

God, not hardly. "I'm getting out now."

"I will heat your food and your tea."

He'd cooked for her. Or he'd just cooked. He made that tea for her. She realized what she was doing. Looking for things that meant more than they did. Noted. She would repay him for everything. She had plenty of money and by the looks of his home, he could use some it would appear. Although he didn't seem the least bit lacking in anything. She'd have to find a way to repay him, one he'd accept.

She also needed to call her father. Once she did that, she'd focus fully on her recovery. She was a victim of a horrific crime, this was her reality. Many women were every day, and they overcame. She would do the same. One day at a time. Then he'd see she wasn't a child, she was a woman of strength and determination to learn from her mistakes. A mature, strong, independent woman. She'd like very much to at least recover some integrity.

By the time she got to the getting dressed part, her will power had taken a dive. She was struggling to remember why she needed to push through the pain.

Focus. Don't stop now.

She eyed the clothes on the floor that she'd dragged in with a foot. She used her toes as tweezers and slowly brought the white t-shirt up and grabbed it with her hand. Another thirty seconds and she was working it over her head. Pulling in the scent, she closed her eyes and let herself get lost in the smell. Almost like…fresh, clean, minty earth and…something else she didn't recognize. Smelled amazing. She'd ask what kind of detergent he used. If she was able to take anything good with her from her experience here, let it be this smell. She'd buy a lifetime supply of it.

The flannel pants were a little rough feeling, more so than the t-shirt. Definitely no fabric softener in his laundry. But not so rough it would bother her. Mild panic hit at remembering she had no clean bra or panty. The thought of putting on the dirty ones made her skin crawl. But it was all she had, she needed to wash them at least.

The last thing on the endless impossible tasks was her hair. She faced herself in the small mirror over the sink and gasped at the sight. Dear God, what a mess she was. Her hair, her face. She angled her head, trying to see herself for the first time. Was difficult to see anything around the swelling and discoloration. Did he really see her as an adult teenager? She'd honestly thought she looked older than her age.

She glanced down at her chest where her very un-child-like nipples pushed against the fabric. Oh God, that wouldn't work. She'd wash her bra and wear it wet. She wouldn't let herself come across as an absent-minded nipple showing-off tramp. She knew the kind, she'd seen them before in her own circle of friends in college.

She got back to the matter of her hair while her bra and panty soaked in the sink. She looked around in the small cabinet and located a wooden tray with a small black comb. She'd likely get it lost in her hair and need his help to cut it out. Not happening.

Eyeing herself in the mirror, her waist long hair felt suddenly very stupid. She blinked back a rush of burning tears, steadying her shaky breaths while running her fingers through it. Felt like thirty minutes before she finally worked through all the major knots.

"I'm just checking on you Ma Petite," he gently called at the door, making her jump.

"I'm almost done. Sorry," she said, her words shaking with the rest of her. She held on to the sink, closing her eyes as pain ran hot circuits through every muscle she had and then some. She was sweating now, she realized. This was stupid.

She carefully squeezed the soapy water out of her undergarments then put them back in and repeated. She let out the water and filled it up again, rinsing till the water ran clear. Ringing them out turned into a quick joke. She had zero strength. Mercy. They'd have to drip dry on her body.

Slowly lifting the shirt, she fought with everything left in her to wrap the bra around and fasten it. "Oh God," she gasped, after managing. She leaned her forearms and head against the mirror as black spots swam in her vision.

Five more minutes and she won the bra war. All that was left was putting her arms back in the t-shirt. The panties could wait. She'd let them dry somewhere inconspicuous.

Finally done, she realized she needed to pee, and the idea brought tears to her eyes. Lowering her body to that toilet brought her will power back to ground zero. She fought the need to cry, slowly shaking her head with her eyes closed. *No more crying. Not now. Maybe later in bed, not when you're about to face Sahvrin.*

As she made her way down to the commode, she stifled and choked back the pain in her sides and ribs. Jesus, Jesus. She lost track of how many times that man had kicked her. Surely, he'd broken something. Or fractured.

At last done, she took hold of the bathroom door handle and turned. She gripped the door jamb as the door opened.

"Ma Petite!" he said, hurrying to her. "You made it." The pride in his tone was suddenly worth every ounce of agony. "Such a fighter, you are," he said at her side, taking hold of her arm. "Let me help you."

The moment she traded the door jamb for his arm, her legs gave out. As if expecting exactly that, he scooped her up in his arms again. "I'm sorry, I—"

"Don't apologize," he scolded, this time his voice firmer as he hurried her to the bed. "You've done too much already. Are you hungry?"

"Yes," she said, wincing even though he lay her so carefully in the bed.

"I have your food, I will feed you."

"I can…probably manage."

He turned and pulled the small table next to the bed again and sat. "Ahhh, I should have sat you up."

She began to move, feeling like she could possibly raise herself on her elbow. He assisted her until she was sitting up again. Probably better, pain had flared to a constant throb in her right shoulder. She slowly reached for the bowl, intent to not be an invalid but he shook his head.

"Let me, Ma Petite. You overworked yourself."

She stared at him, torn between not wanting to look weak and giving him what he seemed to need. Why did he need it? *Because you remind him of his baby sister.*

She put her hands in her lap, closing her eyes briefly, and when she opened them, he said, "Amen?"

He thought she'd prayed. The idea that he was a religious man returned and she lowered her head. "No, I… should have though. I am now," she added, closing her eyes, and thanking God for everything. She wasn't nun material, but she tried her best to be a good person. "Amen," she mumbled, finding him watching her with a small smile that made her uncomfortable. "What?"

He shook his head and lowered it, stirring her food. "Nothing, Ma Petite. It's not important." He ended the possible discussion by presenting a spoonful of food. Her stomach took over and she opened her mouth carefully and took the bite. Not even the pain in her busted lip and jaw could keep the desperate "mmmmm" from pushing up her throat. She'd closed her eyes, savoring it, but swallowing brought another round of agony and flashes of strangulation. She forced the food to stay down as another bite waited. She latched her will-power to his perfect, full lips like a life preserver.

"You like it?"

She took the bite, again her mmmmm coming, louder than before as she nodded. "What is this?" There was fish and other meat.

"Fish coubion and sausage." He stirred it and brought the spoon to her mouth again. "The trout is fresh, and the sausage is made by my father. Beef and chicken. The rest I grow myself, all the herbs and vegetables."

Wow, he grew his food? Amazed, she ate the bite, never remembering loving any food so much as she did this. Was it because every appetite she possessed was starving and being fed all at once? No doubt. She took the next bite, not letting herself care. She couldn't control any of that. It was what it was, and she would enjoy the good things that came when they came.

After the bowl was empty, he presented blue metal looking cup. "Your tea, ma che`re."

She didn't say a word as she gulped it down and finished with a huge sigh. Eyes closed, she began the process of laying back down, beyond ready to sleep. She welcomed his arm around her shoulders as he aided her in the agonizing feat. "Thank you," she finally managed after she lay there with her world spinning. "For everything."

"It is the least I can do," he said softly. The slide of his warm finger across her forehead felt like heaven. "Ma Petite, I should let you sleep but I need to ask you some questions."

She tried to nod. "Okay."

She felt him sit on the bed, happy he stayed close. "How did you find yourself in this terrible situation?"

The question seemed bigger than life and complicated. What had brought her to those final moments of stupidity that led to the abduction? It was far more than one wrong decision or turn. "I...always wanted to visit Louisiana," she said, starting there, since it seemed to apply. "My father never wanted me to. Fought me all the way till the day I left. He wanted me to go to *Paris* with him instead. Guess he thought that was more romantic to his little girl, but I wasn't like most girls, I had dreams of coming for the famous Crawfish Festival ever since I did a school report when I was fourteen. My dad *hated* that I even wanted to live here. What else would a good daughter do but not listen to him?"

Silent tears of remorse rolled down her cheeks. "In the end, my father just begged me to take a friend. He was just worried, I realize now. But... I want to think that it's good I didn't because she might have..." She swallowed, focusing on the stuff she needed to tell. "They were going to sell me," she remembered. "To the highest bidder. A...virgin," she added, hating that she had to give such personal information. She wanted to ask how they even knew she was a virgin while being worried what he thought of a twenty-four-year-old being one. She realized how stupid it was to care about that, now.

"Can you tell me how you got away, Ma Petite?"

She welcomed the question away from the humiliating virgin expose. "I...found something in the boat I was in...and managed to cut the rope around my ankles then wrists. I waited for a place to...escape into the water." She opened her eyes as the terror of that moment in her escape returned. She focused on his handsome face. "I went into the water...very quietly. And I swam under water for as long as I could hold my breath. When I came up, he was far away, and I swam into the trees. I didn't stop swimming..."

"Shhh, don't cry, Ma Petite. You made it, yes? And I found you."

She nodded, closing her eyes while fighting the tremble in her lips. "I was so scared he would come back and find me," she strained around the constriction in her bruised throat. "When he didn't, I got scared I would die out there, or get eaten by an alligator. I could hear them, I think, all around. That was my luck at that point," she said between breaths, bringing a hand to cover her eyes while he stroked her hair. "And then you came," she quipped before a sob gushed out. "You were just there somehow, and you saved me. You tried to save me before and I didn't listen," she strained out.

His shhhh's had never been more welcome as he took her hand between his and pet it repeatedly while she cried.

"You are safe now, Ma Petite che`re." The sudden warmth of his lips pressed on the back of her hand, clobbering the mess inside her. They were small kisses he'd likely give to a distraught child, oh God, her mind honed in on the feeling of that perfect part of him pressing so softly into her skin. Everything about this side of him was so contrary to the man she'd originally met. And the agonizing hunger it woke in her brought new pains and cravings that cut way deeper than the physical ones.

****

Sahvrin wrestled with himself and the need to take her agony and pain. Maybe he shouldn't have kissed her hand, yet it seemed right and necessary for her. He would have to ask more questions later. She'd overdone her bathroom excursion and the tea was already taking effect. He placed her small hand next to her, petting it one last time, vowing to find the people who did this then give them the most horrific death he could dream up.

A virgin. This was a surprise for her age but not at all for her personality. Such an innocent, pure spirit she had, a perfect lure to that wickedness. They couldn't hunt these demons fast enough.

After eating, he considered his next steps. Meet his brothers and Pah-Pah or get some sleep. He'd stayed up all night as promised, watching over her, and exhaustion siphoned the strength from his muscles. He didn't have all the answers he wanted yet. Two hours was all he needed and when she woke, they'd talk again. Then he'd meet his father and brothers later that evening when she rested again.

A moment later, the sound of a boat reached him, and he quickly got his gun and hurried out. His stomach loosened at seeing Lazure's boat. Merci Dieu, his Mah-Mah wasted no time coming to check her.

Helping her off the boat and hugging her, he explained everything he knew so far and didn't know as they hurried to the house. She tried to make him stay outside but he insisted on coming in to at least make sure she wasn't scared.

It took several attempts to rouse her to half coherency. "Ma Petite," he whispered. "My mother is here to check your injuries, okay? She will be touching you everywhere and I don't want you to be afraid. You understand?"

"I'm...I'm not dressed," she mumbled.

"You have clothes on," he reminded while stroking the stress from her puckered brow.

"I mean...I don't...I need to be dressed... better..."

Mon Dieu, she was worried about impressions with his mother. "Mah-Mah doesn't care about such things."

She reached and flopped her hand toward him. "But...I do..."

"Shhhh, you must not care about this. I need her to check you, can she do that?"

She finally nodded and he stood, eying his mother who stared at Beth with a distraught look, taking in her battered condition.

She turned her gaze to him and placed a hand on his arm and nodded. "You're doing perfectly," she whispered, somehow knowing the very thing he worried over before quietly sending him out.

He waited outside with Lazure, focusing on delivering his previous plans to him. Sounds of His Petite crying froze him, and his father stopped him from going in. "Your Mah-Mah knows what she's doing, let her do."

He forced himself to comply, unable to even speak as her broken wails filled every part of him until he burned with a rage he knew would never be satisfied.

****

After his Mah-Mah came out of the house, Sahvrin was beside himself with uselessness. "She is sleeping and is fine."

"What did you find?" he asked, bracing for the worst.

"I don't think anything is broken. Fractured yes." She handed him a sheet of paper showing him all the injuries on a stick diagram she'd drawn. To see the extent of the damage in such a list made him sick.

"Everything you need to do for her is here. There's clothes and medicines," she said as he read through the list. "I wasn't sure what to expect so I brought more than enough. It's all in the satchel on the little table. If you need anything, call me."

"Thank you Mah-Mah," he said, hugging her goodbye. She held on to him tight and rubbed her hand along his back.

"You are such a good man, son," she said. "And she is a very strong girl. She just needs time, good food and medicine, and lots of rest." She stroked both hands along his face and the affection made his skin crawl. She wouldn't be wearing that beaming smile if she knew his actions with her before she was abducted. Maybe she did know and wasn't bothered. Well, he fucking was and would always be.

"Thank you again," he said, beyond desperate to check on her himself.

She gave him a look-over and said, "Go," as if seeing he needed to. He wasn't trying to hide it. He didn't think he could if he wanted to. He just knew that getting her whole again and protecting her while that happened was his job, nobody else. Not even his mother.

CHAPTER 4

Sahvrin took the couch to get some sleep so he wouldn't be useless. When he woke and looked over the couch at his bed, he found it empty. Sudden panic hit him, and he shot up, hurrying to the bathroom. He knocked on the door. "Beth?"

He looked around when he got no answer and hurried to the front door. "Mon Dieu!" he said at seeing her sitting at the end of the pier. But she was in a yellow dress, and he wondered if he was dreaming or seeing a vision. "Ma Petite, are you okay?" he called as he went.

She turned only her profile from where she sat and nodded before staring out again. He lowered next to her in open wonder and worry. "You had a bad dream?"

She looked over at him and shook her head. "I actually feel a lot better," she said, sounding relieved. "Wanted to get fresh air. Guess your tea is working. And food."

"Ahhh, mercie Dieu," he said in relief, still wanting to touch her to make sure he wasn't dreaming. He remembered his Mah-Mah brought clothes and let out a breath. "You changed."

She looked down. "I found the clothes your mom brought. *Love* this dress."

"I thought you were an angel," he said, seeing she might be worried over what he thought. The risky comment paid off with her genuine laugh. He looked out across the cove, realizing it was the afternoon. "Mon *Dieu*, I overslept."

"You needed it," she said, her concern coming through. "How long have you lived out here? I have never seen a more beautiful place. It's like another world."

He regarded the look on her battered face and the sincerity in her voice as she studied his paradise. "All my life, Ma Petite," he said, looking out where the sun lit up the water beyond his little cove. "Glad you like it."

"I love it," she said. "So different from where I live."

He looked at her, remembering. "Ah yes, you are an ice princess if I recall correctly."

"You remembered," she said, smiling a little, like that made her happy. "Lots of cold and snow."

"Mon Dieu, I would not survive."

She gave a small grin and brought her finger to the split in her lip.

"I put alligator grease on your cuts while you slept, I hope it's okay." She turned curious eyes and he laughed. "I tease, Ma Petite. It's just herbs and oils Mah-Mah left."

She grew serious. "She came," she said. "Thought I dreamed it."

"I asked her to come look at you. Seemed good for a woman to do this."

She regarded him only a second. "That was thoughtful. Thank you." She added a small smile. "I thought your Mah-Mah was an angel, and I was dying. She's very kind and gentle and beautiful. Like you." He fought not to laugh at her words and now distress. "Kind like you, I meant. And gentle. Not that you're not…handsome…"

He let out his laugh now. "Ma Petite, you are digging yourself into a grave with this."

"I am," she gasped, seeming glad he wasn't bothered.

And he wasn't, at least not like she probably thought. He'd never met a person like her and was more fascinated with that difference than anything.

She touched her lip with her finger, casting shy glances toward him. "That's why it's so much better?"

"My great ma-ma's recipe. For sure, good stuff."

"I want to repay you for all your help."

"Repay? Mon Dieu, that is not how it works."

She regarded him, appearing confused. "Then… how does it work so I can repay you?"

He couldn't stop his laugh at her sincerity. "You do not repay something like this," he said, wondering over the customs where she came from. "Do you expect payment for saving a person's life where you come from, Ma Petite?"

The sharp look she gave him reminded him of the woman with that pride and spirit he'd ran head into that night. "No, of course not. I guess repay was a poor choice of words. How do I…do something nice to say thank you?"

"I didn't mean to imply anything bad on your part," he assured with a smile, liking that fight in her. "I know customs can be different." He gestured with an arm around them. "Breathe the fresh air in my paradise is a nice gift to me?" He studied her a moment. "You are repaying me every second you draw breath. Now, I'm rich."

She lowered her head, and he noticed the difference in her hair then. "You have so much hair, Ma Petite, how do you manage?"

The worried look she gave made him laugh.

"I mean it gets everywhere when you try to…live and such?" he explained. She looked very different with her hair clean. Nothing child-like about it on her.

"I usually wear it up in some way. Or braided."

"Really," he said, surprised. "In the North Pole, I think you would want to let that beautiful fur cover you."

She laughed and he pointed at her. "See, Ma Petite? You give me more payments with your joy."

She shook her lowered head and looked out over the water. "You are too kind Sahvrin."

"When I'm not being a prick," he agreed, casting a look at her, needing to see what she thought of that.

She might have smiled before muttering, "And a Bishop prick at that."

Laughter ripped out of him at that priceless comment. "Mon Dieu, you are more right than you know."

She eyed him, smiling with a shy look. "I thought of all the people to approach, you seemed the safest since you were dressed so nice."

He considered how to tell her the truth without scaring her. "I'm not bad. Not in the way you might think."

"Oh really," she said, smiling. "How are you bad?"

Her disbelieving tone and look had him ready to repent of all his sins just to make her world as pure as she saw it. "I'm only bad to bad people," he said, feeling like he'd just dirtied her with the confession.

"So, you're a mean bishop who does bad things to bad people."

He stared at the water below their feet, not able to look at her. "Something like that, yes."

"And you're mean to stupid women," she added.

Her words clobbered him. "Mon Dieu, you *gut* me."

"What? No," she cried. "I'm…I was teasing, I know you were angry because of how foolish I was. You were right to be, and I just wished I had understood that and…taken more precaution."

"I shouldn't have left you alone, Ma Petite," he said, forcing the words past the self-loathe in his chest. "What I did was unforgivable."

"Oh my God, no, please, you can't do that, you can't blame yourself for my stupidity."

"You were innocent and naïve." And sweet and kind.

"I'm twenty-four!" she cried. "I should have had more sense, don't you dare say otherwise. And fine, you could've been nicer and made it harder for them to…do what they did but that doesn't mean they wouldn't have at the end of the night when you were gone."

He knew this was true but… "My anger and reckless decision increased the odds."

They sat quiet for several moments and she sighed. "Fine, you're part to blame, is that what you want?"

"No. It's just what it is," he said firmly.

"Then you'll have to find ways to make it up to me, I guess. A year of private fishing lessons? Cooking lessons!" she shot out, pointing at him with a smile that stole his breath.

"I would do that for free, Ma Petite," he said grinning out at the water.

"Oh, *what* a discount," she said, pretending to write on her palm. "The very gallant Sahvrin Bishop—not the Mean Mr. Bishop—agrees to teach Beth how to fish and cook for a year." She held her hand out to him. "Sign on the dotted line."

He grinned and took her hand in his, looking at how small it was then traced the lifeline in her palm.

"That's a strange signature," she said, the delicate softness in her voice making him release her.

"I was measuring your lifeline," he said, angling a look at her. "Can't have you dying before the year is up."

Her huge laugh shattered the darkness enveloping him, making it suddenly easier to breathe. Mon Dieu, the power this woman had.

"Sahvrin Bishop is also a comedian," she said finally.

He smiled and shook his head.

"What? You are."

"I like the way you say my name."

"Oh?" She grew worried and studious. "How do you say it, I want to say it right."

He had to look at her, amazed with her need to care so much about a thing. "I just said I like the way you say it, Ma Petite. Tell me what you do in North Dakota."

She let the name issue go. "Well...I just only graduated college a couple of months ago, so, everything was school until recently."

He nodded, remembering about her college. "What did Ma Petite go to school to learn?"

"I...started out with one major then switched halfway through to digital mapping."

Digital mapping? How interesting. "I have never heard of this."

She explained to him everything, and he nodded in approval at seeing her passion. "You love maps, this surprises me."

She smiled and nodded. "Why does it surprise you?"

He shrugged, looking out onto the water. "I guess I imagined it something women would not be interested in. But I know the world is different than it used to be." He angled his head at her. "I think it's good you learn anything you set your heart on to learn." He wondered then. "Why did you change your first major halfway through?"

"Ah, yes," she began, gathering her hair in both hands and twisting it into a thick rope. Her slow movements reminded him she was hurting and bravely pushing through the pain. "I started out majoring to be a therapist." She gave a little half-laugh, and her blush showed through her battered cheeks. "The story is kind of embarrassing."

Sahvrin was immediately curious and tsked three times. "I am very nosy Ma Petite. I'm afraid I must know this."

He smiled that she knew he joked and even laughed at him. "Fine, I was old fashioned. My mother and my father were…not so happily married, and growing up, when I figured that out, I decided as a young girl I wanted to help them."

Sahvrin was beginning to wonder if she was an angel. "Why would you be embarrassed about wanting to do such an angelic thing, Ma Petite? And what made you change your mind?"

"My mother died two years into my studies, and it suddenly felt pointless, I guess."

"Ahhh, Ma Petite," he whispered, so sad for her. "But why on earth does this embarrass you?"

"Ah, yes," she said, indicating there was more to the story that she didn't want to tell.

"You hold back information. Not nice to do with nosy people."

Her laugh was worth his antics as he waited for the missing details. "Well…the embarrassing part is what kind of therapist I decided to become."

He raised his brows with that, waiting. "You want me to beg for this information?"

"Uuugh, no, I don't. It was stupid. Is stupid. I was glad to switch and that's enough information, really. As you have said to me before, it's not important."

It was his turn to laugh and tsk again. "But I am nosy, Ma Petite," he reminded her. "You are not."

"Nooo, I'm nosy too," she assured with a light laugh. "I just know how to respect people's privacy when I see they want me to."

"Really," he said, tickled with her insult while placing a hand on his chest. "See, I have no respect for such things."

"Now is a good time to learn," she laughed, nodding.

He looked out at the water, perplexed now. "I am trying to understand what sort of therapist would warrant such shame." He looked at her. "Shall I guess?"

"Sexual therapist. Okay?"

Mon Dieu.

"See what your nosy got you? I tried to spare you."

"You did, yes. But now this information brings more questions."

"What made me choose that, I know," she mumbled without looking at him. "Because I learned *that* particular thing is usually at the bottom of all marriage problems, or somehow connected. And I was serious about helping them and wanted to choose correctly."

That particular thing. He smiled, liking that she didn't want to say it. "And helping yourself, yes? Because we are products of our parents?"

"Yes, for myself," she said, like the residual benefit was welcomed. "I certainly do *not* want to become like them or end up like them."

"Mon Dieu, how bad was it? Lots of fighting?"

"Oh, not at all," she said, staring into the water near their feet. "They were the most…civilized people you'd ever met. They could have easily been brother and sister and you wouldn't have known otherwise."

"Ahhh, no la-passion?"

She shook her head. "Not a drop. No hugging, no touching—other than the occasional peck on the forehead by my father."

"Mon Dieu, like a child?"

She gave a humorless laugh and nodded. "Like a child. Although he never kissed *me* that way. So, more like a stepchild."

This news added to the anguish he already had with her. "He never kissed you, Ma Petite? What about your other siblings?"

"I'm an only child," she said seeming unaware how tragic these things were.

He redirected, curious. "And when did you figure this was not how marriage was supposed to be?"

"When I was thirteen. I had friends with parents who were in love." She gave a deep sigh. "I knew right away when I saw it." She swung her legs a little as she thought. "I realized I always knew. Deep inside, I knew something was missing. And when I saw the missing piece, I said *there it is*."

"And you wanted to help them. Such a sucree fille." She looked at him, cheeks flush with curious eyes. He realized they were gray, with flecks of dark blue. "A sweet daughter," he translated. "And you are terrible at receiving compliments, Ma Petite."

She nodded, not denying it. Such purity. How far did this purity go, he was very hungry to know. "So, your mother died before you could help?"

He watched her lowered profile lift and stare with that quiet strength he'd seen in her. She took in a huge breath.

"It's okay, Ma Petite, I'm not really nosy, I was teasing. I can piss off."

"No, it's okay. I did help them, I think. Passively." She offered him a small smile and coming from a face filled with cuts and bruises and tragic childhood, it made it that much more potent to him. "I dropped things I learned to my father and mother. They'd call to check on me, ask how my studies were going and I'd tell them all the amazing things I was learning."

She looked at him, then at his smile. "What?"

"I like this. You are a sneaky snake and a harmless petite dove at once. And you seen a difference in them?"

She nodded, seeming sure. "I heard it, really. I never got a chance to see it. My mother died when she got pneumonia one winter while I was at college. I should have gone home to visit but I just didn't realize how sick she was."

The idea made him ill to imagine. "I am so sorry about this, Ma Petite."

She gave him a small nod. "Thank you for that, Sahvrin." She stared at him for many seconds. "I think you may be the nicest man I have ever met. I'm serious," she cried lightly, seeing his need to beg to differ.

But he wouldn't do anything but accept her beautiful gift without arguing.

"I have a question for you," she said suddenly.

"Anything you want to know, Ma Petite."

"I know your last name is Bishop, but…*are* you…like…a *priest*?"

He let his laughter go at that as she nodded with a smile. "I guess that's a no."

He finally angled his look at her, shaking his head. "I tell you I do bad things to bad people and yet you wonder if I'm a priest?"

"I honestly don't think it's so bad to do bad things to bad people. I mean, God did it."

"Oh Ma Petite," he muttered, shaking his head. "There is nothing godly about who I am and what I do. There is a fine line between a righteous judgment and revenge. God knows the exact sins of a man and I have to guess at those. I always assume the very worst even while knowing I will receive the same manner of judgment one day."

The Twelve actually judged the guilty by a set code that involved rolling dice. But only members were allowed to know that even if he'd likely trust her with his soul.

He eyed her troubled look, suddenly unable to break free from her intense gaze. "Then you need to quit that."

The soft words rode over his skin, making him smile. "That's it?" he asked, amazed. "Just quit it?"

Her eyes roamed his face before giving a nod. "Yeah."

She'd paused and thoroughly double checked her answer, further confirming his angelic suspicions. "Now I have a question for you." He eyed her expectant gaze. "Are you…a nun by any chance?"

She gave another one of those dark shattering laughs and this time it was contagious. "A cherub perhaps?" he said, chuckling with how funny this was to her. "Ma Petite, so much laughter over these sincere questions. You meet a Biship who is La Captain Prick, and *still,* you are an angel to him?"

Her laughter subsided and he decided he had to know. "Tell me this. Do you have someone special waiting for you in North Dakota?"

She shook her head, carefully dabbing the happy tears from her bruised eyes. "No," she said.

What a shock. And another tragedy. And yet not. "You are still very young. There's time."

"I'm not in a race about it. What about you?" she asked.

"Me?"

"You have someone special?"

"I do, yes. Gras Jean, my pet alligator is madly in love with me." She erupted in more laughter. "Ma Petite, this is not meant to be a joke, I am serious." More squeals of laughter. Such good medicine for her. "Truthfully, I choose not to date in my line of work."

She sucked in a breath, giving a concerned look. "This is why you're so grumpy," she diagnosed, making him laugh.

"There isn't a woman I know that would put up with the likes of me." It was half true.

She gave a cute pfft sound. "Then you need to find other oceans to fish in."

"Not worth the trouble," he said, shaking his head.

She drew back a little, staring right at him. "You're going to sit there and tell me you're better off alone?"

He laughed heartily at that, nodding. "I have been alone, as you say, for fifteen years."

Her jaw dropped with that. "Why?"

"Because of my line of work," he reminded with a grin.

"So you can't have a girlfriend *and* work?" she wondered, perplexed. "We're made to be with a soul mate, you know" she added, sounding truly disturbed with his situation.

"A soul mate," he said, regarding the setting sun. "If you say so."

Her frustration came in a tiny huff. "I do," she said, like she was trying to convince him.

"Ma Petite, I'm glad you think this. It's a very good thing to think but it's not for everybody. You understand?" And even though his celibacy was no longer required for him, old habits died good and hard in that department for him.

She'd turned away finally, the pout on her lips making him smile for some reason. "You are going to be angry if I don't share this belief?"

"No, just…sad for you."

"Mon Dieu, I saved an angel who won't be happy until I have everything her heart desires? What if I'm not that kind of man, Ma Petite?"

"I don't…care if you believe differently and I'm totally fine if you never have a girlfriend for the rest of your life."

The anger in her mutter said otherwise and he really needed to change the subject while knowing what was likely in that pretty head of hers. If he'd ever be with a woman, it should *never* be an angel like her, but she would argue and say she was no such thing.

He focused on the ugly reality, namely the people he needed to hunt and kill slowly. "Can I ask you some serious questions, Ma Petite?"

She regarded him with that eager sincerity. "Whatever you need to know, I'll tell you. I want to catch these people. Not for myself," she said, somehow knowing the direction his thoughts had taken. "For those who didn't escape or won't escape. There were other girls with me that didn't get away, you know."

Fuck, that was bad. He gazed forward, thinking. Whoever abducted her would know all about who she was and where she lived by now. She couldn't go back to the same place. Her father was not safe now, either. It was a sad thing to be thankful she had no siblings but in this case he was.

"I need names, Ma Petite." He glanced at her. "Any name you might remember would help."

"I remember three names." She focused a moment then gave, "David… Blanchard… and Brisco. I don't know if it's first or last names. And I can probably draw you somewhat of a map of where they kept me." She looked at him. "If you think it would help."

Sahvrin was desperate to know who these names were but came up with nothing. "How long did they have you?"

"Two days. And I really need to call my father."

"You understand that these people know who you are and where you are from. This means they know where your father and any other family is."

The look she gave said she'd already thought the same thing. "I know. I need to warn him."

"They're already looking to see what they can find out."

"Who is?"

"Like-minded people in the business I work for is looking, Ma Petite. This is not the first time we've dealt with this evil and we take it very seriously. We will find out everything that we can. Our men are preparing to hunt these demons. We will find who did this, I promise you. I am meeting my father and brothers this evening. You will give me your father's name and I will call him personally."

She suddenly moved to stand, a painful feat judging by her stifled groans. He stood too, watching the panic in her face. "I need to talk to him."

"Listen to me," he said, holding her shoulders carefully. "You have to stay here where it's safest. I will not risk you being seen." Or possibly calling her father after they got to him and set him up as bait. "Trust me, please."

She suddenly appeared dizzy, and he stepped into her, holding her steady. At feeling her sag, he lifted her in his arms and made his way into the house with her, glad she didn't protest. Laying her in his bed, he said, "You need more rest, you're still too injured for all of this."

She pulled his arm when he straightened. "Please don't leave yet. I don't want to be alone."

He sat on the bed next to her and smoothed the hairline along her forehead, something he needed as much as she did. "Get some rest, Ma Petite."

"Please lay with me," she mumbled, tugging his arm.

Mon Dieu, he really shouldn't.

Until she fell asleep.

He lay down, keeping plenty of distance between them. That plan fell apart when she scooted herself closer and pulled his arm over her shoulder and clutched it tight. His plan to get up when she drifted off also fell apart when he slept too.

CHAPTER 5

Sahvrin woke to fingers stroking along his arm. He tensed at realizing he'd fallen asleep, and Ma Petite was now awake, tracing patterns on his skin. And he was aroused. Something he was *not* accustomed to being.

He took in a deep breath, and she went completely still, telling him she preferred him not knowing what she was doing. That was good, he would happily pretend ignorance for her. Since she feigned sleep, he carefully moved her hand off his and sat up. He made his way outside to relieve himself in case she needed the bathroom, realizing it was the next morning. Mon Dieu, he'd slept long and hard.

His cock jerked as pieces of a dream came. Of her. He closed his eyes as his mind replayed him doing sexual things to her, craving to make her feel good. His cock ached with the real memory of it and how she'd responded in the dream, craving it, needing it just as much as he needed to give it.

This was… so *fucking* not good.

He quickly slammed the door shut in his mind, focusing on what was next with her. Protecting her was the most important thing. And that external threat came with enough danger, he'd have no problems fixating on that alone.

He made his way back in, seeing the bed empty. "I will put on coffee. You want some?" he called.

She opened the bathroom door and he attempted to inspect her facial injuries while not seeing her beauty. "Healing nicely," he said, failing on the latter while getting the small jar of ointment on the shelf near him and handing it to her. "Apply liberally."

She looked up and that smile shattered his focus. She was not a child, this was more obvious than ever in the morning sunlight. He realized that when she healed completely, she'd become that beautiful woman he'd first met. Mon Dieu.

The sound of a boat spun him around. He was suddenly torn between reaching for his gun and his phone. Had to be his Pah-Pah.

"Somebody's coming?" she seemed to just realize.

"Yes, Ma Petite. My Pah-Pah."

"Are you sure?" The panic in her voice brought him to her, only to face the new problem between them. *She's your baby sister.*

With that, he kissed her forehead like he'd done to Juliette so many times. "I am sure. He is the only one who knows the way here." He checked his phone anyway and let out a breath of relief at seeing his *I'm on my way to you.* "It's him."

"What do I do? What about the dress?"

He regarded her, not understanding the reason for her distress. "He knows what happened, the dress is beautiful on you Ma Petite."

She eyed the screen door then him. "But he's your father. I just...this is a first impression."

She was becoming more confounding to him with every exchange. "He does not care about impressions, Ma Petite."

"But *I* do," she fretted, sounding more distraught as the boat drew closer.

"Do you want me to stay outside with him?"

As though thinking that strange, she sagged a little and looked around. "If you're sure... I can...maybe cook, or...make coffee."

The sight of her tears brought him back to her. "Ma Petite, why are you crying?" He wiped the tears from her cheeks, and she pushed his hand away.

"I don't know, I'm...I probably just need coffee myself."

She said this in a tiny wail, and for some reason it made him smile. What a peculiar little thing she was. "Go take a shower, Ma Petite. By the time you are done, he will be gone, yes?"

She suddenly shook her head and wiped her eyes. "That's silly," she said in a shaky whisper. "I'll cook breakfast for you and..." Her words trailed as she stared at his kitchen. "You don't have a stove?"

"It's right there, Ma Petite." He pointed to it, smiling. "It's a wood burning one and I will need to show you how to use it." He pointed next to it. "That's the coffee pot."

"Oh," she muttered. "Is that what that is?"

At hearing she had no experience with a drip pot, he couldn't help but chuckle, oddly okay with her ignorance. It wasn't a spoiled by modern conveniences kind of ignorance, but more never having been introduced to it before.

His phone buzzed when his Pah-Pah's boat came to stop at the pier. He looked at the screen. *I have your brothers too. Can we come in? We have more clothes for her.*

Mon Dieu. "My brothers are with him."

The suck of her breath said her limit had just been pushed too far. And he was suddenly sure he didn't want his brothers around her.

"I will tell them now is not a good time."

****

Get it together, you're acting like a child. "Sahvrin, I'm fine, really. Just...quickly tell me how to work this pot at least."

He studied her a moment, and the intensity in his dark gaze made her swallow. "We stay outside."

His tone held a finality she'd not heard from him before and didn't fight. "Whatever you want," she said.

"Take a long shower for your muscles, Ma Petite. My Pah-Pah has brought more clothes. You can change if you want to."

Change? Did he think she needed to?

She watched him walk off, taking in the sight of him. Blue jeans and white t-shirt was a stark contrast to that outfit he wore when she originally met him. She was torn between which was more drool worthy. The jeans and t-shirt took first place in that second.

She snuck a peek at the family unloading on the dock. She spotted silver hair and figured he was the dad. She was shocked to see what a lumberjack kind of man he was. Fit as a fiddle and wearing blue-jean overalls. Her heart went berserk as she watched them all exchange hugs. Did they always do that? How amazing.

She backed her way to the bathroom, not wanting to stop watching them. She measured the brothers to Sahvrin and wondered who was the oldest now. Several were a bit taller than him but only a little, and maybe thicker. Nothing fat about any of them. Like a pack of…swamp warriors.

The conversation suddenly turned serious, judging by the grave looks on their faces. She really wanted to know what they were saying. Would he tell her everything? She continued to study each of them, deciding they were all *almost* as handsome as Sahvrin. She was likely biased with the whole savior sickness plaguing her. That's what it was. After having their chat on the pier, she'd confirmed it when he'd lay with her. It took all her will power not to repay that man in whatever sexual favor he wanted. How was that for angelic.

God, she couldn't be that person. It was the trauma. She had all the symptoms. But she'd met him before the trauma and liked him—until he opened his mouth, but nevertheless. So, it wasn't *just* the trauma.

While in the shower, a knock sounded at the door. "Ma Petite, there's a bag of clothes hanging on the door for you. I am going to take a ride with my brothers and Pah-Pah, you will be okay here."

It wasn't a question but a statement. "I'm fine. Go on and have fun." She cringed at her word choice. He wasn't going have fun, they're hunting human demons. No wonder he thought of her as a child.

Fear froze her. Were they going hunting now for them?

He hadn't said anything more and she guessed he was gone. They wouldn't be hunting them now. He said they were preparing to.

She finished her shower, getting nervous and eager at remembering the clothes. What kind were they?

She listened before opening the bathroom door. Hearing nothing, she turned the knob and pushed it enough to create a six-inch crack that she looked through. Pushing it more, she peeked around while reaching her hand out. Feeling the something on the door, she yanked it into the bathroom and shut it back, locking it. She smiled at the cute sack of clothes. Like you'd see in an old-time store filled with…rice or flour, maybe.

Opening it, she pulled out the first thing, something red. Her heart raced in hope. Could it possibly be another dress? She gasped with a laugh at finding it was. A beautiful red sundress with straps. And long, thankfully. Would hide most of her bruises.

She'd leave her hair down to cover anything that might show on her back. Her beautiful winter fur as Sahvrin referred to it. Did he like it? She wished there was a body mirror. She smiled at the soft red material. Please let it fit. She carefully pulled it over her head, every muscle in her body screaming for mercy. She was pushing too hard as usual. She never knew when to stop, when to quit. This was her personality every day, all her life. But that stubbornness helped her through every hard time, and she'd had plenty.

"Yes," she gasped at seeing it fit perfect. The top was that stretchy, crimpledy material like the yellow one she wore, so she didn't need her bra.

She remembered there was more than one thing in the bag and carefully lowered to pick it up. Opening it, she spotted white and a light orange, pulling them both out. Ohhhhh the white one! She dropped the red dress and held the white piece up.

"Oh wow," she breathed. Another beautiful summer dress only it had more layers of material with a sheer lace on top. She loved it. Dropping it on the floor, she began the tedious, painful task of removing the first dress. She decided to get out of it in reverse, removing the straps then pushing it down her body.

She was ready to pass out by the time she got the white dress on. Thank God it fit because there was no way she could change again. She didn't even care what it looked like at that point.

She saw the top was designed to wear on or off the shoulders. That was easy. Off the shoulders would be a loud and clear calling card and she was not about to stoop that low even if she actually did want to call him. She needed to nurse her dignity back to health, it was plum broke. Never in her life did she contemplate doing the things she now did with him.

*****

Sahvrin's anger boiled. Boiled past the point of logical. His brothers and Pah-Pah were one hundred percent right, he just hated the idea of her being put on the stand about any of it while freshly battered. But time was not fucking on their side and if they were selling her to the highest bidder as a virgin, they needed to learn all the details surrounding that. The puzzle of how they even knew she was a virgin returned. If somebody close to her was involved in this, they needed to learn that, God forbid it be the case.

As if reading his mind, Jek said, "Her father is stacked. And an investor. I'm not saying he's guilty of anything but if he *is* involved in any kind of way, whether knowingly or ignorantly," he said raising both hands, "then it changes a lot."

"I know this," Sahvrin said, swatting the air in annoyance. "I understand all of it, the dynamics. I realize there are missing pieces and that her father may be a dirty player in this, and I realize we need answers that only she can give at this point."

"We don't like it any more than you do," August offered in a low mumble. "But the sooner we find out the better."

"If this turns into a ransom--"

"But they don't have her, we do," Sahvrin interrupted Lazure."

"Yes, but her father doesn't know this, does he?"

It hit Sahvrin what he was saying. If whoever took her was doing this as a ransom.... "But they were selling her, they were in the process of moving her to someplace? If this was a ransom, why move her at all?"

"If," Jek began cautiously like he knew he was treading on thin ice, "her father is dirty in all this, then contacting him would compromise her safety."

"So she doesn't speak to him until we know more on that," Sahvrin said, and they all agreed.

"The quickest answers would be through Brisco," August said, not hiding his bloodlust. "And I know where to find him."

Sahvrin knew there was no other choice where His Petite was concerned. "When we return, we will speak to her and learn whatever more we can. But I'm warning all of you," he said to his brothers. "Watch what you say to her and how you say it. She is *nothing* like the women any of you associate with. Understood?"

They all agreed, and he ignored their smirks, not giving a damn what conclusions they drew. Just so they did as he said, then no heads would need to be ripped from shoulders.

****

The sound of a boat sat Beth up from a dead sleep. Her heart pounded as she remembered where she was. Crap, he was back. She scrambled out of bed, gasping through the pain as her stomach joined in the attack on her sudden frayed nerves. It was night already. She'd slept nearly the whole day!

She made her way through the darkness to the bathroom to check herself. Thank God the lights were off, she didn't want to be seen floundering like a nervous bride or a guilty intruder.

She did her best to smooth out her hair then splashed water on her discolored face. She touched the few spots that were still a little swollen, hoping she didn't look too much like a freak.

A soft knock sounded on the bathroom door and she nearly vomited. "Ma Petite."

She almost didn't recognize Sahvrin's voice. Curious and concerned, she opened it two inches. "You're back?"

"We are," he said, his tone sounding…odd. "I'm sorry it took so long, are you okay?"

"I slept the whole time," she said, not wanting him to worry. "What's wrong?"

He gave a sigh. "Will you…be willing to speak to my father and brothers? They have questions, Ma Petite. I will be with you. Unless you're not well."

She tried to understand his tone. "I'm…well to talk. Yes, of course I will." That was the only answer there was, it seemed. What did he mean by *I will be with you*?

"Meet me outside, Ma Petite. Okay?"

She closed the door, staring for several seconds. She panicked at realizing she'd rather walk out with him. Opening the door, she saw he was already halfway there.

What did they want to talk about? Why did she feel like this would be difficult? *You're not a child. You have training in dealing with people. These are people.*

Despite the lecture, her legs trembled as she headed for the door. She suddenly worried how the dress looked. Without a long mirror, she could only guess.

She made her way toward them on the pier where they all stood with lowered heads, all but two. Sahvrin and one of the brothers. Sahvrin looked right at her with an intensity that made her nervous.

"Beth, I would like you to meet my family. This is my Pah-Pah, Lazure. My brothers, Jek, August, Bart and Zep." He motioned to each one.

They all looked at her now and she smoothed her hands repeatedly over the front of the dress, feeling like a plague. "It's very nice to meet all of you," she said in her strongest voice. She looked at Sahvrin who stayed put where he was, making the plague feeling worse. The brothers all greeted her in nearly matching replies of hello, hey, hi but their tones were low and... something she couldn't put her finger on. Guilty?

She fought with a full-body tremble while trying to figure out what bothered Sahvrin. "You can...ask your questions," she said, wanting to get it over with.

Sahvrin spoke in low French and the brother who had looked at her, Jek, she realized, spoke something back to him. Then they were all speaking it, gradually getting louder as they went with Sahvrin moving closer toward the Jek brother as he did.

The father yelled something in French, and they all went silent, like a magic switch. The man finally turned to her and raked his hand through wavy silver hair that went to his shoulders, her tremble getting worse. "Forgive us Miss Beth," he began in a deep voice. "There are things we need to ask you."

She glanced at Sahvrin, not sure why this felt threatening. "Okay. Like what? I'll do my best to help."

The father began again. "If this...is bad people running the operation—" Sahvrin spoke French and his father said, "Yes, not if, we know these are bad people. But if..."

At seeing his difficulty, she looked at Sahvrin. "Sahvrin, what do they need to know? You have my father's name and the names I gave? Ask what you need, I may be able to help, I...I want to, that's what I told Sahvrin." Embarrassment filled her at knowing she pronounced his name wrong. "Sorry if...I talk funny," she muttered, not sure what else to call it.

They all spoke French again, obviously about her or they'd say it in English.

"How about we do more reconnaissance with what we do know and go from there?" She believed the one named August suggested it, looking like he had other places he'd rather be.

"Miss Beth," the Jek brother said. "In their world, there's trafficking and then there's business as usual. And please…pardon this next question…" He eyed Sahvrin before going on, "But would you have any idea how these men would know what the…status of your sexuality is?"

"The reason we wonder this," Sahvrin said, "is…" He suddenly seemed to consider something then lowered his head in a mumble of French which prompted his brothers to mumble back the same manner.

"I can't really help you if I don't understand what you need," she said, hoping they realized that included the language barrier while wondering what the Jek brother was getting at concerning her virginity.

"Like I said before," the August brother interrupted. "More time digging into the things we do know, run down that name? Pretty sure we'll get plenty from that."

They went back to murmuring like she couldn't hear and the words *her father* froze her. "What about my father?" She looked at Sahvrin as he finally approached her, making her nervous. "Is he okay?"

"We haven't tried to contact him yet."

"How long did you say you were missing, Miss Beth?"

She looked at the father, her mind suddenly racing too fast. "Uh…" She closed her eyes, focusing. "I…how long was I here? I'm sorry, time has been…"

"Now don't fret," Miss Beth," the father said in a gentle scold.

"You've been here three days this night. You told me they had you for two days?"

She nodded, her mouth too dry. "Yes, then…that's right."

"So, she's been missing for five days," Jek muttered, his tone implying that meant something.

"Maybe ask her when her father expected to hear from her," the brother who seemed to want to be somewhere else mumbled.

"Well, you just sort of did," Sahvrin muttered back. "She's not deaf."

"I was supposed to call him…when I got to my room. I-I had…a hotel room, a bed and breakfast."

"The Breaux Bridge Inn," Sahvrin said, remembering.

"Yes, that's it," she shot out, feeling out of breath and a little dizzy.

The French flew again, low but faster all while her mind fought to put together the fractured pieces they seemed to be playing with.

"How many days did you book this room for, Ma Petite, do you remember?"

"A week," she said, nodding. "Seven days. I wanted plenty of time to…sight see." The murmur of French buzzed with the rest of the confusion in her head. "When can I call my dad?"

Sahvrin turned from his conversation, looking at her. He suddenly strode quickly over and captured her face in his hands. "Are you okay, Ma Petite? You don't look well. Do you need to lie down?"

She shook her head, fighting back the tears and losing the battle. "I need to call my dad." The words strained out, only half audible. "He'll be worried, and I don't want him worried, he's my only family," she said, the words gushing out around a sob.

He pulled her into a hug and held her tightly. "Shhh, okay, Ma Petite. I hear you."

"Is there something wrong?" she asked in his chest? "Do you think they might have hurt him?"

"No, Ma Petite, that's not it."

"Then what?" She pushed him away to see his face. "You're not telling me something. Why? I'm not a child."

"We're not sure if maybe this was a ransom type situation given who your father is, Beth."

She stared at him, blinking. "Ransom?" She considered that. "You think…that's possible?"

He nodded and she searched his face for signs he was hiding something. "What else? I want to know everything."

"Ma Petite," he said, quietly. "Somebody knew you were a virgin, yes? We can't understand how anybody would come by this type of knowledge."

Wait… "Are you saying… you think my dad…"

"No, no, that's not what I think."

"But you're saying it's possible!" She pushed him, so angry and hurt he'd think that. "You don't even know him! He may have been a… shitty husband but he was a good dad! Is!" And why was she sobbing? She fought out of his embrace that seemed to only make her weaker. "I'm fine," she insisted, holding up a hand between them. "I'm…not a child," she said. "I was abducted, and I was beaten, okay, fine. I escaped. I'm alive. There were other women… girls," she corrected. "Who did not. I will do whatever I can to help, I'm not afraid. I mean it," she said, making the words hard and wrapping her arms around herself. "I don't need or want pity." She was sick of being useless and broken.

"And as far as how they knew I was a virgin, your guess is as good as mine." She said this to the brothers and father. "How do you determine that? I have no idea. I don't recall filling out any resumes that asked about my virginity. The only people that knew that was me, I didn't have long chats with girlfriends over such…private things. How would they prove that to a buyer? A hymen test? Mine was ripped to hell at my first pelvic exam thanks to a jerk of a doctor who didn't know what he was doing."

And now there were twelve eyes of concerned judges glued to her. She stood there shuffling her feet, all her pride in shreds. "You have any other questions?" She was ready to be alone.

Silent humility hung in the air when the Jek brother saved her from basking in it. "Can you tell us from where exactly you were abducted?"

She thought back. "I attended the festival and had some drinks. I don't even normally drink, but in a stupid attempt to fit in, I did and then I was invited to a party by some kind people—or I thought they were kind—and I don't have much memory after that."

"Do you happen to remember the name of the bar?"

She wasn't even sure which one asked that. "It was…No, I don't know, I don't remember."

They began listing names of bars.

"That one," she shot out.

"The Roulette?" Sahvrin asked.

"Yes, I'm sure of it."

They exchanged extra heated French now.

"I even remember the layout of it. I can draw a map."

"Thank you, Ma Petite. And that was the last bar you remember going to?"

"Yes," she said, nodding again and hugging herself.

"Do you remember at what point you realized you were…abducted?" Bart asked.

"I woke up tied to a bed in a room. There was…tape…over my mouth," she said, her voice lowering.

"You said there were others?" Zep asked.

"Not at first. But later, I was put with other girls. We couldn't talk because of the tape. On our mouths. Sometimes they…removed it to ask questions." Sickness churned her stomach at recalling the one girl she tried to protect. "They did…really bad things to some of the girls." She fought the shake in her voice as she shifted on her feet. "I was tied, but I tried to…to stop him, he was…hurting her so bad and…" She pushed Sahvrin away when he tried to come to her. "I don't want comfort!" she yelled. "I don't care if they beat me half to death, I'm free and she's not, she's stuck there and she…" The painful memory closed off her throat. "She was so… so young." She covered her mouth and turned with a sob, not able to fight Sahvrin's arms from behind her, holding her tight. "I've never had a sister, but she seemed just like a little sister…" He spoke French over his shoulder and not long after the sound of the boat signaled they all left, but Sahvrin never let her go. He held her and shhhh'd her until exhaustion won and dried up all her tears.

CHAPTER 6

Sahvrin sat on the edge of the pier, needing to think about what was coming but His Petite took up all the space in his mind. They'd decided to use the guns as leverage, ship them to the heart of the swamp then lock the Roulettes out until they gave up the guilty and their blood to pay for the crimes. They'd get the royal treatment at their Weigh Station before they got the luxury of death.

Agony welled up in him again at what his angel said about why they beat her. Beat half to death for trying to help a child. And without even looking or seeing it, he knew after that meeting, his brothers were taken by her, battered condition and all. She was different and you'd have to be blind not to see it. But they were not taken with her like he was, not hardly.

His father insisted he take four more days to take care of her. Felt like he'd been sentenced. Damned to Heaven and only allowed to observe, not partake.

He'd develop a plan and stick to it. She needed to rest, eat, get fresh air, and that was it. And he needed to be that protector he'd neglected to be from the beginning. He was getting his chance to make up for that horrific mistake. But if he was going to survive, he'd have to be that Bishop she'd met. His Saint Sahvrin was too soft, too giving and she was too vulnerable and hungry for everything to not devour that and him whole.

Just from the little experience he had with her, she'd be a difficult patient. Her kindness and selflessness and wanting to help with everything while being too fucking sexy for his celibacy vows was like kryptonite. Fighting demons was a lot easier than fighting this angel. Not even the hard-ass Bishop was equipped but it's all he had.

She was not an option on his life menu that he could or should contemplate. That idea needed to be shot dead. She was still recovering from trauma, she was still very young, and she was not cut out for swamp life. And she was especially not cut out for the demands that came with his leadership of The Twelve.

****

"So, are we clear?" Sahvrin asked from the kitchen after giving His Petite the strict schedule she had to follow.

"Very clear," she called. "Think like a zombie, lay like a zombie, walk like a zombie."

"It's only four days," he said, getting her dinner while realizing they were already having their first confrontation. "You must agree."

"I agree," she assured. "And after four days, I can start doing things to get stronger?"

"Yes, after four days, I'll allow you to do more."

"I get to do more than nothing?" She eyed the tray he brought to her. "Am I allowed to eat on the couch?"

He stepped aside. "Yes."

"Thank you, sir," she muttered, scooting out of the bed. "All of this is very kind of you," she said on the short trek to the living room. "I don't want you to think I'm ungrateful, that's *not* what this is."

"I know what this is. It's you being unable to let others do for you without returning the favor somehow."

She sat on the couch, looking up at him while he set the tray on her lap. "That's a good trait, I thought."

"Not when you need to heal, no."

"Well, I know my own body and ability better than anybody." She picked up her spoon, smelling the delicious aroma.

"Ma Petite."

She looked up at him.

"You took a two hour shower the very next morning after I found you half dead. That's not knowing your body's abilities."

Her mouth opened for a couple seconds. "I went that slow because I knew my ability."

"And you prove my point by missing the point. You shouldn't have showered." He ended the discussion and walked back to the kitchen for his own food. "You know I admire your strength, but there's a difference between being strong and being stupid."

"Okay," she cried lightly from the couch. "I get it. I just…don't like feeling useless."

"You're not useless."

"Yeah? What am I good for?" she wondered around the food in her mouth, pausing with a dramatic 'mmmm, this is so good.' The orgasmic tone made him smile while challenging him.

"Tomorrow, I have work in my shop."

"What shop?" she asked.

"The one in my back yard."

"I never got to see the back yard yet."

"You're free to stroll the docks, but beyond that, ask me." He made his way to the sitting area, taking the single chair near the couch.

"Docks? Is there more than one?"

"The dock surrounds the house and has piers leading to small pieces of land."

"Oh how neat," she said, smiling and doing that mmmm again. "You must show me how to cook when I'm better. I can at least do that. And clean, I'm very good at cleaning."

"I'm sure you are," he said, not looking at her. She was too easy to stare at and once he started, it was hard to stop. The fact that she was oblivious made it easy which didn't help.

****

Beth woke up and stretched, so relieved to not encounter excruciating pain. She still hurt but nothing like those first three days. The smell of food lifted her head and she looked around, wondering what time it was. She didn't hear anything which meant Sahvrin might be already working in his shop. She forgot to ask what he did in it. Guess she could *stroll* and find out.

She made her way out of bed, forgoing a shower since she'd had one before bed. Dr. Bishops orders. A long one. Hot as she could take it. She decided on the red dress today and worked it over her head after her bathroom business. She regarded her hair in the mirror with a sigh. Seemed more stupid by the day. Especially in the heat. She got the brush they sent with the clothes and the little baggie of hair accessories. She'd spied a hair clip three times too small. But the hair ties worked.

She decided to go with two braids wrapped around themselves. It was childish but whatever. Not like he was looking. More like ignoring it seemed.

She slipped on the cute brown sandals that were only a little small and found a plate of food with a note on top of it on the counter. She smiled, picking it up. *Eat all of it.* Her grin crumpled at the curt message then returned full-blown when she uncovered the plate. "Wow." Bacon, eggs, fried cubed potatoes…what was that pile of white stuff? She picked up the fork and moved it around then tasted a bit. "Mmm." The buttery salty flavor danced on her tastebuds as she carried the plate to the couch, glancing out the window for signs of her strict babysitter.

She happily sat with her plate, holding it at her chest near her mouth. She didn't mind him babysitting her at all. Pretty sure there wasn't a time in her life that she didn't feel more royal than at his little shack in the swamp. "Dear God, the man can cook," she murmured with non-stop mmmm's. Would be nice if she learned how to do that. She could follow directions pretty good but definitely had to have them.

****

Sahvrin mixed the final coat for the outdoor tub in the wheelbarrow. His Petite was still sleeping, which was good. Hopefully she stayed that way till he was done. She'd be able to test the tub tomorrow afternoon if the weather cooperated.

Small footsteps approaching on the back dock said he'd wished too soon.

"Oh, there you are. Morning! Or afternoon, I overslept."

He straightened and his gaze did its usual inspection, starting at her face. The swelling was all gone, and the bruises were fifty percent less colorful making her fifty percent more beautiful. "Morning. You ate?"

"Yes, I'm *stuffed*." She regarded the pier leading from her to him. "Am I allowed?"

"Yes. Just be careful, it's wobbly."

He watched her eyes get big as she stared at the fifteen-foot narrow walk with worry.

"I'll help," he said, setting his shovel down.

"No, I can get it," she fussed, like he was taking one of the few privileges she had.

He paused and eyed her red dress, wondering where all her hair was while she navigated the bridge with both fists at her chin.

When she made it across, she hit him with her bright smile. "And I put my dish in the sink without even washing it," she bragged, as if she'd waited to finish her sentence. "Pretty sure it's more stressful not washing it than washing it," she informed.

He turned back to his wheelbarrow with a grin. "Where's all your hair, Ma Petite?"

"Oh, it's still there. I just braided it and wound it up out of the way. And I was thinking how useless it is to have all this hair while in the swamp."

He paused at the hint of her doing something to it. "You won't always be in the swamp," he reminded. "And you need it where it's cold."

He caught her looking at his sweat soaked shirt as he pushed the wheelbarrow to the tub. "Maybe I'm tired of living in the snow and ice," she said.

Sounded more like a fishing statement. What was she fishing for? How he felt about that?

"Plus, I *was* coming here to see if I wanted to live here," she reminded.

He dumped the bucket of mix. "Right. And your experience so far?" he teased, glancing at her.

She inspected one of the sitting logs nearby and sat. "It's not been all bad." She smoothed her hands over her dress. "Aside from the obvious nightmare, I happen to love it out here. Well, not *here*, here. I mean, I *do* love it here too, just in the swamp I mean, I love the swamp."

He laughed at the mess she made with her words, while spreading the mix. "So you want to live in the swamp?" he said.

"I don't see why not," she said. "I wouldn't want to live in town, that's for sure."

"You don't know what you're saying," he assured.

"What? Yes, I do. What's to know?"

"Oh Ma Petite," he said, breathless. "The swamp life isn't for northern women. The heat would likely kill you, for one."

"I would adjust," she argued lightly. "If I can survive extreme cold, I can survive the opposite?"

He laughed at that. "I would think it doesn't work that way."

"How would you know?" she challenged. "And it's not like I'd be chained here, if I didn't like it, I could leave."

"Yes, you could," he said, knowing that's exactly what would happen.

"Doesn't mean I would. There's things I can do to adapt. Get a tan for one. Cut all this hair off is another."

He straightened, looking at her. "If you cut your hair and change your mind, you won't get it back for years."

"It's just hair," she muttered. "I've been wanting a haircut for years. What's the point of all this hair, it's nothing but a hassle. More product, more time to upkeep, more *annoying*. Especially here."

"Fine, cut your hair," he said, not wanting to argue with her over it.

"You think? What kind of hair cut should I get?"

"None," he said.

"You just said to cut it," she cried.

"Because you seem bent on doing that, so do it."

"So you *don't* want me to cut my hair?"

He went to the hose and turned it on, rinsing his hands. "I don't care what you do with your hair, Ma Petite. It's your hair to do whatever you want with it. If you want to cut it all off, do it, but don't ask me, okay?"

She eyed him, looking confused with his dick answer. Fuck. "You want to know what I really think? I think your hair is beautiful and I'd be pissed if you cut it all off. But it's your hair, not mine."

"Why would you be pissed?" she wondered, curious.

"It's a figure of speech, Ma Petite. I wouldn't really be pissed," he said, shaking his head.

"I get it," she said after a few moments. "You love my hair and think it's beautiful. Noted," she said lightly.

Mon Dieu, she was like a trap he always walked into.

"So what are you doing?" she asked.

"Finishing this outdoor tub so you can have a proper soak."

"A *what?*" she gasped, making him turn to see what she looked like when making that sound. "You lie!"

"It should be cured enough to use by tomorrow afternoon."

"Oh my God, I can't believe you built a *tub!*" She made her way over and inspected. "It's huge! Like a small pool! You're truly amazing, aren't you?"

The overloaded compliment sent him with his tools to the outdoor shower. He turned it on and parked his wheelbarrow next to it then removed his shoes. He decided to leave his shirt on at feeling His Petite's eyes all over him. Amazing how she did that not realizing he could see her. He glanced at her, and she quickly looked away, proving his point.

He turned so he could finish without distraction.

"Oh my God, is this your garden? How cute!"

He rinsed himself first while she explored his small paradise.

"So much sun here, wow! It's like a tiny little paradise all by itself." She sucked in a breath. "Is that lavender? I can't believe you know how to do all of this!"

He started rinsing his tools now.

"You *have* to teach me this stuff," she said, her voice getting distant.

"Ma Petite," he called, needing to warn her about swamp creatures.

Her screams erupted and he threw down the shovel, nearly colliding with her as she flew out of the garden, arms flying. "It's on me, it's on me!" she shrieked, slapping herself everywhere.

He managed to catch her and search her body and hair. "I don't see anything," he yelled over her as he brushed her down with a hand, permanently etching her soft curves in his brain.

She ended up in his arms, clutching his wet t-shirt with uncontrollable shaking. He stroked her back as she let out a verbal shudder. "I *hate* spiders! I want to go back inside," she said, making him grin.

"I'm thinking Ma Petite doesn't have these kinds of swamp creatures in the North?" He led her back and she paused at the bridge. Not wanting her to end up in the water next, he scooped her up and carried her across.

He couldn't keep from measuring her weight, not happy as he set her down. "Mon Dieu, you feel malnourished."

"What?' she said, sounding offended. "I'm not *malnourished*. All I do is eat and sleep!" She shuddered again. "And no we don't have many of those creatures up North. But that doesn't mean I can't…get used to them."

He let out a laugh at how hard she shuddered when she said that.

"You're wet, I can…get you a towel."

"I can get it," he said, passing her as he headed inside.

"Fine, get it," he heard her mumble. "Get everything. And I decided I'm not going in," she yelled now. "I'm sitting on the pier."

"Good, the sun will be good for you," he called back from the fridge, amused at how she saw his therapy as some kind of attack on her.

"Spiders are part of God's creation," she said, possibly trying to convince herself.

He got a dry towel and clean clothes. "Ma Petite," he called. "I'm changing, don't come inside."

He removed his clothes and dried off.

"Oh shit!" she gasped, spinning around and hurrying back out. "What are you *doing*?" she demanded incredulous.

"I'm *changing*," he said, just as emphatic. "That's why I said *don't come inside*."

"You said *come inside*! You need to be *louder*!" she fussed, sounding more traumatized than she'd been with the spider.

The idea made him chuckle.

"Are you *laughing*?" she wondered.

"Yes, I am," he admitted, pulling his dry jeans on. "I'm decent," he announced.

She walked in and walked right back out with another shrill, "A man without a shirt is *not* what I'd call *decent!*" she let him know.

God, she was so funny. "I'm sorry. No shirt in the swamp is like common attire."

She gave her cute sputters. "I imagine you *don't* say that for women. Do you?"

The way she added *do you* was priceless. "I don't say anything to women."

Before he could add, *because I don't date them,* she choked out, "So you're fine with women going without a shirt?"

He made his way outside, needing to see her while she was so pissed. It reminded him of the first time he'd met her, and he really regretted not enjoying her more then. "I was going to say I don't say anything to women because I don't date them."

He studied that fiery spirit in her, drinking it in. "But surely you have an opinion? Are you saying I should go around the swamps without a *shirt?*" she wondered, super incredulous. He didn't answer her fast enough and she said, "Wowwww, so you *like* women parading naked in front of you?"

Mon Dieu, how did it go from women not wearing shirts to him *liking* them parading naked in front of him. "If you would let me answer."

"Your either know or you don't, I'm not so sure what there is to think about!"

"Well, for one, you keep switching from women and you, and those two things are not the same in my mind."

She went quiet, eyeing him and now he realized where she'd go with it. He couldn't win. "I'm not okay with any woman going without her shirt in front of me to answer your question."

She stared at him with an angry suspicion that made him grin. "And that was *so* hard to say?"

"With you interrupting me, yes."

"You think this kind of thing is funny," she said, nodding at him, not at all happy about that. And that made it fucking hilarious.

"I don't," he said even as he laughed.

"Right. Right. This is so disappointing," she muttered, turning to face the cove.

"Mon Dieu, Ma Petite, stop," he begged, still laughing. She answered him with a hand up while walking toward the end of the pier, muttering how wrong she was about him.

He followed her, amazed at how easily their conversations ended this way. From day one, he realized. The more arousing thing was how she didn't even realize what her offense plainly said to him. That she did *not* like the idea of another woman parading naked in front of him. The only reason he hesitated in that whole conversation was because she'd entered the scenario and that was different. Having her parade without a shirt in front of him was *definitely* something he wasn't against. But he couldn't tell her that, obviously.

"For the record," he said behind her, ready to set it straight. "I don't wish for any woman parading naked in front of me. Ever."

She turned with a screwed-up face. "Wish?" She faced forward again. "What a weird choice of words. Try *want,* Mr. Bishop. You don't *want,* not *wish.* Wish is what you do when you see a shooting star or throw a penny in a well, not decide whether or not you want to ogle tits."

Fuck, he couldn't believe she'd managed to arouse him out of his mind with her jealousy. Obliviously, of course.

CHAPTER 7

Sahvrin lay on the couch that night, unable to sleep as every moment of the day kept revisiting him, particularly the tits fight. She was *still* pissed, and he was sure she always would be as long as she thought what she did. The more he tried to fix it, the worse it got, so he quit trying, not wanting to hurt her even if she was doing it to herself. He didn't like her thinking he was into women outside of her and he couldn't really tell her either without causing things he didn't want to. No, he wanted to, but he wouldn't because if she'd proven anything to him today it was how she was *not* made to live in the swamp.

And she'd better not fucking cut her hair.

The sound of thunder rumbled, and he listened for signs of His Petite being awake. He needed to wean both of them from his initial hovering now that she was healing. A minute later, the thunder rumbled louder.

"Sahvrin?" she whispered loudly.

"Yes?"

"Uh… you're awake?"

"Yes."

She was quiet. "Okay… Night."

"Do you need me to lay with you?"

She didn't answer and he got up, making his way to the bed. "Push over."

"I didn't answer," she said as she scooted over.

"You didn't need to," he said, laying at the edge of the bed.

"I was actually about to say I didn't need you to."

"Well, I can go back on the couch."

"That's silly, you're already here. Unless you want to, then obviously you can."

"I don't want to."

The thunder boomed and she was suddenly glued to his back. "Turn over, Ma Petite."

She quickly turned and he did as well, draping his arm over her. She clutched his arm tightly between both hands and he pulled her closer at feeling her tremble.

He spoke soft French, stroking her forehead with his other hand till she fell asleep. When it sounded like the storm passed, he moved to untangle himself, getting her soft moan and relatching to his arm.

Mon Dieu.

He settled back down, resolving to just sleep. Tomorrow, he'd finish the tub and start working on the bracelet he'd get 8-Bit to embed a tracker in. That way he didn't have to worry about losing her again.

Sleep finally claimed him followed with more of those naughty Petite dreams. This time when he woke up, her fingers were in his hair and her leg covered his hard on with his hand on her leg. Mon Dieu, was this where his dreams came from?

He eased her leg off and sat up, then stood. Glancing back, he froze at seeing half her breast pushing out the top of the nearly sheer tank she wore. He lowered his gaze and the plump strawberry shapes topping her delicate mounds clobbered his cock and tickled the Bishops ruthless vengeance. How big would her nipples get when aroused?

He forced himself away from the torment, heading out the door to relieve himself. He hadn't done it in years, but he was convinced if he didn't jack off soon, he'd do something worse.

****

It had taken everything for Beth not to move when Sahvrin realized it. At some point in the morning, she'd waken to him pressing her leg into his erection. She didn't dare disturb him because…well, she didn't mind him feeling good, even wanted that, God did she ever. And technically she wasn't doing anything, just being asleep and oblivious while he didn't realize what he was doing. Why say anything? It was an awkward they could do without after the stupid crap that happened yesterday. When she'd finally heard the outside door, she opened her eyes and let out a breath. She looked down to see if she was decent. God, he no doubt saw her nipples through her top. Wasn't like she knew a storm would come and he'd sleep with her. If she had she'd have dressed differently.

Now she wondered what he thought of them. Her clit tingled as visions of his naked body returned from when she'd walked in on him. It had been cycling non-stop in her head.

Dear. God. She'd only seen his backside but that was traumatizing enough. He'd had a huge tattoo on his back and now she was curious about it. But his tight, muscular butt was forever etched into her mind as was the dark tan line right above it.

Such a delicious tan he had. She wanted one. The no shirts in the swamp argument returned, chilling the heat in her body. She recalled there were shorts in the clothes and a sports bra. That could serve as tanning attire. Where would she find the sun? Sure as hell wasn't going back in that garden. Yet.

The dock in the back would eventually have sun on it. She'd ask Sahvrin. There was nothing wrong with getting her skin prepared for the swamp. It was a necessity, really. And it didn't require work so he shouldn't have a problem with it.

Couldn't handle the swamp, she'd see about that. Sure, there were things to get used to, duh. She was a survivor; she could handle it. Spiders and all.

She hurried out of bed and into the bathroom before he could come back in. She took down the bag of clothes hanging on the hook and found a little happy surprise. The white top she'd seen wasn't a top at all but a whole piece bathing suit! Yes!

She put it on and ran into a life-long plague. Her fat butt. Ugh! She couldn't wear this damn swimsuit around him, no way! She could wear the shorts over it. People tanned that way, didn't they?

Who cares, she could tan anyway she wanted. She could ask him to stay on that side of the house so she could. He could handle that, Mr. never wanting to see women naked. What a saint. What a Bishop.

She paused then smiled remembering one thing. He loved her hair. For that, she'd wear it loose for him but in a ponytail for her. Happy medium.

By the time she came out the bathroom, Sahvrin was cooking at the stove. She'd decided to pretend they didn't fight yesterday and today was a new day, clean slate. "Morning, how did you sleep?" she asked, panic slamming her at the worst question she could possibly ask if he'd remembered or been aware of what happened.

"Slept hard," he said in his low, sexy voice, making her womb jerk.

"You must've been tired. Musta needed rest." Shut up now. Move on. "Is that coffee I smell?"

"It is," he said. "Want a cup?"

"I was about to get it. Did you have a cup yet?"

"Was fixing to."

"I can get it," she said, grabbing a second cup before he could deny her. "Whatcha cooking? Always smells amazing."

She watched him in those delicious jeans and white t-shirt, chopping onions. "Crazy Omelet."

"Oh, yum. What's crazy about it?" She looked down at the coffee and glanced at him, catching him staring at her shorts. Or was he looking at her butt in them? God, how embarrassing. Bet he wasn't thinking her malnourished now.

"What's crazy is the order you cook it. You fry your meat and vegetables first then crack the eggs right on top before gently flipping it."

"Sounds more genius than crazy. I'm so hungry!" She brought his coffee to him, and he set his knife down, wiping his eyes on his sleeve right as the sting of onions hit her.

"Whoa," she said, backing up and blinking around the sting.

"Usually I cut them quick and miss the eye mutilation."

"Eye mutilation," she said with a little giggle. "Sorry," she added, sipping her cup.

"For what?"

Hmm. She was always assuming the wrong things with him. "I was thinking I may have caused it somehow. The uh…" she wagged her fingers at her eyes "…distraction."

He chuckled. "You were thinking right." He walked over to the sink and turned on the water, splashing his face then patting it dry with a dish towel while she burned to know what that meant. He went back to the stove and dumped his onions and other colorful things in a big black skillet, creating a hiss of smoke that soon turned the kitchen into a nose paradise.

"I was thinking to start working on my tan today. Where would I find the best place to do that here? Anywhere but the garden."

He let out a laugh, angling his sexy look at her. "The back dock at two has sun for a couple hours, but that's too long for you."

"Why?"

"Because the ice queen might get heat stroke."

"I just need an hour," she said, getting his head shake.

"Thirty minutes for your first time. Fifteen minutes on one side, fifteen on the other."

"That's *all*?"

He nodded and she wanted to argue but bit her tongue. "Fine, thirty minutes it is. I was thinking you could give me privacy. Mah-Mah packed a bathing suit and I'd like to use it to suntan."

His humored look made her feel stupid.

"What?"

"You need privacy with a bathing suit? I would think you might if you were planning to sunbathe naked."

Her pulse sped up at just the word. What was he saying. "I've...never sunbathed naked. Not even in a tanning bed."

He shrugged, cracking eggs in the pot now as she wondered what he was thinking, why was he saying that? "I don't...really care to show off my body is all," she added.

"This must be difficult at pools for you?" He stirred without looking at her all while she felt like he was proving some point rather than making casual conversation as his tone implied.

"I don't like doing it there especially."

"But you do?"

"Yes, but if I had a choice, I would rather nobody see."

He nodded, hitting the spoon on the edge of the pot. "It's unfortunate you think you have no choices in these situations."

Okay what the hell was he saying? "I guess I could choose to not go to swimming pools and even beaches, yes. I just...figured I was odd for having an issue with it since everybody else seems to be fine about it. So I pushed through it."

"Well, now you don't have to push through anything. If you want to you can, if you don't, then don't do it. It's your life, your body, your preference. Nobody else. You want to tan alone, then you will tan alone. You want to tan nude, tan nude. I will not look if you don't want me to."

Her brain sputtered at those last words. If she didn't want him to? Was he saying he wanted to watch if she wanted him to? He'd said yesterday, very clearly, he didn't want to see any women naked. Ohhhh wait a minute, he'd said her being in the scenario changed it. Mercy. Was he telling her he wanted to watch her naked?

"Okay," she finally said, realizing she'd not answered. "Thank you." Wasn't sure what she was thanking him for now. And if she wanted him to watch, how was she supposed to tell him that? The idea had her beyond aroused. She set her coffee down, needing a cold water.

****

Sahvrin was playing with fire, he knew. And he was caring less and less. But seeing her ass in those shorts and her wearing that bathing suit top had done a number on his self-control. The idea of her suntanning on his deck had him so fucking provoked and he'd said more than he'd meant to. Every second with her was beginning to feel like fighting a war. There was no telling what she got out of his mixed signals given her inability to understand even plain English. He'd need to jack off now. After waking up aroused out of his fucking mind and now seeing her ass and her cute tits in the same moment finished him off.

There was no reason not to jack off, he wasn't into masochism, and walking around with a hard-on was just that.

At one o'clock, Sahvrin exhausted himself with workouts. He even let His Petite watch him. Which meant he'd pretended he didn't know she did. He'd given her a good show, even doing it in only his briefs, not caring that his cock was hard the entire time, knowing her eyes were all over it.

He knew it was wrong to hope it caused a *little* of what she triggered in him, but Saint Sahvrin was slacking, leaving Bishop to handle things, who interpreted everything she did as an attack on his sex-less ethics code. This called for retaliation to him. Didn't matter that fighting fire with fire would incinerate everything. The Bishop lived to burn things down and was more than happy to burn with it.

He showered outside then checked the cure on the tub before making his way back to the house. At the front door, he paused and angled his head at what he was seeing inside. He opened the door and His Petite shot up from the bathroom floor.

"What are you doing?"

"I uh…spilt…something and was just…wiping it."

He made his way over, eying the rubber gloves on her hands then inspected the bathroom. Seeing his bottle of home-made cleaner on the sink, he leveled a look on her. "You're cleaning?"

"No, just a little, I spilled—"

"Spilled what, cleaner?"

"Well, I was just cleaning the toilet and a little spilled so yes, I was cleaning it up."

"We had a deal. You agreed."

"It was barely anything, my God, you're acting like I'm a criminal! I cleaned a little, so what. I'm not an invalid but if I go another day unable to do something, I'm going to wither away or go crazy!"

Anger bristled along his nerves as the Bishop once again saw this as a transgression that needed answering even as he struggled to take her out of that category. "It's two-o'clock. You have a date with your tan," he muttered.

She stared at him, fully seeing and feeling his anger and still it wasn't enough for him. She lowered her gaze with a quiet, "I'm sorry. You're right. It was wrong, I shouldn't have, even if I think it's stupid."

He held his jaw shut, not giving in to her need for his reassurance. She finally turned and walked off, and the sight of her ass brought his anger straight to his cock.

He stood there, boiling for many seconds then decided she should wear sunblock. He made his way to the back dock right as she lay on the blanket he'd put out for her.

"You need to wear this," he said, ignoring her startled reaction as she clutched a towel to her chest. "Lay down, I'll put it on your back."

She hesitated then did as he said while he poured some in his hands and rubbed them together. He paused. "This bathing suit isn't for tanning, it's got a million strings in every direction."

"Well…it's all I have," she said, sounding confused.

"Why not remove the top since you're laying on your front. Nobody is here looking."

"Well, I…ugh," she finally mumbled, angling her head toward him. "Can you turn?"

He did, then said, "Turned," and waited while his cock hardened.

"Okay, I'm done."

At seeing the fading bruises on her exposed back, hunger filled him. He added more sunblock to his hands and rubbed them together, moving his palms gently over her warm skin. "Do the bruises hurt still?" he asked, wanting to French kiss each one.

"Not...really."

"Am I hurting you?" he asked, making his touch even softer.

"No," she murmured. "Feels... so good."

Fuck, she was starved for touch. He focused on feeling her, not wanting to forget what that was like, sure he'd never get the chance again. Her skin was silky and soft as he glided his palms over every inch of her back, painfully aware he was doing what he swore not to. Touch heaven.

"God this feels amazing," she said, making his cock throb.

"Your body needs this."

She answered with an innocent, delicate mmm. "As long as I'm not working?"

"Yes," he said, moving his hands up her sides allowing his fingers to dip down too low. He stroked along her arms too then back, digging his thumbs gently into her shoulder muscles, ready to devour her.

"Oh my God," she murmured, lost to it.

He went all the way down to her waist now, focusing his thumbs at the very bottom of her back, getting more of those pleasure sounds. His eyes lowered over her ass, and all Bishop saw was sin that needed punishing.

"Why you're tanning in these shorts? Do you *want* a boy's tan."

"What? No, I don't," she murmured, sounding lost to the feeling as he kept his pace sensual.

"Then take them off," he said, his cock aching to see her ass.

"I...I don't like showing my butt."

Fuck, did she think it wasn't gorgeous? "That's fine, I won't look," he straight up lied, prepared to coerce more.

"Can you turn?"

Fire raced through his veins as he did. "Turned." He waited as heat pounded his cock. He really needed to stop before he couldn't.

"Okay."

The delicate way she said it made him brace for war. He stared at her ass, struck completely dumb. Fucking Dieu, how did she not know she had the finest ass on the fucking earth? He returned to rubbing her back before she got worried, getting her to that point he had her before. It didn't take long. And the sweet sounds of pleasure were getting less innocent as he memorized every rib, contour and vertebrae.

Out of nowhere, Saint Sahvrin made a return and said, "Done," then moved to stand. "I'll let you know when fifteen minutes is up, then you can turn over."

"Thank you," she said weakly, the lust in those sweet words licking his cock.

Fuck, he was going to explode. "Second thought, I'm going to go check traps. I'll be back in about an hour. Fifteen minutes on the front," he reminded as he went. "Don't go over that."

"Okay," she muttered. "Have fun," she added in a sweet voice.

Yeah, fun. Going have tons of fucking fun burning in the memories of that heaven.

****

While out, Sahvrin ran into more signs of trafficking and followed the possible trail as far as he could, not finding anything more. Stopping at one of the Swamp Shops, he pulled his phone out and located Spook.

"Eveque, it's been a lil bit," Spook answered.

"Yes, too long," Sahvrin said. "I'm gonna send you coordinates where I'm finding signs of demon networking. Need you to come see what you can see."

"Send it. How's everything going with that?" Spook asked.

"Good. I'll have more details in a couple days."

"Usual meeting's still on?"

"If you're meaning my mother's party, yes. If we need to do anything before that, I'll let everybody know."

"Sounds good. Send the coordinates and I'll get on it right away."

"Thanks. How's your father and mother?"

"They're good. Still embedded in the swamps like a couple of old warts on a toad."

Sahvrin grinned "Good to hear it. You should bring them."

"I will if I can talk them into it."

The odds were low going by Spooks tone. "Text me anything you find. If you need to reach me quick, I'm at the shack."

"Got it. Later."

Sahvrin hung up and tied his boat to the dock, hopping onto the pier. "Com-on-sah-vah," he said to Ms. Bernadette as he entered the small house on piers.

"Lil-Eveque," she called with a toothless grin. "Meh, I don't see you hardly?"

"I've been around," he said, looking to the right.

"What you need, sha?"

"Not sure, really," he muttered, walking the first aisle.

"Meh you shoppin?" she asked with a laugh because he did that never.

"I guess I am," he said, spotting a sun hat and picking one up. He grabbed everything he thought she would like, finally realizing he might be apologizing without words. Was mostly all pleasure foods of the healthy kind since she'd not had anything like it yet. He remembered her boredom comment and added various forms of entertainment to keep her occupied. He put a pair of flip-flops in the bag and said, "Say-to, fini."

"Meh you done got the whole store," the old woman laughed, writing all the items down. "You sure you don't want dis?"

She put an alligator necklace on the pile, and he nodded it in with the rest.

Fuck, he'd been gone almost three hours, he realized as he left. A cool front had snuck up on him and the next couple of days would offer cooler weather, thank Dieu. He'd cook her a gumbo, she should like that.

CHAPTER 8

Beth cried as she stared in the mirror at her red tits. She'd fallen asleep in the sun and now Sahvrin was going to be so pissed. To make it worse, since he wasn't there, she'd gone topless. And to do something to make up for the tanning crime, she'd organized his desk which required zero work effort and broke the cute stick art sitting on top of it. Probably some family heirloom. Then while looking for glue to fix it, she saw a tablet and thought to make a paper fan to help cool off her burn. She had no idea it was a journal when she opened it. She didn't read anything intentionally. At first, she was captivated by the beautiful cursive writing, not really paying attention to what was written. And when she did, she'd shut it. It seemed like a love letter of some kind, and she still wasn't sure if he'd written it or somebody else had. The handwriting didn't look like the one on the note he'd put on her food. And now she couldn't look again to compare or ask without him knowing she'd snooped. No, it wasn't really snooping, but he still might get mad, and she'd already done enough for him to be mad about.

She'd tell him, just not today. Maybe in a couple days. But the real fear was the art piece she'd broken. He didn't have many things in his house and the few pieces that seemed like collectibles were obviously of value to him. She was over-reacting. It was sticks and could be glued back, no big deal. She'd intended on gluing it and not saying anything, but she knew hiding that would eat her up. One secret was enough with him. Not to mention, she seemed to feel more guilty with him when she'd done something wrong or stupid.

While going over her Sahvrin crimes, she remembered how horny she'd gotten when he'd simply rubbed her back. What was wrong with her? God, he was. Everything about him aroused her. But it seemed... more, way more than what would be normal. She froze, considering. Was it something in the tea he made her drink? Some exotic herb in the medicine? She closed her eyes with a helpless moan at remembering his large hands moving on her. He'd been so gentle, so careful. So...sexy about it.

More heat flooded her cheeks at the no-going-back-now shame of him seeing her butt. She knew he looked, of course he did. She was ninety-nine percent sure. And the one percent chance that he hadn't, actually bothered her. She wanted him to look, she realized, confirming her sluttiness.

She needed to stop this madness with him. Probably why he'd left suddenly, he was seeing it and was disgusted with her behavior since he wasn't into women. Not like she totally believed that but come to think of it, he showed no signs other than the ones with her which she was likely reading way too far into.

God, what if he was seeing what she *really* wanted? She sucked at hiding things, and he was especially clairvoyant with her.

Shame and desire warred as she fanned her chest with the little make-shift paper fan. She made her way out of the bathroom and gasped at seeing he was back. "Oh *crap*!"

She hurried to the bed and lay down, not ready to face him. She remembered she'd borrowed one of his dress shirts because it hurt to wear anything tight on her chest. It was nothing to worry about, but she worried anyway.

When it took him a long time, she sat up to see what he was doing. She spied brown paper bags on the pier and a childish excitement coursed through her. He'd gone shopping? She decided he might need help and made her way to the door and called, "You need me to carry stuff?"

"No," he called back, making her stomach knot up at his tone. Was he still mad?

She waited as he made his way, carrying all the bags in both hands, his rubber boots and jeans making him look sexier somehow. What a *ridiculous* thing to be that beautiful.

She backed away from the door, ready to get it all over with only to hurry back and hold it open for him as he approached.

He froze before her. "Mon, fucking Dieu," he muttered in shock.

"I fell asleep," she said with her head lowered as he walked in. She eyed him as he put the bags on the floor next to the counter and braced as he walked over to her.

"What are you doing?" she gasped, grabbing his hands when he began unbuttoning the shirt.

He glared at her. "Looking to see what *degree burns* you have."

"I don't…have anything on under it."

"Then you'll have to be *embarrassed*, I guess," he said, pissed.

"I'll do it," she gasped, stepping back and unbuttoning the first four then looking to the right with her eyes closed as she opened the shirt.

****

Sahvrin stifled the groan when her tits came into view. It was another brutal war of lust and anger, as usual. "Fucking Christ," he whispered.

"I'm sorry." Her mouth clamped together with her eyes as tears rolled down her cheeks.

He hurried to her and closed the shirt, stifling the lust pushing in his vocal cords, then held her face, wiping her tears. "Okay, don't cry," he said, giving in to the need to put his lips on her. He pressed them to her forehead with his shhh, shhh," as she choked out sobs.

"And I broke your stick art on the desk accidentally. I tried to find glue and couldn't and then I accidentally found a journal I swear I was just looking for paper to make a little…fan to cool my burn, I wasn't meaning to read it and stopped the second I realized what it was."

Journal? He held her head to his chest, stroking her hair. "I can fix anything, Ma Petite. And I don't own a journal, maybe you found my sisters." He'd confiscated it when he found out she was breaking the dating rules.

"I'm sorry, if you show me how, I can maybe fix it."

The genuine concern touched him more than it should, it was her magic, he realized. He wasn't used to a woman caring so much about him aside from his sister and mother. She'd been this way at her most broken state, even.

He closed his eyes as images of her bright red chest flooded him with fire. Poor baby, that was going to fucking hurt, while *killing* him.

He led her to the bed and made her lay down. "Be still while I get something. Have you put anything on it yet?"

"No, I wasn't sure what to put," she said, covering her eyes with a hand.

"Don't cry, Ma Petite, I'm not mad, okay?" He kissed her forehead again, fighting the need to do more.

He found his burn salve and made his way back, sitting on the bed. "Keep your face turned away. I will dress the burn."

"Oh God," she strained, facing as far away as she could while he moved the shirt aside.

"I will try to go quickly but I don't want to hurt you." He started with her upper chest and gradually worked his way to her breasts, fighting not to stare. He lost that fight. His gaze locked on her nipples, tall and tight. His attempt to use a non-sensual touch caused her breast to bounce under his careful dabbing.

"Almost done," he said, feeling terrible for her while his cock raged the closer he got to her nipples. "This might be…sensitive," he said before dabbing the ointment on the first one.

"Oh my God," she shot out in strain.

"Sorry Ma Petite," he whispered, carefully covering every inch of it then moving to the other one.

A strained "Mmm," flew from her with the kick of her legs as he quickly finished.

"Done," he said, his own breath releasing with hers as he stood. "Don't cover it."

"Oh God, I have to stay this way?"

"Your payment for not listening," he muttered, back to furiously aroused-pissed.

"I fell asleep!"

"Because you were so exhausted from doing nothing?"

"Because I'm *bored* out of my God *blessed* mind, maybe!"

"Maybe," he said, staring when she sat up.

"Don't look!" she cried, raising the sheet before her chest. "I thought you didn't look at women's breasts!"

"I don't. But I don't see you like other women."

"Oh, right, you see me like a child, I remember."

He unpacked the bags he'd brought in. "I *sure* never said that."

"You don't need to. Or a little sister, that's what I am."

"And that's a problem for you why? Did you want to be something else to me, Ma Petite?"

Her silence got him hard, and her, "I never said that" lie, even harder. Mon Dieu, she was something.

"I bought you things to entertain you," he said, making his way over with the bag.

She held the sheet up before her like a wall with only her head sticking out, misery, guilt and eagerness on her pretty face. "What did you get me?" she wondered, seeing it as a personal gift, he realized.

He dumped the bag on the bed, and she gasped, "A coloring book! And colors!"

His cock ached that she picked the most childish of them as her favorite. *Because she's still a child,* he reminded himself. *Still injured, still fragile, still everything you need to stay away from.* She was also sweet as fuck. He'd not met many twenty-four-year old's, but he was sure she took first place in cock-sucking sweetness out of a million.

"And jacks! I haven't played that in years! Ohhhh, cards, I don't really know any games other than solitary, maybe you can teach me."

"I don't play."

The disappointed look she gave said he'd be making an exception.

She fought to drape the sheet over her shoulders as he contemplated ideas he had no business thinking about. "I'll teach you a card game later," he said.

The happy smile that earned him set fire to his cock. He wouldn't break code-rule and gamble, but that didn't mean he couldn't win certain things. If she lost, he'd consider it fate's punishment. If she won, he'd consider it fate's gift to him. Either way, he'd win.

****

"That burn cream is amazing," Beth said from the bathroom as she added more to her tender nipples. "The pain is almost gone." There was no way she could stand him doing it again, God she'd nearly moaned from the pain and pleasure he'd caused. How horrifying that would have been.

"Good," she heard him say from the kitchen. "Gumbo is ready. Come eat."

His bossy tone had an odd effect on her and not a bad one. She liked it, she realized. Maybe because she knew at the bottom of it, he did it out of concern. Yeah, she'd go with that.

He'd wanted her to go without a top, which she informed was *outrageous* of him to even ask. It was a medical matter to him he'd said. Right, maybe so, but it wasn't for *her*.

She held his dress shirt away from her chest as she went out. It was still the best thing to wear next to everything else.

"Sit on the couch, I'll bring your tray."

She did as he said, unable to keep her smile back at realizing he was the nicest bossy person she'd ever met. She watched as the tray lowered to her lap, not touching it until he let it go. "What is *this?*" she wondered, picking up one of the crystalized brown squares with nuts in it.

"Your dessert."

She smelled it. "Mmmmmm, that smells sooooo gooood. You bought me that too?"

"I bought it," he said.

"For me," she added with a smirk as he took his seat near her. She leaned and smelled the main dish. "I had intended to try gumbo while I was here," she said, stirring it while he busily ate his.

She took her first bite and Mmmm'd with a "Dear Lord, how do you *cook so good!*"

"Glad you like it," he said, right as she choked.

"Sorry, a lil spicey," she said around wheezing and sputtering.

"Milk?" he asked, getting up.

She nodded, coughing it out.

He returned and she gulped half of it down then cleared her throat. "Wow," she strained, her esophagus still wanting to shut down business.

"Too much red pepper," he said, taking her bowl to the kitchen. She watched him do something to it then returned with it. "That should help."

"What you do?" she wondered, stirring it.

"Just added a little water to dilute it."

She tried some more and got back to the mmmm-mmm business, nodding at him. "That did it, thank you."

She could hardly wait to finish her gumbo, eyeing the delicious translucent square every other bite. When she finally got to it, she took her first nibble and had a mouth-gasm. "This is sooooo gooood," she called to Sahvrin who was busy doing everything in the kitchen while she sat like a lazy, fat-assed pig.

"Figured you'd like that."

"Why does Louisiana have such good food?" she wondered, in tastebud heaven. "Why can't the people up north figure out cooking?"

"You can take the skills back with you."

She gave an annoyed look, hating how he was always trying to discourage her from living there. "I can mail recipes home," she said. "While I live here, in the swamp. And cook them myself. And not *here*," she clarified, "I would get my own place."

She heard his sexy chuckle, hating how it aroused and annoyed her.

"I have plenty of money, I can buy whatever land I want and hire…swamp men to build my dream *shack*."

"You would be hiring me or my brothers," he informed. "We're the best. But I charge a lot."

"Betting one of your brothers would give me a discount."

His snort made her grin, while she wondered what he'd muttered after. "Or I would."

This piqued her interest. "Are you being serious?"

"Yes."

"For real?" she double checked.

"Yes," he said, making his way over and taking her tray.

"Aren't you going to ask if your crippled patient wants anything else?"

"Does my crippled patient want to learn how to play cards?"

Excitement made her mouth drop. "Yes!"

He grabbed a couch pillow and put it on the floor next to the coffee table across from her then headed back to the kitchen. "Want something before we start?"

"No thank you, I'm stuffed! And it was *so* good," she added. "You're the King." She smiled at his grin as he sat across from her with the cards. "What's your poison?" she asked.

He cast her that sexy look, shuffling the cards. "Five Card Draw."

"Ohhhh, sounds dangerous. Is that a big casino kind of game?"

"It is."

"Well, let's do it!" she said, crossing her legs on the couch.

"What are we betting?" he asked, dealing out cards.

"Betting? Like money?"

"I don't gamble with money," he informed.

"Oh…. Well, I don't know, you tell me."

"You tell me first." He placed the deck next to him after passing their cards out.

"Hmmmm," she thought. "What can I bargain for?"

"Anything you want."

She gave a laugh. "Anything? Like…you building my house for free?"

"Damn, that's steep," he said, making her laugh. "Fine."

Her jaw dropped. "No! I would never let you do it for free."

He gave a mini-eyeroll with his, "Of course you wouldn't."

"How about if I win, I get to do something, like…"

"Clean the toilet?" he wondered. "The stove? The fridge?"

"No, not clean! What about take me fishing? Tomorrow," she added.

He shook his head. "The sun is the last place you'll want to be tomorrow," he assured.

"Oh." Shit. Crap. "Then you let me…do something for you."

He eyed her, mildly interested and yet guarded. "Like what?"

She shrugged. "I'll let you pick."

He gave a real laugh at that. "You'd let me pick?"

"I trust you to be reasonable!"

"Do you," he said, like she were very stupid to do that.

But she did trust him, and she nodded with a confident, "I do."

"Fine. And if I win," he said, eying her. "You sleep without that shirt."

She swallowed, heat hitting her privates. "And you'll sleep on the couch," she said, making sure.

He nodded then gave a light shrug. "Unless there's another storm."

She couldn't even be mad since he wanted to ease her pain and speed her healing. "Deal," she said.

He picked up his cards and she picked up hers. "What do I do?" she asked.

He explained how the points worked and she nodded, getting it. "So, I'll keep my two Aces," she said, making him laugh. "What? No?"

"Yes, but don't tell me."

"Oh, okay."

"You get to throw away the cards you don't want and draw that many more."

She threw away three of them and he gave her three. She picked them up and threw those as well.

He laughed and shook his head. "You can't throw those three, you're stuck with them."

"Crap," she said, taking them back. "Now you know I have only two aces!"

"I do," he said, drawing his cards and looking at them. "But it beats my two tens," he said, laying his cards down.

"So I win?" she wondered with wide eyes.

"This round, yes." He scooped all the cards up.

"I get the prize, right?"

"You do. You get to do something for me that I pick. Because you trust me."

Her heart hammered at his tone. "Yes. So, what do you pick? Remember I trust you!" she laughed.

"I remember," he said, his stare burning her. "I'd like a massage."

She went serious. "Oh," she said, heat filling her cheeks. "What kind?"

"Guess you can massage my…back," he finally said, bringing a breath of excitement while she tried not to show what that did to her.

"That was very nice of you," she realized.

"It was," he assured, maybe implying he could've named other parts of him.

He shuffled again then dealt out five cards. "Now what are you playing for?" he asked, holding the deck. "I'm still playing for the same."

Mercy. "Uhhh, let me think." What did she really want to do for him? She looked around for inspiration then snapped a smile to him. "You let me cook breakfast! After you show me how to use the stove!"

"That's two things," he said.

"Ugh, then you show me how to use the stove and when I beat you again, I'll get the breakfast."

He laughed until only his sexy panty-melting grin remained. He picked up his cards and she did the same. This time she didn't give her answers away. She only had two threes. She threw three cards, and he gave her three more. He drew two cards. Crap.

She looked at her cards and didn't stifle her gasp. She'd gotten two fours.

"Loser shows their hand first?" she asked.

He lay down his cards. "Three jacks."

She lay down hers. "Four pairs!"

He grinned. "That's two pairs. And three of a kind beats that."

"What? But I have four cards!"

"Three of a kind beats a pair. Even two pairs."

"Uuuugh."

"No shirt for you tonight," he announced, gathering the cards back into the deck. "Another round?"

"Yes," she said. "And if I win, I want you to teach me to make gumbo."

"And if I win, I want you to take off your shirt now."

Her jaw dropped. "I *can't!*" she cried. "Why are you asking for that? I thought you didn't like women parading their tits in front of you?"

He shrugged, propping his knee up and draping his arm over it. "I don't. But you're not parading, you're letting your burn air out."

"What if I just...leave it unbuttoned?"

His eyes went to slits on her. "Deal," he said, passing their cards again.

She drew her cards and dropped her jaw at the crap he gave. She tossed all five.

"You quit?" he asked, grinning with raised brows.

"No, I need five more!"

"You should keep at least one, you might get another like it?"

"Is that what I should do?"

"You don't have to."

"Then...no. I want five more."

He gave her five more and took two again. Ugh. She slowly picked up her cards. "Oh my God, five more pieces of crap! I should've kept that king!"

"I have three fives," he said, laying his cards on the table.

"Are you cheating?" she wondered, unbuttoning her shirt while eying him.

"I'm not," he assured.

"How would I know if you were?"

"You likely wouldn't," he said, laughing.

"If I see you looking, I'm buttoning it back."

"Fine," he said. "Now I'm playing to give you a massage. First."

The memory of his last massage had her sick with horny excitement. "Where? As in what…body part?"

"I'll trust you to choose for me."

"Why not just make me if it's something I need?"

"I could," he said, like it was her choice.

"My feet," she hurried, before he changed his mind.

"Deal," he said, passing their cards. "Last game," he said. "Then we cash in."

Oh God. Was just feet. "Okay."

CHAPTER 9

Sahvrin was wondering how he'd survive this without having an orgasm. She'd won the last game and he was spreading a blanket on the floor for his massage. Mon Dieu, maybe he *was* a masochist.

"Shirt on or off?" she asked, as he removed it. "Guess off," she said, her nervous excitement showing. "I should warn you I don't have a lot of knowledge about this."

He lay on the floor. "I'm sure you have a decent amount about the male body given your two years of education."

"But, a sex therapist doesn't learn about how to massage."

"What does she learn?" he wondered, waiting with his hard cock pressing into the floor.

"Not about massaging," was all she managed to finally sputter.

"It's a good thing you switched majors," he said, smiling to himself.

"I'm starting. Do you mind if I…kneel above you, uh straddle your…hips?"

Mon Dieu, did she forget all her vocabulary? "Please do," he said.

"And why is it a good thing I switched majors?" she asked, stroking her hands softly over his back.

"Because you can't hardly speak to the opposite sex without getting worked up."

He wished he could see her face. "I talk to the opposite sex just fine," she said, her hands like silk along his skin as she seemed to absently rub.

"You know that massage involves working the muscle, not just masturbating my skin."

She gasped and he chuckled when she smacked him. "I was distracted by this tattoo. Is this like a seal?"

"Mmm. Yes. Of the organization I belong to."

"Like…a swamp gang?"

"Something like that."

"How interesting."

"You're tickling me."

"Sorry." She got busy with pressing her fingers into his muscle and the feeling was fucking orgasmic.

"You like it?" she asked when a lusty groan slipped.

"Yes," he mumbled.

"You're so tight," she said, sounding amazed. "And hard."

The Bishop stepped up to war with Saint Sahvrin, insisting she was purposely tempting and needed to answer for it. "You sound surprised."

"I am. You're laying here and it feels like you're using your muscles."

"I am," he assured.

"Well…try to relax." She tried to help by roaming her silky hands all over his back.

"That's not helping," he said fighting back another cock-burning groan.

"Does it tickle?"

"Yes." All over his fucking balls.

"I told you I don't know what I'm doing. Where did you learn how to massage, you're like a professional. Never mind, maybe I don't want to know."

She'd done it again, obliviously told him she was jealous. "Why wouldn't you want to know, Ma Petite?" he decided to push.

"I just…don't. It's not my business."

"I learned it from my first girlfriend," he said, or the Bishop said.

She didn't speak for a moment. "Good for you." Her touch gradually went from delicate to a baker working dough. "I did learn things," she added now, making him grin as he waited to hear. "I learned tons of sex stuff in the Kama Sutra book."

His eyes slowly opened with the throb of his cock. "The what book?"

"It's supposedly an ancient text on all the ways to have sex. Emotional, mental, and physical."

"Emotional sex?" The hell was that?

"Right, so, it's all about breathing, and sighing, and feeling."

"So you think this is bullshit?" At least her tone implied it.

"I mean, I don't know, it kind of sounds a little…circus-ish." He grunted when she began karate chopping all over his back now. "And the *positions!* Talk about a freak show. Like…humans-are-not-made-to-bend-at-those-angles kind of freak show. Am I doing good?" she wondered.

"Yes, very," he strained, wishing she'd sit on him. "If you get tired and need to sit, you can."

"Oh…. Okay." But she didn't. "Soooo," she said lightly. "Your first girlfriend, huh? And how old were you? I didn't start dating till I was eighteen," she volunteered. "Daddy's strict orders."

"I had no such strict orders," he muttered. "But I was seventeen."

"And how long did that last?"

"Not long enough and too long," he said.

She paused briefly then seemed to use her elbows now. The new position brought her inner thighs against his waist which in turn brought images of her riding his cock. "That sounds like an oxymoron."

"She broke up with me."

Again she paused very briefly before getting back to the job she was so terribly good at. "So not long enough because you didn't want her to break up?"

"I'm glad she broke up," he said.

"Then how was it not long enough?" she wondered, pausing again.

"The stupid boy didn't want it to end, but the man in me wished it had never begun."

"Was she a tramp?" She sounded hopeful.

"Definitely," he said.

"So she…slept around on you?"

"Probably."

"You don't know?"

"Nope. Don't want to, either."

"So how do you know she was a tramp?"

"Ma Petite. I won this massage fair and square."

"Oh, sorry!" She got back to work, her touch much softer now. "So how do you know she was a tramp?"

"I guess it was just a figure of speech."

"Ohhh, I see. I understand. In that case, she was definitely a tramp. A very *dumb* tramp," she mumbled.

"Ma Petite, you don't even know her," he said, grinning.

She gave a cute snort. "Well, she broke up with you and I'm guessing this was your pre-Prick Bishop days which means you were likely so sweet! Am I right?"

He had to laugh at that while fighting the urge to throw her on the floor and take what she teased him with. "Maybe," he grunted, so fucking hard now, moving his hips.

As if by some miracle, she scooted down and worked his lower back muscles now. He gave an appreciative groan.

"Oh, this feels good?" she asked.

"Fuck yes," he said, too aroused to care.

She went quiet as she tended that area, seeming to focus. "Tell me if I'm doing it too hard or not hard enough."

"You can go harder," he said, wishing she'd put all her weight into it. He gave a thick groan at her renewed efforts. "Where'd you learn that?"

"Maybe from you," she said, the sweet words sounding winded.

"Mmm, remind me to thank myself."

She gave a breathy laugh, getting quiet again. He jerked when her fingers hit a ticklish spot.

"Crap, sorry," she gasped.

"Didn't hurt, just sensitive there. And I'm ready to do you now, then it's bedtime."

"Oh, okay," she said, sounding surprised and disappointed as she stopped. "You can do me tomorrow if you're tired."

Do her. "I'm not. The bedtime is yours." He turned, finding her with the shirt closed as she quickly sat on the couch and put her feet on the coffee table.

He moved it out the way and knelt before her, holding one of her feet in his hands.

"Ohhh," she said with wide eyes when he began massaging, making him smile.

"You like that?"

"Yessss," she moaned, seeming pleasantly surprised. "Wow, yes," she said again, eyeing him with shock.

He worked on her ankle after a bit, letting his fingers creep up her calf.

"God that's amazing," she said, closing her eyes. He eyed the closed shirt, all too aware of her disobedience. He wouldn't force the issue. Yet. "Did you…learn that from your girlfriend too?"

"I did," he decided to say, bracing her reaction.

"So she had a lot of…skills."

"She was older than me."

"Oh, so you were jailbait?"

His cock jerked at hearing her jealousy. "I guess I was."

"There's no guessing. You were."

"Then I was. Very willing jailbait."

"So she…molested you and taught you about sex, I'm guessing."

God, she could make him laugh. "Yes, she did," he said, happy to chat about sex with her in any way. "She was into young men."

"That's disgusting. How did you meet?"

"At one of my mother's many parties. I guess you could say she raped me."

"Is that a figure of speech?"

"Not this time, no."

"Are you shitting me? And why is this funny to you?"

"*You're* funny to me."

"What a bitch."

He shrugged, debating on what to tell her about it. "Maybe seduced is a better word."

"What a *tramp*," she fumed as he caressed and stroked her soft skin, ready to know what that would feel like on his tongue and lips. "If I had been your mother, I'd have killed her *so* dead."

He had to smile at that, eying her sparkly gaze while taking her other foot. "I bet you would have. My feisty angel."

She gave a huge eye and head roll that made him laugh. "No angel here, I promise you."

"Says the twenty-four-year-old virgin."

The pink in her cheeks made him almost sorry for his words. "I don't believe in screwing just to screw."

"Neither do I," he said, watching the pleasure of his foot rub fight against her anger.

"Is…that when you decided you weren't meant for a soul mate?" she wondered.

"*And* a perceptive angel."

"Oh my *God*," she said, smacking the couch. "This bitch ruined your whole *life?*"

Her mini tantrum caused the shirt to gape open and his eyes devoured the little gift peeking out at him.

"The bitch created Bishop and for that, I can thank her." But didn't and never would. He moved his touch up her calf now, allowing himself to stare at her tits every few seconds.

"I can't believe it," she said, sounding so disappointed about the whole thing.

"What about you, Ma Petite," he wondered, ready to be out of that spotlight. "You had boyfriends, yes?" He placed her foot against his chest and worked over her calves, glad she didn't protest.

"I…had a couple."

"But no sex."

"No. No sex."

He eyed her, wanting to know what she *did* do. "Just kissing?"

"Um…a little. Not a lot because of what it could lead to. Didn't want to be a tease."

He couldn't speak because Bishop suddenly burned to know if she teased other men the way she did him. Obliviously. "Such a smart angel," he decided to say, his fingers creeping up to her knee now, insanely jealous of the ones who got to taste her. "But how are you to learn about sexual things?"

"Well… " she began, her tone timid. "I kind of imagined that the one I ended up with would…teach me or…we could learn it together."

She was breathless now and he wanted to know why. He also loved her answer as much as he hated it since he was experienced, even if it had been a while. "So, if you end up with an experienced partner, that has its pros, yes?"

"I mean…I guess, but…"

He waited for her answer, but it didn't come. "But what?"

"Maybe I wouldn't… want him to have done that with another woman."

"But… if you steal his heart, he will not remember another girl's name, I think?"

The slow smile she gave was a winner. "I guess if I managed that, then…that works. I kind of get my cake and eat it too."

Mmmm, he wanted to eat her cake. "I think Ma Petite can easily manage this."

"You do?" she asked, as if she thought he would know.

"Absolutely."

"Why do you say that?" she wondered, her toes pressing into his chest. Right at that moment, she glanced down and realized her tits were bare to him. She gasped and snapped her head up. "Why didn't you tell me!" She shoved him with her foot, pushing him onto his haunches. He realized it was a chance to get out of the fire while he could.

He stood and went around the couch while he still had the willpower to. "Taking a shower, Ma Petite. You should get to bed."

****

Get to bed. Like a child. She lay in said bed, the heat from her burnt tits and now boiling privates in an all-out war. He'd been starting at her breasts and not saying anything! Why did that bother her so much when she actually *wanted* him to *want* to look? She was such an idiot. He was clearly in the process of…doing something with her. His foot massage was slowly moving up her leg and she hadn't intended to make him stop!

Why couldn't he just be bossy in that and force her?

Because that would be *rape. Stupid.*

Ugh.

She froze and got up on her knees in the bed at hearing sounds in the bathroom. Was that…was he… She crawled on her knees to the foot of the bed, pressing her ear against the wall. "Oh God," she gasped, pulling away and pressing her ear again. His thick breaths and moans echoed in the wall right into her ear. "Oh God," she whispered, closing her eyes as she imagined what he was doing and what that looked like.

His breaths picked up speed as did the grunts and moans and hisses. A deep growling sound strained out of him with a *"Fuck yes, yes."*

She knelt there, her privates throbbing with so much pain as she panted on desire. She was going to die if she didn't have an orgasm now. If he could masturbate, then she could too, she knew how to do that much. But later when she knew he was sleeping.

CHAPTER 10

Beth woke up feeling lost and confused and dying of thirst.

She sat up and looked around. What time was it? She leaned and peeked over the couch, then listened in the silence. Where was he? Sliding out of the bed, she made her way to the little fridge, looking at the front door as she went. The sight of Sahvrin in only jeans on the pier froze her and tightened her womb. What was he doing? Her eyes devoured the delicious sight of him, especially that tattoo. Mercy, could a man be more delicious? Not in a million lifetimes.

Pure lust brought her to the screen door where she pressed her nose to stare. He gave a brisk shake of his head and swiped his hands through his dark black hair. It was wet, she realized as she watched with renewed awe at the ripple of muscles. What was he doing out there?

Pushing through her inadequacy, she opened the door. She'd just go talk to him and ask questions like normal people do. Five steps into her bravery, he turned, and she stopped in her tracks. He stared at her now, and she felt like a deer in headlights. God, the intensity in his dark eyes weakened her knees.

He was coming toward her now, a half-naked, slow-moving swamp storm, his eyes fixed on her chest.

"I'm sorry," she announced as he approached, because saying random things at the wrong time always seemed right. She *was* sorry. About something. Shit, the shirt. She reached up and made sure it was unbuttoned but not *open!*

Her eyes locked on *his* beautiful chest. "I see you had another shower, that's nice. The night is sultry enough for one," she went on, her voice quivering and cracking as he closed in on her. "I...I don't think I ever told you how much I love the way your family hugs and...and even the fighting and the..." He stopped just before her and took her face carefully between his hands and lowered his head. He pressed his lips on the center of her forehead and before she could think *like a child*, his kiss moved just to the left. Then to the right. "...and... the love," she mumbled with eyes closed, really wanting to stare at his chest this close up. The smell of that soap or shampoo from the shower permeated the space between them until her mouth watered.

"Ma-petite," he whispered, gliding his hand along the hair next to her face. "Please forgive me for not being stronger."

He continued pressing soft kisses onto her head. "Stronger?"

"My brothers--"

"Probably hate me," she gasped, sure he would never kiss a child like this.

"No, Ma Petite. They are all madly in love with you. But they will *never*... lay a single fornicating finger on my angel, this I promise."

His hands and lips vanished, and she slowly opened her eyes, fighting to catch her breath. He was gone too. She swallowed, licking her dry lips. His angel? What did all that just mean? Those kisses. They were...

She drifted back down to earth, shoving her inner negative Nancy back before she had a chance to shit on everything. Those kisses were not childlike. And they were damn amazing. That was her treasure, no matter what it meant or didn't.

What was this sudden, deep conviction to protect her from his brothers who...were madly in love with her? What on earth was he seeing? And they were fornicators? That was a shock, she wasn't sure why. *And they will never lay one single fornicating finger on my angel, this I promise.* Heat flashed through her body. He said that while kissing her. That was big, that meant something.

"Ma Petite, come inside before Gras Jean pays you a visit. He's always hungry and very jealous."

She hurried in at the mention of hungry alligators, but she kept her smile to herself about the jealous part. She didn't want to be walking around with a grin while something bothered him. And something obviously did.

"I must've taken a cat nap. What time is it?"

"Around midnight, I think."

"You…take showers at odd times."

"I couldn't sleep," he said, at the coffee pot, making her wonder what had him so bothered that he couldn't sleep. Had she angered him or…disappointed him?

"Want coffee?" he asked, without looking at her.

"Yes, sure."

She watched his muscles moving in his arm and back as he did the simple task of making coffee. Her gaze got stuck on his hands. Mercy, those thick veins beneath the smooth tanned skin. My God he had beautiful hands and fingers. Big and long. So long.

He chuckled and she snapped her eyes up. Shit, what was funny? What'd she miss?

"Ma Petite, you're being a scientist?"

"A scientist?"

"You were studying me so intently."

"Sorry, I was uh, comparing." Crap, what was she saying?

"And how did I measure up?"

She moved to the other counter, wrapping her hand in her hair while double checking the shirt was still mostly shut. "Fine. Good."

"Fine and good?" He tsked a couple of times, setting the coffee pot back on the little stove to heat. "How can I improve?"

His question threw her in all the wrong directions. "Why would you want to?"

He shrugged, placing his hands on the counter, basically an invitation to devour him with her eyes. And resisting brought embarrassing eye twitches. "I am always trying to improve myself, Ma Petite."

"Nothing," she said. "You can't."

"I can't improve?"

"I mean….there's nothing to improve."

His head went back with a laugh.

"You…don't have shortcomings," she added. "That I can see. That you should change."

The look on his humored face said she was a mess of contradictions, but he didn't mind at all, maybe even liked it. Loved it if she was being dreamy.

"So, I am perfectly fine and good?"

She could agree with that, so she did, with a nod.

"Where did Ma Petite learn her science skills? In her first major or her second?"

He was teasing her. Toying with her. Or just making conversation. She tried to appear as one considering a conversational response. "Both, I'm sure."

"So… this has puzzled me for days. Why does Ma Petite not have someone special?"

Why that stupid topic? "Why are you curious?"

He returned his hands to the counter, back to staring deep into her eyes. "It fascinates me that somebody has not abducted…" he closed his eyes "…stupid word choice…taken you…. Mon Dieu, another stupid choice…"

She smiled, saving him the trouble. "I didn't find the right one. I mean I found plenty, just not the right one."

He angled his head, looking at her. "And how does Ma Petite define the right one?"

Somebody like you? "Just..." She gradually pulled her shoulders up. "Smart…kind…caring. Not stupid," she added, considering her must have's. "Has to be affectionate,"

"La passion?"

She swallowed and nodded with a wispy, "Yes," before lowering her eyes.

"And you...cannot find this person all through college?"

"Well, you always think you have, but people are not...always honest about who they are or maybe they just don't know who they are," she explained. "I wouldn't say they lie or are bad, just..." she shrugged, suddenly feeling like a wife justifying an abusive husband. "Selfish," she ended, ready to be redeemed from her deluge of relationship mishaps.

"Ah, yes. I see this in my fornicating brothers."

"Oh," she said, not wanting to lump them with the bad guys. "I'm not anybody's judge and it's not my business what people do."

"Except with you," he said.

"Right. I developed a system," she informed, regretting her words at realizing where it ended. But his nosy button was pressed. "I just...had requirements when I dated."

The cross of his arms over his chest and raised brows meant don't stop now. His eyes lowered to where she wrapped and unwrapped her hair around her hand. "Ma Petite has more secrets," he said, eyeing her. "You're nervous."

"Not secrets, just...I don't like talking about private things."

He nodded, smiling again. "A good thing you changed majors, yes?"

Ugh, sexy smartass. "It wasn't anything outrageous, I just...didn't allow for sex in dating because it was the only way I would really know what they liked me for."

"Why are you so defensive about this brilliant system you developed? It should be required learning."

She gave a relieved laugh, amazed with him as usual. "I think so."

"So how many imbeciles did Ma Petite have to sift through?"

Laughter shot out at those priceless words. "I'm too embarrassed to say."

His look turned painful. "Mon Dieu, that many?"

She nodded and smiled at his grin. "I quit trying after about four."

He turned and pulled their coffee cups closer to him. "You might be the wisest person I know." He picked up the pot and filled both cups, then handed her one.

"And what about you?" she asked, taking it. "How on earth did you manage not to get *raped* again all this time?"

He lowered his cup, smiling. "You sound like that's a hard thing to do?"

She held back her snort. "Surely you must know how ridiculously cute you are. Don't tell me all the girls you meet don't try to get you in bed, I'll be…insulted."

God that laugh. "Ohhh, Ma Petite, you always go too far," he said, confusing her. "My line of work requires a level of focus," he said with an easy shrug. "Women can be a risky distraction."

Surely, he wasn't always in this line of work. "So, you're saying you seriously only had sex with *one* woman, and that's it?"

"Is this hard to believe for you?"

She gave a shrug, her head swiveling oddly. "Maybe."

"Perhaps Ma Petite can help me."

"Help you? How?" Her heart hammered at what he could mean.

"I seem to have need of one of your majors."

Her heart skipped several beats. "Hoping you need a map?"

It was hard to stay serious with him when he laughed like that. Was like getting drugged with happy rainbows. "Maybe you can draw me one to the real treasure."

The real treasure. It made her a little nauseated that she wasn't a real enough treasure to him. "Some things can't be taught. Some people are blind to the obvious before them. Or they just don't really want what they think they do."

"What do you think I want, Ma Petite?"

She shrugged, looking down at her cup and seeing her shirt gaping. "No clue," she said sipping her coffee and discreetly shutting it a little. "Mmm. Good as usual."

"Let's pretend I'm looking for a woman. The first requirement I'd have is she *has to* love the swamp as much as I do. Enough to marry it till death parts them. I'd want her funny, kind, strong, independent. Beautiful. And with a body that haunts my dreams."

Dear God, felt like he was describing her. Did her body haunt his dreams? She was the one dreaming. "No possessive women?" She was damn possessive.

He thought a second then, said, "I definitely want her possessive of me and only me."

Felt like she was auditioning for a part. "And would you be possessive of her?"

He nodded with absolution. "Dangerously so."

She laughed at that while her insides jittered everywhere. "I think any woman would want nothing less."

"And you, Ma Petite?" He eyed her over his coffee cup again.

"Yes, I supposed I do since I think I belong in the woman category," she said, heat burning her cheeks.

"You think?"

"Well, I'm trying to think that."

He set his coffee down, clearly intrigued. "Is this hard for you to imagine?"

She sputtered a little. "Well, with people thinking of you like a child or..." She almost said little sister. "You haven't helped," she decided to come out and say.

"Me!" he said, hand on his gorgeous chest in amused shock.

"Yes, you." She wasn't letting him off the hook anymore. "I mean...you call me little all the time, I remind you of your little sister, you *see* me as your little sister, you *treat* me like your little sister so yes," she nodded setting her cup down before she spilled it everywhere. "It's hard identifying as a woman when around you." She crossed her arms over her chest then uncrossed them at encountering her second-degree burns, ready to vanish now.

"And you think there's something wrong with being a woman and little at the same time?"

As usual, he pinned her against the wall with his fail-proof logic. "No."

"Clearly you do, Ma Petite," he begged to differ oh so lightly.

"Maybe I just don't like being thought of as the little sister." There. She'd said it straight.

The heat in his eyes got three million degrees hotter. "Ma Petite," he said, a whole octave lower. "I did that to protect you."

****

Bishop had officially declared war against Saint Sahvrin. Ever since their little card game, he decided it was time to *burn* it all down. And now that it was burning, even Saint Sahvrin was ready to meet the needs of his starved angel. One by one, Bishop tossed little pieces of tinder into the flames and His Petite added her own with that angelic oblivion.

"Protect…from what?"

The whisper called Bishop right to her front door, eager to punish something.

"From me."

"You?" Her confusion mounted next to her excitement as he watched her try to think around it. "And…now you're…."

Years of pent-up hunger spilled out everywhere. "More dangerous, Angel."

She loved this, he saw. Craved it. And her fight to hide that brought fire to his blood like it did when he tracked and hunted the guilty.

"How…are you dangerous?"

Such a brave petite fleur. He remembered that her panties hung in his bathroom, and therefore were not on her. He imagined walking over and doing whatever he wanted because she would surely let him.

"It's okay if…you don't want to tell me."

"I want things, Ma Petite," he said, not caring about what would be incinerated by this fire, only interested in how hot he'd make it burn.

"W-what...kind of things?"

He let his gaze lower to what kind of things, staring at her breasts peeking at him from behind his shirt. Mon Dieu she was beautiful. The years of deprivation had him needing to stare at her tits for hours. If he had been under his celibacy contract, he'd surely forfeit his position if it meant having just a small taste of her. He raised his eyes to assess her condition and at finding her gaze boiling with need, he knew he'd get a lot more than a taste.

"Has Ma Petite... ever felt pleasure?"

The heat in her shocked stare reached him. "I...I'm...a virgin."

His cock throbbed at her answer, loving it very much. "You have *never*... felt sexual pleasure, Angel?" he asked, his pulse hammering now.

She licked her lips and looked down into her cup again. "Not...with a man, no."

Mon *fucking* Dieu. Images of her rubbing her sweet pussy with her legs wide open filled his head and cock. Seeing her in that kind of pleasure was suddenly air he'd die without. "You have touched yourself before? Ma Petite?"

She closed her eyes, and he knew without a doubt that it was arousal she now panted on.

He made his way slowly to her, ready to turn everything up. She remained with her eyes closed when he stood next to her. "Tell me," he urged in a whisper, wanting to tear into her. "Have you ever touched your pretty pussy?"

She gave a gasp, followed by another with her soft whispered, "Yes."

He leaned and put his mouth near her ear. "Do you want to feel good, Ma Petite che're?"

Her breaths shook out more, then she finally gave him what he craved to have. "Yes."

He realized that answer still wasn't enough. "Do you need *me* to make your pussy feel good?"

"Yes," she said weakly, still not looking at him.

His cock pounded as he reached up and stroked his finger along her face, getting a tiny whimper as she leaned into it, hungry. "Follow me."

He made his way to the couch and turned, finding her several feet behind. "Sit," he told her, his cock fighting to burst from his jeans.

She looked at the couch as if it were a most difficult decision. He waited for her to make up her mind. There could be no wrong decision with her.

"You do not have to, Ma Petite," he said softly. "You can say no. But once you say yes…know that I will make you helpless."

She finally gave her breathless yes with her eyes closed. That was enough for him.

He decided at the last burning second that she'd better not touch him while he pleasured her. He would already be burned alive but once His Petite was in the flames, she could easily rise up and render *him* helpless. She was still mending but not completely there yet. He'd give her any and every form of pleasure, but not sex. Not until she proved she wanted all that it came with.

He sat carefully next to her, placing one arm on the top of the couch. "Ma Petite… you must hold your hands behind you and tell me you will not touch me. Will you do this?"

Her decision came faster than before, but the slow way she did as asked said she still battled with herself.

That fight was all but over.

Once she sat, it was his turn to battle. Mostly what part of her did he want first and with what part of himself did he want it? He eyed her breasts barely visible between the gap in his shirt, his mind erupting in hotter flames. Mon Dieu, he'd start there. She needed his tongue and lips soothing that tender flesh.

He moved her hair gently aside and her frantic breaths burned him alive. "Do you trust me, Ma Petite?" He leaned in close to her face and paused at her mouth, feeling her breath. He glided his thumb on her lower lip, drawing her sharp gasp then moan. So new to pleasure, Mon Dieu. He stroked her face like he had so many times, kissing her temple while trailing his fingers along her jaw, making his way to her neck.

"Lay back, angel. Relax for me."

She did as he said, keeping her eyes closed. The reclined position made her like an offering he couldn't resist.

"I'm going to kiss you," he warned before brushing his lips along her parted mouth, moaning in her hot whimpers. Pulling back a little, he stared at her while carefully opening one side of the shirt, then the other, exposing her completely. Angling his head, he took in the red, delicate mounds. "Ma Belle Angel," he whispered, marking his brain with the painful vision before moving back to her mouth. "I need to lick your beautiful nipples."

He didn't wait for her permission, lowering and carefully circling the burning, hard tip with his tongue.

"Oh my God," she gasped when he suckled it between his lips. Mon Dieu, the thick flesh in his mouth made him insane.

"Please, oh please," she begged, driving him.

He licked all along her hot, small mounds, placing tender, open mouthed kisses on them. He pulled up, watching the rapture in her face, psychotically fixated by it. He'd have to have this again. And again. And fucking again.

He looked down at her squirming hips, ready to drive the fire higher. She wore a thin skirt, the short length making it easy to slide up. His cock hammered cruelly as he uncovered his treasure.

"Mon *Dieu*, Angel," he breathed when the perfect dark triangle appeared. He tucked the material down at her waist, not wanting any interference. Her legs were now closed almost as tight as her eyes. That would change very soon. He glided his fingers along the seam of her closed legs, brushing the soft pussy hair then moving back to her knees again. When he moved along the same path, she gave scared, hungry moans, opening a little. "Yes, Ma Petite. Open for me."

By the time he was at her pussy, she was open enough for him to slide his fingers softly over her mound, feeling her shape. He added a little pressure as he moved along her lips, till her hips pushed back. He watched her pussy reach for his hand, his breaths thick at the sight. He turned leaned for her breast, kissing the nipple closest to him as he dipped a finger between her folds.

"Sahvrin!"

He couldn't speak. He groaned while exploring her nipple with his lips and tongue. Up and down her slick heat he glided the pad of his finger till he was quietly swearing in French. He wouldn't enter her, not yet. He moved to her mouth, wide with the shocking pleasure, recalling her pelvic exam confession. He would soon kiss her there and remove all the painful memories.

"Please, yes," she gasped between sharp breaths as he barely pushed his finger in her. "I need it."

He pulled up to see her face as he pressed his palm into her clit and pushed his middle finger carefully in her. Her mouth opened more, and she looked down, watching. He watched with her, groaning hungrily. "Your sweet fucking pussy," he said when she twirled her hips and flicked for more. He sank deeper inside, exploring her wet heat while moving his palm in circles on her clit.

"Sahvrin, oh," she cried, her hot walls spasming.

He pushed in deeper until his hand pressed into her body. The fucking clamp of her pussy, Mon Dieu. "Open *wider*, Ma Petite," he said at her mouth. "Give me more of your pretty pussy, so much *fucking* more." He looked down at her creamy legs doing exactly as he said while he pressed harder until he seethed with lust.

"I'm coming, I'm coming," she cried.

He gripped her jaw and forced her to take his kiss, forgetting to be gentle. He filled her mouth with harsh groans, licking at her tongue while grinding his palm against her clit. The way she bucked and cried in his mouth nearly caused him to erupt in his pants.

Sahvrin finally broke the kiss, wanting to see her as he slowed his pace. She remained with mouth open, repeating "Oh my God," between many breaths. The sound of her shock said she had never experienced such a thing and the idea had a million unhealthy things racing through him. He was the creator of this first pleasure, and nobody else could give it now. He'd just signed an unwritten contract between them. Only *he* was allowed to give her that.

"Ma Petite," he whispered at her mouth. "Tell me how much you loved it." It wasn't the intended thing he meant to say but realized he needed to be sure. "Have you ever felt this pleasure before?"

He watched her eyes open barely, staring at him as she confessed the breathless whisper. "Never in my life."

So much hunger she stirred in him. He gripped her lower jaw, again too hard, making her to take his kiss. The sounds of her arousal mixed with surprise told him she liked this hunger in him. Merci Dieu. But he had too much of it. And he couldn't be hard with his delicate, sucre fleur, not yet.

She suddenly wrapped her arms around his neck. He should stop her but her fingers exploring his back felt too fucking amazing and sacred to disturb. Her breaths picked up again with light moans of need followed by scraping nails along his back. "Ma Petite," he croaked with need.

"Make love to me," she sighed in his mouth. "I want you to be my first."

CHAPTER 11

Mon *fucking Dieu*. He grabbed her face and held it tight, ready to bow before her, codes and rules be damned.

He hurried to stand, and she eyed him with a look that said she might be devastated if he didn't accept the beautiful gift she'd just offered him. *Fuck.* He raked both hands through his hair remembering all the things that should give him the strength to stop. She was too injured… and she needed time to know how she really felt. Without being influenced by codes and rules. He needed to see it too.

"Oh my God," she said, misreading his hesitancy. "You… you don't want to. Oh my God."

"No, no, no, Ma Petite, I very much *do* want to."

Confusion gradually replaced the shock and devastation as she stared at him. "What's wrong?"

"You are not entirely healed, Ma Petite. I can't risk hurting you." He could stick with that for now.

She stared at his mouth then raised her offended gaze to his eyes. "You wouldn't hurt me."

Her bold faith in him did things he never imagined. "This is true, Ma Petite, never intentionally."

She seemed to consider what he meant.

"You drive me out of my mind," he explained, shaking his head. "I'm very sure I would accidentally hurt you." That was pure fact.

Her brows tugged together. "You can…be gentle."

He shook his head, especially sure he couldn't be that. "I won't risk it."

Her sweet gaze softened, as she stared at him. "Well...when?"

The eagerness in her tone made his cock ache. As if she felt it, she lowered her gaze. "I can at least..." she raised her eyes back to his. "Make you feel good?" Her tongue swept innocently over her lips and the erotic gesture convinced Bishop it was the perfect solution. "I...I can't say I'm skilled at anything, but...I did have certain classes, and...you can help me. Tell me what to do, what you like."

Sahvrin closed his eyes, needing more air. He'd been planning all this on a one-way street. Her pleasure, not his. Her sweet offer was suddenly debilitating.

"Please?"

"Mon Dieu, you're killing me," he said, back to staring at her. "I can wait."

She didn't like that answer. "Wait for what? I just want to make you feel good. I can't get hurt doing that."

He let out a single laugh around his insane arousal.

"You need it," she said gently. "And I want to. A lot."

"Ma Petite," was all he could say, his mind lending logic to her sweet argument. He sought for an anchor and sat in the single chair behind him, holding the arm rests.

"I can't believe you're making me beg to give you pleasure," she said with a mix of mild offense, surprise, and maybe amusement. "Are you scared *I'll* hurt *you*?"

He let out a laugh at that, needing the comic relief in that second. "I'm scared you'll drive me crazy and make me do something I'll regret."

A look of eager curiosity filled her hot gaze. "What would you do?" she asked, like it was a pleasure option on the menu. And it was, God, it *was*, but she wasn't ready for that kind of fucking even if she was the right one. But his arousal was like a demon-bull he'd locked away for years that had grown during captivity.

"When you're ready, I'll show you," he promised, winded at the idea.

Now she was winded too and very curious. "What if...I make *you*?"

"Ma Petite, stop," he gushed, shaking his head, not even smiling at that boiling idea.

She suddenly rolled her eyes and dropped her head back with a cute growl. She had no idea how close she'd just come to getting anything she wanted. He realized a sudden problem. He already wanted to pleasure her again, but now she'd find that unfair. "But *you,* Ma Petite, need pleasure," he said, ready to plead his case.

"I'm not arguing *that* one," she said, waiting for him to elaborate.

"*I* can wait. *You* don't need to wait."

She stared for a few seconds, confused. "What are you saying? I feel like you're telling me a riddle."

He smiled, lowering his head. "I want to pleasure you again."

Her jaw dropped after a second and remained that way while she sputtered attempted words. "That's not fair."

"To me?" he said in a chuckle.

"And to me! I want to just like you want to."

Her selflessness was turning out to be the most unanticipated weapon. "Tomorrow night."

She eyed him, surprised and looking suspicious. "What about it?"

"You can pleasure me."

She melted right before him, lowering her gaze to his chest in open lust. "And... me?"

"You let me pleasure you twice more."

Her eyes nearly glowed with her arousal and his cock ached, waiting. "What...will you do this time?"

She asked in curiosity, but her tone said she was bargaining. Wanting to know if the deal was worth taking. "I will do many things to you Ma Petite, but this time I want to lick your pussy until you're pulling my hair in orgasm.

"Oh my God," she gasped, her eyelids going heavy, cheeks pink with maybe shame and arousal at the idea. "You said you will show me when I'm healed…what you'll do." She licked her lips, drawing her knees up. "Tell me."

Mon Dieu, she was full of provoking surprises. He would expect her to be too embarrassed to ask such a thing. "The first time, I would make love to you." He was now praying there would be a first time.

Her lips parted immediately as she crucified him with her hot stare. "And the second?" she asked on a light gasp.

His own lips parted from the heat consuming him. "The second time, and probably every time after, Ma Petite… I will *fuck* you."

She let out a moaned gasp that jerked his cock. "And what's…"

"The difference is…" he began, closing his eyes from the potency of his desire. "One is soft, slow and sweet." He opened them, staring at her. "The other is not."

Judging by the lust in her gaze, he was thinking he could possibly make her orgasm just with conversation. "What…will you do?"

Fuck, she wanted to hear him say it. "Are you sure you want to know that, Ma Petite?"

She nodded barely with a positive, "Yes."

His pulse rammed his cock as he stared into her innocent gaze. "I will fuck you too hard, too fast and too long. And yet it will never be enough of any of those, this I am sure, Ma Belle Petite Fleur."

The delicate sounds this produced from her had him at reckless again. "I will let you fuck me right now, Ma Petite. In my bed. You will sit your beautiful pussy on my mouth and fuck my lips and tongue until you orgasm."

He was so desperate, he couldn't even laugh at her unexpected wide eyes and quick headshake. "She finally gasped, "I can't…I can't do that!"

He wasn't sure if she meant can't or wouldn't. "I will help you, Ma Petite," he promised, winded still, assuming the best. "You don't even have to work, I can take care of *everything* once you climb on."

Her mouth fell open wider, and he wondered if it was the climbing on part she had problems with.

She was beyond fun to be with. "You don't want this?" he asked, ready to laugh now.

She began to sputter again. "I…I *do,* I just…that's…so…"

He waited for her description, kind of needing it. "So what, Ma Petite," he pressed when she took too long.

"So…"

"Unimaginable?" he tried to help, wanting an inkling of where her mind was.

She shook her head at that. "Nooo, it's plenty imaginable. That's the problem."

He gave in to his laugh finally, surprised that he could still be surprised by her. "Is it the climbing part, Ma Petite? Or the sitting? Or the fucking my mouth? You haven't thought of doing this before?"

"Oh, I've thought of it plenty," she corrected, suddenly serious as can be. "I was required to *see* all the positions, and there are many I told you."

"Mon *Dieu,* I cannot believe there is a book like this."

She nodded with slow severity before assuring, "Trust me… you wouldn't want to try *half* of what's in it. I thought some of it was a joke, the positions were so *insane.*"

For nearly a full minute he laughed before she demanded what was so funny.

"You laugh, but this stuff was not for normal people, maybe if you were in a *circus* and could bend the laws of physics."

"Where can I find this book?"

She regarded him sharply like he'd asked for the plague. "God, I'm not *telling* you."

"How many positions did they *have* Ma Petite?" he wondered, hungry for all of them with her.

Her mouth dropped open even more with wide eyes. "A *ridiculous* amount!"

"Ma Petite," he laughed, shaking his head. "Will you describe *one* at least, please."

She appeared to mentally sift through her useless sex databank for the best of the worst. He didn't know what he enjoyed more, that there was so much sexual ground to explore with her or how stupid she thought it was. He was ready to seduce her into trying all of them before ever learning if she was the right one.

"Oh!" she remembered, glancing around. "I'll need something to draw it."

Sahvrin hurried to his desk and brought her a pen and notebook, flipping it to a clean sheet.

She took it and shooed him with little flicks of her fingers. "I can't draw this while you're looking," she said, making him laugh as he sat several feet away from her on the couch.

He studied her profile as she drew, her brows raising while her head barely shook. "I can't even…hardly draw this."

She finally presented it to him, and he took it. He angled his head several different ways at her stick figure diagram, unable to hold his laughter in.

"I told you it's crazy!"

"Ma Petite, I haven't even figured out what I'm looking at."

"Right? That's how crazy it is!"

"I mean…show me what part is the woman and which is the man."

She scooted closer with the pen and began circling things. "Her head. His head. This is her…you know what and this is *his* you know *what*."

God she was fucking adorable, and he couldn't stop from laughing at the derisive tone she had. But even with her circling things, her drawing skills prevented him from fully grasping what was being done. "Where are her legs, Ma Petite?"

"Here!" she cried, tracing the lines. "One going north and one going south."

He finally saw it and hissed in pain.

"Right?"

"Maybe this is special sex for Olympic gymnasts?"

She threw her head back and laughed and the sight of it had him instantly hungry. Mon Dieu she was beautiful. She caught him staring and paused, eyeing him with a curious heat. "What?"

The soft word made him realize how close they were and what led to their discussion. He could do it here.

She seemed to read his mind and a look of arousal and worry slowly filled her. "What?" she demanded lightly, her voice a whisper.

"Did they have positions for oral sex?" he asked, moving to that topic, sure they did and sure he'd get that book too.

She gave a nod after a few seconds, confirming as much.

"Any that made you think... that looks amazing, I can't wait for Bishop to do this to me?"

The sudden way she went serious made him realize what he'd called himself. Before he could worry, she bit her lip in pure lust. "The position's not... just for her," she said, breathless. "It's for him and her."

He immediately knew what she meant and somehow managed to say, "Tomorrow night" while wanting to think about the Bishop dynamic unfolding in his head.

Before her disappointment could go too far, he moved off the couch and knelt next to her. He gently pushed her hair over her shoulder on the left, then the right. Avoiding her burnt chest, he gently held her jaw and neck and eased her back.

She responded with those delicate whimpered gasps when he slid the shirt aside, exposing her beautiful breasts. Her soft full nipples made him forget his plan other than to make those tips tall and erect. He started with the left one, circling the plump softness with his tongue, her hot breaths on his face as she watched him make it hard. He moved his hungry gaze to hers, leaning to kiss her lips before going for the nippe on the right, groaning as he circled his tongue around it. "Does it make you hot, Ma Petite?"

"Yes," she gasped, holding her hands in fists at her sides.

He continued the torment, pushing his cock into the couch as her desire grew hotter, bolder. "Where is it hot, my Angel?"

Her mouth flew open when he barely touched both tips with his fingers. "In my…" She gave several gasps. "Where you're going to lick me."

He slid the small skirt up, exposing the smooth triangle again. The years he went without suddenly crashed down on him in hungry revenge. He raised his eyes to hers. "Open your legs wide for me, Ma Petite."

She struggled briefly then slowly opened them.

"More," he said, his gaze moving between her tormented face, and her gorgeous pussy. He suddenly wanted to see her touch herself more than anything else. "Show me," he said when she pulled her knees up a little. "Show me how you make it feel good." He dipped the tip of his finger in her entrance, ready to build her courage. "My Angel is so wet," he said around a shudder. "So tight on my finger."

She finally made her move, sliding her hand between her legs. The sight of her stroking her clit was an instant addiction. He'd finger her while she masturbated until she came undone. Then he'd eat her pussy after she showered in the morning.

Her knees went back more with her growing moans and he pushed all the way in, learning her with careful touches. He watched his finger slide slowly out, groaning at the shine on it. "Ma Petite," he said on a harsh breath as she moved her fingers in slow circles while he fucked her with deep, in and out strokes.

Her moans soon turned into cries that had him pumping his cock against the couch with thick breaths. "So tight on my finger," he said harshly, picking up speed.

She arched her back, gripping his shoulder with her other hand. Gasps came with every moan now as she rubbed her clit faster. Fuck. "Come for me Angel," he ordered harshly.

Her legs widened more, and she gave a strangled cry as the pleasure seized her so hard, only the sound of his finger ramming in her wet heat could be heard. Finally, her voice broke through, with gasp after gasp, like somebody fighting for their life.

Fucking Dieu, he'd never seen anything like it. Another instant addiction, watching her orgasm.

When everything slowed, he leaned and kissed her open mouth to taste the aftermath. "Ma Petite," he breathed, winded from the rush of it while pumping his raging hard on against the couch.

"Oh *God,* that was…" She swallowed between breaths. "…amazing."

Sahvrin groaned as he slid his arms under her body and lifted her off the couch. "Time for your beauty rest, Ma Petite. I'll wake in the morning for your next orgasm."

A slow sweet smile filled her face as he carried her around the couch and lay her in his bed.

"Sleep with me," she begged, latching on to his arm.

"Tomorrow night, Ma Petite. Or I may sleep fuck you."

She gave a gaspy hot look and licked her lips. "Okay," she said, turning on her side and staring at him.

He needed to jack off before he exploded.

"Aren't you going to kiss me goodnight?" she asked when he'd turned to go.

He returned and leaned down, placing a soft, lingering kiss on her forehead. "Goodnight Ma Petite, Ange."

He half expected her to try to get more but instead she looked at him with a dreamy smile. "Goodnight Sahvrin Bishop."

He stared at her a moment then went lay on the couch. Sahvrin Bishop. Hearing her say those names together in that order started a fight in him. Bishop wasn't into sharing or being second to anybody, not even Saint Sahvrin. He'd fight till he had it all, every bit of that heaven he wasn't supposed to touch.

But only if she wanted all of him. He'd never give himself to a woman again unless she proved she wanted his family, his swamp, and all the Horde that came with it.

CHAPTER 12

"Ma Petite, wake up."

Beth bolted up too fast, gasping in pain from unhealed injuries.

Sahvrin's lips pressed hard against hers with a groan before he turned. "My brothers are here. Get dressed. And not in anything that show your belle tetons."

"Show my *what?*"

"Your tits, Ma Petite, your beautiful tits. I don't want to kill a brother for looking," he said, pulling a black t-shirt out of his drawer and glancing out one of the windows. The look he snapped her way made her try to hurry faster while a long string of French flew from his sexy mouth.

Oh, he was so mad. In the bathroom she pulled the yellow dress off the peg on the back door, hoping it was the right one in his eyes. God, it would hurt her breasts to wear. There was only one other choice, the red and she was thinking the color might be too related to la-passion.

She smiled to herself as her heart hammered wildly with Sahvrin memories. Sahvrin *Bishop* memories. Her heart fluttered that he'd referred to himself as that. She was glad because she really did miss the man she'd first met. He was different but not in a bad way now that she knew why he'd been a prick.

Oh God, she still couldn't believe he'd done all that to her. She fought for air when the memories got too real. She snatched the brush up and pulled it through her long hair. A quick knock on the door made her jump then she opened it.

"I cannot tell my brothers about you and me, Ma Petite. I will explain later. Trust me?" he asked, leaning in to press his lips on hers again.

"Yes. I do," she said, grabbing his face and kissing him back.

He glared at her, then whispered, "I should fucking gut them for wrecking my morning plans with you."

She bit her lip as though considering. "We still have tonight."

His gaze lowered to her mouth, and he leaned with a groan, kissing her again. "Come." He grabbed her hand.

"But…I need the bathroom."

He gently pushed her back in. "Hurry."

"I was going to do something with my hair."

He paused abruptly, snapping his eyes to her. "I'll get rid of them."

She shut the door, smiling as she did her morning bathroom business. While sitting on the toilet, she pulled all her hair to one said and began braiding it just in case he couldn't get rid of them. Her braiding slowed a little. Why didn't he want to tell them about them?

Before a yucky feeling could sicken her stomach, she remembered he'd said to trust him. She definitely did. With her life, obviously.

He met her on her way out of the bathroom, appearing distraught. "I have to go and meet with the men, Ma Petite. I'm sorry."

"Oh, don't be sorry. What men?"

"My father and brothers and a couple friends. I don't want to leave you here alone so I'm bringing you to my Mah-Mah."

His tone said he wasn't negotiating, and she was surprised at the amount of joy that gave her. "Whatever you think," she said, wanting him to know she trusted his judgment while her stomach went to jittering at the idea of meeting his mother while coherent.

"They are expecting you." He looked her over and she held her breath at his fierce expression. "They are ready to meet la femme pour qui je suis follement tombée amoureuse."

Wow. "That's going to need a translation," she said, burning with curiosity while still wondering what he thought of the dress.

He eyed her. "I cannot give that to you now, Ma Petite."

Her mouth dropped. "That's *rude.* Should I ask your brothers?"

He leaned and gave her a kiss, his lips soft as silk on hers, contradicting his pushy mood. He suddenly gave a frustrated growl and pushed her into the bathroom, his kiss turning passionate as he shut the door. "Ma Petite, you make me crazy."

He yanked her dress up while she held on to his neck. The hungry stroke of his fingers on her pussy made her gasp.

"Ma Petite, you are so fucking wet."

"Yes," she said in his mouth.

"Who are you wet for?" he demanded, his tongue stroking hers.

"You, I'm so wet for you."

"*Who*, are you *wet* for?" he demanded again, plunging his finger inside her.

"Oh God," she shot out, wondering what he wanted to hear. "Sahvrin," she confessed, breathless.

His fingers bit at the back of her neck as he palmed her clit and wiggled his finger so deep. "Try again, Agnel."

She lifted her leg and opened herself, her moans building. "Bishop," she gasped, her orgasm there.

"Fuck yes," he groaned, hot and greedy in her mouth then hammered his palm against her. "I can't wait to *fuck* this soft pussy."

She came instantly, fighting to be quiet.

"You fucking want that," he said with a note-taking lust, as she shuddered and trembled into pleasure delirium.

He continued feasting with low, hungry sounds at her astonished mouth and she watched him from a slitted gaze, the most sexy, handsome man she'd ever seen. And he liked her. No, *Bishop* liked her. He'd just made that crystal clear and dear God she could never be more thrilled about anything.

He gently pulled his finger out and sucked her juices off, making her gasp at the nasty act. He made her weak kneed and giddy with emotions she couldn't begin to name.

A terrifying notion almost made her sick. What if he didn't want her for more than this? She remembered he'd also thought sex was more than screwing. Had that been Sahvrin or Bishop who thought that?

His kiss turned tender, making her forget silly doubts and fears of doing everything backwards with him. When his hands and lips and eyes were on her, what else mattered?

****

The first big worry was how to hide her feelings for Sahvrin. Or Bishop. Lord, she hoped this didn't get confusing or challenging. Bishop almost sounded jealous of her affections for Sahvrin, which was kind of funny and sweet. And yet the jealousy felt entirely serious.

She wasn't sure how it would feel to have him not show his feelings for her. She'd be mature about it. He'd tell her later why he had to. Wasn't a big deal. There were plenty of reasons he might want that. Like…wanting it to be a surprise, or wanting to see their reaction when she wasn't around in case they hated the idea which they likely could. Getting hooked up with the rescued, maimed girl from up north might be a tradition breaker. Oh God, some peoples did have traditions like that.

Looking toward the boat, her stomach turned over at seeing they all watched her. It was only her guess what they saw, what sort of impression she was making. She let herself look at Sahvrin, not wanting to see judgment in their eyes as she held on to her thick braid with both hands. Then she remembered she wasn't supposed to say anything about them being…intimate and she was sure her ogling Sahvrin would give it away. Was she messing up? Sahvrin's face was unreadable, so it was hard to tell.

She focused her eyes on the boat and how she was supposed to get in it. It wasn't small like the one Sahvrin had but it wasn't huge either. Sahvrin's hand suddenly extended out to her, and she eyed the boat and it, wondering if she was supposed to put her foot *in* the boat or on the ledge.

"I'm…I'm not used to boats," she said, not sure how to express the problem.

"Put your foot here," Sahvrin directed, tapping the edge of the boat.

"Okay," she said, carefully stepping. The boat dipped with her weight when she pushed off the pier and she gasped, latching both hands to his arm as he helped her the rest of the way.

They all cheered like she'd crossed the Grand Canyon and despite her shame, a smile flew across her lips. Sahvrin directed her to the front of the boat. She spotted three seats between the front and back, the middle ones big enough for two. Sahvrin sat in the seat directly in front of her and the other brothers were in the two seats behind him.

Laughter erupted amidst the French conversation, and the sudden eyes on her made her cheeks heat up with worry.

"Hi Miss Beth." The brother sitting just behind Sahvrin greeted her with a swampy flair. It was true up close; all of them were handsome and she was pretty picky on those standards.

"I'm sorry," she said to the brother who'd greeted her while Sahvrin used an oar to push the boat away from the dock. "Which brother are you again?"

"Bart. The black sheep of the family. Nice to see you again."

She leaned and shook his extended hand with a smile while much French and laughter erupted.

"I'm Zep. Pleased to meet you," he waved from the seat behind Bart.

"You too," she said with a wave back before standing and leaning to shake the third brother's extended hand over Bart's shoulder.

"August. Swamp life sure does agree with you."

She nodded politely, wondering if he was mocking her sunburn. "Nice to meet you August."

"And I'm Jek," the one driving called from the back as he maneuvered the boat without giving her a glance.

"Nice to meet you again," she called, glancing at Sahvrin who talked over his shoulder to one of his brothers. She wished they'd speak English. She'd love to hear their banter. She caught Zep watching her with a grin and he gave her a wink, like he knew something she didn't. If she was judging between the brother's—and she obviously was—he was second in line to looks next to her glorious Sahvrin. Sahvrin with the beautiful smile and heart, and mocha eyes that could melt panties.

She stole a glance at him, still busy with his brothers. They talked and laughed like best friends, and she soon found herself smiling even though she didn't understand a word they said. French might be their first language judging how freely and quickly they spoke it. She wished she knew a little of it.

The boat moved out of the cove and scene stole the show, its beauty drowning out the brothers. She craned her neck to see as much of her surrounding as she could, thrilled to pieces at the beauty. Leaning left, she glanced behind Jek with the feeling of being in a parade on a float. She just wanted to wave at everything. They'd pulled out of Sahvrin's hidden yard and onto his water driveway, and now they were moseying down the tiny lane. To where, she wondered, turning forward to see.

Something moved in the water, and she gasped at a pair of otters. "Look!" she cried, wishing she had a camera. "It's like we're driving down a winding water road," she said, watching the swamp go by next to the boat.

"You like it?"

She didn't even turn to see who asked, only nodded as she sucked in the warm fresh air. "I love it! So different than back home."

"You don't have bayous?"

She turned to see who asked and guessed it was Zep. "No, and if we did, it'd likely be frozen most of the time."

"Sahvrin tells us you live at the North Pole." He gave a shiver and shook his head. "We would not survive that, sha."

Sha. She smiled a little at the expression. Did they all have these kinds of terms?

"It's always oooohh and ahhhhh at first," Bart said, leaning toward her from his seat. "Then they leave. Like my Pah-Pah says, the swamp life is either for the retired or the retarded."

They all laughed, and she did too, catching Sahvrin staring, sending her pulse racing. She curbed her giddy joy, not wanting to come off as immature. She still felt like she was proving her womanhood to him. And that she actually *did* love the swamp.

"Mah-Mah wants us all to marry," August said, grinning. "Meh, I don't really wanna marry a retired or a retarded woman, thank you."

This brought raucous laughter that had her giggling.

"I'm sure there's women out there who would die to live out here with you all," she said over the boat motor."

Apparently, that was funny as hell. She eyed Sahvrin, hoping to learn what on earth she was saying wrong to be laughed at. He seemed to be holding back a smile. "I don't get what's so funny," she finally said to him, not as loud. "I feel like I'm missing a joke."

"Don't worry," he said to her. "It's not really that funny. Cajuns just know how to make the best out of hard things."

Hard things? Was he suggesting that these handsome men couldn't find a woman to be with them out there? Might have something to do with their fornicating ways. Maybe if they were more like Sahvrin, they'd have a better chance. You can't expect to find anybody serious by looking in social dumpsters. "You guys can get a mail-order bride," she said, smiling.

They all looked at her, curious.

"It was a joke," she said. "I mean maybe there's such a thing, there used to be, I don't know."

This got them all talking in French again which pushed her out of the conversation. She glanced at Sahvrin, finding him looking pensive. She suddenly missed being alone with him. He was so much more…attentive. She couldn't seem to get enough of that with him.

She gave her attention to the scenery, again getting swept off her feet by the view. Didn't take long for her smile to return. She closed her eyes and took in a deep breath of the air again, holding her hand out to feel the warm breeze as the boat sped along the winding waterways a little faster now.

She turned to find Sahvrin staring at her again and her pulse raced at the hungry look in his eyes. "How far is it?" she asked.

He leaned forward and she did too. "Vous êtes belle like the swamp, Ma Petite."

She looked at him, gaze narrowed with a small smile, mouthing "What?"

He didn't tell her with words, but he did with his eyes and whatever it was, she really liked it. She fought to hide what his mysterious words did to her, remembering their secret.

"Thirty minutes," he finally said, grinning at the trees.

She regarded him, confused. "What's thirty minutes?"

He turned his smile at her. "How long it will take to get there."

Wow, thirty minutes. "How do you even find your way?" she wondered, realizing how impossible it seemed to keep track.

"Sahvrin has a gift," Bart said, smiling at her.

She looked at Sahvrin who dismissed the claim with a headshake.

"No?" she wondered, looking back at Bart for more details.

"I just don't drown my brain cells in booze," Sahvrin explained.

Beth tucked runaway strands of hair behind her ear.

"Sahvrin's our Swamp saint," Zep said with a beaming grin and bounce of his brows.

Again, she regarded Sahvrin, finding him absorbed in the scenery passing by. Either he was ignoring him or bored.

"Hey, Sahvrin," Jek called. "Your lil girlfriend is waiting for you. Look alive."

Girlfriend? They turned a corner in the bayou and Beth spied a dock on the right with people on it. Girls, she realized. In bikinis. Great.

Sahvrin held his hand out to her, and she took it, sitting next to him where he directed. As they passed the girls, the brothers whistled and hollered French, and Beth watched all four of them stand and holler back. She gasped and turned away when one lifted her bikini top and yelled Sahvrin's name.

"The view is much better to the left, Ma Petite," he said, looking in the opposite direction. She realized what he'd just done, and relief flooded her.

"Wow," she awed, staring at the tree line. "Very friendly neighbors."

"Qui," he said, dryly.

She regarded him out the corner of her eye. "You have not so secret admirers. I'm not surprised." She gave him a smile to show she wasn't the jealous type. Wasn't true but she could control herself about it. Plus, he hadn't done anything to provoke her jealousy, he can't really control what women do.

They finally turned off the main waterway, or what seemed like a main waterway and drove through a series of small water roads. Much like Sahvrin's house, theirs also had a winding driveway. She was eager to see what was around the next bend.

"Oh, look, turtles!" she cried, pointing them out to Sahvrin. "Sunbathing."

"You like to sunbathe, Miss Beth?"

She glanced over her shoulder at Zep's smiling face. "I like the sun," was all she cared to say. He added something in French, irking her, especially that he laughed after whatever it was. She remembered she was nearly fluent in Italian and turned with a pleasant smile. "Non lo sai che è scortese parlare degli altri in una lingua stranierato?"

She turned back around with a light smirk in the sudden silence.

"What language is this?" Sahvrin asked, smiling like she'd surprised him yet again.

"Italian."

He spoke French over his shoulder with a laugh then looked at her. "I told him you are nothing like the simpleton women he's accustomed to and should be careful."

She gave him a full-on smile. "Well thank you for that interpretation." She faced forward again. "Maybe it's a northern thing," she said. "But when we want to say things about people that we don't want them to hear, we do this neat thing and say it *behind* their back, not right in their face in another language."

Sahvrin laughed loudly at that and turned a little to his brothers. "Ma Petite says she would like to learn French so she can understand everything we're saying." She turned to him with raised brows, making him laugh more. "Don't you?"

"I do, yes, but obviously I won't learn it as fast as you all speak it."

"How about I translate when it's something I feel you would want to know?"

She considered while feeling it was a half-ass deal but agreed.

"So do I get to know what you said to him, Ma Petite?"

"I asked him if he didn't know it was rude to speak about people in a foreign tongue."

He gave her a look of pure delight. "Allow me to translate in French, Ma Petite." He proceeded to, and they all hissed with painful noises around their laughs.

"We stand corrected," Bart said. "No more being rude with our native tongue."

Crap so French *was* their native tongue? "English isn't your first language?" she asked Sahvrin.

"Ah, no, Ma Petite," he said easily. "We are strong believers in preserving our culture and only speak the Cajun French unless we don't need to."

Dammit. "I should've learned French," she said, a little sad.

"It's not quite the same, but if you knew it, you would better understand us."

"Oh, so it's a different dialect?"

"More like a language created out of necessity from when our people moved here from Acadia. We created new words in a new place to describe all the new things. It is a mix of our fancy French and the mother language of this land, English? Yes?"

She remembered some of the terms. "Is that the same as Creole?"

He gave an indifferent shrug. "People like to fight over identity, Ma Petite. Who is called this and who is called that, who came first and who came second. But I call it a dish we love to eat here-- jambalaya? We put all sorts of amazing ingredients into a dish, and we mix it up into one thing. That's what this country is. A big pot of jambalaya. Full of the best tastes from every culture."

"You done woke the professor," Jek said from the back of the boat. "Goes to college and comes back too smart for his own britches."

She snapped her gaze to him. "You went to college?"

"Hell, he left too smart for his britches," August said. "Went to college at *seventeen*."

They all laughed while she stared at him for an answer.

"Guilty," he said, like he wasn't proud of it.

"Why didn't you tell me? Where? What did you go for?"

"I told you our brother was gifted," Bart bragged.

"It's not a gift it's hard work. You would have managed the same if you had listened to Mah-Mah and Pah-Pah."

"Sorry, bro-dearest, my job as the middle child was to cut up, and I did."

"He's a grand master of it," Sahvrin agreed.

"So where did you go?"

"I went to the University of Louisiana, Ma Petite."

"He's an *artist*," Bart said, or accused.

"An *artist*," she gasped, jaw dropped. "How amazing! What kind?"

"Every kind," Bart went on. "There ain't nothin he touches that don't come away with the Sahvrin smack."

"Well, my favorite talent of his happens to be the one that is making me rich, "Jek said.

"Which one is that?" she wondered over her shoulder when Sahvrin seemed happy to sit on all the details.

"Mechanical Engineer. That boy can modify anything—and he does."

She shoved him with a gasp. "Holding back on me, I see. Maybe I want to renegotiate what you teach me now."

"That ain't all he can do," Zep said. "The man is a genius with paint brushes."

"Dude, really?" Jek said, sounding angry.

Beth eyed Sahvrin, finding his face dark. Were they giving him grief because he didn't pursue every talent he possessed? "I think a mechanical engineer is an amazing art," she said, truthfully. "I would love to see some of your work."

"You'd love to see some of his paintings," Zep went on, clearly pushing buttons.

Beth realized there was more to it than they were saying, and she burned with curiosity now. But the mood it put Sahvrin in was really pissing her off.

"Sometimes we switch passions when we realize which are more important," Beth said.

"We're under strict orders to not talk about it, Miss Beth," August informed, buried hostility and all." This prompted French from Sahvrin which remained untranslated. It also ushered in a silence that lasted till they pulled up at another pier.

The sight that came with it changed the subject and the depressing mood.

"Oh my God," she said, gawking at the mini mansion of yellow and white painted wood set back on a huge piece of land enshrouded in Cypress trees. "This is just…*beautiful.*"

Sahvrin got out the boat and turned to help her. "I will introduce you to my family and then we have to go," he said, not quite making eye contact with her. "You will be okay?"

She nodded, holding his sudden stare while worry knotted her stomach. Was he upset with her? The idea made her sick since he was leaving, and she'd maybe never find out. She glanced up to see a group of women headed toward them, waving and smiling. Dear God. "Sahvrin, they dressed up? Oh my God, how do I look?" she hissed in distress.

Why he found humor in that, she had no idea but any smile on his face after the college thing was worth seeing, even at her expense. He leaned in and whispered in her ear, "This is how they always dress, Ma Petite. And you are the most beautiful thing I have ever seen in my life. *Never* forget that." His lips brushed her cheek as he pulled away, heading down the pier while she stood there breathless, her heart dancing in her chest.

"I think he likes you," Bart muttered as he passed her. "And that's a good thing," he added, over his shoulder with a wink.

"Yeah, keep chipping away at that square mile block," Jek mumbled as he passed her next.

What? What block? And why was it a good thing that he liked her? So many clues creating so many questions and no time to ponder with the royalty parade approaching. She never would've dreamed people like this existed, not in this remote location. The house and massive yard was like a hidden paradise, another world, just from the little she could see. They reminded her of Victorian royalty only the Swamp edition. Dresses that were fitted and flowing. Nothing flashy, just natural colors and beauty.

A beautiful woman came toward her, long silver hair flowing, huge smile on her face. She looked familiar and could hardly believe that might be his mother. "Beth," she called, arms stretched out as she came, wrapping her in a tight embrace for nearly a whole minute, hand stroking her head. "Oh *honey*," she soothed, finally pulling back while the shock of such an affectionate welcome threw her right off her composure horse. "It's so nice to see you again! I'm Claudette, Sahvrin's Mah-Mah? And now I'm *your* Mah-Mah, yes?"

Wow, she was so young looking. The kind woman didn't wait for an answer as she turned and introduced her to about half a dozen more ladies, all beautiful and giving her the same welcome.

Before it was over, Beth wept as she finished out the heartfelt hugs with '*thank you*'s, feeling like Dorothy leaving OZ, only she was just getting there and wondered where these people had been all her life?

Then just like that, the atmosphere changed to excitement as his Mah-Mah held her hand and tugged her to the great huge house. They walked up the incline and more of the paradise came into view and she gasped at it all. Was like a tiny *village*. There was the big house, then other small matching houses scattered about. She was in some strange fairytale dream in another time it felt like. She caught Sahvrin's hot eyes on her and knew it wasn't a dream at all. It was wonderfully real.

CHAPTER 13

Sahvrin signaled his Mah-Mah to the laundry room next to the kitchen, recognizing that look. She had it every time they tried to set him up with a pretty face, convinced he just needed to meet the right girl and he'd get over his obsession with celibacy. He wasn't obsessed with it, he'd just adjusted to that life after fifteen years. The idea of a relationship with a woman had been an alternate reality. And now, that reality was right there in His Petite Ange.

The problem with his Mah-Mah was her uncanny ability to read his mind. Already he could see by the look on her face that she knew everything he felt about her.

"You are okay that she stays here while we meet at The Weigh Station?"

"Of course!" she cried, like that was a stupid thing to ask. Her face suddenly softened with a huge smile. "She's so *beautiful*, Sahvrin." She put the tips of her fingers over her smiling mouth. "And she *really* likes you!"

"How could you know that," he said quietly, shaking his head at her. "That's not what we're here for, Mah-Mah."

Her face went serious. "Pah-Pah has told me everything and I'm sure there will be no problems hunting these devils down. We'll be here cooking up a celebratory feast for when you all return from your meeting. Oh Sahvrin, she's *different!*"

"Yes, she is." He wouldn't argue that.

She shook her head with a slow severity. "She's *more* different than that," she said, squealing in excitement.

"And she's recovering from being beat half to death. While defending another child," he added, wanting her to know that for some reason. All that got him was more joyous nods like he was proving her point instead of focusing it on the right thing.

"You have anything to add, Mah-Mah?"

"No," she said, going aloof.

"Show her around, make her feel like family."

"Oh, I will," she said, back to huge smiling plans. "Before I'm done, she'll want to live here forever. *Watch*."

"I don't want you doing that," he ordered, getting mildly pissed. "I do not want that forced."

Her grin said she thought otherwise, and he gave up. "I always have your back," she assured, scratching the light beard along his face with both hands. "She looks so *cute* in the dress we sent."

"Mon Dieu, she got second degree burns," he remembered. "She fell asleep sunbathing. You have ointment?"

"Of course!" she said, like he were dense.

"See that she has everything she needs?"

She whacked him on the shoulder. "I *will*!"

"She may want a bath," he remembered. "To soak her deeper injuries. She tries to hide the pain, but I see it."

She nodded slowly and smiled like he was again proving all her cupid points. "Pah-Pah said she has *spunk* and is very strong spirited. This is good?"

"It's good for her, yes. In this life, she'll need it."

"And good for the swamp life?"

He hugged his mother and kissed her on the cheek. "Yes, Mah-Mah," he said, deciding for once not to crush all her stubborn dreams. "She's perfect for everything, are you happy?"

This earned him giddy clapping and light jumping up and down. "But before you leave, talk to her?" his Mah-Mah said. "She is very nervous! Make her at ease."

The sharp look his Mah-Mah gave wasn't one he'd ever cross even if he wanted to, which he didn't. And he had every intention of talking to her before leaving.

"Why don't you show her around before you go?" his Mah-Mah cooed, hands clasped dreamily under her chin. "Your brothers are getting ready, you have time!"

****

Sahvrin found Beth in the living room with his aunts all around her. He waved to get her attention and the moment she looked at him, the need to kiss her slammed his gut. Yes, she was fucking perfect. Nobody had to tell him that. But he really needed to keep everything reigned in until she spent more time there.

He signaled she come, and he watched her smile and politely make an exit like she did this kind of thing every day. Maybe she did. He never did learn what kind of circles she ran in. Given her father's wealth, no doubt high ones. Highly civil. The only civil thing about the swamp life was right here at this house. Everywhere else, including his shack on the water, was the kind of life most women from a city would consider a wrong turn. Especially women from a northern city. She'd bake out there, just as she did yesterday. And his position in The Twelve and what that entailed added a challenge to any favorable odds. Her angelic ways would be the biggest hindrance. She'd sacrifice herself to please others and he wouldn't let her do that, not for him or anybody else. She deserved what she wanted, not what he wanted and he'd cut his own balls off to make sure she got that.

"Mah-Mah wants me to show you around," he said to her.

She gave half a smile before worry stole it away. "You don't have to if you need to go."

That was the sweet angel he had to protect with all that he was. Before he'd had one touch, one taste of her, she'd owned his soul without question, and every time she said something sweet like that, she owned it that much more.

He gave her the grand tour, showing her the homestead, watching her reaction the entire time. He'd meant to look for red flags that said she could never live such a life, but instead he'd gotten saturated by the many facets of her, particularly the stuff beneath her silky skin. "And this is the soap house," he announced, ready to bathe her.

"A *soap house?*"

She hurried up the five wide steps, her gasps flowing non-stop along with giddy laughter. "I cannot believe you have a soap house! I had no idea that was even a thing to do? Of course it is, somebody has to make *soap!*" she answered herself with a contagious exuberance that made him laugh.

He followed as she race-floated from one room to the next. "The areas are separated by the various soap-making processes," he explained as they went.

"The *smells are heaven!*" She spun to him with wide eyes. "Is this where you shop for your yummy soap?"

"It is. This was my favorite place to visit as a child," he confessed, watching her smell and touch everything until his hunger boiled.

"I can see why! And you should know that the smell of your soap makes me drool. Must be formulated to attract females."

He grabbed her as she raced to see another room, pulling her to him. He groaned, kissing her perfect mouth with great restraint before pressing his forehead to hers when his pulse fought to beat out of his veins. "Ma Petite," he whispered with eyes closed.

He looked to see desire and worry flit across her face, making him need to feed the first and erase the other. He kissed her again, opening himself more when she moaned in his mouth, like a secret confession of what it all meant to her. He stroked her tongue with awe, adoring her.

The front door opened with, "You in here, bro?"

Sahvrin broke the kiss, winded but glad for the interruption. He was in the process of thinking his gut instincts were right enough, she was the one, and what better time and place to make love to His Petite than now, in the soap house? "Coming," he called, stealing one more kiss. Then another. And another, making her giggle.

"You can't get enough of me?" she mouthed with a bright smile that wrecked the darkness in his mind.

"Ma Petite, you have no idea." His answer lit her up more somehow and he realized he wouldn't see her for the rest of the day. He wrapped her in his arms and lifted her up in a tight hug, burying his mouth in her neck until she squealed with laughter.

"Later, when I get back, I will show you the bath house."

"The *what* house?" she wondered with her dramatic incredulity that made him chuckle.

"A house for bathing. I was saving my favorite places for last."

Her mouth hung open with wide-eyed disbelief. "A whole house? *Just* for bathing?"

"Well, not technically a house, but we call it that. The soap house and bath house were always a hard choice for a favorite," he said, leading her out the door. "But I hated baths growing up and it didn't become a favorite until later."

"You preferred bathing in the bayou?"

"I did. And I bathed every day and more than once in the summer. But Mah-Mah said she wouldn't have her sons smelling like alligator shit."

She gave him a big laugh and the sight and sound made him crave to have her with a la passion, consume that magical stuff bubbling out of her, but especially murder in cold blood anything that threatened it.

"I will also show Ma Petite my childhood bedroom later," he announced as he pulled her down the stone path.

She suddenly jumped in front of him with a sparkling look in her eyes. "Your childhood *bedroom*?"

Her slow smile gave him an instant hard on.

"Are you thinking what *I'm* thinking?"

"I am now," he muttered, staring at her mouth while knowing his thoughts were a lot more vulgar than hers. "We can spend the night," he said, his logic born of pure lust. "Mah-Mah would be delighted. She may secretly have a priest over to marry us while we sleep."

She threw her head back and laughed before leaning up and pecking him on the lips. "I would immediately file for an annulment!"

"I would tie you to the bed so you couldn't," he teased back, testing the marriage talk with her.

A different light entered her eyes with that, one that made him go serious. "I might fight you," she countered.

He lowered his mouth to hers, kissing it with reverence. "I would win," he warned softly.

"Because I would *let* you, Mr. Bishop."

Mon *fucking* Dieu. He plowed his tongue in her mouth, gripping her jaw in hunger until her frantic, delicate moans filled his mouth.

"There's the love birds!"

Sahvrin pulled away at hearing his Mah-Mah, fighting to catch his breath. Of course she wore a giddy joy on her face, wrapping her arms around him for a tighter than usual hug. "My beautiful son," she murmured against his chest before pulling back and holding his face in both hands. Then she pointed a finger at his nose with raised brows and a nod. "I'm taking over from here. Your brothers are ready and your Pah-Pah is antsy. Us women will be over here making a feast. I was hoping Beth would join us for the fun?"

"I would love to!"

He watched her leave as every letter in those words and the way she spoke them resonated in him. He'd always believed words had this kind of force, but he'd never seen it so potent outside of evil. She'd had it when he first met her in town, he realized. He'd stupidly mistaken it for overcompensated pretense. Like an artist oversaturating a real-life scene, making it cartoonish. But her perception of reality and life *was* that vibrant color. He'd wanted to correct it, show her that she was going about living all wrong, that the world was colored by evil and she needed to play by those rules.

She suddenly glanced over her shoulder twenty feet away, and soaked him with her sunny yellow smile. Mon Dieu, *she* was the master artist. She colored reality as she saw it or wanted it and didn't hold back. Even when life dumped black goopy paint onto her canvas, her gift turned it into another outlandish work of genius. He was fucking riveted by it. Needing to touch and feel its texture while playing in it. But he especially needed to protect it. Because if there was anything he'd learned, it was that the most beautiful things in a person broke the hardest of all.

****

The first odd thing Sahvrin noticed was not a word was mentioned about Beth once they were on the boat. Instead, they talked speed French about gathering the small passe to comb the swamp for traffickers. He'd prepared himself for the mocking at least. The great and terrible bishop had finally fallen.

Surely, the burning stake His Petite had him on was worth any amount of sibling torture.

"I think all we need is Spook and Big Rex," Jek said. "Next to us, they know the swamps the best. We divide up and crank open the eyes on every waterway they could possibly use."

"What are these eyes you speak of?" Zep asked.

Sahvrin turned when it got quiet, finding them looking for his input. "The ones we installed last year to monitor the main waterways. I just need to reset a couple of boxes and hit the switch for a live feed."

"So we have to just let the women get *trafficked* meanwhile?" August said, pissed.

He didn't like it either. "I think the arms shipment is our best angle for leverage. We drive that blade in deep then every move they make is in our control."

"I just wanna skin em, then make cracklins with their filthy hide and feed it to their prez."

Everybody turned to August, finding a dark bloodlust in his gaze.

"May as well grind up their brains and balls too," Jek said, staring ahead as he steered. "Some juicy links of boudin dick."

August nodded with a satisfied grin. "Now *that's* a menu."

Nothing but the hunting and capturing, judging and sentencing now. After long and heartfelt confessions. And of course, the First Bishop's blessing.

CHAPTER 14

Sahvrin led the way to the Weigh Station, fighting to find every hidden marker.

"Ain't no fuckin' way Lester's been maintaining this place," August said for the third time, smacking himself. The mosquitoes were starving for human blood in these woods.

"How did Lazure find his way is what I'd like to know," Jek wondered through a round of coughing. He didn't envy his allergies in the dead of summer. Points to him for not giving a fuck. His stubborn streak would have him eat what threatened him, just to spite that it did. Then he'd build an immunity instead of die, because that's just how Jek worked. He did all the shit that should kill you and somehow lived and grew stronger. And dumber.

"He's probably with Big Sha Leblanc," August muttered, smacking his face again. "Pew-tan mosquitoes are affeme. Big Sha knows the swamps better than the alligators, they won't get lost."

"We still keeping everything the same as last time? I sure as hell hope not." Again, it was August with another smack. "Be the first thing I'd like to take a vote on."

Bart chuckled. "You don't like scribing no more?"

"Hell no. But if I have to write the minutes of the meeting, I wanna vote to use my phone. Then I'll just record it while I text Melissa."

"Still can't believe you're dating the same chick for a whole month," Jek said. "Aghhh, thank a good fuck, I see it!"

He wanted a good fuck. It was all Sahvrin could think about now. But truly, if the wrong person ever found this place, Sahvrin would cut his own head off and lay it on a golden platter for them.

"Sweet Christ almighty," Zep huffed, leaning over. "Now one of us has to climb a fucking tree. Remind me again why Lazure had the bright idea of putting this funhouse fifty feet high."

Sahvrin walked up to the doorbell system and yanked on the rope, ringing the bell up top. Lazure was likely already there.

They took several steps back and stared up.

"Hey! Rapunzel, you home?" Zep yelled. "Let down your nappy hair!"

Faint footsteps clopped above, bringing a round of relieved sighs. "I hope they stocked the fridge, I'm thirsty as a mo-fo," Bart muttered.

"How long's this gonna take?" August wondered as the five-man crate pen lowered down.

"No clue," Sahvrin said, grabbing the rope on the door when it got low enough.

"I got land business," August informed.

Sahvrin glanced at him. "Unless we have swamp business first."

"I'm counting on it," August said. "That's why I need to get to land."

"What you got?" Jek asked.

"Some new toys I wanna pick up."

"Don't want you going alone," Sahvrin said. "I need some things too. We can all take a ride." Sahvrin opened the gate door.

"And what are *you* getting?" Zep asked, with a curious smile. "Flowers, maybe?"

"Some parts for a prototype I'm designing."

"Better be making me one," August said.

Sahvrin eyed him, flipping the wench switch. "It's for the Swamp Dragon."

"Ohhh, early Christmas," Jek said, grinning. "Do tell."

Sahvrin looked up, eying the groaning rigging. "Remind me to bring oil for this beast."

"Don't leave us hanging," Jek said, eager.

"It's a harpoon I originally designed for alligator hunting. Non-lethal. More of a wench."

"Ohhhh," Bart said, his tone going lusty. "A human wench for our upcoming swamp party?"

"Probably."

"Pic or you lyin," Jek said, grinning. "I know you have one, hand it over."

Sahvrin pulled out his phone and opened his design folder, scrolling. He hit the harpoon and handed him the phone.

They all crowded around it with low whistles and dark laughter. "That's fucking sick. And I thought I was the sadistic one."

"It's non-lethal," Sahvrin reminded.

"Oh, we know all about your methods," Jek said.

Wasn't really a choice. Every guilty party had their day in the Bayou Bishops court system right there at The Weigh Station. All The Twelve's hunting equipment was designed to catch, not kill. Once in confession, the tools changed, just as they did for execution.

Sahvrin took his phone back when they reached the top, pushing thoughts of His Petite back. He needed to hone his focus since the threats they were meeting about were directly tied to her.

"Well if it ain't mah lil tinker toy podnuh."

Sahvrin shook Big Sha's hand, grinning at his strong grip. "Long time Big Sha. You doing good?"

"Doing *great!* I hear you done caught yousef a fish in the sea?"

Fucking Lazure and his swamp news flashes. "She's one of a kind."

"Meh yeah," he said, laughing and patting his back hard enough to rattle his spine. "We don't have no secrets when it comes to our lil' ones. You know T-Randal has a new fish too, yeah?"

"Is that so?"

"Sho nuff!" Big Sha's wide eyes indicated there was a story to be told behind this *catch* and Sahvrin wasn't about to ask.

"Who else is here?" Jek wondered.

"La-Fawnse!" Lazure yelled.

"Hole up yuh ass," he drawled from behind the kitchen door. "Coffee can't make its gawdamn self, now can it?"

"Let's sit," Lazure said, pulling the chair out at the head of the table.

"Same places?" Jek asked.

"Same places," Lazure said. "And same positions. August, you're recording."

"I was hoping to take a vote on that."

"Not now. Your Mah- Mah has big plans over the next few days, and we need to get done with this as quick as we can. Grab your writing gear out of the desk."

August pushed up with a sigh while Sahvrin contemplated his parent's marriage for the first time in maybe ever. There was nothing in the world the man seemed to love more than pleasing his mother and Sahvrin had found it amusing, and often annoying.

"It's like a gawdamn family reunion," La-Fawnse muttered as he took a seat at the table, looking around at each of them like a pissed off judge. "Coffee's fresh," he added as a sentencing.

"I'm good," Jek muttered.

"Anybody want a water?" Bart asked at the small fridge.

All but the coffee drinkers raised their hand.

"How the hell can you drink coffee in this hot as hell heat," August wondered after chugging his water and opening the large ledger.

La-Fawnse eyed him and raised his cup to his mouth and sipped loudly, then set the cup back on the table. "Just like that, boy," he said in a low rasp. "When you grow swamp balls, you'll figger it out."

August laughed and shook his head. "I'd rather be oblivious."

While Lazure opened the meeting with the traditional language, Sahvrin got out his knife and stone, sliding the blade slowly along it to help focus.

"So, we have a dilemma," his father said when the meeting officially started, eyeing each of them. "We need to pick between the trafficking and the arms deal. I say we choose the arms deal. Bigger snake pit and likely both are intertwined. Anybody have a reason we might not want to do that, speak."

They all remained silent and Lazure palmed the table. "Then we vote. All who favor us pursuing the arms deal first, say I."

The round of I's began with Sahvrin and went around the table.

"Now we need to talk about the particulars of the arms deal. We want to avoid suspicion with the Roulettes and need to decide how to approach them for renegotiation. Any suggestions, Sahvrin?"

He nodded. "I think I'll have talked sense to my hot headed Pah-Pah and as leader of The Twelve, take over the renegotiations seeing as we need the money for…." He shrugged and went with, "…guess because we want it."

Lazure leaned back, staring into the air before finally nodding. "I like it. I *am* getting old and ornery."

Big Sha laughed and smacked the table. "Gettin'? You was born *ornery*."

"So, we find out what and how many arms they're shipping," Jek said. "Any time frame we shooting for?"

"The sooner the better," Lazure said.

"What about The Twelve?" Sahvrin asked, twirling the tip of his knife on the table.

"They will be at Mah-Mah's celebrations. We'll meet at the Basilique when they come, same as always. By then, we'll have enough information to strategize."

"How are our numbers?" Zep wondered.

"Should be in the last recording," La-Fawnse said, sending August flipping through pages.

"Found it." He scanned the page. "According to the Keepem's records for last year, the numbers of The Horde total two hundred eighty-two. Damn, I do *not* remember writing this," he said, amused. "You want the break down in each Hatch?"

"No," Lazure said. "We'll get that later from Nickels. He should have every detail about current supplies. We'll ensure every man has their choice of defense. "Sahvrin." Lazure eyed him now. "Put off all current jobs that you can and get as many men as you need. Time to get your war game on. I want every Hatch loaded with plenty of everything they specialize in to bring these sick motherfuckers to Church for judgment."

Adrenalin rushed through Sahvrin at the bloodlust dripping from his words. Was just what he wanted to hear. Nothing would give him more satisfaction than giving these demons the royal treatment right there at their Weigh Station Church.

"Anybody learn anything new?" Lazure moved his gaze over them.

"A reliable source said they saw Francois son, Beaux, get in the car of a Roulette member," August said. "Might wanna inquire into that."

"Damn," Lazure said. "You boys were gonna pay him a visit, first chance. Do it sooner rather than later." He looked at Sahvrin again. "You make any more headway on the eyes you installed?"

Sahvrin drew a blank at what he was talking about. "For what exactly?"

"Tracking the waterways."

"Our boy's got ma-petite-on-my-mind syndrome," Zep muttered with a low giggle. "Can't say I don't see the—"

Sahvrin jammed the tip of his knife inches from Zep's arm on the table. "Do not... talk about her," he said, his sudden rage making everything calm in him.

Zep raised his brows with exaggerated wide eyes. "Yes sir yes sir three bags full."

He jerked his knife out of the table. "I need to run a few wires and turn it on. Can probably have it finished tomorrow or next day."

"Oh yeah," August said. "Just heard there's a hurricane headed this way."

"I already felt that bitch in my ole bones," Big Sha said.

Lazure's sigh weighed heavy. "They say when and where?"

"In about five days," August said. "Spose to hit New Orleans."

"Ain't that where the mutha bitch chapter is?" LaFonse wondered.

"It is," Jek said.

"And we *do* know Breaux Bridge Roulette is involved with the trafficking which means so are they," Zep said.

"How do we know that?" Sahvrin wondered.

Zep grinned. "I *just* so happened to be with a woman last night that knew Blanchard, one of the dude's your *petite* named," Zep said. "She was complaining about being forced to help recruit pretty girls for a *modeling* business they were running. When I asked how come she wasn't their top model, she said because it wasn't really modeling, it was a whore shop. And she was *nobody's* whore." Judging by his look, she was probably giving him head under a table while informing him.

"Any more information on Beth's father?" Sahvrin wondered.

Bart raised his hand. "Was going to tell you this in private but realize it needs to be said here. So, I did a deep dive on her father *and* mother. Turns out there was a dispute the day of the funeral about how the mother died. Apparently, her mother's sister claimed the husband poisoned her."

"Beth would've known about that," Sahvrin was sure.

He shrugged. "The sister lives in an institution so I'm thinking they may have wrote it off as psycho-dookie."

"What about her mother, you find anything of use?" Sahvrin wondered.

"Not a thing. It's like she didn't exist before him."

"You search her maiden name?"

"I looked but couldn't find anything other than her Sweetling name. Maybe you can ask Beth for it."

"I'll give it to you tonight." Sahvrin looked at Lazure. "Does Mah-Mah know about the hurricane coming?"

He tucked his chin and aimed a glare at him. "What do you *think*?"

Sahvrin figured. "So we'll be having a hurricane, birthday, boudin festival party all in one, and the whole swamp is invited?"

"You know it," Lazure said, stroking his beard again while Lafonse and Big Sha's laughter rumbled around the room.

"You and the boys gonna be performin, right?" Big Sha asked. "My girls wanna know." He leaned in with a gleam. "They's in love with them Bishop boys."

Weren't they all. But the last thing he wanted to do was party while evil circled them like vultures. He especially didn't want to *perform*.

"Your momma is expecting as much, I'm afraid," Lazure said, eying him sideways and making Sahvrin sink inside a little.

"Miss Beth will have fun."

Sahvrin eyed Bart, finding his smile innocent enough. "I'm sure she will," he said, already brainstorming for excuses to get out of it. Then again, maybe a party would be the best thing for her right now. She earned a day of fun.

"One other thing," Bart said. "You might want to ask Beth if she knows a Julian Abshire. His name keeps coming up in connection to that Blanchard dude. Maybe he's connected somehow, I don't know."

"I'll find out," Sahvrin said, curious now.

****

Beth felt like the queen of the ball up until Lucas and Luseah arrived. Spoiled swamp child, Aunt Rena told her—Luseah, that was. "Don't pay her no mind. She likes to stand out."

"How old is she?"

"Oh, she's sixteen going on thirty." Aunt Rena giggled. "Remember that age?"

She did. She was in boarding school, missing her mom and trying not to be seen. Not sure why the girl would have a problem with her. Would it have anything to do with Sahvrin? Was she jealous? But they were family. Pretty sure they were, but she wasn't about to double check.

"Am I doing something I need to fix?" Beth asked, just to be sure it wasn't a culture offense.

"Oh no, honey. It's not you. It's her," the woman said with a fan of her long nails toward the raven-haired beauty." She's probably bothered that there's a prettier face than hers around. She'll get over it. Those two aren't blood, no how. They're children of the Dark Swamp."

Beth learned they'd been rescued fifteen years ago in a war against devil worshippers in the bayou. Her gaze strayed to the twin, the male replica in looks. What beautiful people they were. But his attitude was completely opposite of his sister, thank God. At least toward Beth. As much as she was thankful for that, it seemed to make things worse with Luseah. What a unique name. And Lucas reminded her a little of Zep, but his genuine kindness was all Sahvrin. There was nobody sweeter in the world she'd ever met than the swamp version of Sahvrin. Nothing at all like the Mr. Bossy Bishop. Memories of her recent hot encounters with him made her pulse race. She'd gotten to know his sweet side and was very eager to get to know his mean side. Or bad side as he called it.

She listened to Lucas talking and smiled. He had the *cutest* accent, like maybe French might not be his first language, unlike the brothers.

"Beth, would you come give me a hand?"

Beth looked toward the kitchen then hopped up at seeing Mah-Mah's waving from the doorway. Finally, she might do something else useful. She'd helped peel potatoes—fifty of them—which took her the whole time all the cooking went on. She didn't mind. They played music and laughed and danced while she watched and peeled to the tune of it all. What wonderful people they were. So happy and…alive. La passion, as Sahvrin would call it.

Her stomach danced in sick excitement when the thought of tonight returned again. She couldn't wait. It was nearing dark, and she wanted to ask how long they'd be but didn't want to look too interested. Mah-Mah seemed to know and love that they were *together*, but she wasn't sure who else did.

Entering the kitchen, Mah-Mah waved her over. "The men are on their way back," she announced in a whisper when she got close. "I want you to go wash up, you can use the inside bathroom. And then I'd like to give you some party clothes to change into. Would you like that?" she asked, smiling.

"I would love it," Beth said, trying not to grin too big.

Mah-Mah hugged her suddenly, long and tight then pulled away. "I know you came here by terrible circumstances, but look what gift God has wrought out of this wickedness?" The woman nodded with raised brows and Beth wiped the sudden tears, agreeing.

"Yes, he has." She fought for air, getting another tight hug from his mother, making her tears come faster.

"Oh Shaaa pee-chay, you are such a soft-hearted flower?" she observed after pulling away again.

"I...my family was different from this. Sahvrin calls it...la-passion."

His mother laughed, and the sound of the pure joy made Beth smile. "He would know, yes?"

She seemed to be asking her and Beth's cheeks warmed with a nod. "Yes, he definitely does."

This got tiny claps and more giddy laughs. She held out her hand. "Come, I'll show you where everything is!"

The mischief in her eyes made her laugh as she followed and got a tour of the spacious, adorable bathroom. The first jaw dropping feature were the two fat black pots sitting in a wooden frame for a double sink. The wood holding it glowed a warm polished brown with two Victorian framed mirrors over each pot with tons of flowering décor. Then she spied the tub hiding in the corner and gasped. "Oh my Gosh! It's like a giant witches pot!"

Before she could worry over offending, Mah-Mah laughed, sounding tickled to death. "That's what Sahvrin always called it! Lazure would make jokes about throwing me in it and making a gumbo and Sahvrin would cry and cry," she said, smiling at the memory. "He was so in love with his Mah-Mah," she informed with a serious nod. "Up until he was ten, he was dead *set* on marrying me!"

The story warmed Beth beyond belief before Mah-Mah jumped back to the present and hurried to show her where everything was and how it all worked. "Oh, and *look!*" she said, closing the bathroom door to reveal a dress hanging on the back that dropped her jaw.

"Oh my goodness, that's *beautiful.*"

"And *sexy?*"

Beth laughed and nodded. "You took the words from my mouth."

"Oh, I went to the soap house and got you something special to wash your lovely hair with." She opened a cabinet and turned with a delicate glass jar filled with something lavender colored. "Sahvrin *loves* this smell. It's his *very* favorite. You can use it for hair and body! It's my royal *luxurious* recipe!"

Beth took it and opened the top for a whiff. "Oh my, now it's *my* favorite."

"Perfect! Now hurry up. I would like to help you with your hair!" She spun to leave then spun right back. "And those towels near the tub are for using, not for looks!" She gave a sudden gasp and hurried to a cabinet then floated gracefully back with another jar. "I want you to take at least a thirty-minute soak in the hot water," she instructed with a firm tone that made Beth smile. "Use *all* of it."

"The whole jar?"

She nodded once. "The whole jar."

"I will. Thank you so much."

She turned again, the layers of her pretty dress flying about. Reminded her of angel's wings. "I will lock the door on the way out, my dear," she announced without turning. "And I will call the men and tell them to take the long route home!" she said alarmed, as if realizing there wasn't enough time.

Finally left alone, Beth went up to the dress hanging on the door, her dreamy smile spreading. From the waist down, the soft lavender flowed in various shades and soft materials. The top of the dress had sheer strips that seemed to be for draping over the arms, but not sleeves. She fingered the tiny lavender flowers covering the princess cut top and straps. How fantastical. Like Cinderella. But in an enchanting swamp kingdom with a devilishly handsome Swamp Prince.

CHAPTER 15

Mah-Mah was on the final flowers in her hair when three fast knocks rattled the door, making them both jump.

"Mon Dieu, they better not be early!" Mah-Mah whispered, hurrying to the door.

Beth examined herself in the mirror, fighting the wave of nervous nausea. She could actually say she looked beautiful. Not brand-new *Cadillac* kind of beautiful like Luseah, but more like… new Toyota kind of pretty.

The door opened and Mah-Mah came back in, shutting it back. She then turned to her and the look on her face sent a sick dread slamming her stomach. "What?"

She hurried over and grabbed her hands. "There's somebody here," she said, her fretful look bringing panic to mix with the dread.

"Who?"

She closed her eyes briefly then opened them right as another knock pounded the door.

"Mah-Mah, are you in there?"

Beth stood frozen in place as the woman hurried and opened the door, letting in Lazure who looked like he'd seen a ghost of a dead loved one. That he may have hated.

The French speaking erupted in whispers and hisses, making Beth's panic skyrocket.

"Is Sahvrin okay?" That's all she needed to know.

Mah-Mah hurried to her, nodding as she did while Lazure continued in hushed French. "He is fine."

"Is he here, is he back? Who else is here?"

Lazure spoke French that sounded like a panicked question.

"I just found out! I haven't had time!" Mah-Mah cried.

"Please stop speaking French!" Beth gasped, bringing a shaking hand to her mouth with, "I'm sorry, I just…I can't understand what's happening." She smoothed her hands over the soft dress, her smile quivering under the strain of panic she held at bay. But something said she should be panicking and not knowing about what or why was doing her head in. "Can I see him," Beth wondered, suddenly wanting to be back at his little house where everything was quiet and simple.

"Go and see about this, Lazure!" Mah-Mah hissed before grabbing both Beth's hands in her warm ones. "I want Sahvrin to explain everything to you. A woman from his past is here, but don't worry, I will get rid of her immediately!"

A woman? "She's here now?"

Mah-Mah nodded before her pretty face darkened and she looked away. "How dare that bitch come here. How did she even remember the way?" She snapped her eyes back to Beth. "I won't lie to you, little one. He was madly in love with her," she said, nodding and wiping her tears. "She broke my son into a million pieces. He used to be an *artist*, a *brilliant* artist and when she left, she took that passion with her. He never touched a paint brush again."

It all hit her. That's why he didn't want to talk about the art. Oh God, that was the *woman!* The one who taught him everything about *sex*?

The need to comfort Sahvrin and run from what she was sure was coming made her ill. *He was madly in love with her* kept playing over and over in her head.

"Why do you think she's here?" she heard herself ask, already numb.

The answer to that was lost to the buzzing fears in her head and what was coming. She needed to prepare for whatever it was.

"I need to change," she realized in a mumble.

"No! You are not changing!"

The sudden image of him in the next room with a beautiful ex made her need to hide. Escape. And just as quickly, without thinking, she headed to the bathroom door. She would not run from him. From this. She just needed to know where she stood, where he stood, how he felt about this woman.

After much confusion, she finally made her way outside, gathering that's where they must be. She spotted them on the pier, ignoring the call of two of his brothers as she headed toward them. She would be civil, this was *not* a big deal.

She focused on the fact that this woman broke him into a million pieces, rather than all the sex they'd had. The idea had her pulse pounding on every frayed nerve, and they were *all* frayed.

She stared at the woman, unable to look at Sahvrin as she closed the distance. With ten feet between them, she held out her hand in greeting, almost dumbstruck with her beauty. "Hi, I don't mean to interrupt, I just wanted to introduce myself. I'm Beth, I'm just a friend."

"Katrina," the woman greeted, sounding as kind as she was beautiful. "Very nice to meet you, Beth."

"Wow, aren't you gorgeous!" Beth gushed, unable to stop her dumb laugh. "Well, I see you are here to…catch up. I just wanted to welcome you."

"And why the hell would you want to do that?"

Sahvrin's angry question snapped her gaze to his, and the fury in his dark eyes stole her breath. "I…I was just wanting… to make sure you were okay and…"

His burning eyes bore hard into her. "Your concern is almost as beautiful as you are, but it's not necessary. I will speak to you at the house in five minutes."

Her head was nodding then finally her "Okay," flew out. *Go to the house. Get your ass to the damn house.* "I'll go to the house." She took a step back and tripped on the air, arms flailing ungraciously. "Whoops, got it," she said, turning and hurrying back the way she came while her heart hammered so hard in her chest, it felt like it might shatter.

****

Sahvrin stared after His Petite, burning to know what was going through her head now.

"I actually didn't come here to fight with you."

He stared at the female demon from his past. "What *did* you come for?" he really wanted to know. Her associations ran too close to his current problems, that was for damn sure and her remembering how to even get out there was now another problem.

"I just wanted to see how you were, sue me."

"You're about fifteen years late, Katrina. And I don't want to fight with you either. I'm over it all."

"I see that. Is she your girlfriend?"

Fuck. Definitely no accident her coming here. And now she could identify Beth.

"No," he decided to say.

"You always call your friends beautiful?"

The jealous fury in her blue eyes was laughable. "We're related," he said, in sarcasm, watching her reaction to that while digging for something to buy time. "Now that you're here, you can take the jewelry box you left behind."

The sudden softening in her face was the win he needed. "You kept it?"

"I kept everything." In ashes scattered in the swamp.

Her fighting stance slacked a little. "So, how is she related?"

"Cousin," he said. The look in her eyes said she didn't believe him. "I put everything in the guest house." He allowed his gaze to touch her half-exposed breasts then raised it to her face. The heat in her eyes brought an acid to his tongue, making him want to spit. "Follow me."

The sound of her boots behind him meant his little trick worked like a whore's charm. She was here for more than just information. What, exactly, he didn't know. If she thought he'd have anything to do with her after what she pulled, she had a very vulgar revelation coming.

He didn't allow himself to glance at Beth who watched them from the porch. He didn't need to look to know there was hurt and confusion and fear on her beautiful face and being unable to do a fucking thing about it had his rage boiling.

"Your cousin looks worried about you," she said.

She definitely knew the cousin thing was a lie. But she didn't know he knew she knew. "She'll get over it."

Once in the guest house, he lit the wall lights and locked the door while she was distracted. He pulled out his phone and opened Jek's message box.

"What are you doing?"

"Just letting Mah-Mah know I'm okay. I'm sure she's worried I'll do something stupid with you." *Meet me at the guest house. Katrina is here and she knows something. We can't let her leave. Have August get rid of her boat.*

He put his phone in his back pocket, looking at her. "Like, fuck you," he added, repeating the dirty breast gazing trick and replacing the sudden worry in her eyes with a little too much lust.

"So, you came all this way to see me?" He leaned against the door and crossed his arms on his chest.

"Yes." She lowered her gaze over him, and he realized it was partly true. "Are you still painting?"

The hopeful smile on her face made his fury burn. "Never touched a brush since you left."

A knock sounded on the door, and he turned only his head. "Who is it?"

"Jek."

He opened the door and let him in, locking it back. "Well, well, look what the swamp dragged in. Hello Katrina."

She eyed him, all that fear returning. "What's going on?"

"That's what you're going to tell us," Sahvrin said. "I know you were sent. Jek, find some rope. And get Zep in here to interrogate her."

"Texting him now."

"Listen, you don't have to tie me up, I do know what's going on. But I wasn't going to tell, I was coming to ask for your help."

"Have him bring some of Mah-Mah's truth serum," Sahvrin said eying her, already sick of her lies.

"I'm telling you the truth. I need your help with my daughter."

He stared at her, hating that he had no way of verifying much since he'd forbidden anybody to utter her name. "*What* daughter?"

The tears pouring now hardened every muscle as he stormed up to her and grabbed her jaw hard. "What…daughter."

"Yours," she gasped, clenching her eyes tight.

Sahvrin stared at her for many seconds then shoved her back onto the small couch. He turned to Jek who had a clueless look then back to her. "Prove it," he seethed, ready to kill something.

"How am I supposed to *prove* it? When I left, I was pregnant and didn't tell you. I planned on having an abortion and found out my father used me as leverage because he was being blackmailed by The Roulettes. He was part of their trafficking," she said, her mouth twisting with rage. "Then Remy Dupre, the president of Roulettes in New Orleans decided he wanted me, and I had no *choice* in the matter," she shot out, telling him he'd raped her. "I eventually told him I was pregnant, and he assumed it was his. I thought he'd want to abort it and instead he became a proud *father*," she said with a pent up loathe that said she'd gotten her punishment and then some.

Sahvrin paced in the fiery hell she'd just unleashed. "Where is she? How old is she?" he demanded.

"She's with him. Always. Like a prisoner. A well cared for and provided for sixteen-year-old prisoner. We both are. I know about the arms deal he wants to do and so when he needed information, I saw my chance of getting her out and I volunteered to get it."

Sahvrin spun and pointed at her. "You didn't say a damn word about any of that."

"I had come to you for help," she yelled back. "I...I was sorry about leaving, I *am* sorry. I knew it was a slim chance you'd forgive me, but I had to try and if not for me then for our daughter. If he ever finds out that she's yours, he'd..." She shook her head, covering her mouth. "I don't know what he'd do, Sahvrin. But she's all I have left."

"Left of what? *Us*?"

"Of anything!" she screamed back. "I have *nobody* and *nothing* but her, and she means the fucking world to me, you sonofabitch, do you understand?" Her face had turned hard and furious, a look of somebody who'd been forced to do unthinkable things to survive. "I will *kill*. And *die* for her if that's what it takes, but you have to get her out of that *life*. She deserves this," she spread her arms around, "this life here, this beautiful world I *stupidly* threw away."

Sahvrin turned his back to her, gritting his teeth and eyeing Jek who was still riveted in shock.

"What's her name?" Jek wondered to Katrina as Sahvrin closed his eyes.

"Savvie," she whispered. "I have pictures on my phone, look," she gasped, pulling it from her pocket.

Sahvrin stormed over and snatched it from her, not trusting her. "You were ready to fuck on this floor," he muttered to her. "What's the password."

"Savvy2507" she said, making his stomach sick. 2507 was their fucking anniversary. "And I told you I will do anything to protect her," she said, back to seething pissed. "That includes say what I have to, do what I have to and *fuck* who I have to."

But the heat in her eyes had been nauseatingly real. He knew it and she knew it.

Another knock came and he looked at Jek before calling, "Who is it?"

"Zep... August."

Jek opened the door and they entered, eyeing Katrina with wonder as Jek locked the door back.

"Where's Beth?" Sahvrin asked Zep.

"I think she's being distracted while we sort this out."

He typed the password into the phone and the image of a beautiful young girl popped up on the screen. He aimed the phone at Katrina.

"That's her."

"What's going on?" Zep wondered.

Sahvrin stared at the girl, fighting a million thoughts and emotions. She was so fucking sweet looking and could've been Juliette's twin. "Meet your long-lost niece," he said, presenting the phone for two seconds before hurling it across the room.

He paced several steps, needing to kill something more than ever. His brothers stood guarded and ready as he fought his rage. Savvie. "You cold, fucking, bitch," he gasped, leaning over and holding his knees, unable to get enough air.

"What's he talking about?" August mumbled behind him.

He listened to Jek tell him the sordid story as plans began filling his head. "Where is she?" He went to Katrina, fighting the need to jerk her to her feet and shake all the answers from her. "I want every detail."

"What if she's lying about all of it?" August wondered.

"I'll happily do a DNA test," Katrina said.

"Oh you will," Sahvrin assured even though he believed every word she said. If there was one thing he knew about her, it was when she lied.

"She doesn't have a clue what's going on," Katrina said.

"So she doesn't know she's a prisoner," Sahvrin interpreted, looking at Jek. "We find her, we take her. She comes here."

"She can't come here!"

He snapped his gaze to Katrina.

"They know I know this place," she said. "They may not be able to beat it out of me, but I would sing like a fucking bird if they threatened her, and they *would*."

"Not if we get her before they know. And they won't beat anything out of you because you're not leaving."

She flew at him, and his brothers caught the clawing cat. "I have to go back! You can't go near her, they'll fucking know, I'll kill you!"

"Text Lazure," Sahvrin told August. "We need to do this as soon as possible. When they won't expect it." He faced Katrina again. "What about Beth, what do you know about her?"

Her mouth twisted in disgust. "What do you *think*? That a very valuable piece of merchandise went missing in the swamp, and he wants it back. Hope you didn't fuck the virgin value out of her."

He held her stare, ninety percent sure she'd spoken the truth. He wanted more than anything to say he *did* fuck her, and it was the *best* fuck he'd ever had, but his need to protect His Petite was way fucking bigger than his hate for this woman.

He went back to pacing and arranging the information racing in his head. Sahvrin closed his eyes briefly then looked at Katrina. "Who are the dealers for these guns?"

She swallowed, shifting on her feet like she might try to run.

"Tie her to that fucking chair," Sahvrin said, before pointing at her. "Fight and I'll make you sorry. Please try me."

She eyed him, her chest heaving for many seconds before she slowly sat in the chair and let them tie her. "The Diablos De La Guerra, that's who are supplying."

"Who are they?" Sahvrin asked, stopping before her.

"They're your worst nightmare for seven of your fucking generations."

He nodded, eying her. "Then I'd say this arms shipment is a big deal."

"Anything with them is a big *fucking* deal," she said, like she wanted to spit.

He considered that and turned to Jek. "I have to renegotiate that contract now. Once that deal is sealed with the supplier, then King Cock won't renege, not for his whore or his child if he wants to keep them alive. But something tells me he'd be more worried about his own hairless sack than he is about them."

Sahvrin turned at Katrina's maniacal giggles, meeting her giddy gaze. "King Cock already signed the deal. And stupid Thadious told the Diablos De La Guerra that the swamp was *ready* to go and *open* for business," she finished with a delighted smirk. "Both of them motherfuckers, and their *extended fucking family*," she yelled, pulling on her restraints, "are the walking dead if they don't get the Holy *fucking Bishops* to help them! Now do you see why I was sent here? To fuck you into this agreement, of course, but that's not why I was going to fuck you, oh no no no, I was going to fuck you for our *daughter's* freedom and protection."

Sahvrin spun to Jek, his adrenaline pumping hard. "You. Me. August and Zep are having a drink at the Roulettes tonight. Bart will stay with Katrina. We're negotiating these gun on *our* terms."

CHAPTER 16

After texting everything to Lazure and asking him to pass it to Mah-Mah, Sahvrin psycho walked his way to the main house, making it there in under a minute. He entered the kitchen and the sight of Beth at the sink stopped him in his tracks. He drank in her beauty, the lavender dress no doubt something special she'd worn for him. He heard her distraught mumbling before she lifted a shoulder and wiped her eyes.

"Ma Petite," he called softly.

She spun and glass shattered with her gasped, "Oh shit," as she hurried to the floor.

Right as he made it to her, she jerked her hand back, blood gushing.

"Ma Petite," he whispered, pulling her up and holding her hand over the sink.

"Crap, crap, crap," she said, looking away as he turned on the water. "Oh God, don't wet it!"

She tried to pull her hand out of his and he held it tight. "I have to see how bad it is, I'm just passing it under the stream for one second."

She hissed and strained as he did.

"It's not bad," he said, his breath releasing. "Hold it up and over the sink." He reached for the paper towels and ripped a square off, wrapping her pointer finger tight then holding it in his hand. The second her teary gaze met his, he devoured her mouth in a hungry kiss, her surprised breath making him groan at how fucking good she felt.

"I'm sorry, Ma Petite," he said at her mouth, still holding her injured finger tightly between his, while pulling her body against him. "I see the fairy godmother visited you and turned you into a princess," he said, looking down into her face.

The worry and fear in her eyes melted a little and he kissed her again, back to ravenous. This angel should *never* fucking worry about his feelings for her. "I missed you, Ma Petite."

"I missed you more," she said, her fingers running up in his hair. She pulled back and looked at him. "What's going on? Can you tell me?"

The desperate plea in her gaze brought every dirty confession to the tip of his tongue. "Let's take a walk."

Sahvrin would use the band-aid ripping method with this since he didn't have a lot of time. Once on the gravel path, he began with, "I don't know what Mah-Mah may have said but I'm going to tell you everything. He stopped and faced her. "Katrina is my ex. Yes, the one I told you about, my first. She left six months after we were married for her career. Never called or came back. She came here tonight and knowing the circles she comes from, I didn't trust that it didn't have to do with you. They sent her to fish for information and then she saw you. I couldn't let her leave with that information. So, Jek has her at the guest house making sure she doesn't."

"Oh God…"

"There's more." He slid his hands on her arms. "She told me we have a daughter." She froze, and he finished ripping the band-aid off, rushing through the sick details. Once he was done, he studied the emotions filling her face. "Say something," he said, ready to deal with it and be done.

She stared, blinking as she lowered her head. "I'm… so sorry," she said. "That must…all be very hard to process. And accept."

He closed his eyes at hearing it was also the case for her too. Being suddenly wedged between his past and his future with her had his anger coming to a quick boil. "I don't know what's coming in the next couple of days, Beth. I have a daughter I've never met coming into my life and now I'll have to protect her and her mother."

"Well…what…do you need me to go somewhere? I don't want to be a threat to your family."

He stared at her, dumbfounded that she thought that, pissed even. He pulled her face in and kissed her, plowing his tongue in her mouth while his fingers slid up in her hair. "You're not going anywhere. Do you hear? Don't fucking say that."

"I…okay," she gasped. "I don't really understand what…"

He put his forehead against hers, wishing he knew how to say everything without fucking up what they had in progress. "It's been seven days since I found you." He pulled up, stroking her face. "I rushed a lot of things in my life and was made to be very sorry for it. I won't rush us for anything or anybody, past or present, do you understand? There are some things I can't tell you yet and won't. Not until I know it's the right time. I'm asking you to trust me on that."

She kept her face lowered and brushed tears from her cheeks with a nod and soft, "Okay." She turned her gaze up to his, hope in those pure eyes. "Whatever you think we need to do…I'll do it."

"I want to date you," he said, tasting her lips.

"No sex?" she wondered, her delicate hunger tearing through him.

"There is more to sex than just sex, as you say?" He petted her face. "We will not rush."

Her brows pulled together as she cast her eyes down. "I didn't…mean to sound like I only want sex, I just…I need to know what's coming, what to expect so I can…prepare."

"Ma Petite," he said, petting her sweet face. "You will not suffer in this, I promise you. I am yours completely and every need you have, I will find a way to answer it while we take it slow."

"I may have… done something in anticipation of tonight but…. it can wait."

His pulse hammered at what she might mean. "What did Ma Petite do? Tell me." He tilted her face up to his, wondering over her furrowed brows.

"I…I ordered that insidious book you wanted," she whispered, like it was hard to get out. "And another one that looked…interesting."

Fuck. He kissed her, moaning as he played with her tongue, quickly losing himself in the delicate moans she gave. "How did Ma Petite even order this?" he wondered, pulling up.

She struggled to think around her desire before saying, "Well, your Mah-Mah—"

"Ahhhh the swamp Cupid."

She gave a laugh, breaking the shame that had overtaken her. "She… gave me your PO Box and I used the computer in the library. I might have been shocked to discover there was one. But don't worry, I covered my tracks. Nobody will know."

He didn't like hiding anything from her for the reason she'd just shown. She had to guess what and why he hid things and was prone to guess the worst. "I don't care who knows that, Ma Petite. And those things I can't tell you yet have no bearing whatsoever on how I feel about you. Nothing on this earth will change that." He lowered and nipped softly at her lips, his hands roaming over her dress, feeling her shape. "What is this other book you ordered?"

"Just…stuff about… sexual relationships."

"How vague," he said, stepping back and taking her hand, ready to get to the very bottom of that. He'd text his brothers when he got upstairs to see how far they'd gotten with the Katrina code. Then he'd learn everything His Petite had been up to. It was only 7:30. They'd hit their night shift at the Royal Fucking Roulette around midnight.

That gave him about four hours to quiet her fears and blow her mind with pleasure.

****

"Oh my God, I can't believe you lived way up here," she cried as he headed up the third flight of stairs.

"The oldest got the best," he said, finishing the last steps to his attic room.

"This house is so huge."

Her father was rich, so he guessed this was nothing compared. "It's the biggest I have personally ever been in," he confessed, trying to remember the name of the dude he was supposed to ask about.

"How amazing to grow up in such a fairytale place."

He stopped at the landing, fighting another urge to touch her now that they were at the bedroom. "The only thing fairytale about this place is you."

The sweet melt of her face burned him. "Is it your plan to torture me slowly with your bayou charm until I'm on my knees begging?"

Mon Dieu, the visions she'd just created.

He opened the door and she leaned around him. "Oh my gosh, this whole thing was yours?"

"The whole thing." He shut and locked the door, the heat wave hitting him in the face. "Mon Dieu, I forgot how hot it gets up here." He made his way along the fifty-foot wall of windows, opening them, then turned on the four ceiling fans.

"Your bed?" She gasped a laugh and he turned to see his angel climbing up the steps leading to his cypress pirate ship.

"A gift from my uncle." He watched her ass under the dress as she went, hunger to see it again stabbing him. She lay in his childhood bed and rolled around in it before spying it. "A slide?" She promptly hurried to it and slid down with a laugh that stoked new hungers.

"My uncle is an amazing craftsman. And my father. They both built this home."

"And now you are?" she wondered.

He made his way to the far side of the room. "Come see this," he called at the largest window.

She raced over and looked out where he pointed. "Is that…a zip line?"

"It is."

She angled her head, peering harder. "To a treehouse!? I saw that treehouse today!"

She straightened and the joyous look on her face slowly turned into something else that brought his reckless desire. He allowed himself to imagine what it would be like if she became his second in command in The Twelve. She would have to submit to the Bishop side of him and he really needed to test how she'd take that.

He watched her stroll the room as he sat in the chair next to his small desk, balls tingling. "Mr. Bishop might have very little practice in going slow," he warned, feeling like that was a safe starting point.

His lavender angel touched one childhood moment after another, casting him a shy look. "What do you mean?"

He eyed her, his cock raging at what he meant. "He's not been allowed to touch and taste before."

She paused at his stick art collection and picked up a figure. "He must be very hungry," she said softly, peeking at him.

Mon Dieu, he was speechless with said hunger. "More than I ever imagined."

The heat in her gaze from across the room licked his cock. "I'm not afraid of Bishop," she said, moving again along his collection.

Her bold words called him right out of the shadows to step into her light. Sahvrin said he'd not been allowed to taste and touch, but now he realized he'd been tasting from the very start. And he still fully intended to have every bit of her.

This didn't alarm him, if anything, it excited him. Because there wasn't a part of him that wouldn't die or kill to protect her.

"Tell me what you have in mind with these books, Ma Petite."

She made her way closer to his side of the room, stopping at the back wall of the bed, only five feet away now. "I was thinking we can… take turns reading the position one. Maybe… scale them from 1 to 10. 1 could be… God no, and 10 could be…"

"God, yes?"

She gave a timid nod, making his cock pulsate.

"How was your day, angel?" he asked, shifting directions before he went past a point he couldn't return from.

She made her way to the ladder on the bed and climbed halfway up and sat before aiming a secret smile at him. "I peeled like fifty potatoes. Washed a thousand dishes."

He grinned at how she said it. "Ma Petite, you love washing dishes?"

"Not really, no," she hurried, narrowing her brows while still smiling, like maybe she worried he'd think it was a dumb thing to like. "I loved helping though," she said, proud of that. "And so many people were there, singing and laughing. It went by so fast!"

He clasped his hands behind his head, watching her eyes move over him before lowering to her lap. "Most women don't really like life in the swamp."

She angled her head with curious eyes at him, her guard up. "Those women here seemed to. I do."

"That's because they're raised in it. Immune."

Half a smile tugged at her pretty mouth. "You act like the swamp is a disease."

"It is to many. Most who aren't from it don't survive long in it."

She leaned her forearms on her lap and clasped her hands, studying them. "Well, I guess time will tell."

That it would.

"I don't care what anybody says, I like it."

His cock ached with her annoyed swat at his red swamp flag. She didn't say it, but he knew it irked her when he threw them right at her. But she needed to know. Maybe she thought he wasn't rooting for her, but she'd be dead wrong on that. He planned to equip her as long as she wanted it, and she'd need all that stubbornness and determination. Swamp people didn't quit till they died. And they didn't go easy into that night.

"What about you?" she asked. "You had fun today?"

He eyed her with a grin. "We had a blast. Walked about five miles in a thousand degrees looking for buried trails while fighting mah-de-gwan that are as mean and hungry as Gras Jean."

She had on a big smile. "Is that a swamp creature, mahdigwan?"

"Mosquitos."

She busted out laughing and the sound along with her sudden gaze on his cock made it jerk. She looked down. "You were teasing," she said with a soft joy.

"I was," he said back, enjoying the vision before him. His mother was surely trying to kill him. "Did Mah-Mah tell you about the party coming?"

Her face bloomed with excitement, officially ending his desire to skip it. "She did! I get to help set up and I can't wait." She gave a secret smile. "I don't think I'm supposed to know that your birthday is part of it."

Another quick rake of her eyes along his body had him boiling. "She is a fierce party animal," he half teased. "I celebrate my birthdays if I want to continue enjoying the breath she gave me."

Her happy laugh made his blood sing. He suddenly wanted to run his fingers through her hair.

"What?" she wondered, touching her hair, worried. "It's probably all messed up now."

"No," he chuckled, needing to crush those cute inhibitions. "I was admiring Mah-Mah's craft and the materials she worked with."

A hard blush came with a glowing smile. "I don't know about the materials," she sputtered, licking her lips nervously. "But she's amazing. She made me feel like a swamp princess."

A swamp princess. Mon Dieu. "That, you *surely* are. Gras Jean will be jealous of me now." Her laughter rang out and he devoured her joy, while the starved Bishop was pushing to get back to the topic of sex. "Tell me more of these books you got, Ma Petite. Particularly the one about *sexual stuff*."

The topic was a real mood changer and fuck, he loved the one it put her in. "Uhhhh, well," she began, doing what he wanted to, wrapping her hair around her hand. Her desire was fascinating. So many layers. He wanted to bring each one, memorize it. "It's just…about…relationships and sex and…styles."

What an interesting word in regard to that. "Styles."

The amount of squirming she did, meant it embarrassed her. "Well, like…temperaments," she said. "Personalities and…such."

"You're doing so good keeping it just out of my understanding," he teased.

She focused on her hands, wetting her lips. "Well, what they actually call it is also very obtuse if you ask me."

"Tell me. Let me try," he said, ready to beg her.

"BDSM," she gushed with a wave of her nervous hand, doing a terrible job at hiding how nervous this made her. "You probably heard of it?"

If he knew what the acronym stood for, he could possibly answer that. "The acronym doesn't ring a bell. But maybe its meaning will."

"It's…mostly about…dominance and submission. And marriage," she quickly added, breathless.

Mon fucking Dieu, did he hear her right? Dominance and submission and marriage? All three raced through his body with a defining force. B D S M. Dominance and submission. And marriage. "The M stands for marriage, yes? The D for dominance, the S for submission? That leaves the B."

She captured her hair in her hand again. "Actually, the M stands for something else, and the B stands for bondage, but it's not set in stone, it's a style, you can decide what you want and don't want."

Bondage. Images of His Petite tied up while he pleasured her fucking burned him. "What does the M stand for? Ma Petite, perhaps?"

"Masochism," she barely said. "But I'm not into all of that," she hurried, like either she didn't want him thinking she was or was worried he wanted her to be.

"And we get to pick what we like?"

She nodded, bravely meeting his gaze.

"I think I choose BDSM to mean Binding and Dominating and Subduing Ma-Petite?"

She held her gaze in her lap, her lips parted, breathless. "You can choose that," she said, slamming him with desire.

"But what does Ma Petite choose?" he had to know. "You need to tell me this."

She straightened and stroked a hand across her forehead before returning it to her lap. "I don't like saying it," she said.

"But you need to," he wasn't sorry to say.

"Now?"

"I definitely *need* to know it and now is perfect." He also needed to hear her say it.

She covered her face with her hands then looked only toward him. "What if I write it?"

Mmmmm. "I can work with that."

"Good," she cried, like even that was going to be hard. "I'll need your input for that," she said, like she couldn't find her pleasure outside of that. Angelic.

"You write it, I'll put my notes."

He decided he wanted that immediately and turned to his desk, getting everything she needed. He brought the small notebook and pen to her.

"Now?"

"I'm going take a shower. Take as long as you need." He eyed her as she took it from him. "But not too long."

She glanced up and he lowered, tasting those perfect lips while stroking the soft skin of her face. Her erratic breaths said her pussy was likely dripping now. Fuck, he wanted to feel it.

His phone buzzed and he straightened, heading to his drawer as he pulled it out and swiped the screen. Mah-Mah. *I have some more clothes for Beth. Do you want me to bring them up?*

He texted her back. *I'm coming down to shower. I'll get them.*

He looked for more texts, finding none. He'd call Jek when he showered, find out what they learned so far.

He grabbed clean underwear, jeans and a t-shirt. He glanced back at her, finding her writing. Good.

"I'll be back in thirty minutes. You want anything from downstairs? Mah-Mah has more clothes for you. I'll bring them up when I'm done."

She nodded before looking hopeful. "Did you eat? I saved a plate of food for you. It's in the oven."

Mon Dieu, his angel had such decadent power. "I'll be sure and eat it." He wanted to eat her pussy and hoped she'd put that down in her list of wants and needs.

"I put a lot," she said with one of her secret smiles. "Mah-Mah said you eat as much as a horse." And she thought that was cute.

"This is true," he admitted, tucking his clothes under his arm and heading for the door. He opened it and paused, then stepped out, ready to jack off. How would he stay in the same room with her and not fuck her unconscious?

In the bathroom downstairs, he realized that she'd agreed to stay and hold off on the sex. But where would she stay? She couldn't stay at his parents with his fornicating brothers living there too. And having her alone with him at his house was sure suicide.

He'd have to stay at his parents with her. His Mah-Mah would be thrilled, she loved having the whole family in one place.

He put his phone on the counter, realizing he needed to get His Petite her own so he could communicate with her at all times.

CHAPTER 17

Beth fanned her face again while trying to think logically. Wow, she couldn't believe they'd just had that conversation. Now, writing this while horny out of her mind was like food shopping while starving. "Focus. Sex therapy cap on. Maturity. You can do this."

She stood and climbed up the ladder and sat on the bed, smiling as she looked all around again before getting back to the white page before her. She wrote a number 1 then tapped the tip of the pen on the paper. "No. Sex." Starting with the most obvious.

She scratched it out and wrote another number 1 only for her brain to refuse anything formulaic. Maybe numbering was putting her in the wrong frame of mind. Not like a list of dos and don'ts, but a list of…ideas. Right. What kind?

Her mind kept returning to his interpretation of BDSM. *Binding, dominating, subduing Ma Petite.* She fanned her face, craving every one of those. Would he be okay with her just taking his ideas? *I just so happen to want what you want.* Likely not. Was there something else she wanted?

Mr. Bishop has not been allowed to touch and taste before. Oh God, that. All that, every bit of it, of him. But what and how? The obvious answer was her becoming his sacrificial sex lamb and the S part of the acronym was all her, it's who she was at her core, she thought. Giving herself to be consumed by him, dear God yes. Yes, a million times.

She aimed her burning revelations at the page, but her hand remained locked with fear. *Do it. Don't think about it, just do it.*

She wrote, *I want Mr. Bishop to….*

She scratched it out and started again. *I want you to let me…*

Again she scratched it out. *I want Mr. Bishop to participate...* Dear God, why couldn't she get this?

She crumpled the paper up tight and started over. *I want to give myself to Mr. Bishop. To do with as he needs.*

She refused her sudden urge to scratch it out. It's what he wanted, and she wanted. She again fanned her face at all the things he might do when fulfilling that. It brought her to the next question of when and where and how often? It was a lifestyle so that meant doing things outside the bedroom. Her heart was back at hammering at that. Him dominating her in any sense at any time was arousing out of her mind.

But what about giving him pleasure? Directly? She was so desperate to do that.

She wrote number two. *I need...* She scratched that.

I have to have your pleasure. That wasn't even proper English. She scribbled it out.

I have to have the ability to give you pleasure. Again, she scratched it out.

You must give me permission to pleasure you. This is not negotiable! She scratched off the exclamation mark, not wanting to seem bossy.

She hadn't really said anything about domination yet and those particulars and he'd definitely want her input.

Her hand trembled in strain from gripping the pen so hard. She let out a frustrated sigh. "Come on," she cried, "you can do this. Like an assignment in class, you've done tons of these."

I want to learn about submission and dominance with *you.* As vague as it was, it was correct. The Bishop side of him had never been allowed to taste and touch and she'd never been touched or tasted except by him.

She ripped the page out and crumpled it, starting over.

I want you to dominate me. Outside the bedroom first, then inside the bedroom. Maybe in degrees? Non-sexual first then sexual. Slowly?

Pure masochism. She never wanted to hurt him or deny him in this. And she'd suffered long enough with denying herself pleasure.

She tore the paper out and crushed it into a tight ball in her hands, throwing it next to the others.

By the time she was done, she had nearly a dozen balls of trials next to her but forgot to put the Bishop in the final draft. His Bishop. No. Her Bishop. She eyed the pile of papers, ready to see what all she'd missed.

The door opened and she gasped in surprise. The sight of him made her forget all about the slop on the bed as delicious perfection in only jeans filled her vision. "I wasn't done," she said, breathless.

He set a bag down and headed her way. Panic hit her and she gathered all her balls of shame, shooting a glance at him. "These are…drafts," she said, yanking the covers over them.

She turned to find him standing right next to the bed, tall enough to cross both his arms on the mattress and stare at the burial. "Ma Petite is hiding her messy process?"

"Very, very messy, yes," she agreed, breathless.

He looked at her for several seconds. "It's the messy process that holds the real truth of things."

Her mouth hung open before she countered with, "You may be right, but I'd rather it in a neat…finished format."

"Neat," he said, eyeing the pile again. "What if I like messy and raw? Real?"

"This is real," she assured, pointing to the tablet glued to her chest. Oh God, he was actually pushing to see it? "I don't want you to see those," she said firmly. "It's like…watching somebody practice singing a song, there's a lot of stalls and voice breaks and *mistakes*."

He was shaking his head slowly at her. "Not the same. There are no mistakes in this, Ma Petite."

"Just read this one." She shoved it at him before he tried to force the issue more.

He took the tablet and she suddenly wanted to snatch it back. Instead, she buried the papers even further under the covers.

"Ma Petite," he muttered softly, already reading.

No time to cringe and worry, he was now looking at her, gaze all burning. "What?" she finally gasped, unable to take his silence. "I put what I want. Like you told me to."

"You did," he said.

What was he surprised about? That she had, or what she wanted. "You don't have to do any of it obviously."

"Obviously," he muttered as if the word didn't begin to apply. He faced away now, reading.

"There's not much there, it's just a start."

"There's a whole *world* here, Ma Petite," he said quietly.

God, what was that tone supposed to mean? It was almost accusing. Threatening. Definitely threatening. "Well, it is a lifestyle and not that I want to be *in* it or *am* into it like some people."

She stared at his gorgeous inked back. Her hands lay in fists in her lap, needing to touch the broad expanse of silky muscle. Lick it. Suck it. Dig her nails in it.

"Mon Dieu," he muttered, like something pained him.

She remembered that meant *My God*. Really? "You can say no," she reminded, trying not to be upset.

He chuckled, his back still turned. "Like hell I can *or* would."

She swallowed, still confused. "What does that mean?"

He turned and she tensed the second his gaze torched her. "It means exactly what it sounds like, Ma Petite." He looked at the tablet. "There's only one part I'm not sure I understand. You want me to dominate you first in non-sexual things." He eyed her with questioning eyes.

"Uhhh, well…" Crap, she hadn't thought of examples. "Just…when you tell me to do things outside the bedroom, I… submit? Do them?"

He gave a half grin that said he was no more informed than before.

"Okay, I clearly didn't think that one through enough," she admitted, pulling her knees to her chest in a choke hold.

"I would love to make suggestions," he said, looking at the paper then back at her again. "But I'll need a little more to go on. Are you wanting a dog and master type of dynamic, Ma Petite?"

"No!" she cried, not even bothering to think.

"I'm not judging you, I'm trying to understand," he said with that sexy grin, placing his arms on the bed while holding the tablet. "There's nothing to be ashamed of with me. You can do no wrong in my eyes with this. And I'm willing to dominate you in and out of the bedroom, in *every* burning degree imaginable, but I need to understand what you want so I can do it perfectly for you."

She was suddenly on fire with that clobbering clarification. "Oh. I think…I may be asking for things I don't know enough about to explain," she said, inadequate shame creeping up her cheeks.

He eyed her in silence until she was breathless.

"Give me the messy truth under the covers Ma-Petite."

Panic returned. "No!"

He tsked at her, his head shaking. "You don't want this." He tossed her the tablet.

"What?"

"I give you one command outside of sex and you tell me no. Either you don't really want it, or it's not something you can do?" He gave a light shrug of indifference. "Maybe you need to think on it some more. I brought the clothes Mah-Mah has for you. Do you want to shower before bed?"

Her heart hammered in her chest, scattering her thoughts. She focused on what he'd first said, her not really wanting it or unable to do it. Dammit! "Fine," she said, even said it while looking right at him. "Yes, I want to shower and yes, you can have my messy process." Before she could change her mind, she yanked the covers back and began scooping them up and dumping them before him, throwing the final few into the pile.

He was grinning at her.

"Now what?" she wondered, trying not to be pissed.

"I think you also need to finish that dynamic, Ma Petite."

"What do you mean?"

"What are the rules of engagement? When does it start and stop? Or does it not? So many questions that need answering," he said, taking hold of her ankles and tugging her toward him. When he had her sitting at the edge of the bed, he lay his head in her lap. "Mmmm," he murmured. "Don't move."

"Nonsexual," she reminded, winded already.

He lifted his boiling stare to her. "Is this sexual to you Ma Petite?"

She gasped, staring at his mouth. "Everything with you is sexual to me."

He straightened and captured her face in his hands, his mouth hungry on hers, tongue lashing. He placed a hand over her butt and jerked her into his chest.

"I need to make you orgasm and I'm not waiting much longer to do it," he said right in her mouth. "Go take your shower and figure that into your dynamic." Both his hands were on her butt now, fingers pressing methodically until she moaned from it.

He pushed away from the bed and turned. "Go before I can't stop. I need you to help control this."

"Okay," she finally said, unlocking her shaky limbs and making her way to the ladder. She paused, eyeing the slide on the other side and crawled over to it. She slid down, unable to stop her laugh then hopped up and walked around him, feeling the burn of his eyes on her. She

She peeked in the bag at the door and picked it up, then turned to find him still watching. "Doing as you said," she informed, hoping he understood she meant submitting. She couldn't take the boil in his stare a second longer and left out, holding on for dear life as she descended the stairs on limp noodle legs.

****

Sahvrin hated to call Jek and ruin the most intoxicating mood he'd ever been in, but he needed to know what was going on. "What's happening?" he asked Jek when he answered.

"Stepping outside," he muttered before giving a low whistle. "Our Katrina was loaded on the information front. "I asked if anybody else knew how to get here and she swears no. Said it took her all day to finally figure it out."

"Yeah, well I don't want anybody else trying that and accidentally getting lucky. She say anything more about our daughter?"

"Tons more," Jek said, making Sahvrin's stomach tense. "You wanna know?"

"Every detail."

"Well," he began, his tone going lighter. "She's super smart with numbers, and I think we know where she gets that. And get this. She's an amazing artist and doesn't even know she inherited that talent. She's obviously beautiful. That screen guard she had on her phone worked," he muttered with a low chuckle. "I probably looked at a hundred pics of her from birth to present. She's fucking amazing, Sahvrin. I'm really sorry we missed all those years though."

"You and me both," he said, still numb about it. "She looks tiny still."

"She is, barely five feet."

He shook his head, dread eating at him. "You think she'll even want to be here? Out here? She doesn't even know us."

"One way to find out. But it's not like we have a choice about it."

"I know. Does Lazure know yet?"

"I updated him with all the information she gave and put it in our group box. Check it when you get a chance."

"We need to get those eyes live on the waterways first thing tomorrow."

"Agreed. After I get Beth situated, we'll go into town and see if we can't arrange a meeting with Thadious tonight."

"Sounds good. We can chat about the details when it's time. You ask about that name Bart gave? The Julien one? And don't forget to give him the maiden name of her mother."

"I will."

"She doing okay with all this?"

"Like an angel."

"Just so you know, I think she's swamp material from what I've seen and heard from Mah-Mah and Lucas. Lucas might be in love," he said in low laughter.

"He better not be," Sahvrin said. "I'd hate to have to maim the adorable fuck."

Jek laughed. "Wait till the women start lining up for that one."

"And the men for Luseah, trust me, I don't look forward to it."

"I just checked on that storm," Jek said. "Looks like it'll turn and hit Alabama and Florida panhandle. But they have another one a week behind it we'll need to get ready for."

"Good. Anything else on her father or family?"

"Check the group chat, Bart put some things in it, nothing that stands out in my mind.

"I will. Looks like Mah-Mah is still bent on this party. That woman," he muttered shaking his head. "At least there won't be a hurricane on top of everything else," Sahvrin said. "Now that we have leverage, we don't want mother nature bringing tide surges that could drown everything."

"You right about that," Jek agreed. "Well, keep your eye on the group chat. Putting everything we find there."

"Will do. Thanks."

"Night bro. Get some sleep. Katrina is tied secure by the way. I'm not taking any chances with her. And uh… you okay?"

"Yeah…just a little numb."

"I hear you man," he said, sounding weighed down.

"What about you? You holding up these days?" Sahvrin realized how long it'd been since they all really connected outside of work.

"I'm good. Hey you remember Shelly? From Breaux's Mart?"

"Yeah, why?"

"I'm dating her."

Sahvrin's brows rose. "For how long?"

"Going on two months."

"Wow! That's a record?"

"Hell yeah it is."

"You must like her," he fished.

Jek gave a deep sigh and Sahvrin's laughter erupted. "That much?"

"Yep. That much."

"Well, damn. Glad to hear it. Now I won't be the only Bishop walking around with an eternal hard on."

Jek laughed at that. "I invited her to the party. I know it's bad timing, but was thinking we could perform…make an impression on our women?"

Sahvrin grinned, never imagining Jek wanting such a thing. "I'd like that."

"I'm sure Beth would too."

"Maybe, yes." He heard her on the stairs. "I gotta go. Talk to you later."

He put his phone on the dresser and headed to the door. Fuck, she was fast. She knocked and he opened it, making her jump. "You don't need to knock, Ma Petite," he said, smiling at whatever she wore. A long white cotton gown with ruffles on the arms and neck. Then he realized it wasn't a gown but a robe. She climbed up the ladder and sat in the bed, then undid the robe and struggled her way carefully out of it. "Glad you're not wearing that in this heat," he said, eager to know what she wore underneath. At glimpsing something red and lace, his cock jerked, and he slowly went to the bed to inspect.

When he stood at the foot, he smiled at how she now hid in the sheet.

"What are you laughing at?" she wondered, worry and offense on her brow.

He met her gaze, sliding his tongue over his lower lip. "I find it...fucking *delicious*," he decided, "how shy you are around me."

He watched his words light her up as she lay down on her back and pressed the covers at her sides while staring at the ceiling. "Well?"

He moved closer to her face, grinning more. "Well, what?"

She covered her face. "Did you read the junk I wrote?"

Shit, right. He went to his desk, sitting.

"What are you doing?"

"Reading them now."

"What?! I left out of here so you could do it!"

He turned with a laugh. "I thought you left to go shower."

"Yes, but it was a two-part...necessity!"

Mon Dieu, he loved this woman. He opened all the balled-up papers while she whined and complained in shock and disbelief. Once he had them open, he put them in a stack and made his way over to her with them."

"What are you doing?" she asked, sounding panicked.

"I'm coming here to read them."

"No!" she cried, horrified. "It's not funny, Sahvrin, please don't! I mean it!"

"Ma Petite," he said, blocking her from trying to grab the pages now. "Lay still." He laughed when she increased her efforts. "Are these your rules of engagement? Am I commanding wrong?"

"Stop teasing!"

Sahvrin's laughter stopped when her sheet fell. She jerked it back up, breathless. "Fine, I'm...apparently not good at this, but neither are you!"

He drew back in surprise. "I gave two very simple commands. Nice ones," he said, wanting her to know they could so easily be otherwise.

Her pretty mouth remained astonished even as her eyes glowed with a million watts of *make me orgasm. S*he slammed herself back down on the bed, staring at the ceiling with a sigh. "Do it then. Read it right in front of me and make me feel stupid, since that's what turns you on."

"Is that what I'm supposed to be doing? Commanding things that turn me on? That's a huge component in this dynamic, Ma Petite. It changes a lot."

"No, it doesn't have to but…I assumed that's the point of the dynamic, to obtain some form of pleasure."

"Ah, I see."

"And not all pleasure is linked directly to your privates."

"With you, I'm afraid it is."

She gasped, lifting her head at him. "I do *not* get horny about everything."

He laughed, putting his forehead on the bed then looked at her. "I meant it's that way for me with you, everything you do is attached to my cock. And," he said, getting serious as he studied her flush cheeks. "Did you not just say before your shower that everything about me is sexual."

"Well, maybe I meant that in reverse."

"Did you?" he decided to ask, remembering he had commands in his arsenal now.

"No," she finally mumbled. "But it applies in reverse."

"Yes, it does." He eyed her sheet cloaked body, hungry. "I'm going to read now, and you'll lay still and be submissive, yes?"

Her eyelids fluttered in a hard eye roll, and he held back his laughter understanding what it was like to be aroused and angry all in one. Such a sexy fucking look on her.

He stared at the single line on the first page, his body locking up with pure lust. He moved to the second page, then the third, and fourth. By the tenth one, his cock had become a raging battering ram. "Ma Petite," he said, finding it difficult to think past his craving to do what she begged for in those papers.

"What?" she asked, her soft voice a mix of shame and arousal.

"I see you tossed the Mean Bishop to the curb?"

"I actually didn't, I had every intention of adding him back in, but the process was long, and I didn't want to keep writing everything over and over while I worked out the more…difficult things. And you shower *very* fast," she said, blaming him.

All he heard was the mean Bishop was the *easy* part for her. And that she asked for him *first,* and on every page after had him in a lust-crazed predicament.

"Obviously, I want him in, he was the first one I wrote. Of course I want him in," she added yet again, her tone tender like she didn't want him to feel left out.

That *beautiful* fucking angel. And hearing her say it all out loud put a burning ache in his balls. "Consider it done, Ma Petite angel," he said, not saying another word until he finished with the rest of her sexual clues. He wanted all of them.

He went to his desk, getting a pen.

"What are you doing?"

"Making notes," he said, returning to the bed, reading through each paper again.

"What kind?"

He circled all the clue words on every page then handed the stack to her."

She took them and sat up, fixing the sheet so it was under both arms, covering her. She went from page to page now. "You circled words."

"It's the main message."

She was quiet as she continued moving through the pages. "I see," she finally said, her answer breathless.

"Tell me."

She flicked a glance at him. "Make, want, I and me, and…Mr. Bishop."

"Put it in order."

She gave a light sigh then hurried through the difficult confession. "I want Mr. Bishop to make me," she said, handing the stack of papers back.

"In degrees," he added, watching her squirm in that sexy shame. "I just want to know *exactly* what you want," he said, being patient. "And it's good you are aware of it too."

"So… now we both know."

He took her hand and pulled it gently to his lips, placing a kiss on the top of it. "Did Ma Petite decide on the rules of engagement yet?"

"I think so," she said, focusing on his mouth on her.

"Let me hear them." He continued rubbing his lips along the soft skin of her hand.

"I can't…think when you're doing that."

He paused the pleasure and lay her hand exactly at her side and waited, head propped on his palm.

"I can't think while you're staring," she complained lightly, bringing his own sigh.

"Do I need to leave?" he wondered, amazed.

"No, just…give me thinking space."

He made his way to the chair at his desk and sat.

"So…" she finally said after a full minute.

"Mon Dieu, just say it Ma Petite," he begged. "It's just words."

"So for when and how long and…behaviors."

He held his tongue, not wanting to interrupt her, but definitely wanting to know what the last one meant. "That can't be all," he finally said when it was obvious she was done.

"Well, no, but it's the gist."

"Ma Petite." He sat forward looking at her laying there still. "I can't know how to do this with gists."

"Well, what particular thing do you need to know?"

"All of them," he said, laughing.

She got on her side, looking at him. "I don't know all of them."

"Well...how will we know what to do?"

"We discuss it and figure it out."

"*You* have to decide this."

She gave a frustrated breath. "Why am I doing all the work?"

"It has to be you to decide."

"Well, fine, I will, but how about you lay some options for me to pick from?"

He realized she couldn't do it because she based all her decisions on the needs of others. He needed to fix that. "Starting with your top priority. You want Mr. Bishop to make you."

"Not...just Mr. Bishop," she corrected, hesitant.

"Okay, you would like Sahvrin and or Mr. Bishop—"

"And or?" she wondered.

"Because you want both, Ma Petite," he gently explained, ready to kick Sahvrin to the curb now that he knew how she felt about Bishop.

"Why are you laughing at me?" she asked, sounding genuinely upset and making him actually laugh.

"I'm not laughing at you, I'm laughing because you're the most amazing and beautiful woman I have ever met. I guess laughing is how I express what you do to me."

The perplexed, worried look on her face was priceless. Like she must be flawed or doing something wrong.

"I've laughed more with Ma Petite than I have all my life, I think." He gave a little shrug, not at all sorry for it. "One day you will be known in the swamps as the angel who raised me from the grave."

The smile that slowly bloomed on her face along with her dreamy look brought his grin. "Okay, so, starting with *when*," she said, her inhibition gone as though raising him from the dead had vanquished them.

"Yes, when," he said, dying to make her orgasm now.

"I think the non-sex stuff can happen...all day."

Before he got excited, he asked, "What exactly happens all day again?"

"You commanding me."

"So now I just need to know what kind of commands you want." He leaned forward in the chair, resting his elbows on his legs, eyeing her.

"Well…maybe just…asking me to do things."

"Things," he said, annoyed with that term. "Like… go work in the garden, woman, go take a shower, feed the chickens?"

"No. Like… things with *you*."

"Ma Petite, you think I'm being intentionally dense?" he asked, at her snippy tone. "I just need examples. Even *one* would help."

"Like…command me to hold your hand or get you a drink of water or run you a bath or… make me give you a massage."

Fascinating. "I just picked up another theme in your list."

"What?" she worried, as if he considered them flaws.

"All of your examples seem to benefit *me*."

She appeared confused. "Well, yes. That's the idea?"

He had to laugh and when he was done, she was back to annoyed. "So, this is all for me?" Why was he surprised? She was his angel.

"The one dominating commands things he wants, and the one submitting gives it and likes giving it. What? Why are you looking like that?"

"I just wonder if Ma Petite has this right and since you've barely touched on it and can hardly remember even that, how about we wait to see what the instructions say. Or suggest."

"What do you think I'm wrong about?" she wondered.

"Well, for one, you seem to be assuming that the one dominating must automatically use that to serve himself and I don't feel like that's right and if it is, I would want to definitely change that to include me commanding things I know you like as well."

She licked her lips, her brows puckered in curiosity. "Like what?"

"Like me commanding you to give yourself an orgasm is the first one that comes to mind."

The desire that lit her face lassoed his cock, forcing him to stretch his leg to make room. "Oh," she said. "I…didn't think of that."

"But you like it."

"Yes," she said after many seconds. "And I like being commanded to… to do things to you."

Fu-ck-ing-Dieu. "I can manage that," he said, already fiercely aware of her desire to give him pleasure. He definitely understood that. "Would Ma Petite ever…care to switch roles?" Because he was sure being commanded sexually by her was somewhere in his fate.

The look of certain calamity on her face as she shook her head cracked him up. "*Pretty* sure commanding isn't something I'm very good at. I can barely manage you commanding *me*."

"We can practice with small things," he said, ready to negotiate or beg. "You commanding me to rub your back or brush your hair."

A smile spread on her pretty lips. "You want to brush my hair?"

"Mon Dieu, yes," he said, feeling like she should know that.

"Okay." Her smile got as big as her blush. "I think I can handle stuff like that."

He was thinking once she got a taste of it, she may be able to handle a lot more. He wasn't really into commanding her outside of sex and he wasn't really into being commanded by her outside of it either. "Would you like to practice right now? Command me to rub your feet?"

He'd take any form of touching her at this point.

She gave a giggle and held her feet up, wiggling her toes. "Sahvrin, come rub my feet."

The bossy way she said it was another clue to her preconceived ideas about dominance and submission. Sounded more like bully and victim to him. He wouldn't be either of those, but he could damn sure dominate her in sex and submit to her sexual commands.

Dieu, that was like getting two heavens.

CHAPTER 18

Beth got up on her elbows, smiling as Sahvrin took her foot and began barely rubbing her feet. "I can't feel it," she laughed.

He didn't answer her as he continued the same.

"Harder," she said with a softening smile, watching him. He obeyed and it sent a thrill through her along with a million other instant ideas. "God that feels good," she said, seriously, wondering how far she should go on the first time.

She smiled feeling mischief. "Kiss my feet."

He took her foot in both hands and held it before him like a sacred object then began placing the softest kisses along the top. Her smile slowly disappeared as she watched his lips on her. God he was such a good kisser. His eyes were closed, and he opened his mouth more, stealing her breath when he began French kissing her foot, his hot tongue licking. Her pulse raced as he moaned like it was turning him on, sucking and nipping at the skin until she felt delirious.

"Stop," she gasped, ready to orgasm if she saw him kissing anything another second.

He obeyed, setting her foot back on the bed, not even looking at her yet. She was frozen with need and how to meet them without doing too much. What she really wanted was to pleasure him, but he never let her. What was she thinking, she had the power to change that. She could make him let her. And make him…not touch her while she did, as hard as that would be for her. And him.

What if she commanded him to pleasure himself?

Oh God, yes.

"Go get the chair and put it there." She pointed to the middle of the floor where she could see him.

He rolled his eyes to her for a burning two seconds then did as she said. It was official. She definitely liked commanding him.

"Take off your pants."

****

Sahvrin almost choked on shock, never guessing she'd have the courage to command that. His pulse hammered in his cock as he hurried to obey before she got cold feet.

Standing obediently in his underwear, he waited.

"Sit in the chair."

He did, then leaned back, putting his ass at the edge. He propped his heels on the chair legs, opened his knees and rested both hands between his thighs, waiting. But Mon Dieu, he could come under that hot gaze of hers.

She licked her lips, telling him she'd just stumbled into something delectable. Soon, it wasn't just desire in her eyes, but a current of heat that sent anticipation riding his spine. Judging by the delay, this next command was hard for her. He silently willed her the courage to say it.

"Touch it."

The whisper shot out like a whip aimed at his cock. He wasn't about to ask for specifics. He slowly moved his hand over the length, pressing as he did. Her eyes were locked on what he was doing.

"Both hands," she added, breathless.

He groaned, reaching between his legs and cupping his balls while sliding his hand along the length. She watched from on her elbow, her lips parted, eyes like a fire on him.

He opened his legs more, pressing his fingers into his balls while grabbing his length in his fist.

"Take it off."

****

Beth swallowed and licked her lips, nearly panting as he stood, doing as she said. She gasped when his cock sprang free from his underwear, terrifyingly huge. He returned to his position and opened his legs nice and wide, placing his heels back on the legs of the chair. This time he grabbed his cock at the base and held it in his fist, as if wanting her to see how huge and tall it was. Noted. Very huge and very tall. She couldn't stop her moan as he moved his hand slowly up the length, his fingers stroking over his balls again. Oh God she wanted to suck him so bad. Maybe next time she'd have the nerve.

She was desperate to touch herself while watching him. What an orgasm that would be. His breaths thickened and his mouth opened a little when his fist circled the head. She moved her eyes along his abs and chest, terrified to look at him, knowing he watched her watching him. But she had to, his gaze was magnetizing, pulling it to hers. When their eyes locked, she gave another moan. The boil in his stare burned her clit making it ache. She should command him but wasn't sure how now.

She wanted to make him come, see how he looked in an orgasm. "Come for me," she quickly said before she chickened out.

His head dropped back with his eyes closed, breaths strained and hissing as he opened even wider. He moved his fist faster along his cock the muscles in his abs and arms flexing. So beautiful, oh yes. He brought his head forward, his moans thick now as he sped up, watching himself.

"Oh God, yes," she gasped when he reached farther between his legs, those beautiful fingers sinking into his balls and a little beneath.

"Beth," he gasped, his head going back again. She sat up, panting as his hips rolled hard with his orgasm.

"Oh my God," she whispered, devouring the sight of his cum jetting on his stomach in powerful spurts, all over his lickable muscles. His eyes remained clenched tight for endless seconds before harsh groans strained out of him. She had to kiss him when he did that next time.

Her heart pounded fiercely when his hand finally slowed along his cock while his body heaved with deep breaths. His fingers were still pressed into his balls, moving softly and she noted their location, wanting to know every spot on him that gave him extreme pleasure.

His head finally came forward and she swallowed, bracing for the sure lock of his gaze on hers. Nothing could really prepare her and when it did, she literally moaned at the potent look he wore. His chest still rose and fell, and his cock lay almost asleep in the crook of his one opened leg. She'd never imagined a man could be so, so, sexy.

His brows rose a little and she realized he waited for a command. "Uh…get dressed," she said, her mouth dry as he slowly stood. He turned and went to his dresser, giving her another amazing show of his backside. Dear, dear, sweet saints, he was insanely beautiful. His muscular legs, his *butt*. Perfect. But his back was a panty-melter. Maybe it was the tattoo. She wanted to touch that so much. Up close with her lips and tongue. So much she wanted to do to him and with him.

He turned, wiping himself with a t-shirt, boldly cleaning himself. How did he have zero inhibitions in this? She envied his confidence, unable to imagine doing it. She could barely manage him seeing her with the light on. He was like a wild animal, never learning any shame and she was very grateful for that.

"Ma Petite is going to get my cock hard again if she keeps devouring me with her pretty eyes."

She met his gaze, heat flooding her clit and cheeks instantly. "I…" she almost apologized. "You're so beautiful," she said, wanting him to hear it from her. She never wanted to regret not telling him what burned in her heart and mind. And body.

He made his way to the chair and fetched his underwear and sat. She watched him casually put them on as if nobody else was there. He stood and turned, depriving her of seeing what him putting his glorious cock away looked like. She could have commanded him to let her see. She really needed to learn to use that.

He turned and made his way to the bed like a tidal wave of sex appeal about to crash down on her. She braced again. She did that a lot with him. He held so much power over her without trying, it was exhilarating. He put his forearms on the mattress, trapping her in his gaze now, two feet away. "How did I do?"

"Amazing," she said, wetting her lips and staring at his sexy mouth, tugging with a smile.

"I had a good master." His eyes lowered to her mouth and her lips parted.

"I was terrible," she said, bringing his seductive gaze back to hers as he gave her a slow headshake.

"I tremble to imagine what you will do to me when you get some backbone."

Tremble. Hard to imagine him trembling for anything. Right now, she was conflicted with fear of him commanding her. She wanted it so bad but wouldn't ask, she couldn't. She would masturbate later while he slept.

A sudden light flashed, followed by a rolling thunder a few seconds later. "Where are you sleeping?" she wondered.

He took hold of her face and pulled her to his mouth, the firm tug making her clit tingle. He was going to make an amazing dominant. He already did. His lips were tender on hers, pressing softly at many angles like he wanted to feel them every which way. "With Ma Petite, if she can agree not to rape me."

She couldn't stop her laugh at his mouth, closing her eyes at the amazing feeling of his fingers stroking along her face. "I promise," she said, so glad he would.

"And if you agree that tomorrow, I get to command Ma Petite the same way she commanded me."

Her excitement shot out in a slight moan, bringing his hand behind her neck for a deeper kiss. "Yes," she remembered to answer, sliding her fingers along his jaw, feeling it open and close with his devouring kiss. "I need it," she gasped in his mouth, too desperate to care.

"Undress."

The command was so hot and harsh it made her moan again, as if he'd touched her. She moved the sheet and his hand shot out, stopping her. His Mah-Mah had snuck in a naughty sheer red top and bottom.

"Don't fucking undress," he said, his breath rushing out at seeing the sheer panties next. Placing his hand on her outer thigh, he turned her toward him, so her legs hung over the edge. He shoved her knees open, setting off her gasps and moans before he even started. He stared between her legs, a hungry groan leaving his sexy, parted lips.

He took hold of the panties and yanked them down, the bite of material making her delirious. "Sahvrin," she panted when he pushed her legs back open and stared right at her pussy.

He looked right at her now. "Who are you fucking wet for?"

Oh God. Soft moans came on every breath. "Bishop. I'm wet for Bishop."

He placed her left foot on the edge of the mattress then the other. He worked his fingers under her ass and lifted her pussy up.

"Bishop," she panted again, shame and desire battling it out as he kissed slowly along her inner thigh. She couldn't keep from watching as he slid his nose right between her folds, his breaths thick with sounds of lust making everything throb. Already her legs trembled, desperate. The tip of his nose pressed against her clit, right as his tongue licked at her entrance. "Oh my God," she gasped, heat flooding her privates and making her reach for more already. His fingers dug into her upper butt as he pressed his mouth harder against her, groaning as he tongued her. His nose randomly pressed her clit, driving her crazy and forcing her to reach harder, twirling and flicking for more friction.

She gasped when he moved to her clit, his breaths ragged and hungry as he opened her pussy lips so wide with his thumbs. "Oh please," she shot out dropping her head back and rocking against the gentle suction. "Don't stop, I'm begging, don't. Oh God."

He answered with a harsh groan, then slid one of his thumbs in her pussy, moving it in and out, matching the rhythm of his suction. "Oh God, Bishop," she called, clutching and pulling his hair, pumping her hips faster. Her moans turned into cries of "Oh God, oh God, oh God" higher and higher. "I'm coming, I'm coming!" He held tighter, his strained moans vibrating on her pussy as she bucked and shuddered without a bit of shame.

His mouth finally turned soft, his tongue licking gently now. The sounds he still made against her was like its very own sex. She ran her fingers through his silky thick hair, staring at how sexy he looked with his face between her legs, hands still holding her up. He continued his leisure lapping with soft French words fluttering hot against her. When he lowered her butt to the bed, he stared at what he'd feasted on. The back and forth gliding of his warm hands on her inner thighs spread a tingle through her till she smiled.

She watched him slide his mouth on her left then right leg and realized he'd just wiped himself on her. For some reason it made her smile more. "I'm your napkin?"

He promptly returned to the same spot, French kissing the area. Her smile faded at how his jaw moved with his sexy mouth opening and closing with sucks and tongue-twirling on her skin. Winded, he did the exact same to the other thigh before finishing with a gentle kiss on both. Mercy, she was back at breathless. "All clean." He straightened and closed her legs with a reverence before returning them to the bed. She quickly scooted over so he could climb in with her but instead he headed to the door. Her stomach tensed then loosened when he hit the lights.

****

Sahvrin considered getting on his knees like he used to do as a little boy to thank God for His Petite begging for that. Mon Dieu, going slow with her was going to be some kind of heaven he'd never imagined suffering. And not only did she invite the Bishop to play, she'd put him first. Now he waited with wicked cravings locked and loaded on his sweet angel.

He'd intended to sleep on the floor but after seeing the fear in her face when the thunder struck reminded him storms were a trigger for her. Might always be since she was in the jaws of one when he rescued her. Climbing the ladder, he crawled in next to her, careful not to touch the wrong things, lest he lose what little control he had.

She turned on her side and pressed her forehead against his shoulder and laced her fingers in his.

The sweet gesture stirred his violent protective instincts and he reached with his other hand, stroking her head and along her face. Her soft moan came as she wrapped both her arms around his, holding it close to her.

"Ma Petite?" he said, fighting not to feel everything pressing into his arm.

"Hmm?"

"Do you recall a person by the name of Julian Abshire?"

She hesitated then whispered, "Yeah, why?"

Tension gripped his muscles as he continued stroking her forehead. "His name keeps coming up in our recon. Who is he to you?"

"He was…a very annoying person."

"How was he annoying," he wondered.

"Like a stalker kind of annoying. Why?"

Stalker. "I was told to ask you if you knew the name. I'll find out." He wasn't about to have her thinking of that before sleep. "Stalker, huh?"

She stroked his arm with her fingers, and he felt her nod. "Level ten."

"What is that to you?"

"When you can't take no for an answer and keep hounding a person."

"Did you date him?"

"Very briefly. Up until he wanted to break the sex rules."

Sahvrin turned on his side, facing her. He slid his finger along her face then pushed her long hair off her shoulder, his protective urges biting down.

"Why would his name be coming up," she wondered quietly. "You think he's involved? I wouldn't put it past him if he was. He was a real player, that one. Thought I was the most beautiful woman he'd ever seen and that I should be a model."

Fuck. That was a match. "Turn over, Ma Petite."

After a moment, she did and he pulled her into his body, draping his arm over her chest. She wrapped her hands around it and snuggled her mouth against it. Needing her closer, he covered her legs with his, resisting his cock's need to push against her ass. He couldn't wake her *beautiful* appetite it was more lethal to him than his own.

"I meant to ask…" he said, rubbing his lips on her shoulder. "What's your mother's maiden name?"

She gave a small moan. "Sweetling. Amelia Sweetling."

"Her maiden name?"

"Mmhm. Isn't that cool?" she murmured around a yawn. "They had the same last names."

Cool wasn't the term that came to mind.

"Sahvrin?"

He sucked in a breath and opened his eyes, realizing he'd drifted off. "What?"

"Your phone is chirping," she mumbled next to him. "Might be important."

He got up on his elbow, glancing at the lit screen on the dresser. Shit, what time was it? He leaned and kissed her temple several times then quietly hopped down onto the floor. At his dresser, he picked up his phone, squinting a little as he unlocked the screen. Eleven thirty. Perfect timing.

Jek's name was first, and he opened his box. *Kattrina's getting texts from Savvie. She wants to text her, said she's worried and scared.*

Shit.

"Everything okay?"

He made his way back to the bed, standing next to it as he texted him back. "Savvie is texting her mother, worried. She wants to text back but…"

"Oh no, that's terrible," she said. "You think they'll get suspicious if she doesn't text her?"

"Maybe." He dialed Jek's number and the moment he picked up, he moved the phone from his ear at encountering Katrina's pissed screaming. "Jek?" Sahvrin called over the racket.

"Just gag her!" Jek yelled.

"I'm trying!"

Sounded like Bart. "Does she need a sedative?" Sahvrin asked. "I'll call Mah-Mah."

"So she can spit it in my eye?" Jek said, sounding like she'd done that already.

"I'll have her put it in a syringe."

"Good. Have her bring something for a bite. She bit Zep."

"Why the fuck she do that?"

"He pissed her off is her reason. He told her the truth and she couldn't handle it Zep said."

He didn't even want to know. "What about Savvie, what do you think we should do?"

"Was hoping you had ideas. Not texting seems like a bad one."

Sahvrin went over several scenarios, not liking any of them. "I'm coming. I'll call Mah-Mah first. You ready?"

"Yeah, very," he said, like he'd rather fight a legion of demons than deal with Katrina.

The hell was going on down there?

"You have to go?"

He turned, finding His Petite up on her elbow.

He walked over and stroked her face. "I do have to go. I have land business with my brothers tonight. Would you like to come downstairs? I can get Luseah to stay with you."

The look on her face brought his anger. "What? Did Luseah say something or do something stupid?"

She barely shook her head. "But…she doesn't like me for some reason."

"What the fuck she do, why didn't you tell me?" The look of sick worry on her face brought his lips to hers. "I'm sorry, I'm not mad at you."

"She's just a child," she said. "Your Aunt said she's just jealous and would get over it. I'd rather not force anything. But Lucas was very nice to me," she assured, as though that would salvage something with his bratty sister. It wouldn't.

"I'll get him to wait with you, then."

"I can probably manage fine by myself. In here."

He pulled her mouth to his again. "No. And sorry angel, that's a command."

The soft press of her fingers on his face called up all that heaven she offered. He took her hand and held those fingers on his lips. "Okay," she whispered finally.

He remembered her need for Bishop and again pulled her to his mouth, a rush of lust making him groan. "When I get back," he said, holding tight to her jaw before releasing it to caress her neck. "Bishop wants you all to himself."

Desire made her breaths shake and he gripped her jaw again too hard, kissing her with a buried lust that commanded His Petites. Mon Dieu, she was a moldable fire in his hands, begging to be shaped by him. He just had to make damn sure not to hurt her in those flames.

CHAPTER 19

Sahvrin swung his leg over his Land Dragon and gripped the black leather-clad horned-handles. His moss-colored iron beast met his ass and cock like an eager sex slave and that's what set her apart from his Swamp Dragon. When he woke her, she greeted him with growling cock-teasing breaths, and when he opened her up, Mon Dieu, she fucked him like a wild beast. In his celibate world, she was the only one he let turn him on.

The sudden idea of having another seat custom made that fit him *and* His Petite sent a hot current through his balls. He could customize it so she orgasmed on every ride with her tits pressed into his back and arms wrapping him tight. Mon fucking Dieu, clear his schedule, he must create that.

"We got four Bayou Bishops headin' to a pack of demon Roulettes," Zep said with a happy grin. "Sounds like an unfair fight."

Sahvrin stomped down on his beast's kicker. "Time to wake, Ma Belle Noir." She greeted him with a greedy rumble as he worked his hips for that perfect fit in her tight mouth. The night was just right for a free ride on the back roads to town which allowed them to forego the black wide-brimmed hats for Swamp Crushers.

"We goin' cold?" Jek asked on the mic.

"We'll stop at the weapons room and pick up some knuckle busters just in case."

"That's it?"

Sahvrin belted a few barks out of Belle Noir. "Our leverage is more lethal than any heat we could carry."

"Alright," he said, like he hoped he was right.

"If it gets messy, we fight our way out."

"Yeaaahhhh," Zep said with a sadistic glee and "Laissez les bons temps rouler!"

The blood lust festering in Sahvrin since he'd found His Petite roiled with excitement. "Just remember we're not there to start a fight. But if they start it, we kill 'em."

****

Once in town, the festival crowds began to thicken and Sahvrin let Belle Noir clear a path with her thunderous pops. His brothers' dragons joined in, creating a carpet bomb of air-shaking rumbles across several blocks.

It didn't matter the gender or the age, everybody stopped and awed at their Land Dragons. Being the festival, they cheered and did other things His Petite wouldn't like. But his brothers revved their beasts in appreciation, inviting more of the tit show.

Sahvrin switched his blue tooth to intercom. "Lot of young kids in this crowd."

"Yeah, yeah," Zep muttered. "Celibate Sahvrin with the perfect girlfriend wants everybody to be a fuckn' saint."

Sahvrin couldn't resist a grin. "Maybe I'll inspire you to put an end to that cock-rage-war you all up in."

"Or not."

Sahvrin revved Belle Noir, letting her roars beat against her iron lungs. "Keep your dick in for this ride," he said. "You can see tits anytime."

There was no parking near the packed-out Roulettes. The amount of leather in the crowd meant other chapters were likely there for the festival, so parking a block away was as good as it got.

"Set your Dragon alarms to five," he said, climbing off Belle Noir. The modified boat horns he'd installed on their bikes were an auditory killer. Unless you were deaf, level five was like getting a magnified alligator bellow right in the eardrum. .

"I don't like leaving Fer-Noir this far out," August said.

"Make sure your app is on for any alarm alerts. Trust me, Mon Frere, nobody will fuck with her."

They got the usual stares as the four of them made their way in Bishop attire to the front entrance of the club where the deep thumping said a live band played inside.

As fate would have it, the same Mr. T dude from their previous meeting stood at the door, checking membership.

When he saw them approaching, he ducked his head to the guy next to him, sending him inside. They got to Mr. T who acted like they'd pulled Judges on him a week before and now he was ready to even the score. Sahvrin walked up and leaned in his face. "Tell *Thadious* the Bishops are here to speak to him."

"Already *announced* you." The ground words barely managed to escape the fury of his tight lips.

"Very good," Sahvrin praised like he would any dog, adding swamp swagger to his grin. The amount of adrenalin humming in his blood said vengeance had drawn its bow across every muscle in his body.

Another Jethro giant appeared at the door, looking around then eying them with a nod. "Follow me."

Sahvrin stared into Mr. T's eyes as he passed, letting him know his bloodlust burned hotter than his, before heading inside. The six-foot giant led them upstairs to a guarded door that opened when he arrived.

Sahvrin quickly estimated about twenty males and twice as many women packed in the private barroom. He eyed some of those women and his blood burned at seeing most were teenagers. His escort led them to a corner with a large round table where Thadious and four other men sat, two teenagers for each sick fuck.

"Well, well, well," Thadious said sending the girls off. A good thing since Sahvrin couldn't think around the urge to say fuck deals let's just kill. "What can I do for the Royal Kings of the Swamp?"

"Here to negotiate," he said, eying the other men at the table, wondering who they were.

"Where's ole *Lazure,*" he said with that tight smile, dragging his father's name along Sahvrin's raw nerves. "Where's the *First Bishop.*" His glossy eyes lowered down him then back up. "You come to shoot me in my own club?" He spasmed out a laugh that nobody shared and Sahvrin showed he was unarmed as did his brothers.

"Wanna' make a deal."

"And what if I don't wanna make a deal with you?" he sneered.

Sahvrin stared at him long and hard. "Then I'll skip the middleman and do business with the Diablos De La Guerra myself."

A dark coldness settled over Thadious's face.

"What kind of deal you wanna make?" the man on his right asked.

Sahvrin turned. "Who might you be?"

The man's laugh never reached his eyes, now locked on him. "Remy Dupre. President of the New Orleans Roulettes."

Sahvrin eyed his extended hand then raised his gaze back up, right as it hit his brain like a bomb that his daughter might be there in this filth. "I want three things," he said, his rage at a dead calm.

The man shrugged and spread his arms out with the arrogance befitting a child-fucker. "Name it. There's plenty to go around. How much you want?"

Sahvrin's tongue moved slowly in his mouth before his jaw finally unhinged. "I want a woman, her daughter, and a fight."

A brief silence passed before Remy glanced around the table then back at him. "That's it?"

"That's it."

He leaned back, grinning, then spread his arms. "There's plenty of that to pick from but something tells me you have a particular favorite?"

"The woman you sent to my swamps to fuck me for that deal I'm here making. And her daughter."

The mirth in Remy's eyes cooled. "You want my woman and my daughter?"

Sahvrin couldn't have enjoyed hearing him say those words more. "Not *your* daughter. *My* daughter. I'm Sahvrin Wolfgang Bishop. She's Savvie Wolf Bishop. You want my dot-connecting skills, Mon Ami?"

To see the raw bloodlust in his gaze brought Sahvrin's smile. "It's not often a man gets to decide his fate, but tonight, yours and all your brothers is in your hands. But the clocks ticking while the Swamp Horde awaits your answer. You livin'? Or you dyin' at the hands of The Diablos De La Guerra you've *both* signed contracts with?"

Sahvrin stared at him, his smile big enough for all of them.

"What kind of *fight*," Remy asked, biting the bait.

"Fifty of mine against fifty of yours. I pick the place, you just show up. No lethals. We fight till you can't get up."

The cockiness eased back into Remy's gaze. "How about we fight to the death? Unless you're afraid to die."

Sahvrin let himself laugh before shaking his head at him. "And how you plan on dealing arms from the grave, Mon Ami?"

Remy stared at him, rage making his upper lip twitch as he leaned forward with a low, "How do *you* plan to?"

Sahvrin slammed his palm on the table. "Then we fight to the death and figure the rest out later, qui?" He regarded Thadious who looked like a bulldog on a short leash then back to Remy.

The cold calculations in the depths of his stare could only mean good things. "Sure," he said, his voice hard. "And you can have the mother as down payment, but Savvie stays with me until you make good on this fight."

"No *fucking* deal," Sahvrin said, his voice matching his. "Your whore and my daughter I get this very night, or you're done. The fight is lagniappe for both of us. You get the chance to gain all of it back with this bat-tie, yes? You kill me and all mine, and I agree to give you the keys to every waterway in that swamp. And if you lose, well… I win everything."

Remy leaned forward and jabbed his pointer finger on the table. "*I* keep Savvie till the fight. You can have her *if* you win."

"No-no-no-no-no," Sahvrin assured, his rage back at calm. "You give me my daughter *this* fucking night, or you will *never* enter my swamps."

"Brother, if she's not your daughter..." Thadious muttered, earning Remy's fist slamming the table next to him.

"*Shut* your mouth, you fat, *dumb,* motherfucker." He pointed in his face, his breaths seething. "*You're* the reason this shit is at our door."

Thadious's hands raised in deference, his head even bowing a little like a bad dog.

"I tell you what, Mon Ami. I will fight you this night, here on your turf. No weapons but our fists. Last man standing gets the right to the girl tonight?"

The offer brought the man to his feet. "You got yourself a fucking deal." He glanced back at Thadious. "Downstairs. Clear a spot." He removed his jacket, eyeing Sahvrin with a lusty grin. "Hell, let em' place bets."

Sahvrin's adrenalin hammered as he gave a light shrug. "Waste not, want not," he said, following the demon out the room.

"You sure about this?" Jek murmured as they headed down. "I mean on their turf?"

"I'm sure I'm going to knock his fucking teeth in and get my daughter. Let our Freres know to get ready to fight."

Downstairs, the band stopped playing and a voice boomed out, "Ladies and coonasses...can I have your attention." It was Thadious, passing his fat ringed fingers over his head as if he had hair, grin as shit-eating as ever. "Tonight, we have a special treat for you. Something we haven't done before but hell, if it turns out you all like it, then why not do it again?"

So, *clear the floor* meant *mop up.*

"For the first time ever, here and only here at the Breaux Bridge *Roulettes*, we're gonna have ourselves an old fashioned *fight.*"

The cheers erupted and he laughed, nodding with glee. "Two men will fight till knock-out. No lethals and no weapons but their fists. Tonight, we'll let those who want to stay and watch place $20.00 bets. Those who bet on the winner split the winnings after ten percent goes to The Roulette." He pointed right. "Marie at the back will take your name and money. Fight starts in thirty minutes!"

Sahvrin removed his coat and handed it to Jek then worked on his shirt buttons.

"He made a quick buck off of that one," Jek muttered, pulling out his wallet.

"What are you doing?" Sahvrin wondered.

He paused, eying him. "Betting. We're watching," he said.

Sahvrin handed him his shirt next, stretching his neck while eying his own money scheming brother. "The winnings go to charity."

He glanced at Remy's ripped torso covered in tattoos.

"Hello Lord Dumb Bells," Zep muttered. "Hailing from the New Orleans Gym For Pussies."

"Be sure and sand the floor with those cattle guard abs," August added with a low chuckle.

"Remember that seven-hundred-pound alligator you knocked out?" Jek said next to Sahvrin's ear. "Take your time and make it last. Don't wanna scare them away from the war you brilliantly talked them into."

Sahvrin met his grin with his own. "You like that?"

He answered with shuddering orgasmic sounds.

"Is that Savvie?" Zep wondered, nodding.

Sahvrin turned and his heart lurched at seeing her in the flesh. "Holy fuck."

"That's what you're fighting for," August reminded him.

"Fuck," Sahvrin muttered.

Jek leaned in. "What?"

"She's watching," Sahvrin realized.

Zep moved closer. "You ain't nervous, are you?"

"I'm about to beat the shit out of the man she thinks is her dad."

"Ohhhhh," August whispered, while Zep hissed and Jek added a holy shiiiit, right.

"Maybe go easy on him, go slow," August suggested.

"Nah," Zep said. "You need to make it quick as much as I want it to last and last."

He was right. There was no way he was going to force his daughter to watch him beat the man she thought was her father. She'd hate him.

"She might not even wanna leave with us," Zep said quietly.

"Yeah, shit, you're right," Jek agreed. "Maybe we can call Katrina, let her talk to her."

Yeah. Let her lying mother fix that shit.

"What move you gonna use?" Jek asked, eager now.

"Won't know till I see him dance," Sahvrin said, deciding to remove his boots and socks too. Slippery footing was always a problem with alligator wrangling, and if he was going to make it quick, he'd want grip. The knocking out part could be done with a choke hold. His bloodlust frothed at the idea he'd not get many licks on him.

Sahvrin watched Remy talk to Savvie. The expressions on her face started with confusion then went to worry. Her eyes found Sahvrin, and he was stuck in her stare, wishing he knew what he'd told her. Remy yelled at her, and she jumped, snapping her attention back to her warden in obvious fear. But then he grabbed her shoulder and she winched in pain, causing his revenge to boil with new fucking plans.

"Fighters, meet in the circle and shake hands," Thadious boomed, getting a glare from Remy. "Or just meet in the circle," he said, his spazzy laugh like an auditory buckshot across the room.

Entering the circle, Remy moved into a standard boxer's stance.

"Fight!" Thadious yelled.

Sahvrin staggered his feet with his hands up, palms open, watching for that telling twitch. Remy faked a few punches then finally threw a hard right. Sahvrin dodged it while shoving Remy's arm down, putting his face in the path of his thrusting knee. The blow staggered him sideways, and he grabbed an arm, sweeping his leg, then moved straight into a shoulder breaking lock on the floor. Remy erupted in bellowing yells, banging his free arm as his body bowed from the excruciating pain.

Sahvrin released him and jumped back up, letting him get to his feet. "Come on," he called, craving his blood as he kept him in his kill zone. "You like to scare little girls? That makes you feel like a man?" Sahvrin threw a punch, connecting with his jaw. His head snapped back, and he came at him in a rage. Sahvrin side stepped, bringing his foot into his stomach then grabbed his head and rammed it three times into his knee before shoving him off.

Remy staggered back into the crowd, holding his gushing nose while angling his head at him. He shoved people as he came back in the circle with his fists up, same boxing stance. Sahvrin faked left, then right, making him flinch. "You scared, man? Come on. Come on."

He ran again and tackled Sahvrin to the floor. His knee found his ribs once and Sahvrin spun out from under him and flipped him onto his upper back, putting a lock on his leg. Again he yelled and hit the floor with a fist while Sahvrin put more pressure on it, coming just shy of snapping it over and over.

After he screamed enough, he let go and nailed him in the nose with an elbow before jumping to his feet.

Remy fought to get up, but his leg was useless now. Sahvrin walked up to him and slapped him across the face with his open hand. "Come on, King Cock, that all you got?"

On his one good knee, Remy lunged, getting the heel of Sahvrin's foot in his chest. He followed him to the floor again and put his arm in a lock, pulling till he got those toe-curling screams of agony. This time, he yanked till he got a loud crack. The crowd erupted in shocked gasps and yells, while Remy roared in agony.

Sahvrin got up. "Come on, get up!" he yelled. "You like to fuck little girls, you like to sell them?"

Sahvrin's rage was at more, more, more blood. He grabbed the back of his head and held tight, slamming his fist into his face without stopping.

The crowd erupted in yells and Sahvrin didn't quit even when his brothers tried to rip him off of him.

Arms came up under his, yanking him away. "You're gonna fucking kill him!"

"I want to fucking kill him," he roared.

"Think of Savvie!" he yelled back, dragging him away.

The yelling around them became deafening as fighting broke out.

"I got Savvie!" He thought it was August he heard over the noise and spun around. Spotting them, he hurried over, grabbing her by the arm and pushing through the madness in the direction of the exit.

Savvie got ripped from his hold by falling bodies then August snatched her arm, pushing and kicking his way forward with Sahvrin and Jek catching up. They all made it out the door except Sahvrin now blocked by Mr. T, filling the entrance. The second his wild gaze landed on Sahvrin, the bloodlust they'd shared roared back with the giant coming for him. Before he got stuck in his kill zone, Sahvrin shot his leg out and slammed his heel into his knee, bending him just enough to bring that big head in reach. Sahvrin swung three rapid hammer punches at his temple, staggering him back. He ran at him before he got his balance and plowed his left shoulder into his hip, bringing the fat bastard to the ground on his stomach. Sahvrin scrambled onto his back and grabbed under his meaty jaw, yanking back hard. He yelled as he pulled with all his strength, ready to snap his fucking spine.

Jek appeared out of nowhere, knuckle busters plowing into Mr. T's face till he went limp.

"Sahvrin!"

Sahvrin staggered up, looking around and got a fist to the side of the head. He spun and latched on to the first neck he could reach and yanked down, slamming the dude's face into his knee. Fists and boots came from every direction, beating him down to the ground. He rolled hard left then right, grabbing a leg and pulling.

The loud chirps of police vehicles rose above the chaos and bodies ran in different directions while Sahvrin made his way to his feet searching frantically for his daughter.

"Sahvrin!"

He spotted Jek and his brothers at the edge of the crowd leaving with Savvie. He ran to catch up, racing down the sidewalk with them.

"I called Katrina," Jek said, winded. "She talked to Savvie and told her we're taking her to her."

"She'll have to ride with you," Sahvrin said out of breath, remembering his single seat. He wiped blood from his right eye then helped her on Jek's bike, putting a helmet on her. "Hold on tight. Understand?"

She nodded and he climbed on his own bike, glancing at August and Zep finding only scrapes and bruises on them. He stomped down on his kicker and let Bell Noir bark with thunder. His brothers' bikes joined in as they made their way in the opposite direction of the mess behind them.

With his daughter. Mon Dieu, he fucking had his daughter.

CHAPTER 20

Until Katrina explained the truth to Savvie, he avoided talking to her, worried he'd say the wrong fucking thing. He texted the group box and let his brothers know not to say a word till he talked to Katrina.

By the time they made it back, it was nearly two in the morning and Katrina, Lucas and Beth were waiting on the dock. One look at His Petite sent a crippling hunger through his muscles. After docking, he watched Savvie run to her mother and embrace her. A pang of envy cut him at their bond while at the same time glad she had her for that. Maybe even shocked to see Katrina being that kind of mother. She'd assured him she was different, but he hadn't put an ounce of belief in her self-proclaimed mother superiorness. But he'd happily be wrong about that.

"Thank you Sahvrin," Savvie called with a smile and wave before hurrying down the dock with Katrina and his brothers.

He finally turned to His Petite who still smiled happily at the leaving procession. He pulled her in his arms but held himself back from kissing her. "What did you do while I was gone, Ma Petite?"

"Nothing but missed you," she said with the sweetest look he'd ever seen. "Where is your shirt?" she wondered, her hands roaming all over his chest. "And how did you get your daughter? I can't wait to hear about--"

He kissed her, letting his hunger loose. The delicate, eager dance of her tongue along his and her shallow breaths drew his moan. "Ma Petite is so fucking hungry," he shuddered as she raked her nails in his scalp with a gasped *yes*.

"I need you."

The tiny words engulfed him in flames. He gripped her face in his hands, kissing her deeper with a painful groan. "I'm going to make you come so hard, Angel," he swore. "And then I'll force you to bring my orgasm."

"Oh God, yes," she cried weakly, her arms holding on to his neck.

He finally set her before him, making sure she wouldn't fall while grinning at her. "Should I carry you?"

She gave a flustered half laugh. "I think I can float there on this cloud I'm on."

Sahvrin's laugh broke the night, reminding him of His Petites special power over him. He stroked her face with both hands, kissing her forehead and eyes and cheeks.

Her nails raked in his head again, her kisses back to explosive. She broke away, breathless and grabbed his hand, pulling him down the dock now.

"Ma Petite," he laughed. "You're commanding now?"

"At least till we get to the bedroom!"

True to her words, when they entered his room and he shut the door, he found her waiting several feet away like a good Petite Ange. He locked the door and turned.

"Oh my God, what happened to your face?"

She hurried to him, and he winced at the prodding of her fingers on his cheek. "I'll tell you later," he said, not wanting her distracted.

"Are you okay? Is that all that's wrong?" She looked along his body.

He headed for his dresser. "Just a few bruises here and there. Nothing a shower can't fix."

"Your *back*," she shrilled, those soft hands on him again. He closed his eyes at how good it felt. "Maybe I don't want to know what happened."

The sound of her anguish only got him harder. She was before him now, kissing along tender spots on his chest. "I'll see you after your shower?"

"Yes ma'am you will," he muttered, watching her mouth on him. She seemed to realize he was prepared to let her do that all night and stepped back.

He headed for the door while he had the willpower.

"Do you want help?" she asked when he was about to shut it.

He paused for many burning seconds. "You'll help me after," he promised, leaving out.

****

Beth paced in the room while waiting for Sahvrin, unable to be still. Oh, God, she was waiting for Bishop, she remembered. She kept it to a slow stroll, not wanting to break a sweat and start stinking. He'd want to do things that required being clean. God, she couldn't even say the things in her own mind. Really time she loosened up about that. Like him, he was so…confident and sexy and had zero shame. How lucky.

She paused and raced to the bed at hearing him on the stairs. She stumbled out her pajama pants and ripped off the shirt and sports bra, looking around for a place to put it. She stuffed them in one of the boat windows and ran up the ladder, scrambling under the covers. Lying flat and winded, she worked the panties off under the covers then looked around for a spot to put them. She stuffed them at the foot of the bed under the covers and got back in her place, an eager, out of breath sacrifice. No, submissionist. Submissionary. Submiticist. She snickered at herself, and the door opened. Her nosy brain brought her head up to see him.

He was closing the door and she couldn't stop her, "Oh my God, it's getting worse," at seeing the bruises on his back.

He made his way to her with a look of surprise. "Ma Petite is pissed?"

She stroked his handsome face and touched the gash next to his right eye. "Who did this?" she asked, kissing his brow.

"I got jumped," he said like it was the more boring part of his night.

"By who?"

He reached and pulled a strand of her hair to his nose, smelling. "An angry mob."

"Why?" she demanded, watching his handsome face as he slid her hair along his mouth with his eyes closed.

"Because they were angry." He slowly opened his eyes and lowered his gaze to the sheet. "But they can never be more *pissed* than me, Ma Petite."

She swallowed as he slid his finger beneath the sheet and slowly moved it away from her breasts.

"But this…" he murmured, touching the tip of her nipple with his finger. "puts my rage to shame."

The heat between her legs had her straining out moans as she watched his beautiful face, his words stirring her. She felt like they'd come from Bishop, and she waited breathless for more. His eyes moved to hers and the reckless look in his gaze brought a soft cry of need. She wanted the Bishop more than anything, but how to tell him? At seeing the silent torment in his gaze, she moved over. The words, *"Come here"* never made it out of her mind but they didn't need to because he hopped up and sat on the edge of the bed with his back to her.

She stared at the bow in his posture, longing to heal all the pain he hid in that darkness. "Hey," she whispered behind him, stroking the beautiful tattoo with her fingers. "I'm a good listener, did you know?" She leaned and kissed along the warm silky muscles, letting her hands explore his shoulders. "You're so beautiful," she murmured, sliding her lips along his skin, her fingers into his hair. She watched him angle his handsome face toward her with his eyes closed. The idea that she was a force in his life that was able to comfort him, gave her courage. She moved on her knees and wrapped her arms around him, pressing her breasts into his back.

He groaned immediately, with a tormented, "Ma Petite" as she kissed along his neck. She got bolder and moved her nipples against him, causing his breaths to strain with more groans. The feel of him on her lips and hands made her hungry out of her mind and she let herself imagine that she owned him the way he did her. Running her fingers into his hair at the back of his neck, she made a fist and pulled a little. The hot gasp he gave sent her desire through the roof. She turned his head and kissed him, then his own desire exploded as he pushed her back onto the bed. She bowed under the sudden power, desperate for it.

His breaths shook as he took hold of her hands and moved them above her head, kissing her while rocking his erection against her leg. The feel of his hard cock through his jeans had her pushing back, helping him.

"I want you naked," she gasped, needing to feel him the way he did her.

"I'll fuck you to pieces, I swear I will," he shuddered at her mouth, biting her lip with a groan.

"Then do it," she said, not caring about anything else. "Please, I want you to."

"Don't...," he groaned, biting her shoulder then sucking the muscle hard. He moved to her breasts and did the same there, making her cry out, driving her need higher. Now she understood why he held her arms so tight. She writhed beneath him when he rubbed his chest against her breasts while kissing her. Pinning both wrists in one hand, he used the other between her legs. So unfair. She protested with loud moans when his finger slid inside her.

"You are so fucking wet," he seethed at her mouth, moving his finger deeper and faster.

"Oh my God," she cried, bucking under him while opening her legs as wide as she could. "I want to come, I want to come," she said between sharp breaths.

He suddenly slowed as though remembering he had control over that.

"Please," she begged, dizzy with how hot he made her.

This time when he kissed her, it was hungrier than ever. He slid his finger slowly in and out of her then brought it to his mouth and sucked it.

"Oh God," she gasped, unable to take her eyes from his harsh face.

He slid that same finger over her mouth, and she closed her eyes, panting at how nasty he was being. He pushed his finger in her mouth, and his harsh "*Fuck*," flew when she sucked it greedily. He pumped his finger in and out, his groans hot.

"I need to suck you," she begged. "Let me suck you."

"Turn over."

The heated command rocked her womb. She did as he said and he added, "Hold on to something," in the same tone. She reached and found the ledge of the bookshelf above and gripped it tight.

"Don't let go. If you do, we're done. Do you agree?"

She moaned and panted her "Yes" and the second she did, he ripped the sheet away.

"My *fucking* God, your *ass*."

The anger in his tone confused her while arousing her to pieces. She fought with her shame and worry about what he thought.

"Open your legs."

His angry tone was undoing her. She worked them open halfway and felt him move between them. His hands stroked over her calves and moved up. His fingers bit into her upper thighs and shoved, forcing her legs open so wide. "Oh God, oh my God," she gasped.

"Your *fucking…ass*," he said again, sounding shocked as he stroked and squeezed the cheeks with both hands. His thick groans were killing her. She couldn't believe he liked this part of her that much! He ground her pussy against the bed using her ass to move her. "One hand Ma Petite. Touch your pretty *fucking* dripping pussy."

"Bishop," she moaned, working her hand under her.

"Let me see your finger in it," he seethed, lifting her ass off the bed. She moved her weight to her spread knees and held her hips high while undulating them to the rhythm of the intense heat. "So hot," she cried in the mattress, panting.

He released her ass and she kept it held high, already missing his touch. His finger dipped inside her, touching hers then slid out, moving up to her ass.

"Oh my God," she gushed, clenching her eyes tight in excitement and fear. He pressed the pad of his finger against the tight muscle, moving his other hand to her pussy, helping there. "Oh yes, yes," she strained, when his fingers slid under her hand to her clit. "It's so hot!" she shot out, fighting to finger herself faster and deeper.

His mouth suddenly covered her cheek then sucked hard while his finger moved right on her ass like a heartbeat.

"I want it, please, yes," she said, amazed with how good it felt while masturbating. "Fuck me with your finger." She'd meant in her pussy and his finger very slowly sank into her ass. "Oh!" she shot out, nervous. He was only halfway and two seconds later, he moved in and out in short strokes. He slid his other finger in her pussy with a groan, shoving in past hers.

"Two hands," he said, granting her wish for just one more.

She reached under herself with her other hand, moving her fingers over her clit while raising her ass even higher. He bit her then licked and kissed, like she was driving him mad.

"I can't wait to *fuck* you," he said around his hot breaths."

"Then don't," she shot out, her orgasm coming. The new feeling he created in her ass and pussy together with her clit built something gigantic. "Oh God, Bishop," she gasped, astonished. His two fingers moved equally deep now, his pace still slower than she wanted.

"I'm going to bury my cock in your gorgeous ass one day," he swore, pushing his finger as deep as he could go now.

"Yes! It's coming, please!" she begged, jerking her hips for a faster everything. He twirled the finger buried in her ass, then worked a second finger in her pussy. The tight feeling as he stretched her sent her flying over the edge.

"You fucking kill me," he said as she orgasmed so hard. His two fingers flew fast and deep, forcing her orgasm to go on forever. She bucked her hips and shuddered filling the room with non-stop cries until finally the tremors slowed.

The moment she was done, she turned on her side, finding him sitting on his haunches, hands on his jeaned thighs and looking devastated.

"Your turn," she said, moving on her knees and taking his face in her hands. She kissed him, not hiding her hunger and the hot gasp he filled her mouth with lit her on fire for more.

"Fuck," he said, as she pushed him onto his back.

"Hold on to something," she ordered breathless while opening his jeans and yanking them over his hips. She froze when his cock appeared. "Oh my," she whispered at how huge it was before returning to her frantic pace of ripping them off.

In the back of her mind, she worried if her courage would falter, but when he was finally naked, it tripled. He was up on his elbows, staring at her tits and the look on his face said he'd die if she stopped now. "Open for me."

Her command wasn't very strong, but the way it seemed to physically burn him as he obeyed made her feel powerful. He didn't hold on to anything and that was so very fine by her. She wanted him to see what she was about to do. God, and what was that? Devour him like a virgin fool, that's what. The way his body heaved in anticipation said she could probably blow on him and he'd orgasm.

Moving between his legs, she decided to try her hand at jacking him off. She took hold of his cock in one hand and slowly closed her hand around it, gasping at how hot and hard it was. My God, he was like a *rock,* literally. Silky and boiling.

"Ma Petite," he gushed, his head falling back while she slid her fist slowly along his huge shaft.

"You're *so* beautiful." She remembered how he'd touched the head. She used the tip of her finger and circled that thick edge, moaning when he opened his legs more and pumped his cock in her hand. "Oh God, yes," she said, moving her gaze to his face.

Christ almighty, he was boiling right before her eyes. It was amazing and thrilling. She focused her efforts, gliding her hand all the way to the base then back up again, using her second hand in a circle over the top. Again, she eyed him to see if she was doing good, and his look hit her clit like a heat bomb. His hands were fisted in the crumpled sheet and his sexy mouth remained open with non-stop hot hisses and lusty groans.

Mind blown and courage soaring, she lay on his right hip, putting his beautiful cock in easy tasting distance.

A long string of French flew from his sexy mouth when she held it tight in one hand and delivered her very first kiss to the thick head. His torment had her so horny, she decided she needed him to come as much as he did. She opened her mouth and took just the head between her lips, the salty taste pressing into her tongue. She moved her lips up and down over that thick ridge, loving the way it felt. She mmmm'd when his hisses got longer and louder with harsh groans.

"Fucking Dieu," he shot out, bucking his hips several times.

"Mmmm, you want to fuck my mouth?"

"Ma Petite," he strained.

She gasped when his hand shot out and grabbed the back of her head by the hair. She closed her eyes at the amazing feeling of him holding her back that way. God, he was going to come she realized, that's why he'd done it. She let him control her, lowering back to his cock with a deep moan of satisfaction. She was ready to devour him like he was so good at doing. Grabbing the base of him, she went down, taking him all the way to the back of her throat. This time both his hands pulled in her hair and held her still. She could feel his cock pulsing right in her mouth, mother of mercy. She remained unmoving, following his direction while lowering her hand to his balls like she'd seen him do.

More French gushed when she caressed them and moaned at how good they felt in her careful fingers.

"Fuck, Beth, I'm coming," he swore breathless, his hips pumping faster now. She focused all her efforts and fondled his balls. Before she worried if it was just right, he grabbed her head between his hands and forced her to take him fast and deep and dear God what a womb crushing rush that was.

"Oh *Beth*!" His body locked for several seconds before he went into a thrashing of long delicious, hard groans. Hot cum jetted against her throat and she did the only sensible thing she could think and swallowed.

She forced him to take every bit of pleasure just like he did her and he finally grabbed her head again, letting her know there was a finish point and he'd reached it.

Like climbing off a ride, she released his softening cock with a reluctance while eying him and licking her lips. The verdict of how she'd done came in the form of him pulling her on top of him and kissing her like she'd only made him hungrier somehow. They moaned in each other's mouth, a wordless expression of pleasure and satisfaction. It made her smile on his lips.

"Yes, you did fucking amazing," he said in her mouth, petting her face now and pressing her head to his chest. "But you cannot be naked on me like this for more than a minute or I will surely fuck you into oblivion."

She sat up and grabbed the blanket and stuffed it between them. "There. Fire threats extinguished."

He pulled her back onto him stroking her head on his chest with a deep breath.

"What has you bothered?" she asked, pressing kisses on his nipple. "Is it Savvie?" she asked around a yawn. She closed her eyes at the wonderful feel of his fingers stroking her forehead.

"Yes," he said, seeming glad to say it. "I don't think it's a good time to tell her I'm her father and it's killing me not to."

"Then wait a couple days. Does she know she's never going back there?"

"No."

"How do you think she'll take it?"

"No fucking idea."

"She's such a doll," Beth said, smiling. "Maybe her and Luseah will be friends."

He didn't say anything, and she stroked her fingers along his chest. "They're closer in age. For sure Lucas will get along with her."

"Mon Dieu, we need to tell her the truth before she falls for him like all the girls do. That...*fucking* Katrina."

She raised her head, looking at him.

"She's a bitch," he assured with a matter-of-fact gaze.

"Yes, she is," Beth muttered, laying her head back down. "She stole something very precious to me that I might never get to experience."

His stroking paused on her shoulder. "What do you mean?"

She gave a dramatic sigh. "Ohhh, like..." She raised her leg in the air, showing it off. "...getting my nude painting done by a certain talented artist."

She lowered her leg and slid it along his, smiling.

"I've never thought of painting since she left."

"I know, I heard," she said, not wanting to hear it again.

"Until five seconds ago," he said, back to stroking her shoulder.

She popped her head up getting on her elbow. "Serious? You'll paint me? Nude?"

"I'll paint you nude if I get to fuck you in between sessions."

She gasped a laugh and kissed him right on the mouth. "You have a deal Mr. Bishop."

"Fuck," he whispered, grabbing her face and kissing her. "You realize you've fed a monster. He's not well, Ma Petite."

"Mmm," she said, running her fingers along his face now. "He just needs a friend like me." She placed small kisses on his chin. "I think you should know that…I fell in love with him first."

"Mon Dieu, you're trying to kill me this night," he said, wrapping his arms tight around her. "I will tell you a secret about Bishop," he said. "Before he found you in the swamp, he spent many hours regretting his behavior with the Northern Angel."

She lifted her head with a happy gasp. "Seriously?"

"So very much," he assured, making her turn on her side. "We need to sleep. We have a big day tomorrow."

She turned and he snuggled behind her with the blanket between them. "What are we doing?"

"We check on some of our elderly, make sure they have things, go to town for supplies—"

"For the party?" she wondered, grinning in excitement.

"Yes, and check the post office."

"For the books! Oh my God, what if they're in?"

"Then we'll have to schedule classes."

She giggled at that. "And who's the teacher?"

"Figure that out in class."

She stroked his arm, pressing her mouth on it and sliding her lips against the coarse hair. "Do I get to go to town with you?"

"No, but I'll take you on the boat to see the elderly. It's too soon to risk you being seen in town. Still too much I don't know."

"Okay." She wondered about her dad. "I hope I get to find out if my dad is okay at least."

He pulled her closer to him, draping his leg over hers. "I promise to find that out tomorrow."

She closed her eyes. "Thank you. Savvie can come with us to see the swamp too?"

"Mmhmm," he said, sounding half asleep.

She reached behind her and stroked his head, running her fingers in his silky hair. "Night Bishop," she mumbled, smiling when she heard light snoring. "Night my sweet Sahvrin."

CHAPTER 21

Sahvrin helped His Petite into swamp attire, wondering where Lucas and Savvie went off to. "I swear, he better not be stupid with that girl." They decided to play it by ear when to tell Savvie the truth, but just as he feared, Lucas was going to be a problem.

"Oh, stop," His Petite scolded. "They're fine. Plus, it's not like they're blood related and—"

He straightened, eyeing her. "Don't even *say* it."

"You're right, I'm sorry. Are we going to be walking in water?" she wondered, changing the subject.

"No, but if you have to, for whatever reason, you want these boots that protect you from snakes and other creatures."

"Creatures huh? I really like this thing," she said, inspecting her overalls. "It has more pockets than a purse!" She stuck her hands in each one. "Very practical. Like field attire."

He stood and gave her a firm kiss on the lips. If he didn't do that every so often, it built up and became a distraction. "They suit you." And they really did. She looked sexy as hell in black. The muscle shirt under it was black too, making him wish he'd selected one of his white ones. She had in between breasts, not big not small. Just right. And he was the big bad wolf ready to eat her perfect porridge. He'd have put her in long sleeves, but it was too hot. "You will need sunblock, don't let me forget it," he said. "Savvie too."

"Unlike all you swamp soldiers. So tan."

The envy in her tone made him chuckle. "No more tanning for you," he said, making her laugh.

"My burn was nearly completely healed the next day thanks to your Mah-Mah's cream."

"You need a chaperone when tanning," he said, making her laugh.

"Maybe Bishop can watch me sunbathe."

Mon Dieu. He finished tucking her pants into her boots and stood. "Maybe Bishop could fuck you while you sunbathe."

The desire that put on her face made him slam the brakes. "Sorry, I need to behave. I can't have you wearing that look in front of my brothers."

Her eyes widened with a whispered, "Oh God."

"Here," he said, handing her the black cap. "You can manage this."

"You sure you don't want to do that too?"

"You love it, I can tell," he accused lightly.

"I do," she said, giggling. "Dress me, feed me."

He stood and eyed her. "Finger you. Lick you. Suck you."

She shoved him in the chest with wide eyes, making him laugh.

"I'm sorry again," he said, holding up both hands with a head shake. "Feel free to punish me later. Come," he said, taking her hand.

"Wait, I have to put my cap on!"

While she did, he looked around in the supply room, filling his pockets with various foods.

"So where are we going first? I can't believe I get to go on an air boat, I've never been on one. I hope it's not too scary."

He found an empty potato sack and dumped their snacks into it. "It's very loud but lots of fun as long as you have a good driver. And you do."

She fought to get her long hair through the hole at the back of the cap and he put the bag down to help. "Ma Petite, you may need to put your hair in those ugly knots, so you don't look like a swamp creature after this is all over."

She gave another one of her big laughs as he helped her, then took her hand and pulled her to the kitchen. "Grab something to eat, we won't have time for a full breakfast. Lucas," he called. "You ready?"

"Yeah," he called back, hurrying down the stairs.

"Grab food, we need to hurry. Where's Savvie and Bart," Sahvrin asked, putting fruit and whatever edible vegetables he could find in the sack. "Grab the ice chest Lucas. Make sure it has drinks."

"Already did," he said.

"Good boy," Sahvrin muttered.

"Bart!" Lucas yelled over his shoulder. "Let's go! Oh, Savvie is talking to her mom. I'll go get her."

"We ready?" Bart asked, appearing in the doorway finally.

Sahvrin shook his head at his outfit. "Where you think we're going, the north pole?"

"I prefer not getting a bug rash while you do a hundred on the water."

"Beth and Savvie are coming," he laughed. "I'll be driving like a grampa."

"Uuuugh," Lucas muttered as he headed out.

"You don't have to go slow for me," Beth said. "I like going fast. I bet Savvie probably does too."

Sahvrin headed for the door. "Come on, Ma Petite. Time to roday the swamps."

"Roday?" she asked, as she followed.

"Means run around."

"So how fast do you go? Like what, thirty miles per hour?" She hurried down the steps after him. "I seriously don't mind going fast. I ski, I ride snow mobiles."

Sahvrin nodded with a shrug, letting her catch up. "It's like that. Just no snow."

"Our snow mobiles are pretty fast," she said, looking around the yard covered in a blanket of fog. "They go like sixty, but we never go that fast."

"I'm happy to hear that. It's not safe going fast unless you really know what you're driving and the terrain."

"But you do," she said as he took her hand across the narrow bridge at the back of the yard. "Wow, is this *another* boat dock? You know, I can carry something."

"Lucas," he yelled before answering her. "This is the dock for the airboats."

"Oh my God, is that…is that them?" she wondered as they walked along the pier. She shielded her eyes against the bright morning sun rising behind their six Swamp Dragons. "Are those boats?"

Pounding feet and excited screaming erupted behind them and Sahvrin turned right as Lucas and Savvie flew past. "So close!" Lucas said, grinning at Savvie. Sahvrin wanted to be pissed with the look on her face but there was nothing he could find wrong with seeing her that happy.

"Hi Sahvrin," she said with a smile and wave, telling him her mother hadn't said anything yet. Not like he expected her to jump in to calling him *Dad* right off.

"Hello, Savvie, how did you sleep?" he asked.

"Surprisingly amazing, thanks to Lucas."

Sahvrin eyed him.

"I loaned her my blues collection," he said with an innocent enough grin.

"Hi Miss Beth," Savvie said with a cute wave. She was a tiny little thing and beautiful like her mother, but her eyes were his and it was a strange feeling knowing that she was too.

"Well, hello gorgeous," His Petite said, giving her one of her breathtaking smiles. He realized he might covet those. "How is your mother, is she doing okay?"

"Yes ma'am, she *loves* it out here. I haven't seen her this happy in a long time." Sahvrin felt like Savvie might share that love, at least he prayed.

"I'm so happy," Beth said, nothing but angelic concern. "And don't call me ma'am, you make me feel old!" She looked at Sahvrin then. "Maybe Katrina would like to come?"

"Oh, I wish we could," he fervently lied. "Not enough seats this round."

"It's okay," Savvie said. "Zep is keeping her company."

Sahvrin adjusted his cap on that interesting bit.

"So, wow, these boats are amazing!" Beth said. "I've never seen anything like them. Which one are we going in?"

"Miss Beth," Lucas announced, "Miss Savvie," he added with extra flair and his killer smile. "These beauties are the *Swamp Dragons*." He hopped onto Sahvrin's boat like it was his own. Soon enough Mon' Lil Frere. "But *this* one is Sahvrin's and there's not another one like it on planet Earth," he bragged. "Sahvrin modified the *fff—uh, frack* out of it."

Beth turned to him. "You...built this?" she asked, her eyes huge.

"Modified it."

"He built it," Bart argued, climbing on. "He built all these boats."

"I modified all of them."

"Name one thing on this boat you'd find on any other air boat," Bart challenged with a pissed tone.

"A hundred things." Sahvrin helped Savvie onto the boat, then Beth. "The seats, to start."

"Big ha," Lucas said. "Beth and Savvie, let me introduce you to the *infamous*... Night Dragon." He gave a bow, making Sahvrin shake his head as he fished out life vests. "Whom I like to call—when Sahvrin can't hear—" he said quieter right before yelling, "The God of a Thousand Thunders!"

Sahvrin had to laugh as he guided Beth to her seat and lifted her onto it while Lucas bragged on.

"This swamp monster flies across the watery graves of a thousand demons at 130 miles per hour, *and,*" he added with a thrust of his finger, "he creates category *five* hurricane force winds up to one-hundred-and-SEVENTY miles per hour-- *out* of his *ass!*"

Sahvrin straightened and leveled a hard look at him.

"He means from the blades," Bart explained, pointing to the propellers.

He helped His Petite into her life vest. "Foul mouth little shit," he muttered, making her laugh while Savvie over-enjoyed his theatrics.

"Category five?" Savvie exclaimed while Lucas helped her in her seat.

"You know I can swim, right?" Beth asked, distracting him from the love affair in progress between his daughter and fucking brother.

"That's good," Sahvrin said. "You can keep your cap on." He slipped a black headset on her.

"Is it really that loud?" she wondered, seeming disappointed to have to wear them.

"Is it *loud,*" Lucas cried. "The sound he makes is where he gets his *name*—God of a Thousand Thunders!" He struck various Hercules poses while whisper roaring at all his pretend ghosts in the swamps. His Petite and Savvie laughed at his antics, and Sahvrin couldn't hold in his smile at his Swamp Dragon Nerd.

"Lucas, check the hold for extra gas," Sahvrin said, putting his headset on. "Maybe it's time we build your dragon, yes?"

At hearing it, Lucas popped up with huge eyes, making everybody laugh. Sahvrin took several minutes explaining the communication how-to with the headset to Beth. "So, they're not just for saving your eardrums, it's for talking," he said, handing her a two-way radio that worked just between the two of the, demonstrating that next. "When you need to talk to just me, press this. To talk to everybody, press this on your headset."

"You can even listen to music," Lucas said, his smile huge as Savvie called him to sit by her. Mon Dieu. Controlling what was unfolding was like spitting at a fire.

"Lucas, get Savvie a headset and show her how to work it."

"Got it, boss."

Sahvrin looked around, amazed with the humidity at that early hour. Merci Dieu, Fall couldn't come fast enough. He found the sunscreen and covered His Petite's exposed parts with it, then handed it to her. "Your face."

She took it and Sahvrin turned on the main com channel. "Who can hear me?"

They all gave a thumbs up and Savvie broke their eardrums with a "Me!" Then a "Crap, sorry," at seeing them jump.

"The mic works really good," Lucas said, adding a wink that sent Sahvrin's rage through the roof. Lucas caught his *what the fuck are you doing with her* glare, and he lost the smile.

"Strap up," Sahvrin called out.

"Yes sir, Mr. Bishop," Lucas said, getting in the seat with Savvie who gave him a love-struck smile that had Sahvrin shaking his head. Was fucking love-at-first sight. Why now? Why not a month from now? Or never?

He glanced over his shoulder at His Petite in the seat right behind him. It was the highest for seeing. "Ma Petite, you can hear me?"

She shoved her thumb up next to his face and he glanced over his shoulder at her with a smile.

"Tell me in the mic so I can be sure I can hear you."

He braced for another audio rape and got a quiet, "I can hear you."

"Perfect. I hear you too. You ready for this?"

"Yes."

Her low squeal made him smile as he turned on the engine. "If you get scared, tell me, and I'll slow down or stop. I don't mind. I only mind if you don't tell me."

"Yes sir, Mr. Bishop."

Mon Dieu, she was being a temptress. And she liked doing it. He'd say she was being Cah-nigh, but it was more than sneaky behavior, it was like picking a fight with his cock. And he wouldn't say he didn't love it. She was supposed to be *submissive* and seemed to enjoy being the exact opposite at times. And as usual, the Bishop insisted on retribution.

****

The propellers on the back of the boat began to spin or growl as Lucas would describe it and Beth's heart raced as she glanced behind her to see it. The blades were as tall as her!

"You ready Ma Petite?"

The eager words filled her ears and she nodded and gasped her, "Yes."

"I'll go slow until we have more space to ride."

She watched as they moved down the winding roadway lined with towering trees. The thick fog lingered above the water, wrapping around the huge bases of the cypress. So, so beautiful.

"We usually *fly* through this," Lucas informed, laughing in her headset. She forgot they could talk to each other, and his sudden voice scared the crap out of her. Dear Lord, fly through *this*? Now *that* would be terrifying, given how winding and narrow it was.

"Oh God, I'm so nervous!" Savvie said.

"You'll love it," Lucas promised.

"No flying today," Sahvrin said. She still thought it was cute how much Savvie liked Lucas, and even cuter that Sahvrin was so protective about it. But if Lucas was anything like Sahvrin, and he surely seemed to be, then what better person for her to fall for?

"Why are the seats so high?" she wondered, remembering not to yell.

"So you can see what's in the water," Sahvrin said, angling his head toward her. "It's important since the boat has no brakes or can't go in reverse. Hitting anything at high speed would be bad-bad."

She smiled at the *bad*. She noticed he doubled words like that. Not really an accent but a culture thing maybe. His English was actually very good, he didn't skip words or do many contractions like most who were native speakers of English. Like somebody who didn't practice it enough. Wonder how he sounded in French? More relaxed? Did they even have contractions in the language? Now she wanted to learn it to meet and know that side of him.

She remembered his bad-bad remark. "I used to ski a lot and snow mobile on mountains," she reminded, letting him know she wasn't a stranger to recreational danger.

"Now that's something I'd love to try," Lucas said. She realized he was humming.

"What are you listening to Lucas?" she asked.

"Swamp Blues," he said, giving her a profile shot with one of his heart-throb smiles. He was such a cutie, there was no doubt about that. No wonder Savvie was head over heels for him. "Wanna hear?" he asked.

"Sure," she said.

"Gonna put my music on the com," he announced.

"Go for it," Sahvrin said, his deep voice sending a thrill through her. Every now and then his voice sounded deeper and she liked to think it was his Bishop side.

"Shit!" Beth gasped when the twang of a harmonica blared in her hear.

"My bad, I like I loud," Lucas said, turning it down.

She listened to the music, immediately seeing the attraction. The stomping grind had a command to it that made you just want to get up and move. Or at least tap your foot and nod your head, which she did. When the lyrics came, the gravelly voice raised her brows in appreciation. Very complimentary to the tune. Seductive too. Reminded her of Mr. Bishop.

"I think Sahvrin does this one better than anybody," Lucas said.

"Yep," Bart agreed.

"He can sing? You can sing?" she wondered, forgetting everybody could hear.

Bart and Lucas laughed, and she heard Sahvrin's sigh of "*Mon Dieu.*"

"That man was born with a harmonica in his mouth, at least that's what Pah-Pah says."

"You can sing?" she cried, annoyed with how many amazing things he kept from her. "Why didn't you tell me!"

"Ma Petite," he chuckled. "Why would I tell people such things?"

She realized he wouldn't, not him.

"Don't worry," Bart said. "You'll hear us tomorrow night. We have to perform, Mah-Mah's orders."

She gasped now. "You *all* sing?"

"Yep, and play," Lucas said, not hiding his pride. "They say we're famous in the swamps."

Her smile slowly bloomed as she imagined. "I bet you are. What do you all play?"

Lucas looked halfway over his shoulder. "Sahvrin is on the mouth horn, I like the banjo." He aimed a thumb at Bart. "He's *badass* on the drums, and Jek, that dude puts Jethro Tull to shame on the guitar."

"And Zep is boss on the base," Bart said.

"And August is Beethoven on the keyboard," Sahvrin finished.

"Wow," Savvie said with her tinkly laugh. "I have *zero* musical talents!"

"Same here," Beth said. "You and I can take care of the dancing."

"You know how to dance, Ma Petite?" Sahvrin asked.

"Wellll, I have *some* experience with the classical."

"Now look who's holding back," Sahvrin muttered, laughter in his voice.

"What kind of classical?" Savvie asked. "Please say ballet."

"Yes! You know ballet?"

"Yes!" she shot out, turning to give her a look of wide-eyed joy. "And I *hate* it!" she cried, turning back around, making Beth laugh.

"How long have you taken it?" Beth asked.

"Since I was *five*," she said. "My dad and mom *made* me."

Worry tightened her stomach for Sahvrin at that. "Same," Beth said.

"You both will have to perform something now," Sahvrin said, somehow hiding the bite her words had to have caused.

"How long did you go to ballet?" Savvie wondered.

"Till I injured my ankle at sixteen. Oh, I forgot, I do know how to play music. During physical therapy, I learned how to play glass harps."

"Glass harps?" Bart wondered, interested.

"All these secret talents, Ma Petite." Like he was adding up infractions.

"Also known as the Ghost Fiddle," Beth said with a grin.

"Is that where you rub the top of the glasses and it makes music?" Savvie asked.

"Yep," Beth said, laughing. "I learned a couple of songs."

"How did you come by this amazing talent during physical therapy, Ma Petite?"

"Well, the uh, therapist did it as a hobby and taught me."

"Ohhhh," Savvie said, like she assumed a romance.

"It wasn't like that," Beth assured. "I was only *sixteen* and he was in his twenties."

Bart shot out a laugh. "Damn, a senior citizen."

"I'm *very* sure Ma Petite wasn't into boys at that age," Sahvrin mocked, making her stare at the back of his head with a jaw drop.

"Well, even if I was, he wasn't into me. I was jailbait."

"Unless he was a *good priest*," Bart said, "he was into you."

"So where did he teach you this *Ghost Fiddle*?" Savvie wondered over her shoulder with a sweet smile, not helping.

Beth was trying to recall if she'd missed something obvious with good ole Jeremy.

"So quiet," Sahvrin muttered.

"I was distracted," she said, laughing.

"Fond memories?"

"Yes, they actually were up until this interrogation," she half joked.

"So where did he teach you, Miss Beth?" Lucas pressed now.

"Yes, please tell us so we can all get back to breathing," Sahvrin said.

Oh my God, he was being *dangerously possessive* she realized, heart hammering while she grinning like a fool. "He taught me at the place we did therapy, in the kitchen. It had a kitchen," she explained, trying to avoid the answers that she realized would make her the most naïve person on the planet now.

"What kind of a hospital has kitchens with wine glasses?" Bart wondered perplexed.

"It wasn't technically a hospital, it was…a more private facility."

"How private was it?" Savvie drew out the question with dramatic suspicion then laughed.

"Probably his house," Bart said, with a snicker.

The awkward silence grew and then came Sahvrin's mildly incredulous, "Mon Dieu, she doesn't deny it."

This brought everybody's laughter, and Savvie's, "Ohhhh, this changes everything."

"It doesn't change a *thing* because he was a perfect gentleman." She wasn't about to admit or let on that she'd had a crush on him.

"I'm *sure* he was," Sahvrin muttered, sounding almost pissed, which made her cover her mouth to keep from laughing.

"Somebody's jealous," Savvie sang lightly, and Lucas laughed with a "*Yup.*"

"I just cannot *wait* to hear the music he taught you," Bart added, turning his head to show his shit-eating grin.

"There will be no glass music playing in these swamps," Sahvrin said. "I'll post the decree on every tree in the land."

Beth cracked up at that, leaning and stroking his muscular tanned neck. He caught her hand in his and turned his head, kissing the palm. He looked so cute with his black cap turned backwards. "Okay boys and girls," he announced. "Time for a little speed."

The road in the woods came to an end she realized. "Ohhh kay" she said, her heart suddenly jumping into her throat.

"Come on big bro, show the ladies a *little* of what the Night Dragon has!" Lucas begged.

Beth moved the earphone from one ear, wanting to hear how loud it was. The moment Sahvrin hit the gas, the low growling did just as Lucas described and *roared* like a thousand *thunders*! But it was the thrust and speed that had her holding the seat and her breath. Oh *God*, this was way different than snow mobiles!

"Whooooooooa!" Lucas yelled, both arms up.

Beth caught sight of Savvie holding his hand in a death grip while laughing with exhilaration.

"Open her up!" Lucas yelled.

Sahvrin shook his head. "Nooooo, not this time, lil bro."

Oh my God, he could go faster? She didn't need any more speed, this was plenty!

"My petite, I'm on our private channel. You okay?"

"Oh," she said, picking up the walkie talking and smiling. "Yes, I'm amazing, I love it!"

"You *are* amazing. Glad you're enjoying yourself."

"This is so *beautiful,* Sahvrin! Don't you dare try to make me hate the swamp ever again!"

He laughed and she stared at his shoulders and back, needing to touch him. "I won't dare do it anymore."

"Good! You should be trying to convince me to stay!" she said, watching the trees fly by

"Done."

"Where are we going first?" Savvie asked in the main com.

"We have five stops to make and if Ole man Pee Chue doesn't talk too much, we might make all of them," Sahvrin said.

Beth put the walkie talkie to her mouth and pressed the button. "I think it's so sweet of you all to take care of the older people. I love that. It's like a big family out here."

"It is," he said. "It's always been that way."

"What are you guys doing at their places?" Beth wondered.

"We do maintenance inspection on all the essential things, check it's all still in working order. Make sure they have food and whatever else they want. During hurricane season especially. Sometimes it's easier to bring them to the main house during bad storms like that."

She pressed her button. "The *main* house? How many houses are there?"

"We have many around the swamp, but the main house is safest for hurricanes."

Wow. "Where on earth do you put all of the people?"

"Meh, we scatter them all over the place, wherever they can fit."

She laughed at him. "You joking?"

"Nope. It's just a big swamp slumber party. Mah-Mah probably prays for these things, always looking for a reason to celebrate something."

"Awww, that's just so sweet. And I can't believe I get to be a part of it."

"You say that now, but Big Sha's Pah-Pah snores louder than my swamp dragon."

She laughed, staring at the back of his head, pressing the button. "You sure nobody can hear me?"

"Only me, Ma Petite."

She bit her lower lip, nervous now. "I... I love your back and your tattoo. Not sure if I ever told you that. Such a nice view I have right behind you."

"Would be a much better view if you were right on me."

Mercy. "You sure nobody can hear us?"

"Yes, I'm *very* sure, Ma Petite. Why?" he asked after a few seconds. "You want to say something naughty to me?"

"I do," she whispered, her pulse hammering as the boat bumped up and down and the wind whipped her hair.

"So shy," he said when she couldn't bring herself to, like maybe he both liked and lamented that.

"I am, I'm sorry."

"Do not be sorry for that, it's one of my very favorite things about you. My doose petite d-amour escleve."

His sexy tone lit her up more. "What on earth did you just say," she murmured, smiling.

"That you are my sweet little sex slave."

"Hey," Lucas said in the headset, making her jump in her seat as her heart pounded. "Can we stop at Leblancs? I left my fishing pole there the other day."

"If we have time, yes," Sahvrin said.

How did he stay so cool headed? She was burning up with lust in sixty mile an hour wind.

CHAPTER 22

Upstairs in his bedroom, Beth's stomach lurched at the news Juliette was finally coming even if it was just to leave again with Sahvrin and Zep to visit some guy named Beaux. She really wanted to meet her and hoped she was nicer than Luseah.

"I would like you to keep an eye on Lucas and Savvie," Sahvrin said, finally facing her.

"Okay. I'll make sure they're not alone for a *second*," she assured, not wanting him to worry about them. "But…I'm *very* sure Lucas would never hurt her, truly he's such a remarkable young man. Reminds me a lot of you."

He ran a hand through his hair, looking out the window. "I know this may sound wrong, but…it's not her I'm worried about." He looked at her now. "It's him. Lucas is more of a son to me than my brother. Ever since I found him in the woods, him and his sister, I practically raised them. I put my soul into both of them, but especially him." He lowered his head shaking it. "I do not…I *cannot*…" He paused again, shoving his hands in his pockets. "I'm *terrified*," he seemed to correct, looking right at her. "Of the thought of him getting hurt. He's never shown interest in girls, and I knew this day was coming but it came out of nowhere with the *least* expected person." He gave an incredulous breath. "They act like lifetime best friends already and they *just* met!" He ran both hands through his hair. "I want to hope for the best, and I know they're not technically related. And I know with all that I am that Lucas is an *amazing* soul, and if Savvie is his mate, then I'll be fucking thrilled to death. But…" He looked at her with panic shadowing his hot gaze. "I mean, what if she's *not*?"

Beth hurried over and wrapped her arms around him. "Oh God, I'm so sorry, I didn't know that about Lucas and you and Luseah." His arms went around her. "I wish there was something I could say to make it all safe and I hate that there isn't, it's just what you say, terrifying." She pulled away, looking at him. "Now *I'm* scared too, I can't imagine him going through what you did." Tears stung her eyes at the idea, and she realized she wasn't helping. "I'm stupid," she said, stepping back and wiping her eyes. "I should be telling you things to reassure you, not…help build up your fears."

She looked up and the intensity on his face made her swallow and nearly forget what they were talking about. "I should…be like a… a lifeboat in the storms, not a…oh God…"

She braced as he stormed over and snatched her face in a hard grip, kissing her into oblivion. The force of his momentum sent her arms around his neck to keep from being knocked back while his hot breaths brought frantic gasps from her. His mouth was like a fire, on her neck now, and she was walking in reverse or being pushed.

The wall met her back abruptly, making her breath catch. She caused a mess trying to help him with the overalls, getting growls and her hands swat as he dropped to his knees, pulling them down as he went. She was still kicking them off when he yanked down her panties next. "Open," he shot out, winded.

She opened one leg and he slammed it against the wall, his mouth pressing into her pussy with a groan. "Oh! God, Oh my God," she cried, latching her fingers tight in his hair while he sucked right on her clit.

His finger slid several times along her slit then plunged into her pussy with sounds of lusty hunger that was all Bishop. High pitched moans flew out as fast as her orgasm raced up. "Bishop, it's coming, don't stop!"

His fingers flexed hard on her inner thigh, bringing a biting pain with the pleasure as he fingered her faster and deeper, building a massive hot pressure. She pressed her back into the wall when her orgasm hit and shook her, causing her to pull his hair with all her might. He sucked even harder, holding her tightly in place, forcing her to take it while she fought not to collapse, the shove of his finger the only thing holding her up. She'd never had such a long, hard orgasm in all her life, God, yes, yes, yes.

She struggled not to crumple to the floor, using his head as support while catching her breath. He stood and scooped her up in his arms and carried her to the bed, laying her in it. Dear God. Wow. He kissed her, his breaths thick with moans as he made her taste what he'd done. "Let me do you," she said, stroking his face, feeling sedated.

"Not this time, Ma Petite."

"So mean," she whispered, closing her eyes as he stroked her forehead and pressed the softest kisses on her mouth. "Take a nap, Angel," he murmured at her ear. "I'll be a couple hours."

"I'll get up and chaperone," she said with her eyes closed. "Hurry back? But don't be reckless."

She felt him smiling on her lips. "I will go fast-fast, but not too fast."

"Mmm, that was amazing," she murmured. "I'll pay you back for it."

"I'm counting on it, Ma Petite. And you will meet Juliette when we return. Sleep for me."

Mmm. For him. Anything for him.

****

"Well look what the alligators done drug in." Sahvrin hugged his sister tight with a grin. "Bout time, Beth's eager to meet the lady who gave her all the pretty clothes."

She laughed. "And I brought even more," she said. "Some I think you'll appreciate."

"Mon Dieu, I can't take much more of this temptation."

A spark lit her green eyes now wide. "Are you *still* being a *good* boy, unlike our brothers," she said, muttering the last.

"I'm trying, but please pray for me."

She let her laugh go and he grinned, realizing how much he missed it. "Don't stay gone so long, Ma Chere Soeur."

She put her arm around his shoulders. "Awww am I your favorite sister?"

"Shhh, don't say that so loud, Luseah might here. Can you meet Beth when we return if that's okay? I'm ready to get this over with."

"Sure thing, swamp cowboy. Ready when you are."

"Ready now. Zep is waiting in the boat."

They made their way to the small run-a-round motorboat.

"So, we gonna tow us a lil Beux?" Juliette, asked, sounding eager to wrangle something besides alligators.

"Was hoping you could convince him to come kindly," Sahvrin said, amused while navigating the little run-a-round motorboat through the narrow waterway. "And he's not exactly lil' anymore."

She shrugged. "I wrestle six-hundred-pound reptiles on the regular, I'm sure I can handle that lil' swamp boy. Got my rope anyway," she said as he let off the gas to slow down.

Of course she did. She carried it like he carried a knife and probably had as many uses for it. "I'll come with you," Sahvrin said. "Don't want you getting all sweaty."

She gave him her killer quirked brow. "T-Boo," she muttered with a half grin. "You know me, I live to sweat."

Gah-day-dawn, he hated to imagine the poor soul she might one day wrangle and marry. They'd probably have fifty kids.

"Zep, keep her idling in case we need to leave quick for some reason."

Zep stared down at his phone, head shaking as his thumbs flew over the keypad. He shoved it in his back pocket. "You expecting trouble?" he asked, like he might be wanting some of that, making him wonder who he was texting.

"You know how shit happens in these swamps," Sahvrin said, pulling off his headset when they reached Francois dock. Especially if he was involved with the Roulettes.

"Don't I know it," he muttered, doing the same.

The double innuendo in his tone didn't help Sahvrin's nerves. "You got something we need to know, be sure and tell us."

"Nothing you'd be interested in, that I'm damn sure of."

Women troubles? Would be shocking if it weren't.

"So, I'm inviting him down to the house to help set up for tomorrow's party," Juliette double checked.

"Or hurricane preparations," Zep offered with a casual look around.

"Both work," Sahvrin added as they jumped onto the dock.

"Did you bother checking if he was even here?" she asked, heading down the walk with her ass-kicking gait.

"Unless he lied his ass off, he's here repairing Francois nets."

"Alrighty, then," she said, their boots clonking along the wood as they went.

He shot a hand out in front, stopping her. She looked at him brows raised as voices floated nearby.

"Me first," he muttered, stepping in front and leading, now hyper aware he carried his knife rather than his Judge. They made their way around the back of the house, finding Beaux in the fish shed with two men.

His pulse jack-hammered at seeing leather vests bearing the Roulette insignia. That *mother*fucker. "T-Beaux," Sahvrin called, tossing a wave at him while muttering to Juliette, "You handle Beaux, I handle the other two. On my lead."

"Holy mother of swamp sluts, is that *Beaux*?"

Sahvrin didn't have time to appreciate her shock, assessing the other two. One was a pig stand the other was medium build and covered in tatts. He'd have to put Ink-Junction down first. Big boy second. That bull would be slower but need a few licks.

He spied an old fence post as he walked up. "How's it going gentlemen?" All three men had their eyes locked on Juliette while Sahvrin picked up the post. He swung at Tattoos forehead, dropping him then slammed Tub in his kneecaps, bringing him down. Two more to the head put him out, right as Beaux's yells erupted.

Juliette already had his arms behind his back, speed winding her rope around his wrists. She leaned to his ear. "That was fun, wasn't it?"

He grunted then panted with his forehead to the ground. "Yeah, it kinda was."

Stupid boy.

She grabbed him by the forehead and jerked his head back. "You gettin' fresh Lil Boy Beaux? I thought you learned your lesson when I kicked your scrawny ass last time. You need another one?"

Sahvrin dialed Zep's number while Beaux grunted and strained from the painful hold. Fucking depressing having Beaux turn out to be a snake. He liked Beaux. "No ma'am," he strained. "Sorry."

Sahvrin eyed the still bodies on the ground. "Zep, come give us a hand. We got guest parishioners coming to church. Bring the duct tape."

"Uuugh, you fucking shoulda' called me," he cried pissed.

"You can interrogate later." He hung up the phone as the smaller dude gave a moan. "Stay down Crayons," he muttered, still holding the post.

"I don't know what you heard," Beaux said under Juliette who reclined on him like a beach chair. "But I can explain whatever it is."

"Sounds like a familiar line in a movie," Juliette muttered. "Such a shame you turned on your own people. I knew you were a little shit, but that's gator bait crime."

"I didn't," he cried into the dirt. "They were black mailing me!"

Sahvrin looked around, making sure there wasn't anybody else there. Francois was likely fishing. They got busy wrapping duct tape around the hands and feet of the two men.

"What about Lil Boy Beaux here, we tyin' his ankles too?"

"I won't run, I swear."

"Another cliché line," she said, using his head as an elbow rest. "I see you went and got all grown up. Too bad your girls won't get to enjoy all your big muscles."

"What?" he grunted. "I don't have no girls."

"Any girls, you ignorant swamptard." She leaned forward and smacked her hand on his butt. "And with a fine ass like that? I call bullshit."

"Don't flirt with dead men," Sahvrin said.

"Dead? Wait wait wait wait," he said, between breaths. "You're not gonna kill me, are you? Juliette, you know I'm not like that. I care about my home and our people."

Juliette rolled her eyes. "Now, I haven't *verified* but Gramma Lou-Lou says he's been paying for her utilities."

"Are you saying Gramma Lou-Lou *lied*?" Beaux managed, earning a smack over the head.

Sahvrin eyed Zep, getting a clueless shrug. He looked at Juliette. "Let him walk. He tries to run, we'll assume he loves getting wrangled by you."

She got up and yanked him by his shoulders to his knees. "On your feet, Swamp Stud."

"Yes ma'am," he gushed, standing and looking down at her. "Nice to see you too, Juliette. I see the alligators have been treating you *real* good."

She jabbed him in the stomach with her elbow hard enough to double him over. "Why thank you," she cooed, angling her head at his bent over one before ruffling his hair.

"You're welcome," he strained out, slowly straightening.

"You're going to spend time at the Weigh Station with your buddies either way," Sahvrin said. "Lazure will decide what to do with you after I extract every single bit of dirty information your brain holds."

"No need to extract," he hurried. "I'm willing to tell you anything, I told you that."

"Let's go." Sahvrin lifted Crayons by the shoulders and Zep grabbed his feet.

Once both Roulettes were in the boat, Zep taped them to the floor while Beaux went on and on, "I don't need to go to confession, I can do it right now. They have my sister, and if I don't make sure the guns move, they said they'll kill her."

Sahvrin looked at him.

"They have Tammy?" Zep asked.

He nodded. "She went on her own but they're using her man, they won't let her go."

Juliette eyed Sahvrin then swung her hard gaze to Beaux. "She told you that?"

"Yes!" he cried, nodding.

"Why didn't you come to us?" Sahvrin asked, wanting to punch him.

"Because I thought you was gonna run the guns and it didn't matter! Aren't the Bayou Bishops part of their gang?"

"Since *when* do we run guns in these swamps?" Sahvrin said, in his face now.

"Well, how was I supposed to know?"

"It's called a phone," Juliette said, wagging hers in his face. "And I'm verifying that sister story of yours, right now."

Sahvrin believed him but verification meant specifics. They needed all they could get.

"Shit, no signal," she said. "Stop at Gertrudes house so I can piggyback on the signal there."

Sahvrin got to it in less than a minute, then waited while she made a phone call.

"Who you calling?" Beaux asked. "You need to watch what you say, they might hurt her," he said, worried.

She signaled she understood with a nod and hand up. "Nadine, hey what you up to girl?"

Sahvrin waited impatiently as she whittled her way past pleasantries before asking something useful. "Girl, I was down at Gramma Lou-Lou's, and she mentioned Beaux Brasseaux was helping her. Have you seen him lately? My lord, he's done grown into a hunk." She nodded, putting her hand on her hip. "Yesssss," she cried, winding her finger in a strand of hair then laughing. "You think he's got a girl?"

The hell was she doing?

More loud laughing and a huge breath. "I wonder if other parts of him have grown too, you know what I mean." Guffaws of laughter as she winked at Beaux.

Sahvrin waved at her, and she answered with a firm wait signal.

"Well, I knew his sister had grown into a beauty, but not him. Who would guess somebody so scrawny would evolve into a swamp god."

She fucking liked him! Mon Dieu, leave it to her to manage to mix that with this. Shit with shat.

"She did?" Juliette snapped her fingers repeatedly over her head, signaling she was at the target. A huge breath and, "Oh my God, she seems so sweet!" They all watched as her mouth dropped and eyes got huge. Like a mime acting out a soap opera. "You think? I don't know, Nadine, that sounds so farfetched?" More jaw dropping. "She did? Her mother would roll over in her *grave* if she knew!" A gasp. A ridiculous laugh. "Oh Zep, he's still wrangling alligators with me."

Sahvrin waved his hand for her to wrap it up.

"Hello? Nadine? Girl, my signal sucks. I was calling to invite you to the party tomorrow! Zep will be there, yes."

Zep chunked both hands in the air then let them fall, shaking his head. How funny. Too many women at the same party wasn't good for his *fucking* business. Knowing him, he'd make a party fuck schedule so he didn't miss any holes.

She was suddenly off the phone. "He's not lying." She walked over to Sahvrin and grabbed the knife from his side then headed over to Beaux, cutting through the rope. "Sorry about that, Lil Boy Beaux," she said quietly, tapping his chest with a smile then standing.

Sahvrin eyed him, taking the knife from Juliette when she handed it to him. "We'll get these two to church," he said, sheathing his blade and eyeing their catch taped to the boat floor. "Beaux, you'll stay at the house. I'm sure Lazure will want to ask you questions."

The look of terror on his face was warranted. The First Bishop wasn't anybody he'd want to be on the wrong side of either. "Don't worry," Juliette said, climbing in her seat and strapping in. "I'll hold your hand."

The look that put on his face said he'd take a bullet just to be able to hold any part of her.

Mon Dieu, how quick the swamp tides turned.

CHAPTER 23

After realizing how far they'd have to haul their beloved patrons, Sahvrin decided to tie them to the first hidden tree suitable.

"You're going to die, I hope you know," the colorful one said. "And we know you have our missing girl," he added, grinning. "They're gonna get her back and finish what they started."

"Fuuuuckin' shit," Zep muttered. "I wouldn't mind a *bit* if you did, but don't forget you wanted to interrogate later."

Sahvrin's rage peaked into that deadly calm as he stooped down and pulled out his knife, gripping the man's filthy jaw tight. Holding his head against the tree, he stared into those hateful eyes, calling out the visions of His Petite, beaten half to death. He gripped his hair in his fist and slammed his head three times against the tree then put the blade at his mouth. "Open."

Like a late bloomer, he finally seemed to realize his land balls were in the jaws of the swamp. Muffled wails strained out as his jaw gradually opened.

"Give me your *filthy* tongue."

"No, please," he begged. "I'm sorry, I was…I was lying."

Sahvrin forced the flat side of the blade between his teeth then turned it on its side, wedging his jaw open with it. "I'll dig around your fucking mouth for it with my knife till you're choking on blood."

He belted out several screams before finally sticking out his tongue, sobbing. Sahvrin gripped the slimy organ between his fingers and held tight as he slid his blade through it. He stopped shy of cutting it off, wanting it to dangle around in that abyss.

"Duct tape it," he said to Zep around his screams. He put the tip of his blade under his chin and pushed his mouth shut while Zep slapped tape on it.

They stood, watching him gurgle in panic for several seconds. "Drink up or choke to death, demon. Your fucking choice."

"That'll loosen him up for confession," Zep said. "He'll have to write it, though."

Sahvrin walked around the tree. "Big Man," he said, wiping the blood on his blade along his vest. "You have anything to say before we leave you here to think about your sins?"

"No sir," he said, shaking his head a lot.

Sahvrin stared long and hard into his terrified eyes then straightened.

"I'm already praying and repenting," he said, nodding a lot, holding Sahvrin's hard gaze.

"When I come back," Sahvrin said quietly, "we'll have a proper confession, and you'll spill your filthy soul."

"I will, I will," he nodded. "Every bit of it, I swear I will."

****

Beth woke in a panic and glanced around. Shit, shit, what time was it? She spotted a new bag on the floor near the door with her name on it and hurried to it. More clothes, yes!

At finding the cutest overall blue-jeaned shorts, she dressed in it with a red tank top. And more sandals! Please let them fit, please! She gasped in delight when they did, almost perfectly. She needed a mirror.

Hurrying down to the bathroom on the second floor, she entered it and shut the door for a look at her butt in the body length mirror. Of course it filled it out as it did everything but this time, a wave of desire hit her at recalling Sahvrin's reaction to it. Would it be the same in this? Was it too much? It wasn't *super* tight, but it was definitely obvious she had a fat butt. She had no idea how Sahvrin liked it, but she wasn't about to argue him out of it.

Making her way to the kitchen, she smiled at the delicious aroma, wondering if it always smelled like somebody had cooked a feast. She bet it did. Where was everybody? She spied a note on the counter and her heart flip-flopped at seeing *Ma Petite* at the top. Wow, such beautiful handwriting!

Juliette brought more clothes.

"Yep, found them."

I hope you get some sleep. I'll bring you a phone when I get back so you can call me if you ever want to.

She smiled at that. Only every minute of the day.

Everybody is in town for party supplies and hurricane prep. Lucas, Savvie and Katrina are there. Remember what we talked about.

Sahvrin.

Shit, right. Her heart pounded as she put the note in her front pocket at her breast, planning to keep it forever. She hurried out the door to find the love birds deciding to check obvious places first or at least asking. She knocked on the guest house door, peering around the large yard, turning when Katrina opened it. "Hi," Beth said, "how are you doing?"

"I'm good," she answered, looking like she'd just returned from a photoshoot. "Are you looking for Bishop?"

That name out of her mouth hit her like a punch in the gut. "I was actually looking for Lucas and Savvie. Sahvrin asked me to keep an eye on them."

"Ah, you too?"

"Yes," she said with a light laugh, wondering what he'd told Katrina while catching the beautiful ex's brief perusal of her outfit, bringing that timeless *fat-ass* feeling she always got in public.

"Isn't it *crazy* how those two get along?" Katrina said, shaking her head. "Bishop acts like I raised a putan."

"Putan?"

"A bitch," she clarified.

"Oh, God no," Beth assured. "He just doesn't want them getting hurt or doing anything—"

"Like him and I did?" she finished with a smirk and nod while looking around. "I get it. He doesn't want the same *mistakes* to happen. Don't blame him, neither do I."

"Do you know where they are?" Beth asked, ready to not hear another word about their past.

"I'm sure he's worried they'll fuck the first day and every day after like we did," she went on, like Beth hadn't even spoken. "Right under everybody's oblivious nose, every chance they get."

Maintaining composure suddenly got *very* hard. "They *are* young and inexperienced," was all she could manage to get out while wondering what the hell *experience* had to do with Lucas and Savvie.

Katrina did another full-body assessment of Beth, bringing the fat-ass up to a thousand percent. "I'm sure now that Bishop is in his prime, he's one hell of a force to be near." She fanned her face with a hand and anger heated Beth at the gesture. "Hot as hades here still. Sure hope you're on birth control, you'll need it with him. But there ain't nothin' like sultry swamp nights for hot sweaty sex," she said, taking a seat on one of the rocking chairs.

Wow. What a bitch. Right at home talking about the sex she had with the man that was now *hers*.

"Even as a sex therapist, it's been a challenge."

This got her immediate attention. "Sex therapist? You?"

She nodded, putting her hands in her back pockets and looking out at the yard.

"He's having problems? Not that it's my business."

You think, bitch? "With him being a force to contend with, I'm the one with the problems." Beth fanned her face like she had. "He's helping me learn how to keep up."

She gave a light snort. "How noble of him. Before you know it, he'll have fucked you in every room of every house here if he hasn't already."

Beth swallowed, ready to vomit. She couldn't do this. Katrina was way out of Beth's league in the sex with Sahvrin department. No, with *Bishop* department. Hell, there *was* no league between her and Sahvrin *or* Bishop. "I better go find the love birds," she said, heading down the steps.

"I tried to text Savvie about fifteen minutes ago. Check the docks," she called. "All that boy talks about is his *Swamp Dragons.*"

She couldn't even bring herself to say bye. She'd wanted to form a friendship with Katrina for everybody's sake, but like hell could she stomach hearing another word about their *non-stop fucking* while her and Sahvrin or Bishop hadn't even once. Every house and every room? No doubt every position. She'd taught him everything and visions of her fucking Sahvrin burned gaping holes in her brain. *Very first day and every day after, all day.*

Jealousy and pain had her psycho-walking, almost forgetting where she was going. Finally reaching the dock, she stopped abruptly at seeing Savvie and Lucas sitting near the boats. She backed up, hiding in the bushes, watching them for a moment. After a bit, her heart warmed at the way they laughed and carried on. Such sweet kids. Savvie was a doll, a mini version of Katrina, minus the bitch-slut-whore-putan.

Beth gasped when Savvie leaned and kissed Lucas on the cheek, a quick peck then she pulled away. Oh my. Beth held her breath as Lucas now stared at Savvies' profile for several seconds. The girl sat there not moving, maybe realizing she'd just crossed a line and panicked over what he might do or not do now. Lucas said something. Dammit what did he say? Beth's hand went to her chest when he leaned over and kissed her on the cheek. "Oh my, oh my," she whispered, emotion welling up at realizing it was likely his first kiss. She waited, her heart hammering in her chest, ready to interrupt if things got out of hand. Savvie scooted closer to him and leaned her head against his shoulder then Lucas reached around her and put his hand on her outer thigh, angling his head down at her with a smile that turned her into a blubbering mess.

She quickly wiped her eyes, needing to let them know they weren't alone. "There you guys are," she called, walking out, looking at the swamp so they had time to right themselves.

When she saw them standing in her peripheral, she waved and smiled at them now heading her way.

"I was asked to keep you two out of trouble," she said, blocking the sun with a hand at her brow smiling at them. "Then I slept like the dead for two hours." She gave a grin, pretending not to notice the awkward her words had just created. "So, what do you do around here for fun?" she asked Lucas.

"Normally, I'm working with Sahvrin," he said with one squinted eye. "But I have to babysit Savvie."

Savvie gasped and shoved him with a laugh. "You do *not!*"

"I can't have her getting eaten by an alligator. I hear they love New Orleans meat."

He looked down at her with a smile, creating that two's company, threes a crowd feeling. "I was talking to Katrina, she said she texted you."

Savvie gasped, pulling her phone out of her back pocket. "Crap, she did!"

"She's the one who told me to check here. Where's Luseah?" Beth wondered, realizing she hadn't seen her around.

"She's spending the week with a friend."

"Oh, okay. So Savvie hasn't met her yet."

"Not yet," Lucas said, like he might be praying the event never happened.

She realized how bad it would be if Luseah treated Savvie poorly at such a time.

"Oh no," Savvie muttered, panicked. "My dad texted."

Fear jolted Beth at that news while realizing Sahvrin didn't really go into details about what had happened. Now she felt stupid to not have found that out.

"Don't text him back," she hurried, realizing that might not be a good idea. More panic hit her at realizing she could have tracking on her phone. "Can I see your phone?" she asked.

Savvie handed it to her. "I just want to make sure you don't have any tracking services on here. Wouldn't want them showing up, surprise," Beth sang, drawing a whimper from Savvie. "God, I'm so sorry," Beth cried. "I say *stupid* shit when I'm nervous. Excuse the French!" Beth's fingers shook as she moved through the settings. Oh, holy shit. There it was. "Honey, I may need to disable your phone." She bit her tongue on *you're being tracked.*

"Oh my God, oh my God, do it. Can you?"

The amount of panic in her half cry was alarming. "Doing that now." Beth went to the phone identification to see what kind she had. "I'll need tools, let's go back to the house."

Once in the kitchen, it hit her that Katrina likely had tracking on hers too, holy shit. Surely Sahvrin thought of that with her. "I need a tiny flat tip screw-driver," she told Lucas.

He took off running while she went through all the apps, disabling the GPS related ones. "Thank you, sir," she said to Lucas when he returned with the screwdriver.

"Where'd you learn this?" he wondered, on his forearms next to her, watching.

"Plenty of Data Science classes with my Geospatial degree, also known as digital mapping." She opened the casing where the sim card would be located and dumped it out of the tray. "I'll destroy the SIM and he won't be able to use that for tracking. Now I need to look for any hidden ghost apps."

"Oh my God," she cried. "Can't you just get rid of it? He uses that to keep tabs on me, I don't even want it."

She eyed her than looked at Lucas. "Are you allowed to use a boat?"

"Yeah, why?"

She handed him the phone. "Take this about five miles from here and throw it in the water. I'd say feed it to an alligator so they're chasing that if they *are* tracking."

"He is, I promise you! Oh my God, I didn't even think of that!" she said between panicked breaths, pacing.

"She'll stay here with you," Lucas said.

"What? I'll go with you," she hurried, looking scared.

"Lucas, can you get Sahvrin on your phone for me so I can make sure all phones leading to the wrong place are disabled."

"Oh my God, my *mom's phone!*" she squealed, realizing.

"I'm sure they thought of it, honey, try not to panic."

"You don't know my dad, he's…he's very scary and not nice to my mom."

She was sure that was the understatement of the century. Lucas handed her his phone and she covered the mouthpiece while it rang. "Distract her," she mouthed to him.

"Everything okay?" Sahvrin said upon answering.

"It's me, Beth," she said, watching Lucas take Savvie to the huge swing under the tree.

"What's wrong?"

"Savvie's…uh, stepdad texted her."

"She has a *phone?*"

"Yes, I'm having Lucas take it five miles into the swamp and dumping it, she's really freaking out."

"Savvie is?"

"Yes, Sahvrin, she acts like he's a monster."

"Because he fucking *is!*"

"Oh my God, what about Katrina's phone?"

"Fucking Christ," he muttered. "I'll call Jek to see what he did with it. He's the Geek and I'm sure he handled it but I'm calling to make sure. Keep Lucas' phone with you."

"Okay, bye."

She went to the window, watching them on the swing. "Oh how precious," she whispered, seeing Savvie leaning into him with his arm around her. Sahvrin would probably not like that.

The phone rang and she swiped it. "Yes?"

"He says he wiped everything but now I'm nervous. I'll call her and tell her she needs to give Lucas her phone too, we can get her another one."

"Okay," she said.

"What's wrong? She say something to you?"

Was he reading her effing mind? "No, nothing like that."

"Then what?"

"It can wait."

"Okay. I just left the post office by the way. Your items were in."

"Oh," she said, excitement mixing with her anger, making her want to vomit. "Can't wait."

"Ma Petite, you're hiding a lot, I can hear it in your voice."

"Ugh," she mumbled. "I am. But like I said, it can wait."

"Oh, I'm sure it can," he muttered, as if knowing it was about Katrina. "You stay with Savvie while Lucas handles the phones."

"Yes sir," she said, closing her eyes at realizing it sounded like a submissive thing. "I didn't mean it like…in relation to… never mind."

"We'll talk soon, Ma Petite."

She hung up, letting out a huge shaky breath and putting the phone on the island only to snatch it back up and hurry outside.

Lucas and Savvie headed her way the second they saw her. "Sahvrin said to do as I suggested. He's calling Katrina to have her give her phone as well. Jek said he took care of it, but Sahvrin doesn't want to take any chances."

"Thank God," Savvie gasped, holding on to Lucas' arm.

Lucas tried to move out of her hold without being too obvious and Beth decided she'd better talk to him about what was going on, first chance. And Savvie. She sure didn't want Katrina corrupting the girl's mind with the wrong thing, biological mother or not. "Savvie, maybe you and I can find something to cook for our guys while we're waiting?"

She gave her a worried look. "I can't really cook." She glanced at Lucas. "I wanted to go with you," she said quietly.

He eyed Beth and she put her hands on her hips with a sigh. "I hate to break it to you guys, but Sahvrin wants you two chaperoned at all times." The look they gave her made her laugh. "Oh yeah, he's thinking what you think he's thinking."

Thank God they didn't argue. Lucas looked at Savvie. "I hear Betty Crocker makes everything easier. I know we have tons of her dishes in the pantry. Like brownies?"

"Oh, we have an order of brownies," Beth said. "Come on Savvie, I can't be trusted in the kitchen alone. We can talk about what we're wearing at the party tomorrow while we make a mess."

The smile Savvie gave put a big one on Lucas' handsome face. "I'll be back in about thirty minutes," he said to her. "Gonna get some clothes on first," he added, walking backward with his gaze still on her.

"Okay," she said, giving him a small wave and smile. "Be careful."

Beth gave her raised brows and a smile when he walked off. "That was a little painful to watch," she murmured under her breath as they headed to the house.

"What do you mean?" she asked, a smile in her voice. "And did Sahvrin really say we had to be chaperoned? Why?"

Beth laughed as she entered the kitchen. "Because it's so *obvious* you two are head over heels for each other!"

Her jaw dropped and Beth laughed. "You can *tell?*" Her blush was priceless.

"It's hard to hide that kind of thing," Beth said, going to the pantry next to the kitchen and returning with two bags of brownies and a huge grin. "Sit right there," she instructed, pointing to the stool at the counter and handing her a brownie bag. "You can read the directions and I'll make the mess."

After finding a mixing bowl and pans and setting the oven to the preheating temperature, she eyed Savvie. "Soooooo," she began with a huge smile, making Savvie blush.

"What?"

"Tell me *everything* of course!" The look on her face made Beth pause. "What's wrong?"

She barely shook her lowered head. "He's just…*so cute* and I'm…."

"You're what?" Beth pressed, dumping the contents in the bowl. "Drop dead gorgeous like him?"

This got her a huge laugh. "I'm *so* not gorgeous like him," she assured, pink cheeks and all.

"Are you serious?" Beth asked, realizing she might be. "Honey…"

Savvie looked up at her.

"Surely you know how beautiful you are?"

She lowered her head and Beth froze at seeing tears roll down her cheeks. "My mom's pretty, but I didn't inherit that."

Beth gave an offended gasp. "Who on earth told you *that* crock of shit?"

Savvie looked up with a little laugh then lowered her head again with a shrug. "My dad," she said around a squeak as more tears fell.

"Oh my God, he…he must've done that for other reasons."

She wiped her face. "Like what? To make me feel like crap? He's real good at that."

"Yes, that's exactly why!"

She looked at her, brows narrowed. "But why?" Like she'd asked that question a million times and hadn't come up with an answer that fit.

"The first reason that comes to mind is him not wanting you to know your worth. Not that looks define that, but he'd know to a young girl, they do, and if her dad is defining worth by looks then it makes sense you would too. But newsflash Savvie. He straight up lied to you! You are one of the most beautiful girls I have ever seen and I'm not buttering your bread!"

She gave a small smile.

"And Lucas sure agrees with me."

Her gaze shot to hers and the desperate hope and fear there was heartbreaking. "Why do you say that?"

"Oh honey, you don't see how he looks at you?"

"He doesn't seem to look at me. But I look a lot at him," she sputtered, wiping her face.

"Then he's hiding it well from you, but I can see it. And…I may have seen the little kiss that happened on the dock." Beth laughed at her worried look. "It's okay. That was mighty brave of you."

"More like stupid," she gasped. "I don't know what I was thinking other than…I would die if I didn't kiss this boy who was more beautiful than anything I'd ever seen and so kind to me. I'd just meant it as a thank you and when he asked why I did it, I *froze* and couldn't answer him! It was horrible!"

"Until he kissed you back?"

The way her body seemed to melt, and her eyes fluttered into her head made Beth laugh. "Oh, I know *exactly* how you're feeling. I had the exact same reaction with Sahvrin."

"It's like a spell!" Savvie whispered, serious as can be.

"What did he tell you when you kissed him?" she was dying to know.

"He asked *why* I did it!"

"Such a Bishop question," Beth laughed, grabbing four eggs from the basket on the counter.

"And all I could do was apologize!"

"And then he kissed you back."

"Yes," she said, sounding dizzy while putting her hands over her chest. "And he said, 'I'm not sorry'."

"Swooooooon," Beth said, cracking the eggs into the dry mix. "Sahvrin says some of the most amazing things too. I told him he needed to write for Hallmark."

Savvie laughed at that, such a cute tinkling sound before going serious. "But what if…something happens, and I have to leave? I might never see him again."

Beth paused her mixing. "You don't have to leave, you can stay here as long as you like. This can be your home."

Savvie gave her a confused look, maybe even scared to hope such a thing. "You think?"

Beth really wished she could say more. "Sahvrin is a very good man. He'd *never, ever* let anything hurt you."

"My mom says the same." She lowered her head. "She told me all about the swamp life in her younger days." She smiled now, casting her a shy look. "I used to pretend her and I lived in the swamps alone with nobody telling us what to do and where to go. Nobody… being so mean to my mom…"

Beth put down her spoon and hurried around the island. "Come here," she said, wrapping her arms around her. "What if I said you can have that dream? Sahvrin said he's *happy* to have you and your mom here for as long as you want to stay. That means forever if you want!" She pet her head, letting her cry. "Trust me when I say your life is changed forever now. This is your new life, and you can enjoy it. Besides, the Bishops are like the Swamp Kings, and nobody knows the waterways like they do. So, even if they wanted to find you, they couldn't. And if Sahvrin thought they might, he'd move us to a hidden location, even *deeper* in the swamp."

She pulled back, wiping her eyes and looking at her. "How long have you known him?"

At realizing she didn't know him long enough to be so certain about him, she went with telling her how she got there. "I know this is going to sound crazy to you but…about two weeks ago, I was in a very bad situation too that Sahvrin saved me from."

"Really?"

She nodded. "He rescued me, and I was…really in a bad way. He literally nursed me back to health and I fell in love with him and…" She lowered her head. "Well, I'm pretty sure he feels the same." Beth made her way back around the counter. "Just because somebody doesn't say the words doesn't mean you can't know something. I know what Mr. Bishop feels."

"I'm so embarrassed he wanted us to be chaperoned. What if he doesn't…want me to…like his brother since I'm the daughter of somebody he obviously hates?"

Ugh, crap. "He just doesn't want you two going fast, that's all. He wants you to take your time and not do things that…married people do."

"Sex?" she asked, smiling. "I'm used to that word, trust me." Beth's face fell. "Not used to it like *that*," she hurried.

"Oh, thank God," Beth said, pouring the batter into the large pan and licking her finger. "Mmm." She handed her the bowl after scraping. "Wanna lick it?"

"Really?" she asked, taking it.

"Duh, yeah," Beth assured incredulous. "Can't be wasting all that chocolate down the drain."

"Right?" she said, swiping her finger and eating with a huge grin. "Mmmmm, yes."

"Don't try to tell me you never licked a bowl."

She shook her head. "Mom is so funny about that! Germ this germ that."

"Ohhh, my own *mother* was the same way!"

"Really? How annoying."

"My dad however was the opposite, but he had to sneak behind mom because she'd have a fit if she knew."

"Your dad sounds nice," she said with a smile, still licking away.

"He is. My mom died a couple years ago, and it's been hard for him."

"Oh man, sorry," she said, eyeing her while swiping her mouth with her tongue.

"Sooooo, let's talk about what we're wearing for the party!"

The excitement that put on her face made Beth feel like a superhero. God, she could get used to this whole parenting thing. So fulfilling!

CHAPTER 24

Sahvrin finally made it to the dry dock and helped load all the supplies onto the boat needed in the swamp. When it was finished, he called the men together, wanting to touch base.

At the table under the big oak tree, he put his foot on the chair, too wound up to sit. "Just wanted to go over everything before things get away from us. I'm putting it all in our box but wanted to talk about a couple things. The first one being the guns and when we want to run that. Once we figure that out, I'll make the first shipment date official. We have two Roulettes waiting for interrogation at the Weigh Station. When we want to handle that?" he asked, looking at Lazure.

"Tonight. When the women and kids are asleep."

"Good," Sahvrin said, looking at the rest who all nodded in agreement as well. "Please tell me one of you has information on her father or anything surrounding that? She's been asking."

"Nothing you'd want to tell her," Bart said. "I found a connection between stalker Julien and him."

"What kind?"

"Mostly that the father knows his family well and they have financial links to Roulettes. That's about it, nothing definitive yet."

"Keep digging. I may ask Juliette to call her father and pose as a concerned friend she met while down here just to see where his head is." He looked at Lazure. "What about the guns shipment? Any plans?"

"Preferably before a hurricane and since the current one shifted tracks, do it while we can, I say. We'll still meet The Twelve tomorrow night at the party and begin mobilizing The Horde."

"Sounds good," Sahvrin said. "Beaux should be at the house soon enough with Juliette for any questions you might have for him."

"Good, and once that's done, he can help with preparations."

"What about Savvie," Bart wondered. "When we breaking the news to her? Katrina suggest anything on that? And what about her and Lucas?"

"Who and Lucas?" Zep asked, making Sahvrin wonder who else he *thought* Bart meant.

"Lucas and Savvie," Bart said, with a serious laugh. "Those two are falling hard man, something needs to be said before it gets too far. That's fucked up."

"They're not technically related," Sahvrin said, hating to even deal with it but needing to.

"But Lucas should know better, he knows the truth," Lazure said.

Sahvrin dropped his foot off the chair, pacing a little. "Hard to control that kind of thing Lazure. I ask him to help make her feel welcome, and well…he did a great job of it."

"You never see the boy interested in girls and now this?" Lazure said with wide eyes.

"You can't be more surprised than me," Sahvrin assured. "I've had front row seats with it and it's like watching a boat sink. Beth thinks it's sweet."

"I have to say I'm glad to see his testosterone works," Jek muttered.

"You had doubts?" Sahvrin asked, incredulous.

"Maybe a couple."

"So is Katrina and Savvie going to be living at the guest house indefinitely?" Zep asked.

"What the fuck does it matter to you?" Sahvrin asked.

"Whoooa, back up," Zep said, eyeing him.

"Savvie mentioned you *entertained* Katrina and I honestly don't give a shit if you want to fuck her, but take it to the swamps, don't you dare fuck my daughters mother where she would know. She's already seen too much of that shit, she doesn't need her own uncle doing it too."

Zep kept his head down, but the tight line of his lips said he was too pissed to speak. "Didn't realize you had feelings for Katrina still," he finally muttered, eyeing him.

Sahvrin shook his head and aimed a finger at him. "Don't fucking play games with me, not about this. I mean it."

He finally raised both hands, looking him in the eye. "I hear you loud and clear big bro. If I wanna fuck her, I'll take her deep into the swamps where nobody can hear her screaming orgasms."

"Thanks *brother,* I really appreciate that. Always nice to know you have my fucking back."

"Hold the *fuck* up," Lazure said, eying Zep now. "What the fuck are you *saying?* You don't *fuck* your brother's ex *anything*," he yelled now. "You can have any woman you want in Breaux Bridge, but *don't* you fucking disgrace this family by doing something like that."

"I hear!" Zep yelled back. "I wasn't intending that if it makes a fucking difference."

It didn't. Not to Sahvrin. He knew his fornicating adulterous brother too well. He fucked whatever he wanted, single, married, widowed. Young, old, handicap, it didn't matter. He'd *been* a fucking disgrace to the family.

"So, what about business," Jek said in the following silence. "We're still switching to modifying weapons for the shit storm coming?"

"Absolutely," Lazure said, looking at Sahvrin. "Can you manage that?"

"Yeah," he said, not really thinking about it. "I got it." They didn't have a choice.

"Once we meet with The Twelve," Lazure said, "you'll get the current resource numbers from Nickels, after he gets it from the Keepums so we know *exactly* what we need."

"I'm going to tell Savvie tonight," Sahvrin said, deciding he didn't want to wait another minute. "She's terrified of her fake dad, and it'd give me no greater pleasure than to let her know I'm her father and she doesn't have to be afraid."

"I support this," Lazure said with a nod. "She needs to know that."

"Agreed!" Bart said. "Then I get to be *Uncle* Bart!"

****

Sahvrin was exhausted by the time they finished unloading the boat at the main supply house in the swamp and made their way back to the house. His body ached with the need to touch His Petite and the idea that he could suddenly need anybody as much as he did, boggled his mind.

He needed more rest, that's for one thing. He'd been pushing too hard, too long.

He remembered the phone he'd bought Beth, feeling in his pocket to make sure it was still there. He pulled out his phone and dialed Juliette.

"Where are you?" he asked.

"With Beaux at the house like you said to be."

"When'd you get there?" he wondered.

"About an hour ago, why?"

"Did you meet Beth and Savvie yet?"

"I sure did, they're with us now."

"Us who?"

"Beaux and me?"

"Where?"

"We're playing in the soap house, Mr. Fifty questions."

"Sorry," he said, rubbing his eyes with his thumbs and index fingers. "I need a favor."

"Anything," she said, and he knew she meant it.

"I need you to call Beth's father and find out where his head is, fish around for information indirectly. Maybe pose as a friend she made here during the festival or something."

"Can do. Just need a number."

"I'll get Bart to text it to you. Don't use your real name obviously and block your number."

"He may not answer."

"Well…try, then we'll figure out what to do if he doesn't."

"Got it."

"How is everybody doing?"

"Beth is good," she said. "An ange, as you say, and my Lord, you didn't tell me she was so *gorgeous*."

"She is," he said, the pure truth of it making him smile.

"And Savvie, swamp-heavens, she's your little twin!"

"You think" he asked, laughing. "I was thinking more like yours."

She sucked in a breath. "I'll *take it!*"

He laughed nodding. "I'm telling her tonight. Savvie, I mean."

"Ohhh, really?"

"After finding out she's terrified of her imposter dad, yeah. She needs to know she's safe because she's mine."

"Ohhhhh, now that was some sexy daddy talk right there."

"I'll be there in fifteen minutes."

"You want me to tell *Your Petite?*"

"You can if you want."

"I do want. And I hate to break it to you big bro," she muttered. "But Lil Lucas and—"

"I already know."

"Shoooo, you realize he's not technically related to her, right?"

"Yes. I do."

"Good cuz…they are for real and there ain't no hidin' it." She snickered. "It's kind of hilarious to watch, the poor darlings."

"I want to know as much as I don't."

"Awww, is daddy worried?"

"Very."

"Lucas is a *sweetheart!*"

"I know he is and that's why I'm worried about him."

There was a brief pause and a "Ohhhhhhh, I seeeee. Oh Sahvrin, Savvie is literally love struck with him."

"I fucking *hope* so because…"

"Oh honey, I know, I know, and I'm right there with you. But I know what I'm seeing."

"So did I all those years ago. Things fade."

"I'm not gonna pretend there aren't risks in love, bubba, there are, and it's everybody's duty in life to take those risks at some point."

"And are you?" he wondered, remembering her Beaux theatrics.

"Meh who, me? I'm married to the alligators!"

He chuckled. "Call me or text me later with whatever you learn about her father?"

"Will do."

"Pulling up in five now."

"I'll let the desperate one know."

****

After sending Beaux to help with preparations and getting Juliette to babysit Romeo and Juliette, he finally got His Petite alone. They were still in the soap house and the scents had a soothing effect on his nerves. He walked up behind her where she played with soap jars and wrapped his arms around her, moaning into her neck. "I missed you," he murmured, nuzzling his mouth on the warm skin. The feel of her fingers running in his hair was fucking heaven. Almost as divine as the delicate sounds of need in her throat.

"I'm going to tell Savvie tonight," he said before he went past the point of no return with her.

She turned and looked at him. "You are?"

At seeing the approval all over her face, something loosened in him. "Yes. After you told me she was scared, I decided I needed to."

"I agree. And I needed to tell you something else," she said, putting her hand on his arm as a light entered her eyes. "She told me that her mom told her about life in the swamp and she used to pretend that her and her mom lived here by themselves with nobody telling them what they could do or where they could go and nobody to hurt her mother. Sahvrin," Beth gasped, tears entering her eyes. "That was so pitiful to hear."

Her happy reaction confused him. "How is that good?" he wondered, feeling like he was missing something.

Her face immediately fell. "Oh, it's not good, sorry, I didn't mean to seem like it was. I just thought you would want to know she had dreams of living out here because you were worried she might not like it."

"She was a child dreaming things she has no real idea about," he said. "When did she tell you this?"

"When Lucas went drive the phones to the middle of nowhere, I talked her into making brownies with me. She wanted to go with him. Oh, and their love condition has gotten worse," she warned. I saw Savvie kiss Lucas on the cheek."

Panic hit him. "In front of you?"

"No! I...I slept later than I meant to, I'm sorry, and I hurried out to find them and they were on the dock. I decided to watch them for a moment, see the real deal and she leaned and kissed him. On the cheek," she clarified.

"What did he do?"

"Well..." she began seeming to force a serious look, "...he stared at her at first and Savvie told me later that he asked why she did, and she said she'd done it because he was the most beautiful person she'd ever met and so kind to her and she just wanted to thank him."

"She said all that to him?"

"No, sorry!" She grimaced a little before clarifying. "She said it to *me,* explaining why she'd done it but when *he* asked her why, she *froze* and all she could say was *I'm sorry!*" Beth put her hand on her chest. "But wait," she whispered. "Lucas told her he wasn't sorry, and he kissed her back on the cheek." She covered her mouth with her hand. "I think it was their first kiss. Like ever."

Fucking great. "And why is this so amazing to you?" he wondered, confused as fuck now. "Fuck, I'm sorry," he muttered, seeing his words stung her. "I told you to sleep, all of this is on me."

"Sahvrin… Savvie is—"

"For real, I know. Juliette says the same thing. And like I told her, we can be wrong about what we're so sure about."

She nodded, considering that. "You're right, I…I'm being… I'm thinking of all the wrong things."

"No, you're thinking of the right things, and I'm thinking of the wrong things. It just so happens that the wrong things happen instead of the right things in life, and if you don't think about them, you can't do a damn thing to stop it."

She nodded again, then shook her head. "You're so right. I don't know what I was doing. Am doing." She turned to the counter for several seconds. "Oh and then we made brownies and I let her lick the bowl," she said quietly. "Said her mom never let her do that because she had a germ phobia and I told her my mom did too," she said, her words straining. "But my dad used to let me do things when she wasn't looking and Savvie was happy. I felt amazing that I was able to do that for her."

Sharvin hurried over and wrapped his arms around her. "I'm fucking sorry Angel, forgive me." He pressed his lips into her temple. "I'm exhausted and down to my prick instincts."

She took a huge breath and seemed to hold it then let it out slowly, wiping her eyes, turning to him. "Why don't you go get some sleep. I really should've considered how that would make you feel, I don't know what I was thinking. I wasn't, as usual." She covered her face with both hands, her tears coming again. "But I saved you some brownies."

Her whispered words crushed him more. He took her head between his hands. "Thank you. So much," he said, kissing the backs of her fingers. "For being here, for being you." She lowered her hands finally. "There you are. Give me these lips." He devoured them and didn't stop till she forgave and forgot his stupidity.

"Do you think," she gasped around his kiss, "that I should…be there when you tell Savvie?"

He pulled up, breathless, staring at her. "You think?" he wondered, really not sure.

"Are you…having Katrina there?"

"No," he said, shaking his head, stroking her face.

"Are you telling Katrina that you're telling her?"

He considered that and shook his head. "I'm just going to tell her. I don't trust her not to do something stupid."

Beth nodded. "I agree. I don't need to be there, I don't even want to, I mean I do, I'm just thinking…"

"Tell me," he said, kissing softly at her lips.

"Just that…she might feel better having me there."

"You think so?" He smiled on her mouth. "You're going to make a wonderful mother," he said, kissing the tip of her nose and making her smile.

"I was thinking that too," she said, like she'd not thought of it till recently.

Mon Dieu, this woman. He wrapped her in a bear hug and lifted her with a groan. "I can't wait to get you in my room."

"First Savvie?" she asked.

"First Savvie, yes."

CHAPTER 25

"Are you sure I should be here?" Beth asked one more time from the big swing under the tree.

"I'm very sure," he said, raising their clasped hands and kissing hers.

"There she is," Beth said, waving to her, more nervous than he was maybe.

Savvie seemed in good spirits, and she was sure Lucas had everything to do with that but wasn't about to say anything now that she saw how much it bothered Sahvrin.

Beth scooted over to let her sit between them, and at the last second it felt like Sahvrin tried to hold her next to him. Oops.

"What's up?" Savvie asked, sitting and looking at Beth.

"It's Sahvrin that wanted to talk to you," she said, pointing at him. She gave her a wink and smile at seeing the worry in her face.

"Hi Sahvrin," she said. "What's up?"

"Not much, kiddo, how was your day?"

"It was fun. Beth and I made brownies for the guys."

"I heard," he said, smiling at her. "Thank you for that."

She lowered her head. "If you're wanting to talk to me about Lucas..."

"No, that's not what I want to talk to you about."

"Oh," she said, sounding only a little less worried. "Is it...about my dad?"

"Yes, it is, actually," Sahvrin said. "I have to tell you something that's kind of a big deal."

She stared, and Beth took her hand, holding it. "Okay."

Sahvrin leaned forward with his forearms on his legs, head down. "I've probably never been more scared to tell somebody something in all my life," he admitted, warming Beth's heart. Honesty was good. Vulnerable even better.

"What?" Savvie wondered.

"Your mom and I used to be married.... And when she left the swamp all those years ago, she was... pregnant with you. Only I didn't know, she never told me. It wasn't until she came asking for help that I learned this."

He stared at her while Beth stroked her hand.

"So...you're..."

"I'm your real father. And I'm...sorry that I never knew about you. If I had, I would've never left you there. Or your mom. But I will never let you go, you're safe with me as long as you want to stay. And I do hope you want to stay. I don't want you to ever leave."

Beth froze when Savvie tugged her hand out of hers and held it in her lap, looking down. She caught Sahvrin's look, and held up a hand, signaling he wait.

"Does this mean...Lucas is..."

"Lucas isn't blood related, honey," Beth said.

"So... your romance is safe," Sahvrin said, to which Beth nodded approval when he eyed her.

"What now?" he mouthed with wide eyes.

"You okay honey?" Beth asked after many seconds. "There's no wrong way to feel about this. No matter how you feel, it's okay. Mad, sad, happy, guilty, you can't do wrong with this."

"All of it," she whispered, wiping her eyes, looking in her lap still.

"Okay, that's good," Beth said. "Anger is definitely understandable."

She sucked in a jagged sob, wiping her eyes again. "Only I don't know who to be angry at," she said. "My mom? How can I be mad at her, she's done nothing but try to be a good mom even though she mostly sucks at it. Even when she gets beat on by that…stupid man I thought was my father," she gushed, then let out a sob, wiping her eyes more as her breaths shook. "I'm so glad he's not my dad, I hate him. And somehow, I'm guilty about that?" she squealed, confused. "Why would I be guilty for hating a monster?"

She turned and Beth put her arms around her, petting her head. "Because you thought he was your dad, that's all, and you just wanted his love."

"I was never pretty enough, or good enough or smart enough," she choked out bitterly.

Beth eyed Sahvrin, worried over the dark look on his face. God, he was pissed.

"I understand the guilt," Sahvrin said quietly. "I didn't know and yet I can hardly stand to be in my own skin. I let this happen, I let my own blood, my own daughter get hurt for all these years. I'm sorry, this was a bad idea to tell her."

"Sahvrin," Beth called as he walked off.

Savvie flew off the swing with a "Wait!"

He turned and she plowed into his body, wrapping her arms around him. Beth covered her mouth, stifling a sob.

"Don't be sorry, I'm glad, I swear I am. Don't be sad."

He buried his face on her head, hugging her back tight. "I am sorry, and I am so sad," he gasped. "I missed you, I missed everything, you don't even know me."

"I can learn," she wept. "We can learn."

****

Sahvrin climbed the stairs after his shower, feeling more exhausted than ever and yet lighter. He opened the door and froze at finding His Petite presenting herself in the middle of the room in tiny sheer shorts and matching white top. Mon Dieu, she was going to kill him this night.

"Hi," she said, with a small wave.

"Hi," he said back, his cock delivering aching blows as he shut the door and locked it. He remembered the books and made his way to the desk where he'd stored them. He pulled the chair out and sat, opening the drawer on his right, then put the first one on the desk, then the second. He shut the drawer and sat facing her.

She stared at the books, both hands before her. He looked at them on the desk and grabbed the top one, showing it to her.

"That's the one," she said, breathless.

"I read a little of the BDSM one."

"Really?"

He nodded, his gaze moving slowly down and locking on the dark triangle of hair beneath the sheer material. "Come closer," he said.

She took slow steps and stopped right next to him. "What does Ma Petite want tonight?" he asked.

She licked her lips, reminding him how hard those questions were for her. "What are you offering?" she whispered.

His gaze slid up her body, pausing at her hard nipples before continuing to her timid gaze. "Whatever she wants."

She swallowed and again licked her lips, making him rock hard. "I want…you to…"

She lowered her gaze, and he angled his head, finding her struggle arousing as usual.

"I want you to…*fuck* me."

The gasped words sledgehammered his balls while he considered what she really wanted behind that request. She knew they were waiting to do that and yet she was requesting it. "Ma Petite is so rebellious," he mused, grabbing his cock and moving his hand over it. "Always asking for that which she knows not to ask." He eyed her now. "I ask myself why she does this and can only think of one thing. It's not that she's bad at being submissive, it's that she chooses to be bad at various times. The next question I ask is why does she choose to be bad at what she claims to want to be?" He tsked. "She chooses to be naughty because she wants to be punished." He eyed her tits for many burning seconds before looking at her. "Tell me I'm wrong," he dared.

"I...I do sometimes do things that I know are... wrong. On purpose."

"Like now."

She licked her lips, not meeting his gaze. "Not now, no."

He angled his head at that answer. "So... you're genuinely asking me to fuck you when we agreed we'd wait," he double checked.

She nodded but he was far from convinced. "Ma Petite, do you recall what your BDSM book says about disobedient submissives?"

"I...don't really recall. Exactly."

"They get punished," he said, very convinced she knew that much. "Do you know how they get punished in your BDSM book, Ma Petite?"

"I'm...not sure," she said, breathless now.

"I think you know," he said. "I think your ass is tingling right now at the idea of it. When I read it, I actually laughed. But now...." He groaned, lowering his pants to free his cock and stroke it. "I don't find it funny at all. I find it...very reasonable, yes?"

"I...In some circumstances, yes," she gasped with eyes closed.

"Ma Petite, your clit is aching right now at the idea of it."

Her breaths trembled out with her "Yes."

"Because you *want* me to punish you."

"I…I do," she whispered. "But…I really want you to fuck me tonight. Right now," she added.

Sahvrin stared for many seconds before it finally hit him. He put his cock back in his pants. "You were supposed to tell me what happened today Ma Petite. How about you tell me that now."

Her eyes met his then her brows drew together. "Can't we…talk later?"

He slowly shook his head.

"I don't want to talk about that now."

"I know you don't," he said. "But I need to know."

"Why?"

"Because whatever happened has changed our schedule and I want to know what it is. Was it Katrina?" He fucking knew it was. "What did she say to you?"

"Stupid…things," she said with eyes closed now.

"Like *what*?" he asked, holding tight to his slipping patience. Watching His Petite cross her arms over her chest brought his anger. "Do I need to call her and make her confess?"

Her eyes flashed to his and the anger in them rose his brows. "She talked about your earlier days together."

That. Fucking. Bitch. He stared at her, his rage not brining calm, but the opposite. "Did she."

She only nodded but her jaw was hard now.

"What will it take to get it out of you all at once instead of in tiny disgusting bits?"

"I can't say it," she strained, shaking her head, determined.

"Can't? Won't?"

"I won't, I won't say it." She embraced herself while eyeing him with *fury*. That Katrina had brought such an emotion in his angel aimed at *him* had him seething with the same.

"Then I'll call her."

"Why? Do you *want* to hear her say it?" she gasped.

He stood. "I want to hear *you* say it."

"Well I don't *want* to say," she yelled, her fury growing. "I don't want to say how you *fucked* her every day in every room, in every position!"

"Holy fuck," he strained, his rage still going in the opposite of calm. "Is that why you're wanting to *fuck?*" he asked, incredulous. "Because that bitch bragged about the lies we lived? Who are you fucking for? Her?"

"Me!" she yelled. "I'm fucking for me because I want to know what that is with you!"

"Not make love, but *fucking*," he clarified, maybe pissed with that more than anything. He half circled her, his anger boiling. "So, I'm supposed to *fuck* you the way I fucked *her,* is that it? Is that what you want? Is that what it all boils down to? Just fucking?"

She covered her face with both hands then wrenched them away, stalking to his dresser. She yanked open a drawer and pulled out a robe, fighting her way into it as she headed for the door.

Sahvrin beat her to it and slammed his hand against it. "Tell me why. Why are you doing this now?"

"When will I be safe enough for you to love me the way you loved her, the way you risked everything and lost yourself in her in *every room*. How am I supposed to even *stand* being here when everywhere I go, I'll wonder, 'Did he fuck her here? What position? How many times!" She pointed toward the bed. "And here, in this *bedroom*, that *bed,* I have to know that you *fucked* her more times than you can count, you *bastard!*" she screamed, shoving him twice with both hands. "How can you do this to me*,*" she demanded.

Sahvrin grabbed her by her hand and pulled her after him.

"What are you doing?" she demanded.

"Bringing you where I *haven't* fucked her."

****

He didn't even let her change, he stalked with her all the way to the front dock where the normal boats were and put her in one like a child. Thirty minutes later, her fury had boiled over. "Just how *fucking far* does one have to *drive* to get to a place where Mr. Bishop hasn't *fucked* his precious Katrina?" His silence infuriated her, and she threw everything she had at him. "I hate this stupid swamp, I hope you're driving me out of it! I promise you I will *never* come back!"

She finally put her head on her lap and covered her head with both arms, sobbing till the boat finally slowed. She lifted her head and looked around, recognizing where she was. His little home in the swamp. Tears flooded her eyes at realizing it wasn't contaminated by that *bitch*.

He turned off the boat and climbed out, then pulled her onto the pier. Before she could protest, he was kissing her, his hands holding her face tight. "This is us," he gasped, biting at her lower lip between ragged breaths. "Every inch of this place is you and me, do you understand?" He wrapped his arms around her, hugging her so tight. "This place was a grave before you came. Now it's home, *our* home, you fucking did that."

Her sudden regret and pain burst forth on a sob. "I'm sorry, I didn't mean it, I didn't. I never want to leave you, I don't care where you live or go, I never want to leave you!"

He shhhh'd and soothed her just like he'd done from the first day he'd pulled her out of the swamp as he carried her inside. But the hole in her chest from Katrina still ached in her bones.

CHAPTER 26

Sahvrin sat on his bed with His Petite in his lap, not wanting to let her go. He spent several minutes kissing and soothing her, while the mess she made inside him swirled out of control. But the chaos was different, it was all her, a hurricane of energy, so sharp it cut him, so bright it blinded him, so right it shamed him.

And yet, even as he sat there, he knew he'd *not* fuck her, not now, *not* like this. She deserved so much more than a fix fuck and he wouldn't let fucking Katrina take that gift from His Petite.

Her lips nuzzled at his neck, and he closed his eyes, steeling himself against the tiny gift while praying she didn't push him. Her hot tongue against his skin as she opened her mouth wider with a moan slammed against his will.

Her perfect, sweet lips moved along his face and there was no resisting her kiss and he didn't want to.

His hands slid along her waist and hips as he moaned in her mouth, again praying she didn't try to go too far.

She turned and straddled his lap then lifted her top, pulling his mouth to her breast. He took it with a reckless hunger. "Yes," she gasped, her fingers scraping along his scalp. "Touch me, please," she begged, taking hold of his hands and moving them to her ass.

He let go a harsh breath and filled his hands with it. She moved his head to her other breast, her own hunger unravelling him.

"Make love to me," she gasped, pushing against his shoulders, forcing him down onto the bed. He let her but then wrapped his arms around her body, holding her against him.

"Ma Petite," he whispered between breaths while stroking her head and back. "I will *not* fuck you to make this right."

She lay still and quiet on him for too long.

"I won't let her make me hurry this with you, do you understand?"

She rolled off of him and pushed out of his attempt to hold her. "Don't...touch me."

"Ma Petite—"

"Don't call me that," she said, her quiet pain cutting him. "You don't get to call me that anymore."

"What if I made love to you right now, Beth? How would it make you feel knowing why I did?"

"Like a fucking beggar that finally got their way," she said, her voice breaking as she got up and went sit on the couch.

He followed, standing before her. "How could it ever feel right or be right when the reason you want it is because that bitch provoked you to this?"

She shot up and pointed in his face. "*You* provoked me to this, *not* her. You act like you don't want her dictating your life, your decisions, but she's the reason you're making us wait, she's the reason we have to make sure it's *safe*! She's dictating when I get to have you, how I get to have you because if everything isn't just right, then I don't get the man I want, the man who dove into love with all he had. How dare you! How dare you keep the man I love away from me! You are *mine,* Bishop is *mine,* Sahvrin is *mine!* There is no woman on this earth that will ever love you more and I *want what's mine!*" she screamed. "I'm the one you've been waiting for, you found me, I'm right here and I'm *dying*," she wailed now. "Why did you pull me from the swamp if you were just going to *kill* me!"

Sahvrin caught her as she fell, fucking panicked at everything she'd just said. What had he done? He'd broken his angel. Fuck, God, no.

"Ma Petite," he whispered, his breaths shaking as he held her in his arms, rocking her as she wailed like a baby. "Oh fuck, fuck I'm sorry." He sat her on the couch and took her face in his hands, kissing all over it, desperate to undo what he'd done. "Beth, I love you, do you fucking hear me? You have to listen, you have to hear me. I swore, I fucking swore to God I would never let *anybody* use your sweet soul for themselves, including me, do you understand?" He pet her face over and over. "I wanted to give you time to make sure I was what you wanted, this life, this swamp, my family. And I wanted to make love to you so *fucking* bad the first time you asked me to, please you have to believe that," he gasped, pressing his forehead to hers. "I wanted my angel to be sure she got exactly what she wanted, not what I fucking wanted, but the *second* I knew that you wanted me, then you were fucking mine, do you hear me? You were mine before I laid a finger on you." His breaths came ragged. "I know I said…I wanted you to choose without pressure but… I'm begging you to choose the bastard that hurt you the first day we met. And I will spend the rest of my life making you the happiest angel, I fucking swear to it."

Her lips suddenly covered his, her nails clawing his face with desperate cries mixed with her sweet passion. He kicked the coffee table into the wall, pulling her to the floor, his mouth never leaving hers.

"Are you sure," she gasped between moans, her fingers pulling his hair.

"So *fucking* sure," he answered with a bite to her lower, then upper lip, groaning at the soft cry she gave while his hands raced to feel every inch of her. God, he was going to hurt her, he knew without a doubt he wouldn't be able not to.

He held her jaw tight and sat up, pulling her with him. "You need to do it, Angel," he shuddered. "I need you to fuck me." He got on his knees, undoing his pants. "I'll hurt you if you don't."

She answered with shuddered breaths, kissing and sucking along his chest, her hungry fingers piercing his skin everywhere until his groans filled with lust. She helped him out of his pants, and pulled him around the couch, pushing him down on the bed.

"Fuck, yes baby," he whispered, quickly turning on the small light above the headboard. "I need to see you," he said, ready to beg for it.

She removed her bottom then top and climbed back on him and sat.

"Fuck, protection," he said, closing his eyes in desperation.

She went still and he looked at her, heaving with desire. "I know how to check."

Check? "Check what?"

"If I'm fertile."

He let go of a breath while holding her hips. "Do it," he said. "If you need protection, I swear to God I'll go right now to Mah-Mah's love pantry and get some."

She raised up on her knees and he angled his head, watching her reach between her legs and push her finger in and out of her pussy. "Fuck," he breathed, at hearing how wet she was.

She pulled it out and looked at the essence then spread it between her fingers. "Thick," she said, casting him a look.

"What does that mean?"

She reached down and took hold of his cock, moving on her knees till she was right above it.

"Yes?" He grabbed hold of it at the base with one hand and gripped her thigh with the other.

He held it tall for her and she lowered her pussy right onto the head with a delicate, agonized, "Yes."

The feel of her hot silk on the head of his dick had him seething already. His fingers dug into her thigh as he moved himself slowly along her opening, fighting the instinct to thrust while she twirled her hips on him.

"Sahvrin," she gasped, pressing her nails into his wrists.

"Fuck. My cock is on your beautiful pussy," he said between breaths. "I never want to stop seeing that."

He looked up her body, groaning at the way her tits pushed together. "Your fucking nipples." He moved his hips, hurrying his eyes down to his cock, then back up to her face. "So fucking beautiful," he whispered, watching her in pleasure. "Make your clit hot right on my cock, Ma Petite. Then fuck me," he said, fighting the reckless urges tickling his muscles. "And then I'm going to fuck you. Mon Dieu, I'm going to fuck you so good."

With her tight pussy right on the head, she moved with little downward pumps. He let go of his cock and grabbed her hips in both hands. "Oh fuck, you're killing me," he gushed, his fingers digging into her soft flesh.

She pushed down an inch more with an "Oh!" her moans mixing with worried gasps.

"Go slow Ma Petite." The masochistic command burned him more. Her nails pricked his skin as she remained still until her moans softened. She moved back up a little before lowering down to where she was before, Mon Dieu. She was fucking the head and it brought a cock-throb that made her gasp and go still again.

"So good, Ma Petite," he praised, trying not to dig too hard into her soft thighs.

She took her time, and that took every bit of strength to endure. He focused on her face, particularly the sharp lines between her brows and the stab of her nails as she held on. Her moans told him more than he could handle. Right now, they said she was getting ready to take another inch of his cock.

Her head came forward and she tortured him with those two-inch sucks on the tip of his shaft. "Beth," he gushed, staring at himself in her. She answered him with a merciful decent, burying him halfway.

Her next gasp was one of pleasant surprise as she went still again on his throbbing dick. "Halfway, baby," he said between hisses and groans while eying her progress. "Your pussy is so beautiful on me."

She gave a cry while lowering three quarters of the way and a rogue thrust of his hips escaped. "Mon Dieu, fuck, I'm sorry," he blasted at the sharp cry she made.

She remained still, her moans a mix of pleasure and pain as he went back to holding on to her thighs with a bruising force.

"It's so big," she gasped, pain on her brow. At the bite of her nails, he braced for more of her sweet decent.

"So fucking close baby," he said, winded as he stared, willing for her to go all the way.

Instead, she moved slowly back up his shaft, wetting him with her essence. "Mon Dieu, Beth," he strained as she lowered back down all the fucking way this time.

She tugged his hands off her hips and laced her fingers in his, strangling him with her grip as her cries increased again. "Sahvrin," she moaned.

"Touch your clit, my sweet Petite Ange."

She sat still and panting as if afraid to move then slowly released his hand, doing as he said.

"Fucking yes," he whispered, watching her middle and ring fingers moving on her clit. "Make it feel good baby. Get it hot, get it so fucking hot for me."

Her mouth opened with soft moans. He reached with his free hand and grazed her nipple with the tips of his fingers, watching her mouth open more. "Yes," she said, her pussy clenching him tighter somehow as she masturbated. "Oh yes."

****

Beth's heart hammered with every other part in her. God, this was it, her first time, and with the man she was madly in love with. And he loved her. God, the way he'd said it. With all his heart, she felt it. She panted while holding on tight to his one hand, the pleasure from her clit giving her an edge over the pain. His sexy groans were jet fuel to her desire and helped her down that terrifying slide. He was so big and her attempt to hurry was turning into a torture session of pleasure for him and pain for her.

The sting and stretch began to subside and she lifted then moved back down. The careful maneuver brought another barrage of those cock-pulses against her already tight walls. That, and the way his chest and stomach heaved as he fought to be still did insane things to her.

He needed to orgasm first; she wasn't sure she could. She sought his other hand again and he locked his fingers in hers, his grip nearly crushing her bones. To feel the measure of his desire had her dizzy.

She set out with gentle up and down moves, watching his gaze roam from her pussy to her face like both were a source of life for him. But when he locked those dark eyes on hers, it gave her the power to move her higher up his shaft and then lower.

God he was the most beautiful man when in agonizing pleasure. The lines between his brows deepened with the grit of his teeth and hiss. Then his head went back with a groaned, "Ffffuck," so hot it made her gasp.

It suddenly became all about his pleasure and she moved again, high then low, high then lower, watching him. "Fuck me," she shot out with a gasp, picking up speed.

The sudden thrust of his hips brought a shocked cry, but she didn't stop moving on him, the slide of his cock becoming easier. The way she sat felt like a restriction on his hips, so she pulled her hands from his and put them on his abs. The second she did, his own hands shot to her hips with a stinging smack and "Oh yes, fuck yes."

His eyes fixed on him moving in and out of her and the look it put on his face brought her moans higher. "Fuck, Beth," he breathed, moving her hips on him as he gave short thrusts.

The sensation had her mouth open wide, shock overtaking her moans. "Oh my God, oh my God," she gushed when he worked her hips even faster. She dropped her upper body, putting her hands next to his shoulders.

"Fucking *kiss* me," he blasted.

The moment their mouth's clashed, his fast thrusts turned *so deep*. Her cries met his growls as he hammered his cock with no mercy.

She didn't want mercy. She wanted exactly what he gave her—unrestrained passion, reckless and cruel. His hands bit so hard on her hips suddenly, holding her tight as his head went back with a strained roar. He writhed like it burned as he ground her pussy down on him. God, the pain and pleasure was like getting her soul raked over fire, clobbering her humanity until she was a shaking, sobbing mess.

In a dizzying second, she was beneath him, and he was kissing her softly and petting her face. His shhhh's coated her traumatized body and she realized in that second just how real that medicine was to her. Then came his French and the tone said he was pissed. She reached and stroked his face, pulling his mouth to hers only able to express in moans how much she loved all of it.

CHAPTER 27

"Ma Petite."

Beth moaned and opened her eyes, immediately sitting up at seeing Sahvrin next to the bed dressed in his Bishop suit. "Where are you going?"

"We, Ma Petite." He leaned and angled his head, kissing her cheek then holding his hand out to her. "I have business with Lazure and my brothers tonight. I don't want you here alone."

"Tonight?" She took his hand, realizing she was naked when his eyes burned her. Pain throbbed in her privates as she scooted out the bed while her womb clenched with the unforgettable memory of his pounding cock.

He wrapped his arms around her, hugging her tight as his mouth moved along her face in soft kisses and even softer moans. "Where am I going?" she wondered.

"To my other bed at Mah-Mah's."

The memory of Katrina overshadowed the joy she should have going to his childhood bedroom.

"What's wrong, Ma Petite?" he asked, stroking her face.

She leaned into his touch, addicted to the comforting habit followed by her second favorite—kisses on her forehead.

"Nothing."

"Hey."

She looked up and found his gaze hard and hot on her.

"Everything I am, is all yours Angel, just like you said. You own me."

She lowered her gaze. "She called you Bishop," she whispered, pain stabbing her.

He gave her a swooning kiss and she was suddenly back on the sidewalk for the first time with him. "She knows him by name only, Angel. That man did not exist then. But he does now and he is madly in love with His Petite."

Tears welled in her eyes. "I looked for you," she gasped, looking up at him. "That night. After you left, I looked for you." Her lip trembled. "I wanted you so much."

His fingers bit in her hair and tilted her head back. "Ma Petite," he croaked kissing tenderly at her mouth. "I fucking wanted you more, I swear to God. I realized you were heaven and I'd thrown it away. And my soul burned every fucking day over it."

Her back hit the bed as his buckle clinked followed by his cock sliding against her entrance. "You found me again," she gasped in his hungry mouth as he slid inside her with a careful tenderness while caressing and kissing face. Only a few strokes in and she clawed to get more, wanting all of him at once.

"Fuck, Angel," he shot out, shoving in hard and deep. He held her jaw tight and kissed her as he pounded with that reckless, growling fury, his orgasm already there. He writhed and groaned on top of her, grinding as deep as he could as she pulled his hair too hard.

When he'd filled her with all he had, he swore right in her mouth, "I love you, Ma Bell Petite. I love you more than I've loved anybody, I swear to you."

The joy that gave her brought her tears and when he saw it, he gave a groan, like he was destined to cause pain. A rogue laugh burst out from her, bringing another and another until she couldn't stop.

"Ma Petite."

His confused surprise made her breathless with laughter. She finally got a "Sorry," squeaked past before catching a breath. "I'm just so happy." Her tears returned again.

"Mon Dieu, how are you doing this? Laughing and crying?"

His genuine question brought more laughter and she held on to his neck as it stole her breath. "Oh God!" she cried, sucking in air again.

"Ma Petite, I have fucked you when I swore to myself not to and have broken my commitment to be at this meeting."

"What?" She pushed him off and sat up. "I'm sorry," she said, scooting out the bed. "But I won't take all the blame, that's half yours and I'm being generous."

He yanked her back onto his lap, his grin almost boyish, making him achingly handsome. "Anything my angel wants, I will give her however she wants it and whenever. That is my new code."

Her heart beat so hard in her chest at those words. "I like this arrangement. Is this Bishop's code?"

He devoured her again, his fist winding in her hair and pulling her head back. "You must agree right now to call me by that name when we are fucking. Always."

"Oh God," she said, staring into his smoldering eyes. "Yes."

He tilted her head more, exposing her neck then sucking it so hard. After many seconds, he released the suction with a gasp, licking the spot and kissing before moving to her mouth. "When you say that name, you command a darkness in me. A never-ending vengeance and emptiness." He stroked her face, staring into her eyes. "I need you to always call me out of that place, Ma Petite. Don't leave me in there."

Her heart clenched at his words, and she climbed in his lap, taking hold of his face. "You are *My* Bishop just like I am your Petite," she said with tears. "And I will never leave you in the darkness. I will always be your light. I promise."

****

"So, what's on the menu for our parishioners at the Weigh Station?" Jek asked as Sahvrin's Night Dragon roared through the dark swamp roadway.

"I called for The Revelator to come see what he can see," Sahvrin said.

Zep gave a light snort. "Ain't seen his ugly face in a bit."

"You *would* speak that way about The Revelator," Lazure muttered, not even mildly surprised.

"Whatever," Zep said, making Sahvrin wonder what his problem was. "Let em' *reveal all my sins,* then you can call The Auditor to judge my dirty soul."

August shook his head with a "Puuuuhhh, somebody's cranky."

Probably pissed he has to drive somewhere to fuck Katrina. A match made in hell. But Sahvrin didn't just call The Revelator for the Weigh Station business. The last they'd talked, the man mentioned a vision he'd had about him. At the time, Sahvrin didn't want to hear it. Now, maybe he did.

"Y'all still using smoke signals to communicate with The *Twelve* or what?" Zep asked. "You'd think 8-Bit woulda had implant chips figured out by now."

"If you wanna know so bad, why you didn't join The Twelve?" Bart challenged, saving Sahvrin's breath. "You know they don't tell shit to nobody."

"Well, Lazure isn't part of The *Twelve* and he knows everything."

"He fucking founded it," August droned sounding underwhelmed.

"What is your problem?" Jek said, annoyed. "You not getting enough pussy or what?"

"Maybe too much," August thought. "Probably seen more pussy than a gynecologist during a venereal disease epidemic."

They all laughed but Lazure and Sahvrin. He was busy feeling like Zep was hiding more than his fuck feelings for Katrina. His Mah-Mah had mentioned jealousy more than once explaining his randomly *pissed* behavior over the years. There hadn't been anything for him to be jealous over until recently. He remembered his comment about *his perfect girlfriend.*

Definitely a jealous comment coming from a man who wasn't happy till he put his dick in everything.

His phone made cricket noises in his pocket again. Ever since Sahvrin had opened the app that 8-BIT created for The Twelve's phones, it had been popping. Had been a while since they'd gathered all The Twelve. Usually, problems only required one or two Hatches to handle, depending on the issue. Every Hatch had its honed strengths and in times of a major conflict, The Twelve leaders and their Hatches came together and formed the Swamp Horde.

Zep made his jabs at 8-Bit, but the man's genius was no joke. The dude was a tech-legend. Not only did he lead their Tech Hatch, but he also ran all their operations, big or small from a remote location in the swamp. Sahvrin had been in his shack a couple of times and recalled the room full of screens and computers where he tracked every member of every Hatch via a signal on their watches. Now, with the eyes on the waterways, The Swamp Horde would always have the advantage against any enemy that entered their territory.

It'd be good to see The Twelve again. They only met once a year at Mah-Mah's festivities, but the war that ushered in the group's existence would always be their unbreakable bond. He was also eager to introduce His Petite to the leaders. He'd be one of the first of The Twelve to take a woman in marriage, but he still needed to make sure His Petite wanted the position as his right hand. He wasn't sure if she realized that he'd made love to her before he got her official answer. That was because he was prepared to step down as leader. Nothing on God's green earth would keep him from being that angel's husband and protector, *this* he knew.

His phone vibrated against his leg and the special alert jerked his cock. What was His Petite doing up at this hour? Playing with her pussy and texting him all about it, hopefully. Mon Dieu, he'd never get enough of that woman.

The moment they arrived at the Weigh Station, he pulled his phone out and slid his finger over her name. *Can't sleep without you. What are you up to? I know it's stupid to miss you when you just left. But I do. So much.*

Need hammered his muscles as Sahvrin remembered he'd named himself Bishop on her contacts. Would be his official first cleansing sex command with her. *I want you to open your legs wide and play with your pussy slowly while imagining it's my tongue. When you orgasm, call* my *name. Understood?*

He sent it and willed his cock *down* while opening The Twelve app. He tapped the unread message from The Revelator.

Eveque, Eveque, how doth my dark son fare? I have received your invitation to the Weigh Station and will be there at the appointed time.
Looking forward to seeing my wayward son.
The Revelator

The man didn't always make Sahvrin nervous, but he did now. He called him *Eveque* but only those in The Twelve referred to him as that. Technically, The Revelator wasn't under him or part of The Twelve but instead led the whole Hoard in spiritual matters. His gift to see the hidden things in people as well as his visions served the Horde in many ways even if they were unnerving. If you gave a fuck. Which until now, he really hadn't. In the Katrina aftermath, he'd embraced his courtship with Death, waging a war of rage. And during his darkest hours, The Revelator had taken an interest in him and surprisingly voted him to be leader of The Twelve.

Not surprising, it turned out to be the exact purpose his life had needed.

Many found The Revelator's religious flare amusing, but Sahvrin didn't. Like 8-Bit, he was a legend in his in own rite. His visions and intuition made him one of the best trackers he'd ever seen. You lost anything or anybody in the swamp, he'd find it.

There was only one other man in The Twelve with his kind of tracking skills. Spook. The only difference with Spook, he had no spiritual gifts other than the ones he was born with. His survival and hiding skills were next to phenomenal. He showed up and left out like a ghost. He knew where you were, but you never knew where he was. And if he ever decided to take off his tracker, nobody but maybe The Revelator would find him.

Last Sahvrin checked, he only had four members in his Hatch. He hoped he had more. His skills were too great not to pass down. Wasn't often they needed him, but when they did, he was Sahvrin's first choice in the dirty matters. With The Revelator, he wouldn't do jobs if it went against his often-odd principals. And more than once Sahvrin needed a man of zero principals.

They parked and Sahvrin tied the boat off to one of the cypress knees.

"Lazure, it's been a while," The Revelator greeted behind him.

Sahvrin turned, catching the cordial tip of his black wide brimmed hat and nod of his head in the light of August's lantern.

"Samuel." Lazure reached out and shook his hand. "Too long between Claudette's parties."

This brought one of The Revelators signature laughs. The commanding boom and volume made you stop and need to know what brought it. He was no stranger to his Mah-Mah's incessant need for celebrating things and their incessant need to avoid it. The Revelator didn't seem to share the feeling, attending every one of them faithfully even though he was more seen than heard.

For the longest time, he'd assumed The Revelator wasn't into women, but he recalled the way he danced with one at the last party. Sahvrin would've written it off as being drunk but the man never drank a drop of the devil's Kool-Aid.

The Revelator turned as if sensing Sahvrin coming up. "Well look what the *devil* done sent home," he said, his slow grin growing into a full-blown smile as he looked him over thoroughly. Sahvrin wondered if that was part of his method for *discerning* things about people. If it was, the look he wore said he'd just had a *revelation* of everything he'd done with His Petite. Pleasant surprise was the closest description Sahvrin had for his wide eyes, at least he hoped.

The man put his hand out and Sahvrin eyed it, pretty sure he'd never shaken it before for obvious reasons. Felt like he'd meet God face to face if he did. Fuck it.

Sahvrin put his hand in his and eyed the man while giving a firm shake. The Revelator stared into his gaze while pumping his hand slowly up and down, nodding now. Sahvrin kept his gaze locked on his, the thick jagged scar from his eye to his mouth shining in the flickering light. Sahvrin had heard it was self-inflicted. A woman fell in love with him and took her life when he rejected her affections. Said his face would never be a stumbling block again.

Somebody needed to tell him the scar only added bad ass to whatever look he'd failed to disfigure. The strength in his hand gradually receded, then he released him. "The darkness has been overthrown," he said, a curious eagerness sparking in those stormy blue eyes. "Vanquished." He held the brim of his hat and nodded his head once. "I'll need to be meeting this powerful individual soon?"

Sahvrin didn't hold in his grin. "You'll meet her tomorrow at the celebration."

"Indeed, I will," he said, spinning suddenly. "Now *where* be these children of evil wretchedness?" he wondered in light curiosity.

"Let me lead the way for the Good Shepard." This was from Zep who already headed down the path to the trees they'd tied them to.

"The Good Shepard," The Revelator repeated, his deep chuckle echoing in the humid darkness. "Run boy run," he said, with an eagerness. "The faster you do, the quicker you'll meet me in the way."

Zep shined his flashlight beam on the Colorful One's drooping head and Sahvrin reached with the tip of his boot, pushing it back.

"Bled out," Zep muttered, shaking his head.

Sahvrin felt the cold, calculating finger of judgment move down his spine as he knelt before him and pressed two fingers against his neck. He shook his head. "He ain't dead." Yet.

"This one's awake," Lazure called from around the tree as Sahvrin stood.

"Damn, he done shit *all over*," he heard Bart mutter.

The Revelator knelt before Tattoos, angling his head left and right, high and low, as if looking for an entrance, all while making abrupt clicking sounds in his throat that reminded Sahvrin of his alligator call. Maybe it was a demon call for him.

"Mmhm," he started saying repeatedly with nods, as if confirming something.

"You want me to ungag this one?" Bart called.

"Hold on," Sahvrin said, wanting to see what The Revelator was *seeing*.

He leaned back on his haunches, winded like he'd just run a mile. "A very long and dark road in this one," he said, shaking his head. He rose with ease and Sahvrin headed around the tree to their other demon host.

"I had to use the bathroom," the big dude mumbled at seeing Sahvrin. "I'm sorry, I couldn't hold it."

"He's sorry he couldn't hold it," The Revelator said to Sahvrin with a weird excitement like that meant something. He knelt next to the man. "What's your name, son?"

Sweat covered his face and head, both full of welts from all the hungry swamp insects. "Are you the Executor?" he whispered eagerly, like he'd consider dying at this point merciful. He'd be right. "They call me Rooster, but my Christian name is Brandon. The guy behind me is Needles, and his real name is Stephen." He shook his head, his lips pressing together in sudden strain. "Look, sir," he said, the word barely making it out his mouth as he blinked around tears. "I done some bad things and I know I'm gonna die tonight. I knew this day was coming and I think maybe I prayed it would cuz…" His face seemed to cramp up in pain. "I don't like the man I became." He gave a vigorous head shake then looked at The Revelator with clear eyes. "I'm glad to take my punishment. I hope you do it real good, too. But before I go, you gotta let me do some good, somehow."

The Revelator sat staring for several seconds then stood and turned to Sahvrin. "What do you think we should do, fearless and wise leader?"

Sahvrin knew, but the test behind his question made him double check his answer.

"Sirs, I can't meet my Maker like this, please."

Sahvrin walked past The Revelator, standing before the man. "You can start by confessing your sins. Every single one of them. Your sins and the sins of every Roulette you know."

"Oh God," he quipped with his head down, like that was worse than torture and dying. "Sir, that's going to take a long time," he said, eying them with that twisted, guilty face that Sahvrin wanted to smash with a bat now.

"I have *all* fucking night," Sahvrin assured, turning to meet The Revelator's stare he felt burning into his back. He looked around. "Where'd he go?"

"I'm here boy," he called from his right. "Just takin' a piss before we get to work."

"I'll stay and hear his sins," Zep volunteered.

"I will too," August said. "But we'll need to get them to the Weigh Station. I ain't gettin' eatin' alive for these fools."

"I'll stay too," Lazure said. "Got a bad feeling about this night."

Sahvrin glanced at him. "Like what?"

He shook his head, looking up at the skies. "Dunno."

"Storms comin'," The Revelator said, walking up from behind.

"I just checked that hurricane, it's still headed to Alabama, maybe Florida."

The Revelator nodded with a freaky grin at Sahvrin. "That it is. But that's not the storm I mean."

****

Sahvrin let Jek drive them back, too pissed to think. The Revelator's condemnation was a slap in the face even if he hadn't said it, Sahvrin *felt* it in his unspoken words. And what was his storm talk about? Felt more like a threat than a warning. Yeah. Sahvrin could *see* things too. If The Revelator wanted to show mercy to that fat fuck with the *hours* and *hours* of sins so vile, he'd rather die, he fucking could. But like *hell* if he would. Same for the sick sack of ink-shit. If he died before they got his confession, he'd say fate rolled the judgment dice and deprived him of executing him personally.

He opened his phone after they got going, finding His Petite's name. *On my way back,* he texted her. The Bishop side of him wanted her very much awake when he got back, while his sane side hoped she slept and rested.

Waiting for you.

Those words made Sahvrin's cock throb with things he didn't want to name. *Good. I need you,* he texted back. He left it at that because he wasn't sure what he needed. No, he knew what he *needed,* and he'd been denied. Bishop wasn't interested in wiping slates clean, he wanted to punish something. He'd call it divine intervention that his anger and vengeance thought his cock was the perfect tool to satisfy his judgment lusts. And while she was too tender for him to fuck his rage down, she could survive slow, torturous pleasure. And that ass. It was so perfect, it felt like a sin. The way it wrecked his mind and body and taunted him. So fucking bad and guilty.

****

Beth wanted to wait for Sahvrin at the docks, but he'd told her not to. No, he told her No. Wait in the bed. Naked.

Getting texts with the name Bishop was doing a real number on her. She kept rewriting their history, starting from the night they'd met, imagining various outcomes. What if he'd chaperoned her? What if she'd taken him to her room and done you know what?

She giggled to herself at the idea, knowing he'd have done no such thing. Maybe. Not at first.

Footsteps on the stairs brought hammering in her chest. She got up on her elbows, watching the door. Being a scaredy cat, she'd put on his nightlights, which were basically those fat bulbed Christmas lights strung all over the room. She spotted the BDSM book she'd been reading and quickly moved it under the covers. She was still too shy to show her sexual appetite so openly like he did.

Would he want her to tell him about her playing with herself like he'd asked? She was sure he would and braced for that very awkward moment.

The door opened and he walked in with only black slacks, stormy gaze locked on hers till she could hardly breathe.

Dear, dear God he was wickedly handsome when his hair was wet and hanging to his shoulders. And staring like that at her. Was he angry? Did something bad happen?

She sat up, holding the sheet to her chest. "Are you okay?"

"Did you shower?"

Her clit pounded as he made his way straight to the bed, eyes on her body. "Yes," she whispered.

He grabbed the sheet and yanked, ripping it from her hands and off the bed in one move. She panted, hands on the bed next to her, fighting not to be ashamed and too nervous. She wanted to say something but everything that came to her mind didn't apply.

He spotted the book on the bed and reached for it, picking it up. "What were you reading?"

She swallowed, eyeing the book, realizing he'd want exacts. What was she reading. "I…kind of skipped around."

He set the book down, staring at her tits. "Did you read about submission?"

"Yes, some."

"Did you read about discipline?"

Her pulse raced faster. "Yes."

He pulled a black tie from his pocket and slid it through his hands. "Tell me what it said." He draped the tie around his neck, and she heard his zipper while trying to remember what it said.

"He…he decides how to punish her."

"The punishments are usually different, yes?" He stood next to the bed, and she assumed he was naked now, she was too scared to look.

"Yes," she said, with a nod, her fingers in tight fists next to her, legs drawn up tight. She wanted to cover her breasts but knew better, so tried to sit bravely naked before his burning gaze. Had she done something to anger him without realizing?

She watched him walk to the closet, seeing he still had on tight briefs. He pulled a blanket out and spreading it on the floor.

Was he not sleeping with her? He straightened and pointed to the blanket. "I want you right here, on your knees."

Oh God. She stared at him, her gaze moving down to his huge cock pushing at his underwear. At realizing he was at maximum arousal, she quickly did as he said, fighting her inadequacy of moving around nude.

"Put your hands behind your back," he ordered when she knelt where he'd said.

She did, panting now with eyes closed, aroused out of her mind. Oh God, he was tying her wrists. She gasped when he cinched it tight with a formidable feeling knot.

He knelt before her, putting his hot gaze even with hers, staring at her like he searched for answers to something. She wanted to ask if he was okay and couldn't make the words come. She could only stare back, barely.

"Open your knees."

Her breaths hitched as she did, causing her to lower enough she looked up at him now.

"Tell me what you were reading."

"Oh God," she gasped as he slid soft fingers along her tender folds.

"I'm waiting."

"I…was reading about…spanking." His finger found her clit, drawing slow, burning circles on it.

"And why did my naughty angel choose that?"

She gasped on the heat. "Because…I want it."

"I know you fucking do," he said.

****

Every pounding impulse running through Sahvrin screamed wicked. And yet he'd done nothing wrong. He stared into His Petite's face, feeding off the look she wore as he very slowly rubbed her hard clit.

"Tell me what it said." He lowered his underwear and pulled his cock out. "Tell me while you watch me stroke my cock."

She looked down, her mouth opening more with light moans. "It said…" She licked her lips, brows pulling together. "That he should discuss with her… the consequences. They…oh yes," she moaned when he wiggled his finger on her clit then returned to slow torture.

"They what?" he demanded, seething from the heat in his balls.

"They agree, they have to agree," she shot out. "On what is done. Oh please," she begged, looking at him, desperate.

He lowered his head and flicked her nipple with his tongue, bringing her strained moans higher. He groaned on the thick nub, rubbing his lips back and forth across it. He wiggled his fingers quicky again, catching her nipple between his teeth as he did.

"Oh God, yes, please."

He raised up and dove on her mouth, biting at her lip and flicking his tongue against hers, then pulling back when she fought to taste him. Their breaths clashed, his thick with lust, hers delicate with pleading.

"I need to come," she shuddered, fighting to get at his mouth.

"You have to burn first," he swore.

He reclined on his left elbow, opening his legs for her. "Suck my cock. Put your naughty ass right here," he ordered.

She moved on her knees where he instructed, leaning for his cock while he stroked over the perfect round cheek on his right. She took the head in her mouth, and he gave his first spanking, seething when she yelped in shock, her teeth nipping his shaft. He slid his finger inside her dripping pussy very carefully, driving her moans higher.

She sucked faster and deeper and he removed his finger, spanking her again. "Slower," he ordered, returning his finger to her pussy.

"Oh God, please," she begged when he wiggled his touch over her clit.

He spanked her twice. "Oh *God* please?"

"Bishop," she shot out between sucking, focusing her mouth on the head now. "I need you. I'm begging."

"One orgasm," he said, spanking her ass good when she flicked his slit with her tongue, her lusty moans following her yelp.

"Is your pussy hot, naughty Angel?"

She dove on his cock in answer, raking her teeth on the ascent, bringing his hand down on her soft ass again. "You're being so fucking bad."

"Punish my pussy, please."

"Punish your fucking pussy?" he said, ready to tear into her.

Sahvrin grabbed her wrists and pulled her up, then knelt just before her, staring at the pure lust on her face. "I need to come," she said. "Please, make me come, Bishop."

She said the last with her eyes closed, panting.

He took hold of her hair and tilted her head back. "You want me to make you come?"

"Yes, and I want you. I've always wanted you."

He licked at her mouth, her words overpowering him. He moved his finger over her clit again. "Right here?"

Her *yes* wrenched out between gasps. "Punish my pussy, please. Spank it."

Fucking Dieu. Spank her pussy? What had she read? He tapped her clit with his fingers, testing and her mouth flew open.

"Oh God, oh my God."

He looked down, giving one pop every second or two, his fingers pulling harder in her hair as his hunger began to boil. He could fucking orgasm watching this. He turned her head and kissed at her mouth, spanking her plump lips faster until her cries ended with "Bishop!"

He growled and placed three fingers between her pussy lips and wiggled at a frantic pace. "Fucking *come* Angel."

He devoured her mouth when her cries came, intensifying his assault without mercy until she bucked and shook in his arm. He worked the tie off her wrists, deciding he loathed using it on her and not feeling her touch.

The second she was free, she lunged, kissing him.

He lay her beneath him, grunting when she captured his cock in her hand and pulled him to her pussy. Her nails bit into his ass, forcing him deep.

"Beth," he gushed, kissing her neck, then jaw, then mouth.

"Fuck me Bishop."

He snatched her hands and yanked them above her head, holding her while he bucked his hips, watching her tits jerk as sharp moans flew from her fucking mouth.

His orgasm hit like a hurricane, tearing through him until he couldn't think or hear or feel anything but the endless bliss of His Petite.

CHAPTER 28

Sahvrin bolted up in bed at the emergency chirp signal blaring from his phone. He jumped down and raced to the dresser, adrenalin pumping as he tapped the screen.

8-Bit. That meant information.

"What's wrong?" Beth whispered, half asleep.

"I don't know, I'm finding out." He didn't say more as he opened The Twelve's app and found 8-Bit's name then hit his number. The signal was used in any kind of emergency but being 8-Bit meant something to do with Beth's situation. Or maybe the guns.

"Eveque," 8-Bit answered.

"What is it," he said through the adrenalin.

"I found some things on your woman's father you needed to know ASAP."

"Go," he said, glancing over his shoulder at His Petite, making her way on her elbow.

"Turns out Mr. Owens Sweetling has been MIA since she left to come here, and he bought plane tickets for Paris a week before."

He remembered her comment about her father not wanting her to come, and Paris. "She mentioned something about that."

"Well, after searching, I found he checked in at a Fair Field Inn ten miles away from her. No checkout that I can find.

Fucking Dieu.

"She obviously knew nothing about the dirty stuff, which makes me ask why he didn't tell her. If you know your daughter is going where she'll possibly be abducted and you don't tell her, there's got to be a damn good reason. If he's dirty, we know the reason, but if he's not, we need to know what leverage they have on him. And the financial connection Bart found gets muddier. Nearly every investment is tied to all the wrong names."

Fuck, he prayed her dad wasn't dirty, that would kill her.

"But shit goes a little sideways with these plane tickets. Why buy three tickets the week before his daughter leaves? I think he may have been trying to get them out of the country."

Sahvrin was confused. "Three tickets?"

"For him, Beth Sweetling, and Margaret Sweetling, aka Maggie."

Margaret Sweetling? "I'm gonna need to call you right back. Don't go anywhere."

"Qui."

He hung up and faced His Petite who waited with worry on her face. "That was one of the men from my company. He has information on your father, but I need to talk to him in private. Will you be okay here? I'm not leaving, I'll be back in five minutes," he promised, stroking her shoulder.

She lowered her head, obviously not happy with it. "Okay. What time is it?"

He looked at the phone. "Five-thirty. The sun will be up soon."

"I can go take a shower."

He pulled her to him, kissing softly. "I'll find you when I'm done. I love my Angel."

****+

Sahvrin went to his Tree House and called 8-Bit back, pacing. "Who is Margaret Sweetling?"

"Her sister."

He stopped in his tracks. "She doesn't have a sister."

"She does. She's in an institution."

"No, that's her aunt."

"This is her sister who is twenty-nine. The aunt is in California at Eternal Sunshine, her sister is in Washington State at The Wondering Oaks. I double checked."

Holy shit. "What's wrong with her? Why wouldn't Beth know about her?"

"The second part I don't know but the first I have information that could possibly get those answers. Maggie was institutionalized at seven, so Beth would've been two."

"She wouldn't have remembered," Sahvrin realized. "Why would they hide that from her?"

"Exactly what I wondered. So, I looked up Maggie's doctor. He's just been transferred right at the same time Maggie was scheduled to be released, I'm assuming for this trip."

"Coincidence you think?"

"Possibly."

"Where is Maggie now?"

"Still there as far as I know. Whatever plans her dad made didn't pan out. But if anybody would know anything about it, the doctor would. His name is Dr. Zeblon Wiggins and he's been her doctor from day one. I made a call and learned his last day is tomorrow."

"What's going to happen to Maggie?"

"I have no idea, but I think your woman should call and find that out. She's the only one who could get info, being family. Not sure what they'll give over the phone, but if the doctor knows the inside scoop on this, he might talk to her."

"You think he's connected?"

"No, but if he is…"

"Right." He considered something else. "So if her father knew what was going to happen, and followed her, and isn't dirty, and is now missing…"

"Then the odds are grim for him."

Fucking Dieu. "I hate to say it, but that option is better than him being dirty."

"Well, with all the evidence I have, it's pointing to a father trying to get out of a mess he somehow got into, and his daughter not playing by his plan book."

Sahvrin paced, thinking. "And something prevented him from telling her."

"You know how the devil's deals work. Once you're in you can't get out even if you never wanted in to begin with."

His Petite would have a million questions. "What else do you know about her sister? Do you know why she was put there at that age?"

"All I could find out was that she's mute and has been there since seven."

"Mon Dieu, this is sad. But Beth will be very happy to know she has a sister and will want to get all the information she can."

"I can tell you this," he said, warning in his tone. "With your woman not showing up wherever she was supposed to, they'll be looking at all collateral options."

"Oh fuck," Sahvrin whispered.

"I don't know the extent of power these people have, but I'm assuming it would be nothing for them to pull strings and have little Maggie put in the wrong kind of home if you know what I mean."

"Fucking Christ," he said. "Send me the doctor's name and number and whatever else we might need. And you're sure Maggie is her actual sister?"

"Anything can be falsified, but I can't figure out why that would be. The meeting this evening is still on? At the party?"

Sahvrin's brain stuttered a second. "Yes. At the party."

"Does your woman know what you do and who you are?"

He wished. "Not exactly. Things didn't go as planned with that."

He gave a light chuckle. "With women, they rarely do. But this one I may be a little excited to meet."

A streak of jealousy fired through him.

"Given her line of education, she'd be a great asset in The Twelve. Having a geospatial expert is tech-drool"

"Just don't drool in front of me if you want to keep your tongue."

His laugh said he knew he was only half-joking. "Will we be getting to meet La Bel-Eveque? And I'm not the only one wanting to meet the woman that stole your heart."

His stomach lurched at everything he'd said, especially the term that would be her official title if she accepted it. He was sure she was born to become La Bel-Eveque— *The Beautiful Bishop*. "I didn't exactly get to the marriage talk with her yet. But I did plan to introduce her anyway."

"Uh-oh."

"I'm more worried she'll do it because she doesn't know how to say no."

"Well, that's…"

"Not something I want," he finished. "I need to figure that out."

"You can always put her through The Gauntlet."

Sahvrin considered that. "Maybe. Knowing her, she'd want nothing less. She's got everything to prove and nothing to lose in her mind."

"That can be shaped," he said, like he liked the potential.

"It could. I need to go. See you this evening unless something changes."

****

Sahvrin stood there, half numb with everything spinning in his head. But the marriage talk and The Gauntlet were front and center. He didn't have a doubt she wanted to be married to him, it was the other stuff he had doubts and problems with. And the issue wasn't that she *wouldn't* want everything to do with The Twelve, it was that she *would*.

He'd never contemplated taking a wife before so hadn't even considered how he'd feel about that. He was conflicted right down the middle, wanting her in it and not. He liked the idea of working with her, but he also *loved* the idea of her being a domestic goddess. *His* domestic goddess. And either one she chose was acceptable as La Bel Eveque.

She'd have to pick. Which meant not influencing her decision either way.

But that didn't mean he couldn't make the choices easy or hard.

He headed back to the house, eager to give her the information and make that call. Mon Dieu, his sweet angel had a sister. What had happened to make her mute? Given Beth's situation, Sahvrin was sure he didn't want to know.

****

Beth quickly set her coffee on the table next to the porch swing and hurried to meet Sahvrin, searching for answers on his face about her dad. As usual, he was unreadable, other than the intense hunger aimed at her. He scooped her up in his arms and hugged her extra tight.

"Oh God, what?" she wondered, fighting to get down and see him.

"I have extremely good news and maybe not good news, we don't know for sure yet."

She covered her mouth. "Tell me. Please."

"The good news is really big, Angel." He stroked her arms. "You have a sister. She's at an institution in Washington State."

Her mouth dropped with the sudden hammering in her chest. "What?"

"I thought maybe it was your aunt, but he insisted no. Her name is Margaret Sweetling, or Maggie."

"Maggie?" she gasped, trying to remember that name from anywhere.

"Do you remember her?" he wondered.

She barely shook her head, not sure. "What…what happened to her?" she asked, tears already falling.

He held her upper arms, stroking them. "He only found out she's mute and was put there when she was seven."

She stifled a sob. "Mute? Why?" she strained.

"We don't know, but I need to tell you the other news."

"Oh God," she strained, fighting not to give in to her fears. "Tell me quickly."

"Your father followed you here when you came. He left the same day you did and checked in at a hotel ten miles from here. He bought three plane tickets for Paris the week before."

"Three?"

He nodded. "You, him and your sister. She was scheduled to be released at that time."

"Oh my God," she strained, covering her mouth, and clenching her eyes shut. "He tried so hard to stop me! Why wouldn't he just tell me?"

"We don't know, Angel, but something prevented him. We think these people have some kind of leverage on him. We found that nearly all his financial investments are linked to bad names."

"No," she shook her head.

"That doesn't mean he's bad," he hurried. "It seems he got entrapped in something and wasn't able to get out of it and did his best to protect all of you as long as he could."

She lunged on him, hugging his neck and sobbing. "I knew he was good, I told you." She pulled back. "Where is he, what do you think happened?"

"We don't know, baby," he said, holding her face. "But I have the best men tracking that, this I promise you."

She kissed him, then hugged him, so grateful. "What about my sister?" she wondered, stepping back.

"He gave me the name of her doctor and thinks you should call right away."

Panic rose in her. "Why? What's wrong?"

"If she was supposed to leave and they…if your father…" He closed his eyes.

"Just say it, it's okay," she said, tears streaming again.

"You escaped what they had planned for you, and they may look for other ways to hurt your father."

"My sister?" she shrilled, grabbing his arm.

"We're hoping her doctor might have answers we can use to know what to do."

"I need to call now," she demanded, turning. Where was her phone. "I should call him *right* now."

"Yes, Ma Petite, you can call him now. But it's early."

"Then I'll leave a message."

She waited as he got the number and handed her the phone. "Thank you." She tiptoed and kissed him before dialing.

She paced, wiping her eyes, and steadying her breaths. "You've reached Dr. Wiggins office, I'm not able to take your call, but if you leave your name and phone number and a clear message, I will return your call promptly."

The tone beeped. "Dr. Wiggins, this is Elizabeth or Beth Sweetling," she began, as strong and clear as she could. "I'm the sister of Margaret Sweetling, you may know her as Maggie. I was hoping to talk to you about—"

"Hello?"

The shaky voice at the end of the line startled her. "Dr. Wiggins?"

"Who is this?" a British sounding voice demanded.

"I'm Elizabeth Sweetling."

There was muffled banging. "What…what is your father's name?" he asked, sounding winded.

"Owen Sweetling."

"And your mother, what is her name and her maiden name?"

His testing urgency had her heart racing. "Amelia Sweetling, she had the same last name as my father so her maiden name is also Sweetling."

"What is the name of your second-grade French teacher?"

"Uhh…" Beth tapped her fist on her forehead, thinking. "Mrs. Fletcher!"

"Praise *God*," the man shot out, sounding out of breath. "Now you listen closely to me. I assume you're someplace safe. Your father was *distraught* when he called me the day you decided to go on your trip. Apparently, he thought you'd agreed to Paris," he said, sounding dumbfounded. "I must tell you things that might be hard for you to hear Elizabeth. Your father is in a lot of trouble and has been for years. He got caught up in the wrong side of a deal and your sister came to me when she was only seven, unable to speak after suffering a two-week abduction by some of the same people who tried to take you."

Beth covered her mouth, closing her eyes.

"But it was all a set-up, I'm sure of it. He got a call from a Senator who'd heard of it and offered to help get his daughter back, said he had inside connections. Of course your father agreed to *anything* and that's where it started. Since that, they've been using him to hide their dirty dealings and he's been fighting to escape for years and had determined the only real solution was leaving the country with his family and hiding. Of course when your mother died, he was devastated as you know and wanted to leave before you were done with college. I insisted he wait, he'd waited this long."

"Oh God, this is all my fault," she choked out. "Why didn't he just tell me?"

"Of course he *planned* to, once you were all safe. And the day you left, he was in a panic, said you wouldn't answer your phone."

"Oh God," she gasped, shaking her head as tears poured. "I figured he was calling to guilt me, so I didn't even answer. I was going to call him, but I…I never got a chance."

Sahvrin's arms came around her from behind.

"I *told* him not to go," the man said, sounding angry. "He was supposed to just keep an eye on you but ended up in trouble just as I said, and I was right."

"You heard from him?" she gasped.

"I have not, which can't be good. He was to pick up Maggie last week. I'm scheduled for transfer tomorrow, and I will say it a million times it is a *miracle* that you called when you did, do you hear? You *must* come and get your sister immediately. I will release her to you."

"You will?"

"Yes," he assured. "I have prepared her for this day, she will know you."

"What? How?"

"You were two years old when she came here, and I kept updating your picture as you grew."

Beth let out a painful sob. "Why didn't they tell me I had a sister?" she wailed, Sahvrin's arms tightening.

He gave a shaky sigh. "As unscrupulous as this may sound, we felt it safer for you and her if she remained here, *unwell,* if you would. Broken goods. We had every intention of moving her and even tried but she wouldn't have any part of it, she wanted to be here. By the time she was nineteen, it was obvious she had succumbed to institutional syndrome, and taking her from her home was not in the best interest."

"And now?"

"Now, I fear if you don't take her, somebody else will."

"Oh God, I'll take her, of course, but…will she come?"

"She will, provided you give her a place with familiar surroundings. I have a full list of it all. The must-haves and have-nots, the must do's and the must do-nots. What she will eat, wear, do and not do. She may be mute, but she has plenty of communication skills."

"Will she ever talk?"

"I very much do believe she will," he said, his confidence giving her a wave of relief. "She can hum and scream and do all sorts of things with her vocal cords, so we know the ability is there, it's about choice now. I always hoped that when she was reunited with you, she'd find that reason and purpose to speak again."

"When can we leave?" she turned and asked Sahvrin.

"Right away," he said.

"We can leave right away, is that okay?"

"You *must*."

"We'll take a plane," he whispered, stroking her back. "Would take too long to drive."

"Yes, that's what we'll do, we'll take a plane," she nodded.

"Where am I sending the necessary information for Maggie. You will need to see to it that she has her *must haves*. I will code everything so that you know what to provide ahead of time. Thank *God,* you called. I didn't know what I was going to do."

"Where can he send Maggie's information?" she asked Sahvrin.

"Can he send it in a text?"

"Can you text it?"

"I can send it as an attachment, I suppose. I'll need a number."

"He needs a number," she said, nodding.

"I'll get your phone."

He hurried off and she sat on the swing. "Thank you so much, Dr. Wiggins. I'm trying to remember Maggie, and some part of me feels like I might."

"You should, she doted on you like a mother."

Beth covered her mouth, stifling a sob. "Why…do you care, I'm sorry if that's a stupid way to put it."

"Because I'm your half Uncle on your mother's side. I was adopted and kept my father's name, Wiggins."

"Wow," she said, her heart aching. "You knew my mom?"

"Yes, I did, God rest her soul. An angel. She contacted me when Maggie was returned to them mute, and I had them bring her to me to check. For some reason, she clung to me and never wanted to let me go."

The tight tone in his voice said he might be crying. "Thank you so much for helping us," she said, standing when Sahvrin hurried back. "I have a number for you to send the information to."

Beth gave it to him and waited in the silence. "Thank you," he finally said. "Sending it in five minutes. I must go. I have to pack still and now I need to make sure Maggie's ready. If you need *anything* at all, you call me on the cell number I'm sending with Maggie's information."

"Okay," she nodded. "I will."

"And you must call me when she's safe of course," he added. "Please."

"I will," she assured, her chest tightening at his emotion. "Thank you for taking care of my sister, Uncle…"

"Uncle Wigs, that's the kids favorite name for me," he said, crying now, making her cry more. "I took care of little Maggie when she was three when your mother worked and I guess she remembered me, the precious little puppet. I pray every night that the people who hurt her get their due. I'm not a man of vengeance," he said, his voice breaking. "But whatever she suffered broke many things in her sweet little soul and they *need* to pay for that."

Beth was sobbing now. "I will call you," she promised. "Goodbye Uncle Wigs."

She hung up and turned into Sahvrin's arms and wailed, hugging him tight. "I have a sister but they really hurt her," she cried bitterly.

"Who hurt her?" he wondered, squeezing harder.

"He thinks it's the same people that tried to get me."

"We will find these monsters, Angel, I promise you. But first we will go get your sister and make sure she is safe here."

She pulled away, looking at him. "She can live here with us?"

"Mon Dieu, Angel," he whispered, kissing her lips. "Of course she will."

She threw her arms around his neck again, strangling him, his strong embrace telling her that everything would be okay.

God, she just prayed that they were able to give her the care she needed.

"The text," he said, making her pull away. He opened the file the Dr. sent and handed it to her. She held it where he could see with her.

Seconds after she began, she had to give him the phone. "I can't, I'm sorry."

He took it. "You want me to, Ma Petite?"

She nodded, wiping her eyes between sobs.

"She loves most soft things. If she doesn't like it, she'll let you know by ignoring it. She loves stuffed animals but not rodents, roaches or spiders." Sahvrin smiled at her. "Now we know where you get this?"

Beth let go a single laugh, blinking through tears. "What else does she love?"

"It says she loves white lights and gentle voices. Painting. Soft music. I can help with the painting," he said. "She loves open spaces, and independence." His brows suddenly rose.

"What?"

"Says Maggie is a fully functioning adult who can cook, clean, and take care of herself. That she lived in her own small home at the hospital. This must be some amazing place," Sahvrin said. "But if a house is not feasible, a room of her own, or perhaps a repurposed shed would suffice." Sahvrin looked at her. "You know, we have lots of little Swamp Shacks here and there. We can easily get one ready with all the things in this list. I can have them install cameras so you can watch over her or perhaps you would want to stay with her there until she feels safe?"

Her heart ached in her chest at how sweet he was. "But...where would you be?"

"Wherever Ma Petite tells me to be."

"I mean where would you live? I don't want to be away from you."

"Then I will build a small shack nearby, then you can sneak out at night to visit me?" He suddenly laughed. "Why are you crying at this?"

"It's just so sweet that you'd even consider doing that."

He pulled her in his arms, hugging her tight again. "I would give you anything in this world if it's in my power to give, Angel. You *and* your sister."

She nodded, her breaths hitching still from all the crying. "Thank you. And please, I have money," she said. "We should use it, it's just sitting in savings, collecting dust."

"I have more than enough as well. But if it makes you feel better, I can spend yours," he said, laughing a little.

"It would make me feel a lot better." She remembered the list. "What else does it say, what about the no-no things."

He let her go and looked at the phone a moment. "Hmm."

"What?"

"If Maggie is triggered, she is prone to violent outbursts that can include hitting, biting, scratching herself and others. Throwing things, breaking things, screaming, and crying."

"What things trigger her?" she wondered, angling her head toward the phone.

"Says to avoid belts of any color and size, chain jewelry of any color and size, cigarettes, alcohol, loud or abrupt noise, darkness and…Mon Dieu. Most men."

"Oh God," Beth said. "Most. That means there must be some that don't bother her?"

"I hope," he said, sounding sad for her.

"I'll call Uncle Wigs and see what sort of man she feels safe around."

"His number is here. You call him and I'll go arrange that flight and pack. Meet me upstairs?"

She nodded, looking at the phone then paused when he leaned down and gave her a real kiss. She let out a moan, ready to have him in that second.

"I'll take care of that when you get upstairs," he said, adding a kiss to her cheek and a hard heat through her body.

****

Sahvrin yanked the drawstring on the canvas bag shut when His Petite came in.

I talked to Uncle Wiggins," she said, coming to him.

He took her in his arms and kissed her. "What did he say?"

"Not at all what I expected him to."

"Oh? Let me guess, she likes men that look like Santa Clause?"

She laughed and raised her brows with a little eye-flutter. "Actually, not far from that. She likes men with beards," she said, surprised. "Dark hair, but fair skin, light colored eyes and facial hair, the more the better."

Sahvrin's brows popped at that. "Sounds like Spook."

"Who is that?"

"He's in my group. One of our best trackers. But he's also a survivalist. I can probably get him to camp out near there to keep an eye on her. Maybe ask your Uncle the best way to introduce her to people?"

"Yes, why didn't I think of that?"

She turned to take care of it, and he pulled her back to him. The look in his face weakened her knees. "You need to come, Angel."

Her mouth opened to protest, only producing hot air. She heard the buckle of his belt and looked down as he opened his pants. "Undress."

She quickly removed the light blue sundress and turned to find him sitting naked in the chair with his legs open, cock in his hand.

"Oh my God," she cried, weakly, staring at it.

"Come here," he said, caressing his balls with one hand and stroking himself.

She walked to him, her legs trembling. He helped her straddle his legs and she held on to his shoulders, watching him angle his head and slide his cock softly along her pussy.

"Oh God, yes," she cried out at first contact already pulling his hair and moving carefully down his length in shocked gasps. He felt as big as the first time, only without the pain.

"Mmm, fuck, baby," he whispered, his hands gripping her butt hard. He looked up at her when he was buried. "How does that feel?"

"So big, so good."

He moved her hair behind her, pausing to stroke her face before looking back down. "You need to rub this pretty clit for me, Angel." He moved his thumb on it then looked up at her. "While you fuck me, can you do that?"

"Yes," she gasped at the throb of his cock, nodding.

"Do it," he said, eyeing her tits. "I want to watch you get hot."

She put her hand in place, rubbing her clit already tight and hard from his cock stretching her.

"That's it, fuck yes. Such a sweet Angel," he said, looking at her, his breaths thick. His gaze moved to her breasts where he used every finger on her nipples, and oh God, it brought so much fire in her clit.

"So hot," she said, her breaths shaking.

"You're fucking nipples kill me." He looked down at her hand. "Your pussy is quivering on my *fucking* cock." He looked at her. "Kiss me while you make it hot."

She moaned, sucking at his full lips, using her free hand to pull at the back of his hair. His tongue stabbed into her mouth with a lusty groan and hard throb in his cock.

"My pussy is so hot," she gasped.

"Your pussy is hot, baby? My angel is ready to get fucked?"

She moved faster on him. "Please, Sahvrin. I'm going to come."

He looked down, holding her hips. "Fuck me, Angel. Move on my cock. Like that, like fucking that."

She pulled his hair as she cried louder and louder the closer it got. So thick and hot it made her pant and groan.

"My Angel," he said, astonished, his strong hands a vice on her hips as she fucked him.

"Sahvrin!" she cried when her orgasm hit.

"Oh fuck, do it!" he gasped as she screamed and bucked though the hardest orgasm. Before she was finished, he held her tight to him and moved off the chair, easing her back to the floor before grabbing her hips again and stroking several times deep before picking up speed. In seconds he was ramming ruthlessly until her tits and screams jerked with his pace.

He fell forward after his orgasm, with angry sounding French that never failed to arouse even seconds after getting freshly fucked by him. Dear, dear, God.

His mouth was on hers, filling it with those sexy ragged groans. She stroked his face, as a mess of whimpers flew from her.

"So fucking good, Angel," he praised between breaths, making her heart skip around her chest. "Did I hurt you?" he asked, his tone worried.

"Mmmm, yes," she moaned, earning his worried gaze as she smiled.

His face slowly softened as he studied hers then giving a sexy grin. "Mon Dieu, my Angel is si forte."

She giggled, angling her head at him. "What is that?"

"Means so strong."

"Mmm," she said, pulling his mouth to hers. "One day I will fuck you until *you're* screaming."

The huge laugh he gave brought hers then he rolled, putting her on top of him as he howled on and on. When it quieted, lots of satisfied sounds and the most amazing full-body hug followed.

"We should shower before we go," she finally said with her head on his chest.

"Together?" he asked, stroking her softly.

She smiled. "We'll never leave."

"I meant to tell you, our flight is at 2:00. We arrive there at 6:00, that was the best I could get. Then we fly straight back here for 8:00 pm tonight. And we are officially excused from the party."

She raised her head to see how he felt about that. "I'm sorry you'll miss it."

He gave a laugh, looking at her. "It's an answer to my prayers."

"You don't like them?" she wondered, thinking he did.

"I hate them. But I was going to love it for Ma Petite."

She smiled at that answer before going serious. "Do you think Spook will want to…do what you said?"

"He will do whatever I ask him."

God, she loved his sexy confidence. "So bossy."

He gave her a sexy smile. "Because maybe I'm his boss." He leaned up and kissed her. "I have things to tell you about that Ma Petite."

She looked at him. "Like what?"

"Like everything about me. What I do, my obligations. Normally I would tell these things before I fuck the Angel I love, but in your case, I went in reverse. Of course this is your fault," he added, seriously, making her laugh.

"But, what…is it something I won't like? You're not going to leave and work on the other side of the world, are you?"

"No, Angel," he said, sliding his fingers along her hair. "You know that seal on my back?"

She propped herself on her forearm next to him and nodded. "Yes."

"There are eleven other men with that seal. Twelve of us altogether. And one is the leader."

She raised her brows. "You?"

"Qui."

"Qui, that's yes?"

He nodded, smiling at her.

"So you're the leader of this and…"

"And there are rules and codes I am bound by. The most important one is that I'm not allowed to fuck a woman unless I marry her."

She went serious. "What…oh my God, are you…are you proposing?" Her heart hammered so hard, she had to get up. He sat up too, looking at her, his smile stealing her breath even more.

"I surely had other ideas for proposing and I must blame Ma Petite again, she has always made a mess of my head."

She put her fingers at her mouth and gasped when he moved and got on his knees before her and for some reason, she got on her knees too. He took her face in his hands and kissed her repeatedly, smiling as her sobs started.

"Ma Petite, I'm on my knees naked proposing to you and you get on your knees with me?" His face went serious as he stroked her cheek, sliding his thumb over the tears rolling down. "I want to know will my Angel marry me, *but,*" he said, gaze holding hers. "You cannot answer that until I tell you what that will require for you."

His laughter burst forth when she hugged him so hard, he fell back with her. "Mon Dieu, you are like a bull in love!"

"I don't care *what* it requires!" she gasped, kissing him repeatedly. "Tell me every gory detail. Do I have to climb fifty mountains for you? Wrestle Gras Jean to the death? Fight a horde of demon spiders with my bare hands?" she asked with a hard shudder that made him laugh. "There is nothing in this world bigger than my love for you! You have to marry me *this* instant!"

"Mon Dieu," he groaned, kissing her into a dizzying oblivion. "There's nothing but the paperwork left, Ma Petite. And a very big swamp wedding. Everything else is seared on the dotted line in my heart."

****

"Spook," Sahvrin said on the phone, standing on the docks.
"Eveque."

"I'm gonna need you on my side of the swamp for a bit. We have her sister coming here and I'll need eyes that can see."

"When and where," he said.

"You can stay at the shack near here. When I know specifics, I'll let you know."

"The Birdhouse?"

"That one, yes. Might need a little clean up. When can you come?"

"When do you need me?"

"Yesterday."

He chuckled. "I'll pack up now and be there around noon. Anything specific I need to bring?"

"Just your blue eyes, fair skin and dark beard."

"Huh," he said, sounding mildly perplexed. "I'll be sure and pack those."

"I guess you need to know that Beth's sister is mute and has some…triggers we're needing to avoid. *Men* being one of her bigger ones. Except the fair skinned, blue eyed dark-bearded ones. I thought of you right off."

"Mighty fucking thoughtful of you."

Sahvrin grinned, expecting that response given his aversion to women. But that's what made him perfect for the job. "To give you some context, she was abducted at seven and spent two weeks in a nightmare that stole her ability to speak."

"Wow, fuck," Spook muttered.

"And I'm damn near ready to bet my soul they're of the same legion of devils we're now hunting. We'll fly in with her this evening around eight PM. Lazure will answer any questions till then."

"And the meeting?"

"It'll be at midnight tonight. At the main house in the Basilique."

"Got it. See you then, Eveque."

THE WINNERS OF

BAYOU BISHOPS
"HELP ME WRITE"
GAMES!

*Ladies, I had such a blast!
Can't wait for ROUND 2!!!*

Give me a swampy line that means they get their muscles from working out in a gym
I ENDED UP COMING UP WITH "LORD DUMB BELLS, HAILING FROM THE NEW ORLEANS GYM FOR PUSSIES

Need a name for Sahvrin's Land Dragon
BEL NOIR—CHERYL JACKSON!

I neeeeeeeed, is a name for his shop! GO!
SWAMP RATS MODS AND RODS BY DAVINA PURNELL

Give me the name of their land club!
THE DRY DOCK BY STEPHANIE BECK

What's a cajun/swampy type of insult that means a person is no good
HE WAS AS BRIGHT AS A BAYOU ON A CLOUDY NIGHT BY CHERYL JACKSON

Looking for an old house in the woods to call their land club/shop
LINDA KIDWELL!

In the swamp, they call their chapters _____
HATCHES—BY SARA GONZALES

I need 12 names/titles. Editing to say this is not titles of places, more like people!
ENDED UP NAMING THESE MYSELF WITH THE HELP OF MACHETE AND CHERYL JACKSON!

Description they might use in the swamp for "being gay"
WRESTLING THE WRONG GATORS! CHERYL JACKSON

I need a name for a group of 12 swamp warriors
THE TWELVE—BY MYSELF! LOL

Need a name for waterways that are a hot mess.
DESSIE MINDIE BLAKE, PAULA TOOKE, STEPHANIE BECK, CHERYL JACKSON, SARA GONZALAS, ELISE STEPHENS

As you know, I don't like the name "The Dark Barn" and would like a new one
THE WEIGH STATION BY LINDA KIDWELL AND STEPHANIE BECK

I need some funny/crazy/scary nicknames for some of my swamp scoundrels
DAVINA PURNEL, JO-JO KRAYVELD, SARA GONZALAS, ELISE STEPHENS, ALLEY CAREY

Find me this Swamp Mansion!
DIDN'T PICK A WINNER

Find me Sahvrin's little house in the swamp
DOROTHY CALTAGERONE

Name something cool and useful you might go to college
for
ART AND MECHANICAL ENGINEERING BY
TAMARA SIMMONS

CAJUN RECIPES

Crazy Omelet

Ingredients: (put as much of each as you like)
Onion
Garlic
Onion top
Choice of meat (cajun sausage in the story)
Little bit of vegetable oil or used bacon grease
Potatoes
Eggs
Cheese
Salt
Worcestershire
And whatever other seasoning you like. I use a Cajun Creole one.

Directions

1. You wanna cut up your onion, garlic, onion tops, sausage and potatoes ahead of time. Season it with the salt and other seasonings.
2. Then you heat your oil in a heavy skillet or whatever you have, it don't matter, really.
3. I brown my sausage, potatoes and onions first and get them nice and brown. I shake some Worcestershire in it but never really measure that.

4. I might add a little water from time to time and stir up the sticky stuff to keep it from burning and gives my potatoes more time to soften.
5. After that, I will add the garlic and onion tops and let it all have another round of browning.
6. Then when you think you better add water before it burns, add about ¼ cup and turn it down to low.
7. Then you add your eggs and cheese, just crack the eggs right on top of everything.
8. When you see the whites of the eggs start to solidify, start stirring the eggs into the whole mix until that yolk coats everything.
9. Turn the fire off so you don't cook that yolk. Part of the Crazy Omelet is having the yolk uncooked. If you don't like uncooked yolk, meh cook it all the way, then.

Enjoy with ice-cold milk.

If you'd like a copy of the recipe Sahvrin uses for Cajun Gumbo, you can get that in an entertaining recipe book I wrote in the Cajun dialect here:

Cajun Gumbo
By Lucian Bane

FRENCH WORDS/MEANING

Belle Tetons—Beautiful breasts
Bel- Eveque—Beautiful Bishop
Com-on-sah-vah—How are you doing
Doose Petite D-Amour Escleve—My little love slave
Eveque—Bishop
Gras Jean—Big Jean
La femme pour qui je suis follement tombée amoureuse—The woman I fell madly in love with
Mon Dieu—My God
Ma Petite—My Little (can be used for small person in general)
Ma-ch`ere—My dear
Ma-Petite Catin—My little doll
Mercie Dieu—Thank God
Ma Belle Ange—My beautiful Angel
Mahdigwan--mosquito
Ma Amour Esclave—My love slave
On-est proche-la—We are close or near
Pew-tan mosquitoes are affeme –Fucking mosquitos are bad
Petite Soeur—Little sister
Putahn—Bitch
Qui--Yes
Shaaa pee-chay—Aww, how sweet or aww so sweet
Sha—term of endearment
Sucree Fille—Sweet girl
Say-To- Fini—That's it, I'm done

JOIN MY BAYOU BISHOPS GROUP!

Come help me create book 2! We had a blast doing book 1. Hope to you see you there!

BAYOU BISHOPS GROUP